GEORGETTE HEYER

Footsteps in the Dark

GRAFTON BOOKS
A Division of the Collins Publishing Group

LONDON GLASGOW
TORONTO SYDNEY AUCKLAND

Grafton Books
A Division of the Collins Publishing Group
8 Grafton Street, London W1X 3LA

Published by Grafton Books 1987
Reprinted 1987 (twice)

First published in Great Britain 1932
Published by Granada Publishing 1985

ISBN 0-586-06703-5

Printed and bound in Great Britain by
Collins, Glasgow

Set in Plantin

The place had come to her quite unexpectedly. An uncle whom she, in company with Peter and Margaret, had visited at dutiful intervals during his lifetime, had bequeathed the Priory to his nephew and his two nieces. No lover of rural solitudes, he himself had never occupied the house. In his turn he had inherited it some five years before from his older sister, who had lived there through marriage and widowhood. As she left it so it now stood, and no sooner had Celia Malcolm, and Peter and Margaret Fortescue seen it, than they declared it was just the place they had dreamed of for years . . .

FOOTSTEPS IN THE DARK

✿
CHAPTER I

'And I suppose this is the approach-course,' said Charles Malcolm. 'Full of natural hazards.'

His wife, Celia, replied with dignity: 'That is the tennis-court.' Charles made a derisive noise. 'All it needs,' she said, eyeing him, 'is a little levelling.'

'All it needs,' said Charles rudely, 'is a hay-cutter and a steam-roller. And this is the place you wouldn't sell!'

His sister-in-law took up the cudgels. 'It's perfectly lovely, and you know it. As soon as Celia and I set eyes on it we fell for it.'

'That I can believe,' said Charles. 'A mullioned window or two, and a ruined chapel, and I'd expect you two to go over at the knees. But Peter was with you. What did he fall for? Beer at the local pub?'

'There's a trout-stream at the bottom of the garden,' Margaret pointed out.

'So there is,' Charles agreed. 'And another in the servants' hall for wet days. Bowers showed it to me.'

'Simply because there was a pane of glass out of one of the windows!' Celia said hotly. 'Of course the rain came in!'

Margaret tucked her hand in Charles' arm. 'Wait till you've seen your bedroom. It's got linen-fold panelling, and there's a cupboard which is all part of it, and which takes you ages to find.'

'That really is jolly,' Charles said. 'Then if anyone burgles our room he won't be able to find my dress-coat.

1

I suppose I can mark the place with a cross.'

'No, you have a compass, and take bearings,' retorted his wife. 'Come on in, and we'll show you.'

They turned away from the tennis-court and began to walk back towards the house down one of the neglected paths that wound between flower-beds to the terrace on the south side of the building.

'Chas, can you look at it with the sun on that heavenly grey stone, and blame us for refusing to part with it?' Margaret exclaimed.

'I'll wait till I've seen my room,' Charles replied.

But he had to admit that this house, which had been left to his wife and her brother and sister, was artistically all that could be desired. Built originally many hundreds of years before of grey stone, much of it was now ruined, and much had been added at different periods, so that the present house was a rambling structure, set in wooded grounds where oaks, which had been there when the Conqueror landed, reared up huge gnarled trunks from out of a tangle of undergrowth. A drive of about a quarter of a mile in length twisted through the trees to the gates that opened on to the road which led to the village of Framley, a mile away if you went by road, but much less if you walked across the fields at the back of the house.

Down the road towards the village, but set back inside the Priory grounds, were the ruins of the chapel which had so captivated Celia's fancy. Dismantled during the Reformation, and later battered by Cromwell's cannon, not much of it now remained, but fragments of the walls rose up crumbling out of the grass. Here and there part of the walls remained to show the Gothic windows, but for the most part they were no more than a few feet in height.

The Priory itself had been restored so that the many re-buildings and additions had left little outward appearance of the old home of the monks. Celia, who had acquired a book on Old Abbeys, declared that the library, a big room giving on to the terrace, was the original refectory, but she admitted that the panelling was probably of later date.

The place had come to her quite unexpectedly. An uncle whom she, in company with Peter and Margaret, had visited at dutiful intervals during his lifetime, had bequeathed the Priory to his nephew and his two nieces. No lover of rural solitudes, he himself had never occupied the house. In his turn he had inherited it some five years before from his sister, who had lived there through marriage and widowhood. As she left it so it now stood, and no sooner had Celia Malcolm, and Peter and Margaret Fortescue seen it, than they declared it was just the place they had dreamed of for years. At least, the two sisters said so. Peter was less enthusiastic, but agreed it would be a pity to sell it.

It had been to let for quite a long time, but ever since the first tenants who rented the house two years after the death of its original owner, had left, no one had made even the smallest offer for it.

'Your uncle had a good deal of trouble over the house,' had said Mr Milbank, the solicitor. 'When she lived in it his sister never made any complaint, but she was an eccentric old lady, and it's conceivable she wouldn't have cared. But the fact of the matter is, Mrs Malcolm, the house has got rather a bad name. The people your uncle let it to took it for three years – and they left at the end of one. They said the place was haunted.'

'Oo!' said Margaret. 'What a thrill for us!'

The lawyer smiled. 'I shouldn't build on it, Miss Fortescue. I think you'll find that it's nothing more thrilling than rats. But I thought I'd warn you. So that if you feel you'd rather not take possession of a reputedly haunted house you might like me to follow up this offer.' He lifted up a sheet of note-paper that lay on his desk, and looked inquiringly at Peter.

'Is that the offer you wrote to us about?' Peter asked. 'Some fellow who saw the board up when he was motoring in that part of the world, and wanted to know particulars?'

Mr Milbank nodded. Celia and Margaret turned anxiously to their brother, and began to urge the desirability of owning a country house so near to town, and yet so ideal in situation and character.

The trout stream won Peter over. Charles, a young barrister with a growing practice, had no time to waste, so he said, in going to look at a house which his wife was apparently set on inhabiting whether he liked it or not. He placed his trust in Peter.

'And nicely you've abused it,' he said, over tea in the library. 'For two months you three have dashed to and fro, doing what you called "getting it ready to live in." Incidentally you lulled my suspicions with lying stories about the house, till I almost believed it was something like your description. You' – he pointed an accusing finger at Margaret – 'said it was the ideal home. The fact that there was only one bathroom and a system of heating water that won't do more than one hot bath at a time, you carefully concealed.'

'Do you good to have a few cold baths,' remarked Peter, spreading jam on a slice of bread and butter. 'It isn't as though we propose to live here through the winter. Moreover, I don't see why we shouldn't convert one of the bedrooms into a second bathroom, and put in a better heating arrangement. Not immediately, of course, but at some future date.'

Charles eyed him coldly. 'And what about light? Oh, and a telephone! I suppose we can wire the house while we're about it. This must be what Celia called "getting a country-house for nothing." I might have known.'

'Personally,' said Celia, 'I prefer lamps and candles. Electric light would be out of place in a house like this, and as for a telephone, that's the one thing I've been wanting to escape from.' She nodded briskly at her husband. 'You're going to have a real holiday this year, my man, quite cut off from town.'

'Thanks very much,' said Charles. 'And what was it you said just before tea? Something about going to the village to order bacon for breakfast?'

'Well, you can take the car,' Celia pointed out. 'And you might try and get hold of a gardener in the village. I think the garden is rather more than you and Peter can manage.'

'It is,' said Charles, with conviction. 'Much more.'

The door opened at that moment to admit a middle-aged lady of comfortable proportions, and placid demeanour. This was Mrs Bosanquet, the Fortescues' aunt. She accepted a chair, and some tea, condemned a solid-looking cake, and embarked on bread and butter.

'I have unpacked my boxes,' she announced, 'but I twice lost the wardrobe.'

'What, have you got one of those little practical jokes?' Charles demanded.

Mrs Bosanquet turned an amiable and inquiring countenance towards him. She was deaf. When Charles had repeated his question, she nodded. 'Yes, dear, but I have stuck a piece of stamp-paper on the catch. A very quaint old house. I was talking to Mrs Bowers, and she tells me you could lose yourself in the cellars.'

'That's nothing,' said Charles, getting up. 'I lost myself getting from our room to my dressing-room. Of course it would simplify matters if we locked a few of the empty rooms, but I agree it would take away from the sporting element. Are you coming to the village, Peter?'

'I am,' Peter replied. 'I will introduce you to some very fine draught beer there.'

'Lead on!' Charles said, brightening.

The lane that led to Framley was wooded, and

picturesque enough to draw a grudging word of approval from Charles. Peter, negotiating a hairpin bend, said: 'Seriously, Chas, the place has possibilities.'

'I don't deny it. But what's all this bilge about noises and hauntings, and footsteps in the dark?'

'God knows. In the village they all but cross themselves if you mention the Priory. I daresay there are rats. Milbank said . . .'

'Look here, do you mean to say you knew about this haunting before you came down here? And not one word to me?'

Peter said in some surprise: 'I didn't think anything of it. You aren't going to tell me you'd have refused to live in the place if you'd known?'

'Aren't I?' said Charles grimly. 'If you'd left as many desirable residences and hotels at a moment's notice as I have, all because Celia "felt something queer" about them, you'd never have come near the place.'

'She says she doesn't believe there's anything wrong with the house. All village superstition.'

'Does she? Well, I'll lay you six to one in sovereigns that the first rat heard scuttling overhead will spell our departure. Especially with Bowers shivering round the house.'

'What's the matter with him? Been listening to village gossip?'

'That, and natural palsy of spirit. He unpacked my things and gave a life-like imitation of the mysterious butler of fiction while he did so. "All I know is, sir, I wouldn't go down those cellar stairs after dark, not if I were paid to." Oh yes, and I need hardly say that the first night he and Mrs Bowers spent alone in the house before you came down, he heard footsteps outside his door, and a hand feeling over the panels.'

'Silly ass!' Peter said. 'You can console yourself with the thought that it would take more than a ghost to upset the redoubtable Mrs Bowers. Allow me to tell you that we are now approaching the Bell Inn. Genuine fourteenth century – in parts.'

The car had emerged from the tree-shadowed lane into the outskirts of the village, which stretched aimlessly along one narrow main street. The Bell Inn, a picturesque and rambling old hostelry built round a courtyard, was one of the first buildings on the street. Peter Fortescue ran the car up to the door and switched off the engine. 'Opening time,' he grinned. 'Take heart, Chas, I can vouch for the beer.'

They entered into a long, low-pitched taproom, with a beamed ceiling, and little latticed windows that gave on to the street. Oak settles formed various secluded nooks in the room, and behind the bar stood a landlord of such comfortable proportions and such benevolent mien that he might well have stepped from the pages of Dickens.

Leaning against the bar, and apparently engaging Mr Wilkes in desultory conversation, was his very antithesis, a thin, wiry little man, with a very sharp face and pale eyes that darted from object to object with a quickness that gave a disagreeable impression of shiftiness. He glanced at Peter as Peter crossed the threshold, and at once looked away again.

'Evening, Wilkes,' Peter said. 'I've brought my brother-in-law along to try that draught bitter of yours.'

Mr Wilkes beamed upon them both. 'Very glad to see any friend of yours here, sir. Two half-cans, sir? You shall have it.' He took down a couple of pewter tankards from a shelf behind him, and drew two half-pints of frothing beer. Having supplied his patrons with this, he wiped down the bar with a mechanical action, and said affably: 'And how are you getting on up at the Priory, sir, if I may ask?'

'All right, thanks. We haven't seen your ghost yet. When does he usually show up?'

The smile faded. Mr Wilkes looked at Peter rather queerly, and said in an altered voice: 'I wouldn't joke about it, sir, not if I was you.'

Charles emerged from his tankard. 'Has my man Bowers been in here at all?' he demanded.

The landlord looked surprised; the small stranger, who had edged away a little when the newcomers first entered, shot a quick look at Charles.

'Yes, sir, several times,' Wilkes answered.

'I thought so,' said Charles. 'And did you tell him that the ghost prowled round the passages, and pawed all the doors?'

Wilkes seemed to draw back. 'Has he heard it again?' he asked.

'Heard my eye!' Charles retorted. 'All he heard was what you told him, and his own imagination.'

'Joking apart, Wilkes, you don't really believe in the thing, do you?' Peter asked.

The small man, who had looked for a moment as though he were going to say something, moved unobtrusively away to a seat by one of the windows, and fishing a crumpled newspaper from his pocket began to read it.

For a moment Wilkes did not reply; then he said quite simply: 'I've seen it, sir.' Peter's brows lifted incredulously, and Wilkes added: 'And what's more, I've seen as reasonable a man as what you are yourself pack up and leave that place with two years of his lease still to run. A little over five years it is since I took over this house, and when I first come here the Priory was standing as empty as when you first saw it. I suppose old Mrs Matthews, that used to own it, had been dead a matter of a year or fifteen months. From all accounts she was a queer one. Well, there was the Priory, going to ruin, as you might say, and never a soul would go near the place after dark, not if they was paid to. Now, I daresay you'll agree I don't look one of the fanciful ones myself, sir, and nor

I'm not, and the first thing I did when I heard what folk said of the place, was to make a joke of it, like what you're doing now. Then Ben Tillman, that keeps the mill up to Crawshays, he laid me I wouldn't go up to the old ruin after dark one night.' He paused, and again wiped down the bar with that odd air of abstraction. He drew a long breath, as though some horror still lingered in his memory. 'Well, I went, sir. Nor I wasn't afraid – not then. It was a moonlit night, and besides that I had my torch if I'd needed it. But I didn't. I sat down on one of those old tombs you'll find in the chapel, half covered by grass and weeds. I didn't think anything out of the ordinary for some while. If I remember rightly, I whistled a bit, by way of passing the time. I couldn't say how long it was before I noticed the change. I think it must have come gradual.'

'What change?' asked Charles, unimpressed.

Again the landlord paused. 'It's very hard to tell you, sir. It wasn't anything you could take hold of, as you might say. Things looked the same, and there wasn't more than a breath of wind, yet it got much colder all at once. And it was as fine a June night as you could hope for. I don't know how I can explain it so as you'd understand, but it was as though the cold was spreading right over me, and into me. And instead of whistling tunes to myself, and thinking how I'd have the laugh over Ben Tillman, I found I was sitting still – still as death. It had sort of crept on me without my noticing, that fear of moving. I couldn't have told you why *then*, but I knew I daren't stir a finger, nor make a sound. I can tell you, with that fear in my very bones I'd have given all I had to get up and run, and let Ben say what he would. But I couldn't. Something had got me. No, I don't know what it was, sir, and I can't explain it anyhow else, but it was no laughing matter. Do you know how it is when you've got the wind up, and you sit listening like as if your ear-drums 'ud burst with the strain? Well, that's how I was, listening and watching. Whenever a leaf rustled I strained my eyes to see what was there. But there was nothing. Then it stole over me that there was something behind me.' He stopped, and passed the back of his hand across his forehead. 'Well, that's a feeling anyone can get if he's properly scared, but this was more than a feeling. I *knew* it. I'd still got some of my wits left and I knew there was only one thing to be done, and that was turn round, and look. Yes, it sounds easy, but I swear to you, sir, it took every ounce of courage in me. I did it. I fair wrenched myself round, with the blood hammering in my head. And I saw it, plain as I see you, standing right behind me, looking down at me.'

'Saw *what*?' demanded Peter, quite worked up.

The landlord gave a shiver. 'They call it the Monk round here,' he answered. 'I suppose it was that. But I only saw a tall black figure, and no face, but just two eyes looking out of blackness straight at me.'

'Your pal Tillman dressed up to give you a fright,' said Charles.

Wilkes looked at him. 'Ben Tillman couldn't have vanished, sir. And that's what the Monk did. Just disappeared. You may say I imagined it, but all I know is I wouldn't do what I did that night again, not for a thousand pounds.'

There was a slight pause. The man by the window got up and strolled out of the taproom. Peter set his tankard down. 'Well, thanks very much,' he said. 'Cheery little story.'

Charles had been watching the thin stranger. 'Who's our departed friend?' he inquired.

'Commercial, sir. He's working the places round here with some sort of a vacuum-cleaner, so I understand, and doing a bit of fishing in between-whiles.'

'Seemed to be interested in ghosts,' was all Charles said.

But when he and Peter had left the Bell Inn, Peter asked

abruptly: 'What did you mean by that, Chas? Did you think the fellow was listening to us?'

'Didn't you?' Charles said.

'Well, yes, but I don't know that that was altogether surprising.'

'No. But he didn't seem to want us to notice his interest, did he? Where's this grocer we're looking for?'

At the grocer's, which turned out to be also the post-office and linen-draper, after the manner of village shops, the two men were accosted by a gentleman in clerical attire, who was buying stamps. He introduced himself as the Vicar, and told them that he and his wife were only waiting until the newcomers had had time to settle into the Priory before they paid a call on them.

'One is glad to see the Priory occupied once more,' he said. 'Alas, too many of our old houses are spurned nowadays for lack of "modern conveniences."'

'We were rather under the impression, sir, that this particular house has been spurned on account of ghosts,' Peter said.

The Vicar smiled. 'Ah, I fear you must seek confirmation of that story from one more credulous than my poor self,' he announced. 'Such tales, I find, invariably spring up round deserted houses. I venture to prophesy that the Priory ghost proves itself to be nothing more harmful than a mouse, or perhaps a rat.'

'Oh, so we think,' Charles answered. 'But it's really rather a nuisance, for my wife had banked on getting a local housemaid, and the best she can manage is a daily girl, who takes precious good care she's out of the place before sundown.'

Mr Pennythorne listened to this with an air of smiling tolerance. 'Strange how tenacious these simple country-folk are of superstitions,' he said musingly. 'But you are not without domestic help, one trusts?'

'No, no, we have our butler and his wife.' Charles

gathered up his change from the counter, and thrust an unwieldy package into Peter's hands. 'Are you going our way, sir? Can we drop you anywhere?'

'No, I thank you. Is it your car that stands outside the Bell Inn? I will accompany you as far as that if I may.'

They strolled out of the shop, and down the street. The Vicar pointed out various tumbledown old buildings of architectural interest, and promised to conduct them personally round the church some day. 'It is not, I fear, of such antiquity as the ruins of your chapel,' he sighed, 'but we pride ourselves upon our east window. Within the last few years we have been fortunate enough to procure a sufficient sum of money to pay for the cleaning of it – no light expense, my dear Mr Malcolm – but we were greatly indebted to Colonel Ackerley, who showed himself, as indeed he always does, most generous.' This seemed to produce a train of thought. 'No doubt you have already made his acquaintance? One of our churchwardens; and an estimable fellow – a *pukka sahib*, as he would himself say.'

'Is he the man who lives in the white house beyond ours?' asked Peter. 'No, we haven't met him yet, but I think I saw him at the Bell one evening. Cheery-looking man, going grey, with regular features, and a short moustache? Drives a Vauxhall tourer?'

The Vicar, while disclaiming any knowledge of cars, thought that this description fitted Colonel Ackerley. They had reached the Bell Inn by this time, and again refusing the offer of a lift the Vicar took his leave, and walked off briskly down the street.

When Charles and Peter reached the Priory it was nearly time for dinner, and long shadows lay on the ground. They found the girls in the library with Mrs Bosanquet, and were greeted by a cry of: 'Oh, here you are! We quite forgot to tell you to buy a couple of ordinary lamps to fix on to the wall.'

'What, more lamps?' demanded Peter, who had a lively recollection of unpacking a positive crate of them. 'Why on earth?'

'Well, we haven't got any for the landing upstairs,' explained Celia, 'and Bowers says he'd rather not go up without a light. Did you ever hear such rot? I told him to take a candle.'

'To tell you the honest truth,' confessed Margaret, 'I don't awfully like going up in the dark myself.'

Charles cast up his eyes. 'Already!' he said.

'It isn't that at all,' Margaret said defiantly. 'I mean, I'm not imagining ghosts or anything so idiotic, but it is a rambling place, and of course one does hear odd sorts of noises – yes, I know it's only rats, but at night one gets stupid, and fanciful, and anyway, there is a sort of feeling that – that one's being watched. I've had it before, in old houses.'

'Have you really felt it here?' asked Celia, wide-eyed.

'Oh, it's nothing, Celia, but you know how it is when you go to Holyrood, or Hampton Court, or somewhere. There's a sort of atmosphere. I can't explain, but *you* know.'

'Damp?' suggested Peter helpfully.

His sisters looked their scorn. 'No, silly,' said Margaret. 'As though the spirits of all those dead and gone people were looking at one from the walls. That's a bit what I feel here.'

Mrs Bosanquet put down her needlework and said mildly: 'You feel someone in the wall, my dear? I do hope to goodness there isn't a skeleton anywhere. I never could bear the thought of them, for they seem to me most unnatural.'

'Aunt!' shrieked Celia. 'A skeleton in the wall? Don't be so awful! Why should there be?'

'I daresay there's no such thing, my dear, but I always remember reading a most unpleasant story about someone who was walled up in a monastery, or a convent – I forget which, but it was something to do with monks, I know.'

'Oh Aunt Lilian, Aunt Lilian!' groaned Charles. '*Et tu, Brute!*'

'If I thought for one moment,' said Celia emphatically, 'that anyone had been walled up inside this house, I'd walk out here and now.'

'Quite right, my dear,' agreed Mrs Bosanquet. 'One can't be too careful. I always remember how there was an outbreak of the plague when they disturbed the old burial place somewhere in London.'

'On which cheerful thought,' said Charles, as a gong sounded in the hall, 'we go in to dinner. Anyone any appetite?'

In spite of Mrs Bosanquet's gloomy recollections it seemed that no one's appetite had failed. Dinner was served in the square dining-room at the side of the house, and though the undrawn curtains let in the soft evening light, Celia had placed shaded candles on the table, so that the room had a warm, inviting appearance. By common consent there was no more talk of ghosts or skeletons. They went back to the library after dinner, and while Mrs Bosanquet proceeded to lay out a complicated Patience, the others sat down to the Bridge-table. Even when a scutter somewhere in the wainscoting startled them all it did not need the men's assurances to convince the girls that the place was rat-ridden.

'I know,' said Celia, gathering up her cards. 'Mrs Bowers is going to set a trap.'

'I am not fond of rats,' remarked her aunt. 'Mice I don't mind at all. Poor little things. Ah, if that had been a red queen I might have brought it out. I once stayed in a farmhouse where they used to run about in the lofts over our heads like a pack of terriers.'

Margaret, who was Dummy, got up from the table and wandered over to the window. The moon had risen, and now bathed the whole garden in silver light. She gave an exclamation: 'Oh, look how beautiful! I wish we could see the chapel from here.' She stepped out on to the terrace, and stood leaning her hands on the low parapet. The night was very still and cloudless, and the trees threw shadows like pools of darkness. The shrubbery hid the ruins of the chapel from sight.

'You can see it from your bedroom, I should think,' called Peter. 'Come on in: we're two down, all due to your reckless bidding.'

She came in reluctantly and took her place at the table. 'It seems a pity to be playing bridge on a night like this. Does anyone feel inclined to wander up to the chapel with me?'

'Don't all speak at once,' Charles advised them unnecessarily.

'Personally,' said Celia, 'I'm going to bed after this rubber. We'll all go some other night.'

Half an hour later only the two men remained downstairs. Charles went over to the windows, and shut and bolted them. 'Think it's necessary to make a tour of the back premises?' he asked, yawning.

'Lord, no! Bowers'll have taken precious good care to see that it's all locked up. I'll go and put the chain on the front door.' Peter went out, and Charles bolted the last window, and turned to put out the big oil-lamp that hung on chains from the ceiling. The moonlight shone in at the uncurtained window, and as Charles turned towards the door he heard what sounded like the rustling of a skirt against the wall behind him. He looked quickly over his shoulder. There was no one but himself in the room, but he could have sworn that he heard faint footsteps.

Peter's voice called from the hall. 'Coming, Chas?'

'Just a moment.' Charles felt in his pocket for matches and presently struck one, and walked forward so that its tiny light showed up the shadowed corner of the room.

15

Peter appeared in the doorway, candle in hand. 'What's up? Lost something?'

The match burned out. 'No, I thought I heard something – a rat,' Charles said.

CHAPTER II

The Vicar and his wife came to call at the Priory two days later. Mrs Pennythorne wore pince-nez and white kid gloves, and she told Celia that there was little society in the neighbourhood. There were the Mastermans, at the Manor House, but they never called on anyone, and there was Mr Titmarsh, at Crossways, but he was so very odd in his habits that Mrs Pennythorne could hardly recommend him as an acquaintance. Further questioning elicited the explanation that the oddness of Mr Titmarsh's habits was due to his hobby, which was collecting moths. Mrs Pennythorne said that his manners were sadly brusque, and he wandered about at night, presumably in search of specimens for his collection. Then there was Dr Roote, and his wife, and although Mrs Pennythorne was loth to speak ill of anyone really she ought to warn Celia that it was all too certain that the doctor drank. Finally there was Colonel Ackerley, at the White House, who neither drank nor collected moths, but who was a bachelor, which was a pity. Mrs Pennythorne went on to enumerate the failings of various farmers and villagers, and Charles, who, his wife was wont to say, was never backward in devising methods of escape for himself, suggested to the Vicar that he might like to stroll out to look at the ruins of the chapel.

The Vicar was nothing loth, and ignoring a look of mingled threat and appeal from his wife, Charles led him out.

The Vicar discoursed on Norman and Early English architecture in the chapel, and strove to decipher long obliterated inscriptions upon the few tombs that thrust up through the grass and weeds that had grown over the floor of the building.

They returned presently to the house to find that another caller had arrived. This was Colonel Ackerley, and he proved to be a more congenial guest than either of the Pennythornes, who soon took their leave.

The Colonel was a man of some forty-five years, or more, with a manner rather typical of the army, but otherwise inoffensive. He shook hands with great heartiness, and said that had he known of the presence of Mrs Pennythorne in the house he should have turned tail and run.

The girls promptly warmed to him. 'You must stay and have tea with us,' Celia said. 'And does the doctor really drink, or is it drugs?'

'Ah, poor old Roote!' said the Colonel charitably. 'Mustn't be unchristian, I suppose. Leave that to the Vicar's wife, what?' His ready laugh broke from him. 'Still, I must admit poor Roote is rather too fond of the bottle. A good doctor, mind you, and whatever they say I'll not believe he was ever the worse for wear except in his off-hours. Wife's a bit of a tartar, I believe.'

'What about the eccentric Mr Titmarsh?' inquired Margaret.

'Not an ounce of harm in him, my dear young lady,' the Colonel assured her. 'Queer old bird: not much in my line, I'm afraid. Very clever, and all that sort of thing, so they say. Don't be surprised if you run up against him in the dark one night. Gave me the shock of my life when I first found him in my garden. Thought he was a burglar.' He burst out laughing again. 'Told me he was putting lime on a tree, or some such flum-diddle. He's a – what d'ye call it? – entomologist.'

Peter handed him his cup and saucer. 'Well, I'm glad you warned us, Colonel. Otherwise we might have mistaken him for our ghost.'

'You don't mean to tell me you believe in that story?' demanded Colonel Ackerley.

'Of course we don't!' said Celia. 'But our butler does, and so does the housemaid. Bowers swears he's heard ghostly hands feeling over his door at night.'

The Colonel set down his cup. 'Has he, by Gad?' he said. 'But you haven't heard anything yourselves, have you?'

Celia hesitated. It was Margaret who answered. 'Yes, I think we all have, but we put it down to rats.'

The Colonel looked from one to the other. 'Footsteps, do you mean?'

'That and other odd sounds. It's nothing.'

The Colonel drank the rest of his tea in two gulps. 'Well, it's not often one comes across two such sensible ladies,' he said. 'I don't mind admitting to you that if I were in a house and heard what you call odd sounds I don't believe I could stand it. Bullets I can put up with at a pinch, but I draw the line at spooks. Yes, I draw the line at spooks, and I'm not ashamed to say so.'

'I quite agree with you,' Mrs Bosanquet said, bestowing her placid smile upon him. 'I can't approve of this modern craze for the supernatural. I once spent a whole hour with a ouija board, and the only thing it wrote was M about a hundred times, and then something that looked like Mother's Marmalade, which seemed to me absurd.'

'You ought to try again here, Aunt,' said Margaret. 'Then, if there's anything in it, perhaps our ghost will tell you the story of his life.'

'Who knows?' said Peter flippantly, 'he might even lead you to some hidden treasure.'

Mrs Bosanquet merely shook her head, but the idea seemed to take root in her mind, for when Charles and

Peter came back from seeing the Colonel out, she suddenly said: 'Though mind you, Peter, if there were a ghost here I know just what I should do.'

'Of course you do, darling,' said Charles. 'You'd put your head under the clothes, and say your prayers, same as you did when your flat was burgled.'

Mrs Bosanquet was quite unabashed. 'I should instantly summon the Vicar to exorcize it,' she said with dignity.

Charles' shout of laughter was broken off sharply. A sound, like a groan, muffled as though by stone walls, startled him into silence. 'Good God, what's that?' he rapped out.

Celia had grown suddenly white, and instinctively Margaret drew closer to her brother. The groan had held a note almost like a wail, long-drawn-out and slowly dying.

No one answered Charles for a moment. Only Celia gave a little shiver, and glanced round fearfully. Mrs Bosanquet broke the awed silence. 'What is what, my dear?' she asked calmly.

'Didn't you hear it?' Margaret said. 'As though – as though – someone – gave an awful – groan.'

'No, my dear, but you know I don't hear very well. Probably a creaking door.'

Charles recovered himself. 'Not only probably, but undoubtedly,' he said. 'It startled me for the moment. Comes of talking about ghosts. I'm going round with an oil-can.' He left the room, ignoring an involuntary cry from his wife.

'Do you really think it was that?' Margaret said. 'I'm not being spooky, but – but it seemed to come from underneath somewhere.'

'Don't be an ass, Peg,' her brother advised her. 'If you ask me it came from outside. I'll bet it's the door leading out of the garden-hall. I meant to oil the hinge before, and it's got worse after the rain we had last night.'

'If you're going to look, I'm coming with you,'

Margaret said firmly.

Celia half-rose from her chair, and then sat down again.

'I shall stay and keep Aunt Lilian company,' she announced in the voice of a heroine. 'Whoever heard of a daylight ghost? We're all getting nervy. I shall bar ghost-talk for the future.'

In the garden-hall, where Celia was in the habit of filling the flower-vases, Peter and Margaret found Charles with Bowers beside him, holding an oil-can in a shaking hand.

'Oh, so you thought it was this door too, did you?' Peter said. 'What's the matter with you, Bowers?'

Bowers cast him a look of reproach. 'We heard it, sir, Mrs Bowers and me. Seemed to come from somewhere quite close. It gave Mrs Bowers such a turn she nearly dropped her frying-pan. "Good gracious alive!" she said. "Who's being murdered?" And she's not one to fancy things, sir, as you well know.' Gloomily he watched Charles open the door into the garden. It squeaked dis~ally, but the sound was not the groan they had heard before. 'No, sir, it's not that, and nor it's not any other door in the house, though they do squeak, I won't deny. There's something uncanny about this place. I said it as soon as I set eyes on it, and I can tell you, sir, it's taking years off my life, living here.'

'Is there any other door leading out on this side of the house?' Peter said. 'I could swear it came from this direction.'

'There's only the long window in the drawing-room,' said Margaret. She stepped out on to the gravel-path, and looked along the side of the house. 'I can't see any other. I say, it is rather beastly, isn't it? Of course I know things do echo in these places, but... Why, who's that?'

Charles came quickly out to her side. 'Where?' he said sharply. 'Hullo, there's a chap walking past the shrub-bery!' He started forward, Peter at his heels, and hailed

21

the stranger rather sharply.

A man in fisherman's attire, and carrying a creel and a rod, was walking through the trees beyond the shrubs that ran close up to the wall of the house. He stopped as Charles hailed him, and came to meet him. He was a dark young man of about thirty, with very black brows that grew close over the bridge of his nose, and a mouth that was rather grim in repose. 'I beg your pardon,' he said, 'I'm afraid I'm trespassing.' He spoke in a curt way, as though he were either shy or slightly annoyed. 'I've been fishing the Crewel, and a man told me I could get back to the village by a short cut through your grounds. Only I don't seem able to find it.'

Charles said: 'There is a right-of-way, but you are some distance from it. In fact, your guide seems to have directed you to the wrong side of the house.'

The stranger reddened. 'I'm sorry,' he said stiffly. 'Could you point out the way to it?'

Margaret who had come up, and had been listening curiously, said suddenly: 'Why you're the man who changed the wheel for me yesterday!'

The stranger raised his hat, slightly bowing.

'Are you staying at the Bell?' Margaret inquired.

'Yes. I've come down for some trout-fishing,' he answered.

'There seems to be some quite good fishing here,' Peter said, bridging yet another gap in the conversation.

'Quite good,' agreed the dark young man. He shifted his rod from one hand to the other. 'Er – can I reach the right-of-way from here, or must I get back to the road?'

'Oh no, I'll show you the way,' Margaret said, with her friendly smile. 'It's only just across the drive.'

'It's very good of you, but really you must not trouble...'

'It's no trouble. And this place is so overgrown with trees and bushes you can easily miss the way. Peter, you'd

22

better go back and tell Celia it's all right. Come on, Mr – I don't think I know your name?'

'Strange,' said the young man. 'Michael Strange.'

'I'm Margaret Fortescue,' she told him. 'This is my brother, and this is my brother-in-law, Mr. Malcolm.'

Again the young man bowed. 'Are you staying long in this part of the world?' asked Charles.

'Just for a week or two,' Strange replied. 'I'm on my holiday.'

'Er – won't you come into the house?' Peter suggested. 'And have a cocktail or something?'

'Thanks, but I think I must be getting along. If Miss Fortescue will really be so kind as to show me the short cut to the village ...'

'Yes, rather,' Margaret said. 'Perhaps you'll look us up some other time. Come on.'

They set off together, leaving the two others to watch them out of sight.

'Well, there you are,' said Charles. 'Apparently she's got off again. And would you explain to me how a man making for a perfectly well-known right-of-way fetches up under our drawing-room windows?'

Peter was frowning. 'He doesn't – if he *is* looking for the right-of-way. Common sense must tell him that it can't run this side of the house. To tell you the truth, Chas, I don't like your black-browed friend. Just what was he doing, snooping around here?'

'He wasn't exactly communicative, so I can't say. Might have wanted to take a look at the Priory, of course. Lots of people can't keep off a ruin.'

'He didn't look to me that sort,' Peter said, still frowning.

Charles yawned. 'Probably a mere ass without any bump of locality.'

'And he didn't look like that either.'

'Oh, all right, then, no doubt he came to abduct

23

Margaret. Now what about this groaning door?'

But Michael Strange made no attempt to abduct Margaret. She led him round the corner of the house on to the avenue that ran down to the gates, and cut across this into the wood that lay between the house and the road.

'I'm taking you past the chapel,' she said. 'The footpath is beyond that, you know. You must have asked the way of one of the yokels. Isn't it odd that they never can direct one intelligibly?'

'They always assume too much local knowledge on one's part,' he nodded. A smile, which showed a row of very white teeth, put his rather grim expression to flight. 'There's altogether too much of the "past-Parson-Gregory's - and - turn - right - handed - when - you - get - to-Jackson's-farm" about their directions.'

'I know,' she said, laughing. 'I'm one of those unfortunate people who never know which way I ought to go, too. Tell me, do you know many of the people down here, or is it your first visit?'

'My first,' he answered. 'I was told the fishing was good, and the inn comfortable, so I thought I'd give it a trial. You're new to the place yourself, aren't you?'

'Yes, we only moved in a week ago.' Her dimple peeped out. 'I must tell you, because it's really rather funny: when we saw you just now we thought you were our ghost.'

He glanced down at her. 'Have you got a ghost?' he asked. 'How exciting! What sort of a ghost?'

'Well, we're not sure about that. A squeaking one, anyway.'

'That doesn't sound very awful. Haven't you seen it?'

'No, thank goodness. Of course I don't suppose it's a ghost at all, really, but when we came out we'd just heard the most gruesome sort of a groan. Honestly, it made one's blood run cold. So Chas – my brother-in-law – is going round oiling all the door-hinges. Look, that's the

24

chapel. Doesn't it look eerie and romantic?'

'Yes, I don't think I should care to spend the night up there alone,' Strange admitted.

They stood still for a moment, surveying the ruin. Strange glanced back towards the house. 'H'm. It's rather cut off by the trees, isn't it? Can you see it from the house at all?'

'No, not from downstairs. You can from my window, and the landing window. Why?'

'I only thought it was rather a pity anything so picturesque should be out of sight.'

They walked on slowly. 'If the place is haunted at all, I'm sure the ghost lives in the chapel,' Margaret said lightly. 'If I had the courage of a mouse, which I haven't, I'd get my brother to sit up with me and watch.'

'I think it's just as well you haven't,' said Strange, with another of his swift transforming smiles. 'You never know, and – I should hate you to get a fright.'

'Oh, nothing would induce Peter to forsake his bed,' she said. 'Besides, he doesn't believe in ghosts. Here's your path. You can't miss the way now.' She stopped and held out her hand.

Michael Strange took it in his. 'Thank you very much,' he said. 'It was awfully good of you to bother. I – hope you get another puncture when I'm in the offing.'

'How nice of you.' She smiled, and withdrew her hand. 'Do come and see us if ever you feel like it. Good-bye!'

She watched him stride away down the footpath, and turned, and went slowly back to the house.

'Well, did you find out anything about the fellow?' her brother asked when she entered the library.

'Oh, he's just on his holiday,' she replied.

'So we gathered,' said Charles. 'What's his job?'

'I didn't ask. Why were you two so stuffy? You don't think he was responsible for the noise we heard, do you?'

'That solution hadn't occurred to me,' said Charles. 'I

admit he didn't give me the impression of one who would stand under someone else's window and groan at them. Still, you never know.'

Celia held up her finger. 'I protest. We are not going to talk about groans or ghosts any more. Carried?'

'Carried unanimously,' said Peter.

That resolution might have been kept longer had it not been for the happenings of the next night.

It was about half-past ten when a crash that resounded through the house penetrated even to Mrs Bosanquet's ears, and made Celia, who was improvising idly on the piano, strike a jangling discord. The crash seemed to come from the upper landing, and it was followed by a bump-bump-bump, as though some hard object were rolling down the stairs.

'Good Lord, who's smashing up the place now?' said Charles, getting out of his chair. He went to the door, and opened it. 'That you, Peter?' he called.

The study door opposite opened. 'No. What on earth's happened?' Peter asked.

'Dunno. Without wishing to leap to conclusions I should hazard a guess that something has fallen over.' Charles picked up the lamp that stood on the hall table, and walked to the foot of the stairs.

'I believe it was a picture,' Celia said, at his side. 'It sounded to me like glass breaking.'

She ran up ahead of him, and rounded the half-landing. A little exclamation broke from her. 'Oh, there's something on the stairs! Do hurry up with the lamp, Charles.' She bent and groped for the thing her foot had kicked against. 'Whatever can it be?' she wondered. Then Charles reached the half-landing, and the light he carried showed Celia what she held between her hands.

It was a human skull and the hollow eye-sockets glared up at her, while the teeth of the fleshless upper jaw grinned as though in macabre mockery.

26

Celia gave a shuddering cry, and dropped the hideous thing, shrinking back against the wall. 'Oh Charles! Oh Charles!' she whispered, like a frightened child.

He was beside her in a moment, holding her in the circle of his arm, himself staring down at the skull at their feet. For a moment words apparently failed him.

Peter came up the stairs two at a time. 'What is it?' he asked impatiently. Then he too saw, and stopped dead. 'Gosh!' he gasped. Over his shoulder he jerked: 'Don't come up, Margaret.'

'But what *is* it?' she called. 'Why did Celia scream?'

'Oh, it's nothing!' said Charles, recovering his sang-froid. 'Just a skull rolling about the place. You trot off downstairs, Celia, while I investigate.'

'I – I think I will,' she said, and went past the skull with her eyes steadily averted.

'Take her into the library, Peg,' Charles ordered. He watched her go shakily downstairs, and turned to Peter. 'Look here, this is a bit thick,' he said. 'I don't know about you, but I'm all of a sweat. Footsteps and groans I can put up with, but when it comes to finding people's remains lying about the place I've had enough.'

Peter bent and picked up the skull, and placed it on the window-seat. 'Question is, where did it come from?' he said. 'Bring that lamp upstairs.'

They went on up to the landing, holding the lamp high so that the light was thrown before them. At the head of the stairs a big picture had fallen to the ground, and pieces of glass winked at them from the carpet. The lamplight showed a dark aperture where the picture had hung, and when the two men went closer they saw that part of the panelling was apparently missing. Peter felt in his pocket for the torch he carried, and switched it on, flashing the light into the hidden cupboard. It revealed a small chamber in the wall, and something else besides. A heap of bones were huddled on the floor of the chamber.

'Good Lord! A priest's hole!' Peter said. 'And some poor devil got in and couldn't get out. I say – pretty beastly, what?'

Charles set the lamp down on the table against the wall, and in silence looked at the dreadful remains. After a moment Peter cleared his throat, and said: 'Well – that's that. How did it all happen? I mean – there must have been something besides the picture hiding this hole.' He began to inspect the moulding all round the cavity. One of the rosettes was out of place. He put his hand on it, trying to see whether it would move, and found that it twisted stiffly between his fingers. The missing panel at once slid back into place. He opened it again, frowning. 'Odd. It looks as though the corner of the picture must have knocked it as it fell, yet I don't quite see how it can have forced the rosette round like that. Obviously the – the skeleton was huddled against the panel, and when it opened the skull fell out. You know, Chas, the idea of that poor beggar shut up there, dying of thirst...'

'Just a moment,' Charles said. 'Give me the torch, will you? Thanks.' He directed its light into the hole again and closely scrutinized the bones that lay there. 'Take a look, Peter. Does it strike you the bones are in rather a funny position?'

'What do you mean?' Peter peered at them. 'I don't know. There are the leg-bones, and the arms, all right. Difficult to say how they'd fall once the flesh had rotted away.'

'They look wrong to me,' Charles said. 'Almost as though they'd been put there by someone who wasn't an expert. Give me a hand up: I'm going to see if there isn't an answering catch on the inside of the panelling.'

Peter helped him to climb into the hole. 'What are you driving at? D'you mean that the fellow was murdered and his bones thrown in months later?'

'I don't know. No, there's no fastening on this side.

Faugh! what a smell of must!' He clambered out again. 'Let's take another look at the catch.' He tested it several times. It moved very stiffly. 'I shouldn't have said that it was possible for the picture to have pushed it out of place,' he said. He went across to where the picture lay and closely inspected the broken wire. It was old and rusty, and if it had been cut the operation had been performed too skilfully for it to be apparent.

'I agree with you,' Peter said. 'But that's how it must have happened. Hang it all, who could have faked this, and why? Not quite the sort of practical joke any of us would stage.'

'If it was faked,' said Charles slowly, 'I've an idea it wasn't done for a joke. Mind you, I'm not saying it was faked. It may have happened as we think it did. But I'm not entirely satisfied.'

'But who would . . . ?'

'Damn it, I don't know! Put the skull back, and close it up for to-night. To-morrow we shall have to bury the bones.'

'To-morrow,' said Peter, 'Celia and Margaret will pack their trunks and we shall depart.'

Charles looked at him. 'I'm staying. No ghost, or pseudo-ghost is going to frighten me out of this place. What about you?'

Peter grinned. 'Righto, I'm with you. But if you think this is part of a campaign to scare us away I'm going to town to fetch my old service revolver. Not that I think you're right. If the picture caught the rosette a pretty hard knock it might quite well have done the trick. Do you want to search the house?'

'Too late,' Charles said. 'Whoever was here – if anyone was here at all – has had loads of time to make a get-away.' He placed the skull back in the cavity, and closed the panel. 'Bowers had better come and clear away these bits of glass. I think we won't mention the priest's hole to

29

him.' He started to go downstairs, and as he reached the half-landing the door leading into the servants' wing below was burst open, and Bowers himself came into the hall with a very white face, and starting eyes. Charles called to him before he could reach the library door, and the butler jumped as though he had been shot.

A scared face was turned upward. 'Oh, it's you, sir!' Bowers gasped. 'Sir, I've seen it – I've seen the Monk! Oh Gawd, sir, we oughtn't ever to have come here!'

'Rubbish!' said Charles testily. 'What do you mean, you've seen the Monk? Where?'

'Out there in the moonlight, sir, plain as I see you. Gliding over the lawn it was, in a long black cloak. It's more than flesh and blood can bear, sir, and stay in this place I daren't, not for a thousand pounds!'

'Steady, you ass!' Peter interposed. 'Just you show us where you think you saw this Monk of yours.'

'Out of the pantry window, when I was bolting it for the night. Making for the trees at the end of the lawn it was, and it vanished amongst them, sir. You won't see it now: it's gone, but we've had our warning all right.'

'We'll see about that,' said Charles. 'Not a word of this to your mistress, Bowers.' He ran down the remaining stairs into the hall, and selected a stout walking-stick from the stand by the front-door. 'Bring your torch along, Peter. We'll go out through the garden-hall.'

'It's tempting Providence, sir,' Bowers moaned, following at their heels.

Charles was drawing back the bolts from the door leading into the garden. 'Console yourself, Bowers. If it's a ghost it can't hurt you.'

'Don't you be so sure of that, sir!' Bowers said forebodingly.

The door swung open. The gardens on that side of the house were flooded by moonlight, but where the spinney flanked the lawn it was very dark. The stillness seemed to wrap them round; not even a breath of wind stirred the leaves on the branches.

'Better take a look amongst the trees,' Peter said in a low voice.

'Don't you go, sir, you don't know what might happen to you!'

'Well, I'm not asking you to come,' Peter said. 'Do pull yourself together!'

Together he and Charles stepped out on to the gravel-path, and began to cross the lawn towards the belt of trees.

'Bit of imagination, if you ask me,' Peter growled. 'Good job he didn't see that skeleton.' Then he grabbed at Charles' arm, and gripped it hard. Some shadow had moved among the still shadows of the trees. 'There is something there!' Peter breathed. 'Go carefully!'

They stole forward in the lee of the overgrown hedge, and as they drew nearer to the trees a figure seemed to slide out of the darkness before them. They saw a form standing motionless on the edge of the lawn. Its face was in shadow, but it looked their way, and seemed to be awaiting them. Involuntarily they checked, for there was something strangely eerie about the waiting form, nor could they distinguish more than the outline of the figure, which seemed to be draped in some long garment that looked rather like a cassock. Then the figure moved and the spell was broken.

'I fear I am committing an act of trespass,' a mild voice announced. 'I am in pursuit of a specimen rare indeed in this country. Permit me to make myself known to you; I fear you thought me a thief in the night.' As it spoke the figure removed a slouch hat, and revealed a countenance adorned with steel-rimmed spectacles, and surmounted by sparse grey hair. 'I am an entomologist: my name is Ernest Titmarsh,' it said.

31

CHAPTER III

For a moment they stared at one another; then Peter began to laugh. Mr Ernest Titmarsh, far from being offended, beamed affably upon him. Peter pulled himself together as soon as he could, and said with a quiver in his voice: 'I beg your pardon, but really it's rather funny. You see, whenever we catch sight of anyone wandering about in our grounds we think he's a ghost.'

Mr Titmarsh blinked at him. 'Dear me, is that so indeed? A ghost, did you say?'

'Yes,' Charles said gravely. 'It's – it's an idiosyncrasy of ours.'

Mr Titmarsh replaced his hat upon his head, and seemed to give the matter some thought. Light broke upon him. 'Of course, of course!' he said. 'This is the Priory!'

'Didn't you know?' asked Peter, somewhat surprised.

'Now I come to look about me, yes,' replied their eccentric visitor. 'But I fear I am very absent-minded. Yes, yes, indeed, I owe you an apology. You are not, I suppose, interested in entomology?'

'I'm afraid I know very little about it,' confessed Peter.

'An absorbing study,' Mr Titmarsh said with enthusiasm. 'But it leads one into committing acts of trespass, as you perceive. Yes, I am much to blame. I will at once depart.'

'Oh, don't do that!' Charles interposed. 'We haven't the smallest objection to you – er – catching moths in our grounds. Now we know who you are we shan't take you for a ghost again.'

'Really,' said Mr Titmarsh, 'this is most kind. I repeat, *most* kind. Am I to understand that I have your permission to pursue my studies in your grounds? Tut-tut, this puts me under quite an obligation. Two evenings since, I observed what I believe to be an oleander hawk-moth. Yes, my dear sir, actually that rarest of specimens. I have great hopes of adding it to my collection. That will be indeed a triumph.'

'Well, in that case, we won't interrupt you any longer,' Charles said. 'We'll just wish you luck, and retire.'

Mr Titmarsh bowed with old-world courtesy, and as though his hobby suddenly called him, turned, and darted back amongst the trees.

'And there we are,' said Charles. 'Might as well live in a public park, as far as I can see. I wish I'd remembered to ask him if he was interested in skeletons.'

'I admit it looked a bit fishy, finding him snooping about just at this moment,' said Peter, 'but somehow I don't see him in the rôle of house-breaker. We'd better go in and reassure the girls,'

In the garden-hall they found Bowers, who had watched their proceedings with a gradual return to calm. He looked slightly sheepish when he learned who was the visitor, but he advanced the opinion that they had not heard the last of the Monk yet. This they were inclined to believe, but when they rejoined the girls they assumed the manner of those who had successfully laid a ghost.

Celia was not convinced, however. The discovery of the skeleton, she said, accounted for every strange noise they had heard, since its unquiet spirit was obviously haunting the scene of its ghastly end.

'I don't know about that,' said Mrs Bosanquet firmly, 'but I do know that it is most unhygienic to have dead bodies walled up in the house, and unless it is at once

33

removed, and the place thoroughly fumigated, I shall return to town to-morrow.'

'Oh!' said Celia, shuddering, 'you don't suppose I'm going to stay here any longer do you, Aunt? We shall all go home to-morrow. I only wish we'd sold the place when we had the offer.'

'Look here, Celia,' Peter said. 'If the ghost of that poor devil really has been haunting the place it's ten to one it'll stop bothering us once we've buried the remains. Don't fuss, Aunt Lilian. Of course we're going to bury the skeleton, and you can fumigate as much as you like. But I do think we oughtn't to throw up the sponge quite so easily.'

'Easily!' said Celia. 'I don't know what more you're waiting for! I shan't know a quiet moment if I have to stay in this place another day.'

Margaret was looking from Charles to her brother. 'Go on, Peter. You think we ought to give the place another chance?'

'I do. Hang it all, we shall look a pretty good set of asses if we bunk back to town simply because we've heard a few odd noises, and discovered a skeleton in a priest's hole.'

'Shall we?' said Celia, with awful irony. 'I suppose we ought to have expected an ordinary little thing like a skeleton?'

'Not the skeleton, but we might have guessed there'd be a priest's hole. Be a sport, Celia! If you actually see a ghost, or if any more skulls fall out of cupboards I'll give in, and take you back to town myself.'

Celia looked imploringly at her husband. 'I can't, Chas. You know what I am, and I can't help it if I'm stupid about these things, but every time I open my wardrobe I shall be terrified of what may be inside.'

'All right, darling,' Charles replied. 'You shan't be martyred. I suggest you and Margaret and Aunt Lilian clear out to-morrow. I'll run you up to town, and...'

Celia sat bolt upright. 'Do you mean you'll stay here?'

'That's rather the idea,' he admitted.

'Charles, you can't!' she said, agitated. 'I won't let you!'

'I shan't be alone. Peter's staying too.'

Celia clasped his arm. 'No, don't, Charles. You don't *know* what might happen, and how on earth could I go away like that, and leave you here?'

Margaret's clear voice made itself heard. 'Why are you so keen to stay?' she asked.

'Pride, my dear,' Charles said. 'Of course, with me it's natural heroism. Peter's trying to live up to me.'

She shook her head. 'You've got something up your sleeve. Neither of you would be so silly as to stay on here, mucking up your holiday, just to prove you weren't afraid of ghosts.'

'But it's getting worse!' Celia cried. '*What* have you got up your sleeve? I insist on knowing! Chas! Peter!'

Peter hesitated. 'To tell you the truth, Sis, I don't quite know. As far as I can make out, Chas has got an idea someone's at the root of all this ghost business.'

With great deliberation Mrs Bosanquet put down her Patience pack. 'I may be stupid,' she said, 'but I don't understand what you're talking about. Who is at the back of what you call this "ghost business," and why?'

'Dear Aunt,' said Charles, 'that is precisely the problem we hope to solve by staying here.'

'All those noises? The picture falling down?' Margaret said eagerly. 'You think someone did it all? Someone real?'

'I don't know, but I think it's possible. I may be wrong, in which case I'll eat my disbelief, and go about henceforward swearing there are such things as ghosts.'

'Yes, that's all very well,' objected Celia, 'but why on earth should anyone want to make ghost-noises and things at us? And who could have done it? Neither of the

Bowers would, and how could anyone else get into the house without us knowing?'

'Easily,' said Charles. 'There's more than one way in, besides windows.'

'That quite decides me,' Mrs Bosanquet announced. 'No one is a greater believer in fresh air than I am, but if I am to remain in this house, I shall sleep with my windows securely bolted.'

'I still don't quite see it,' Margaret said. 'I suppose it would be fairly easy to get into the house, but you haven't explained why anyone should want to.'

'Don't run away with the idea that I'm wedded to this notion!' Charles warned her. 'I admit it sounds far-fetched, but it has occurred to me that someone – for reasons which I can't explain – may be trying to scare us out of this place.'

There was a short silence. Celia broke it. 'That's just like you!' she said indignantly. 'Sooner than own you've been wrong all these years about ghosts you make up a much more improbable story to account for the manifestations. I never heard such rot in all my life!'

'Thank you, darling, thank you,' Charles said gravely.

'Hold on a minute!' interrupted Margaret. 'Perhaps Chas is right.'

Celia almost snorted. 'Don't you pay any attention to him, my dear. He'll tell us next it's the man who wanted to buy the Priory from us trying to get us out of it.'

'Well, while we're on the improbable lay, what about that for a theory?' demanded Peter. 'Resourceful sort of bloke, what?'

Mrs Bosanquet resumed her Patience. 'Whoever it may be, it's a piece of gross impertinence,' she said. 'You are quite right, Charles. I am certainly not going to leave the place because some ill-bred person is trying to frighten me away. The proper course is to inform the police at once.'

'From my small experience of local constabulary I don't

think that'd be much use,' said Charles. 'Moreover what with Margaret's sinister pal and the egregious Mr Titmarsh, we've got quite enough people littered about the grounds without adding a flat-footed bobby to the collection.'

'Further,' added Peter, 'I for one have little or no desire to figure as the laughing-stock of the village. I move that we keep this thing quiet, and do a little sleuthing on our own.'

Margaret waved a hand aloft at once. 'Rather! I say, this is getting really thrilling. Come on, Celia, don't be snitchy!'

'All right,' Celia said reluctantly. 'I can't go away and leave you here, so I suppose I've got to give in. But I won't go upstairs alone after dark, and I won't be left for one moment by myself in this house, day or night, and Charles isn't to do anything foolhardy, and if anything awful happens we all of us clear out without any further argument.'

'Agreed,' Peter said. 'What about you, Aunt Lilian?'

'Provided the dead body is decently interred, and a secure bolt fixed to my door, I shall certainly remain,' answered Mrs Bosanquet.

'What could be fairer than that?' said Charles. 'If you like you can even superintend the burial.'

'No, thank you, my dear,' she replied. 'I have never yet attended a funeral, and I don't propose to start with this body in which I have not the smallest interest. Not but what I am very sorry that whoever it was died in such unpleasant circumstances, but I do not feel that it has anything to do with me, and I could wish it had happened elsewhere.'

'Well, since we're all making stipulations,' Margaret put in, 'I can't help feeling that I should rather like to have the door between Peter's room and mine open. D'you mind, Peter?'

'I can bear it,' he answered. 'As for the bones, Chas and I will bury them to-morrow, and we'll say nothing about them, any of us. See?'

'Just as you please, my dear,' Mrs Bosanquet replied. 'But I cannot help feeling that the police should be told. However, that is for you to decide. Celia, you had better come up to bed. I am coming too, so there is nothing to be alarmed about.'

'I hate the idea of going up those stairs,' Celia shuddered.

'Nonsense!' said Mrs Bosanquet, and bore her inexorably away.

The two men's task next morning was sufficiently gruesome to throw a cloud of depression over their spirits. Not even the sight of Mrs Bosanquet sprinkling Lysol in the priest's hole could lighten the general gloom, and when, after lunch, Charles suggested that he and Peter might go out fishing it was with somewhat forced cheerfulness that Peter agreed.

But an afternoon spent by the trout stream did much to restore their spirits. The fish were rising well, and the weather conditions were ideal.

They worked some way down the stream, and when they at last set out to return to the Priory they found themselves a considerable distance away from it. Charles' bump of locality, however, served them well, and he was able to lead the way home across country, by a route that brought them eventually to the footpath Michael Strange had so unaccountably failed to find.

It was already nearly time for dinner, and the two men quickened their steps. They had left the footpath, and were just skirting the ruined chapel when the sound of footsteps made them glance back towards the right-of-way. Where they stood they were more or less hidden from the path by a portion of the chapel wall. Thinking the pedestrian one of the villagers on his way home, they were about to continue on their way when the man came into sight round a bend in the path, and they saw that it was none other than the commercial gentleman they had first seen in the taproom of the Bell Inn. This in itself was not very surprising, but the stranger's behaviour caused both men, as though by tacit consent, to draw farther into the lee of the chapel wall. The small stranger was proceeding rather cautiously, and looking about him as though he expected to meet someone. He paused as he came abreast of the chapel, and peeped into the ruins. Then, after hesitating for a moment he gave a surprisingly sweet whistle, rather like the notes of a thrush. This was answered almost at once from somewhere near at hand; there came a rustling amongst the bushes, and Michael Strange stepped out on to the path from the direction of the Priory gardens.

Charles placed a warning hand on Peter's arm; Peter nodded, and stayed very still.

'Any luck?' inquired the small man, in a low voice.

Strange shook his head. 'No. We shall have to try the other way again.'

'Ah!' said the other gloomily. 'I don't half like it, guv'nor, and that's the truth. Supposing we was to be seen? It would look a bit unnatural, wouldn't it? It's risky, that's what it is. One of them might wake up, and I don't see myself doing no spook stunts. Clean out of my line, that is. I done some jobs in my time, as you know, but I don't like this one. It's one thing to crack a crib, but this job ain't what I'd call straightforward.'

'You'll be all right,' Strange said rather impatiently. 'If you'd remember not to waylay me where we might easily be seen together. Go on ahead. I'll follow.'

'All right, guv'nor: just as you say,' the small man replied, unabashed, and moved off down the path.

When Strange had gone Charles looked at Peter. 'Very interesting,' he said. 'What did you make of it?'

'God knows. It sounded as though they were going to burgle the place, but I suppose it's not that. It looks very much as though one or both of them were responsible for last night's picnic.'

'And they'll have to "try the other way again,"' mused Charles. 'Look here, Peter, are you game to sit up tonight with me, and see what happens?'

'Of course, but Celia'll throw a fit.'

'I'll join you as soon as she's asleep. If nothing happens we've simply got to repeat the performance till something does. I wish I knew what they were after.'

'Meanwhile,' said Peter, consulting his wrist-watch, 'it's already half-past seven, and we're dining with old Ackerley at eight.' He stopped suddenly. 'By Jove! Think that mysterious pair will get going in the house while we're out? I hadn't thought of that.'

'No,' said Charles. 'The little chap spoke of one of us "waking up."'

'All the same,' Peter said, 'I move that we don't stay late at the White House.'

In spite of what Charles said, Peter felt ill at ease about leaving the Priory in the sole charge of the Bowers. Clever crooks, he was sure, would know the movements of their prospective victims. Yet if burglary were meditated surely these particular crooks would find it an easy enough task to break into the Priory without shadowing the place at all hours, and searching for – what? There he found himself up against a blank wall again. Strange and his odd companion had certainly been looking for something, but what it was, or what connexion it could have with a possible burglary he had no idea.

He realized that his mind harped all the time on burglary, and was forced to admit to himself that it was an improbable solution. There was very little of value in the house, and if anything so unlikely as hidden treasure were being sought for it was incredible that the thieves should have waited until the house was tenanted before they made an attempt to find it.

Charles obviously connected the affair of the previous evening with Strange, in which case it looked as though Strange's primary object was to frighten the tenants out of the house. He wondered whether he would seize the opportunity this dinner-party afforded to stage another, and even more nerve-racking, booby-trap.

Peter arrived at the White House with the rest of his family just as eight o'clock struck. His sisters, who had reviled both him and Charles for staying out so late, drew two sighs of relief.

'Scaremongers,' said Charles. 'I told you it wouldn't take us ten minutes to get here.'

They had walked to the White House across their own grounds, a proceeding which Celia had condemned, dreading the return late at night, but which had been forced on them, not only on account of its convenience, but on account also of the car, which had developed slight magneto trouble, and refused to start.

They entered the drawing-room to find that Mr Titmarsh, and Dr Roote and his wife, fellow-guests, had already arrived, and Celia was just telling her host laughingly that if they were late he must blame her menfolk, when the Colonel's butler opened the door to announce yet another guest. To Peter's amazement Michael Strange walked into the room.

'I don't think you know Strange, do you?' the Colonel said, to the room at large. He began to introduce the dark young man.

'Yes, we've met twice,' Margaret said, when it came to her turn. She smiled at Strange. 'How do you do? How's the fishing?'

'Splendid!' he said. He turned to Charles. 'Have you tried the streams here yet?'

Seen in such civilized surroundings it was hard to

believe that this young man was the same who had, not an hour ago, held a furtive conversation with a character whose own words proclaimed him to be a member of the criminal classes. Feeling more completely at sea than ever, Charles answered his question with a description of the afternoon's sport. Dinner was announced almost immediately, and the Colonel began to marshal his guests.

'I must apologize for our uneven numbers,' he said breezily. 'Four ladies to six men! Well, I think we'd better go in all together. Mrs Bosanquet, let me show you the way.'

'Too many men is a fault on the good side, anyway, isn't it?' Mrs Roote said. She was a good-looking blonde, grown a little haggard, and with a rather harsh voice. Her husband was an untidy individual of some forty years, whose huskiness of speech and rather hazy eye betrayed his weakness. His address, however, was pleasant, and he seemed to be getting on well with Celia, whom he took in to dinner behind the Colonel and Mrs Bosanquet.

The White House was a solid Victorian building, with large airy rooms, and the boon of electric light. It was furnished in good if rather characterless style, but evidence of the Colonel's ownership existed in the various trophies that adorned the dining-room walls. Mrs Bosanquet remarked as she took her seat at the round table that it was pleasant to find herself in an up-to-date house again.

'Oh, I'm afraid the White House is a very dull affair after the Priory,' Colonel Ackerley replied. 'Suits me, you know; never had much use for old buildings. Full of draughts and inconvenience, *I* always say, but I'm afraid I'm a regular vandal. I can see Mrs Malcolm shaking her head at me.'

Celia laughed. 'I wasn't,' she assured him. 'I was shaking it at Mr Titmarsh.' She turned to her other neighbour again. 'No, I'm absolutely ignorant about butterflies and things, but it sounds *most* interesting. Do...'

Mr Titmarsh eyed her severely. 'Moths, madam!' he said.

'Yes, moths. I meant moths. I've noticed quite a number here. They will fly into our candles.'

Margaret, who was seated between her brother and Strange, said softly: 'Do listen to my sister floundering hopelessly!' She shook out her table-napkin, and began to drink her soup. 'You know, you're a fraud,' she said. 'You told me you didn't know anyone in Framley.'

'Honestly, it was quite true,' Michael replied. 'I only met the Colonel last night. He blew into the Bell, and we got talking, and he very kindly asked me to dine with him. In fact' – his eyes twinkled – 'he wouldn't take No for an answer.'

'I think you must be a recluse, or something,' Margaret teased him. 'Why should you want him to take No for an answer?'

'I didn't,' said Strange, looking down at her, with a smile. 'He told me you were coming.'

Margaret blushed at that, but laughed. 'I feel I ought to get up and bow,' she said.

Peter, who had heard, leaned forward to speak to Strange across his sister. 'Were you on the right-of-way late this afternoon?' he asked. 'I thought I caught a glimpse of you.'

If he hoped that Michael Strange would betray uneasiness he was disappointed. 'Yes,' Strange said tranquilly. 'I was fishing the Crewel again to-day. I didn't see you.'

'Oh, I was some way off,' Peter answered.

In a momentary lull in the general conversation Celia's voice was heard. 'And you saw this rare moth in our grounds? How exciting! Tell me what it looks like.'

'Ah, that oleander hawk-moth,' said Charles. 'Did you

have any luck, sir?'

'Not yet,' Mr Titmarsh said. 'Not yet, but I do not despair.'

The Colonel broke off in the middle of what he was saying to Mrs Bosanquet to exclaim: 'Hullo, have you been chasing moths at the Priory, Titmarsh? Never shall forget how I took you for a burglar when I first found you in my garden.'

His hearty laugh was echoed more mildly by the entomologist, who said: 'I fear I am somewhat remiss in asking the permission of my good neighbours if I may trespass harmlessly on their land. Your husband,' he added, looking at Celia, 'mistook me for a ghost.'

'Oh, have you seen the Priory ghost yet?' Mrs Roote inquired. 'Do harrow us! I adore having my flesh made to creep.'

Strange, who had looked directly across the table at Mr Titmarsh from under his black brows, said quietly to Margaret: 'Is that really true? Does he prowl round the countryside looking for moths?'

'Yes, so they all say. Charles and Peter saw him in our garden last night. He's rather eccentric, I think.'

'What with myself and – what's his name? Titmarsh? – you seem to be beset by people who roam about your grounds at will,' Strange remarked. 'If I remember rightly you said you took me for the ghost as well.'

'Ah, that was just a joke,' Margaret answered. 'I didn't really. And of course Charles and Peter wouldn't have taken Mr Titmarsh for one in the ordinary course of events.'

'You mean that you all rather expect to see the famous Monk?'

'No, but that was the night...' She broke off.

Strange looked inquiringly down at her. 'Yes?'

'Nothing,' Margaret said rather lamely.

'That sounds very mysterious,' Strange said. 'Have you

been having trouble with the Monk?'

She shook her head. Colonel Ackerley called across the table: 'What's that? Talking about the Priory ghost? These fair ladies are much too stout-hearted to believe in it, Strange. It would take more than the Monk to shake your nerve, Mrs Bosanquet, wouldn't it?'

'I am thankful to say I have never suffered from nerves,' Mrs Bosanquet responded. 'But it is certainly very disturbing when...' She encountered Charles' eye and blinked. 'When the servants are afraid to stay in the house after dark,' she concluded placidly.

'I'm sure you've seen something!' chattered Mrs Roote. 'Or at least heard awful noises. Now haven't you, Mrs Bosanquet?'

'Unfortunately,' replied Mrs Bosanquet, 'I suffer from slight deafness.'

'I see you're all of you determined not to satisfy our morbid curiosity,' said Strange.

Mr Titmarsh took off his spectacles and polished them. 'On the subject of ghosts,' he said, 'I am a confirmed sceptic. I am devoid of curiosity.'

'Well, I don't know so much about that,' said Dr Roote. 'I remember a very queer experience that happened to a friend of mine once. Now, he was one of the most matter-of-fact people I know...' He embarked on a long and rather involved ghost story, interrupted and prompted at intervals by his wife, and it only ended with the departure of the ladies from the dining-room.

Two bridge tables were formed presently, but the party broke up shortly before eleven. The Rootes were the first to leave, and they were soon followed by the Priory party and Strange. Strange's two-seater stood at the door, and when he found that the others were walking back across the park he promptly offered to take the three women in his car.

Celia, who had already begun to peer fearfully into the

darkness, jumped at the offer, but stipulated that Strange should not leave them until Charles and Peter had reached the house. 'You'll think me a fool,' she said, 'but the Priory after dark is more than I can bear. Can we really all get into your car?'

'If one of you doesn't mind sitting in the dickey I think it can be managed,' Strange replied. 'And of course I'll wait till your husband gets back. I'm only sorry I can't take you all.'

'Well, really, this is most opportune,' said Mrs Bosanquet, getting into the little car. 'I notice that there is quite a heavy dew on the ground.'

Whatever Strange's wishes may have been it was Margaret who sat in the dickey, while Celia managed to insert her slim person between Mrs Bosanquet and the door.

'We've no business to impose on you like this, of course,' Celia said, as the car slid out of the White House gates. 'It's only a step, across the park, but I do so hate the dark.'

'It's not an imposition at all,' Michael answered. He drove down the road for the short distance that separated the White House from the Priory, and turned carefully in at the rather awkward entrance to the long avenue. The headlights showed the drive winding ahead, and made the tall trees on either side look like walls of darkness. The house came presently into sight, and in a few moments they were all inside the softly-lighted hall.

Celia stood for an instant as though listening. The house seemed to be wrapped in stillness. 'I love it by day,' she said abruptly. 'It's only at night it gets different. Like this. Can't you feel it? A sort of boding.'

'Why are you so afraid of it?' Strange asked her. 'You must have some reason other than village-gossip. Has anything happened to alarm you?'

She gave a tiny shiver. 'I'm a fool, that's all,' she

46

answered. 'Let's go into the library.' A tray with drinks had been set out there. 'Do help yourself,' she said. 'There's whisky, or a soft drink, whichever you prefer.'

'Can I bring you anything?'

'I'd like some lemonade, please.'

Mrs Bosanquet emerged from the cloud of tulle she had swathed round her head. 'My own opinion is, and always will be,' she said firmly, 'that there are no such things as ghosts. And if – mind you, I only say *if* – I thought there was anything odd about a house, I, personally, should inform the police.'

Strange carried a glass over to where Celia was sitting. 'Is that what you've done?' he asked.

'Not at all,' she replied. 'I said "if." '

'Would you do that, Mr Strange?' Margaret inquired. 'Just supposing you heard weird sounds and things?'

'No, I don't think I should,' he said. 'I'm afraid I haven't much opinion of village policemen.'

'My husband hasn't either,' Celia said. She heard a latchkey grate in the lock. 'Here he is!' she said. 'Is that you, Charles?'

'I'm not quite sure,' came the answer. 'It used to be, but since the experiences of the last ten minutes...'

'Good heavens, you haven't seen the ghost, have you?' cried Margaret.

Charles appeared in the doorway, minus his shoes. Over his shoulder Peter said, grinning: 'He encountered a little mud, that's all.'

'If you want to know the truth,' said Charles, 'I have narrowly escaped death by drowning in quicksands. Thank you, yes, and don't overdo the soda! Too much of water hast thou, poor Charles Malcolm.'

'Oh, I know! You must have found that boggy patch,' said Margaret.

'I trust it was not the cesspool,' Mrs Bosanquet said, in mild concern.

'So do I,' Charles said. 'That thought had not so far occurred to me, but – but I do hope it wasn't.'

'Take heart,' said Strange, setting down his glass. 'I think your cesspool is more likely to be down near the river.' He went up to Celia, and held out his hand. 'I'm sure you're longing to get to bed, Mrs Malcolm, so I'll say good-night.'

He took his leave of them all. Peter escorted him to the front door, and when the two of them had left the room Charles said: 'Well, of all the miserable conspirators commend me to you three! I should think by to-morrow the whole countryside will know that something has happened here.'

'Really, Charles!' Mrs Bosanquet expostulated. 'It is true that I was about to make a reference to what happened last night, but I am sure I covered it up most naturally.'

'Dear Aunt,' said Charles frankly, 'not one of you would have deceived an oyster.'

Peter came back into the room. 'You seem to be getting very thick with Strange,' he said to his sister. 'Did you happen to find out what he is, or anything about him?'

'He's a surveyor,' said Charles, finishing what was left of his whisky and soda.

'A surveyor?' echoed Margaret. 'How do you know? Did he tell you so?'

'To the deductive mind,' said Charles airily, 'his profession was obvious from his knowledge of the probable whereabouts of our cesspool.'

'Ass!' said Celia. 'Come on up to bed. What does it matter what he is? He's nice, that's all I know.'

It was two hours later when Charles came downstairs again, and he had changed into a tweed suit, and was wearing rubber-soled shoes. Peter was already in the library, reading by the light of one lamp. He looked up as Charles came in. 'Celia asleep?' he asked.

'She was when I left her, but I've trod on nineteen creaking boards since then. Have you been round the house?'

'I have, and I defy anyone to get in without us hearing.'

Charles went across to draw the heavy curtains still more closely together over the windows. 'If Strange really means to try and get in to-night, he won't risk it for another hour or two,' he prophesied. 'Hanged if I can make that fellow out!'

'From what I could gather,' Peter said, 'he did his best to pump Margaret. Seemed to want to find out how we were getting on here.'

Charles grunted, and drew a chair up to the desk and proceeded to study a brief which had been sent on from town that morning. Peter retired into his book again, and for a long while no sound broke the silence save the crackle of the papers under Charles' hand, and the measured tick of the old grandfather clock in the hall. At last Peter came to the end of his novel, and closed it. He yawned, and looked at his wrist-watch. 'Good Lord! two o'clock already! Do we sit here till breakfast-time? I've an idea I shan't feel quite so fresh to-morrow night.'

Charles pushed his papers from him with a short sigh of exasperation. 'I don't know why people go to law,' he said gloomily. 'More money than sense.'

'Got a difficult case?' inquired Peter.

'I haven't got a case at all,' was the withering retort. 'And that's counsel's learned opinion. Would you like to go and fetch me something to eat from the larder?'

'No,' said Peter, 'since you put it like that, I shouldn't.'

'Then I shall have to go myself,' said Charles, getting up. 'There was a peculiarly succulent pie if I remember rightly.'

'Well, bring it in here, and I'll help you eat it,' Peter offered. 'And don't forget the bread!'

Before Charles could open his mouth to deliver a

suitable reply a sound broke the quiet of the house, and brought Peter to his feet in one startled bound. For the sound was that same eerie groan which they had heard before, and which seemed to rise shuddering from somewhere beneath their feet.

CHAPTER IV

The weird sound died, and again silence settled down on the house. Yet somehow the silence seemed now to be worse than that hair-raising groan. Something besides themselves was in the house.

Peter passed his tongue between lips that had grown suddenly dry. He looked at Charles, standing motionless in the doorway. Charles was listening intently; he held up a warning finger.

Softly Peter went across to his side. Charles said under his breath:

'Wait. No use plunging round the house haphazard. Turn the lamp down.'

Peter went back, and in a moment only a glimmer of light illumined the room. He drew his torch out of his pocket and stood waiting by the table.

It seemed to him that the minutes dragged past. Straining his ears he thought he could hear little sounds, tiny creaks of furniture, perhaps the scutter of a mouse somewhere in the wainscoting. The ticking of the clock seemed unusually loud, and when an owl hooted outside it made him jump.

A stair creaked; Charles' torch flashed a white beam of light across the empty hall, and went out again. He slightly shook his head in answer to Peter's quick look of inquiry.

Peter found himself glancing over his shoulder towards the window. He half thought that one of the curtains moved slightly, but when he moved cautiously forward to draw it back there was nothing there. He let it fall into position again, and stood still, wishing that something, anything, would happen to break this nerve-racking silence.

He saw Charles stiffen suddenly, and incline his head as though to hear more distinctly. He stole to his side. 'What?' he whispered.

'Listen!'

Again the silence fell. Peter broke it. 'What did you hear?'

'A thud. There it is again!'

A muffled knock reached Peter's ears. It seemed to come from underneath. In a moment it was repeated, a dull thud, drawing nearer, as though something was striking against a stone wall.

'The cellars!' Peter hissed. 'There must be a way in that we haven't found!'

Again the knocking, deadened by the solid floor, was repeated. It was moving nearer still, and seemed now to sound directly beneath their feet.

'Come on!' Charles said, and slipped the torch into his left hand. He picked up the stout ash-plant which he had placed ready for use, and stole out, and across the hall to the door that shut off the servants' wing from the rest of the house.

The stairs leading down to the cellars were reached at the end of the passage. They were stone, and the two men crept down them without a sound to betray their presence. At the foot Charles said in Peter's ear: 'Know your way about?'

'No,' Peter whispered. 'We don't use the cellars.'

'Damn!' Charles switched on his torch again.

The place felt dank and very cold. Grey walls of stone flanked the passage; the roof was of stone also, and vaulted. Charles moved forward, down the arched corridor, in the direction of the library. Various cellars led out of the main passage; in the first was a great mound of coal, but the rest were empty.

The passage seemed to run down one side of the building, but the vaults that gave on to it led each one into another, so that the place was something of a labyrinth. The knocking sounded distinctly now, echoing through the empty cellars. Charles held his torch lowered, so that the circle of light was thrown barely a yard in front of him.

Suddenly the knocking ceased, and at once both men stood still, waiting for some sound to guide them.

Ahead of them, where the passage ended, something moved. Charles flashed his torch upwards, and for a brief instant he and Peter caught a glimpse of a vague figure. Then, as though it had melted into the wall, it was gone, and a wail as of a soul in torment seemed to fill the entire place.

The sweat broke out on both men's foreheads, and for a second neither could move for sheer horror. Then Charles pulled himself together and dashed forward, shouting to Peter to follow.

'My God, what was it?' Peter gasped.

'The groan we've all heard, of course. Damn it, he can't have got away!'

But the place where the figure had stood was quite empty. An embrasure in the wall seemed to mark the spot where they had seen it, yet if the apparent melting into the wall had been no more than a drawing back into this niche that could not solve the complete disappearance of the figure.

The two men stared at one another. Charles passed the back of his hand across his forehead. 'But – but I saw it!' he stammered.

'So did I,' Peter said roughly. 'Good God, it *can't* be ... This is getting a bit too weird to be pleasant. Look here ...

Damn it, that was no ghost. There must be a secret way through the wall.' His torch played over the wall. It was built of great stone slabs each about four foot square. He began to feel them in turn. 'We must be under the terrace,' he said. 'Gosh, don't you see? We're standing on the level of the ground here!' One of the blocks gave slightly under the thrust of his hand. 'Got it!' he panted, and set his shoulder to it. It swung slowly outward, turning on some hidden pivot, and as it moved that hideous wail once more rent the stillness.

'So that's it, is it?' Charles said grimly. 'Well, I don't mind telling you that I'm damned glad we've solved the origin of that ghastly noise.' He squeezed through the opening in Peter's wake, and found himself, as Peter had prophesied, in the garden directly beneath the terrace. There was no sign of anyone amongst the shrubs near at hand, and it was obviously useless to search the grounds. After a moment both men slipped back into the cellar, and pushed the stone into place again.

'Might as well have a look round to see what that chap was after,' Peter said. 'Why the banging? Is he looking for a hollow wall, do you suppose? Dash it, I rejected hidden treasure as altogether too far-fetched, but it begins to look remarkably like it!'

'Personally I don't think we shall find anything,' Charles answered. 'Still, we can try. What a maze the place is!'

Together they explored all the cellars, but Charles was right, and there was nothing to be seen. Deciding that their nocturnal visitor would hardly attempt another entrance now that his way of ingress had been discovered, they made their way up the stairs again.

As they crossed the hall towards the library door a glimmer of light shone on the landing above, and Margaret's voice called softly: 'Peter.'

'Hullo!' Peter responded.

'Thank goodness!' breathed his sister, and came cautiously down to join him. In the lamplight her face looked rather pale, and her eyes very big and scared. 'That awful groan woke me,' she said. 'I heard it twice, and called to you, Peter. Then when you didn't answer I went into your room and saw the bed hadn't been slept in. I got the most horrible fright.'

'Don't make a row. Come into the library,' Peter commanded. 'You didn't wake Celia, did you?'

'No, I guessed you and Charles had staged something. Did you hear the groan? What have you been doing?'

'We not only heard it, but on two occasions we caused it,' Peter said, and proceeded to tell her briefly all that had happened.

She listened in wondering silence, but when he spoke of the part he believed Strange to be playing, she broke in with an emphatic and somewhat indignant headshake. 'I'm sure he isn't a crook! And I'm perfectly certain he'd never make awful noises to frighten us, or put skeletons where we should find them. Besides, why should he?'

'I'm not prepared to answer that question without due warning,' Charles said cautiously. 'All I know about him at present is that he's a rather mysterious fellow who holds distinctly fishy conversations with a palpable old lag, and who – apparently – knows how to get round persons of your sex.'

'That's all rot,' Margaret said without hesitation. 'There's nothing in the least mysterious about him, and I expect if you'd heard more of it you'd have found that the fishy conversation was quite innocent really. You know how you can say things that sound odd in themselves, and yet don't mean anything.'

'I hotly resent this reflection upon my conversation,' Charles said.

'You've got to remember too, Peg, that when we heard that groan before, we found Strange close up to the house,

55

and on the same side as the secret entrance,' Peter interposed. 'I don't say that that proves anything, but it ought to be borne in mind. I certainly think that Mr Michael Strange's proceedings want explaining.'

'I think it's utterly absurd!' Margaret said. 'Why, you might as well suspect Mr Titmarsh!' Having delivered herself of which scornful utterance, she rose, and announced her intention of going back to bed.

To be on the safe side, Charles and Peter spent the following morning in sealing up the hidden entrance. An account of the night's happenings did much to reconcile Celia to her enforced stay at the Priory. Human beings, she said, she wasn't in the least afraid of.

'I only hope,' said Mrs Bosanquet pessimistically, 'that we are not all murdered in our beds.'

Both she and Celia were agreed that the latest development made the calling in of police aid imperative. The men were still loth to do this, but they had to admit that Celia had reason on her side.

'There's no longer any question of being laughed at,' she argued. 'Someone broke into this house last night, and it's for the police to take the matter in hand. It's all very well for you two to fancy yourselves in the rôle of amateur detectives, but I should feel a lot easier in my mind if some real detectives got going.'

'How can you?' said Charles unctuously. 'When you lost your diamond brooch, who found it?'

'I did,' Celia replied. 'Wedged between the bristles of my hair-brush. That was after you'd had the waste up in the bath, and two of the floor-boards in our room.'

'That wasn't the time I meant,' said Charles hastily.

Celia wrinkled her brow. 'The only other time I lost it was at that hotel in Edinburgh, and then you stepped on it getting out of bed. If that's what you mean ...'

'Well, wasn't that finding it?' demanded Charles. 'Guided by a rare intuition, I rose from my couch, and straightway put my – er – foot on the thing.'

'You did. But that wasn't quite how you phrased it at the time,' said Celia. 'If I remember rightly ...'

'You needn't go on,' Charles told her. 'When it comes to recounting incidents in which I played a prominent part you never do remember rightly. To put it bluntly, for gross misrepresentation of fact you're hard to beat.'

'Time!' called Peter. 'Let's put it to the vote. Who is for calling in the police, or who is not? Margaret, you've got the casting vote. What do you say?'

She hesitated. 'I think I rather agree with Celia. You both suspect Mr Strange. Well, I'm sure you're wrong. Let the police take over before you go and make fools of yourselves.' She added apologetically: 'I don't mean to be rude about it, but ...'

'I'm glad to know that,' said Charles. 'I mean, we might easily have misunderstood you. But what a field of conjecture this opens out! I shall always wonder what you'd have said if you had meant to be rude.'

'Well, you'll know in a minute,' retorted Margaret. 'And it's no good blinking facts: once you and Peter get an idea into your heads, nothing on God's earth will get it out again. You will make fools of yourselves if you go sleuthing after the unfortunate Mr Strange. If he is at the root of it the police'll find him out, and if he isn't they'll find *that* out weeks before you would.'

After that, as Peter said, there was nothing to be done but to go and interview the village constable at once. Accordingly he and Charles set out for Framley after lunch, and found the constable, a bucolic person of the name of Flinders, digging his garden.

He received them hopefully, but no sooner had they explained their errand than his face fell somewhat, and he scratched his chin with a puzzled air.

'You'd better come inside, sir,' he said, after profound thought. He led them up the narrow path to his front door, and ushered them into the living-room of his cottage. He asked them to sit down and to excuse him for a moment, and vanished into the kitchen at the back of the cottage. Sounds of splashing followed, and in a few moments Constable Flinders reappeared, having washed his earth-caked hands, and put on his uniform coat. With this he had assumed an imposing air of officialdom, and he held in his hand the usual grimy little notebook. 'Now, sir!' he said importantly, and took a chair at the table opposite his visitors. He licked the stub of a pencil. 'You say you found some person or persons breaking into your house with intent to commit a robbery?'

'I don't think I said that at all,' Charles replied. 'I found the person in my cellars. What he came for I've no idea.'

'Ah!' said Mr Flinders. 'That's very different, that is.' He licked the pencil again, reflectively. 'Did you reckernize this person?'

Charles hesitated. 'No,' he answered at last. 'There wasn't time. He escaped by this secret way I told you about.'

'Escaped by secret way,' repeated Mr Flinders, laboriously writing it down. 'I shall have to see that, sir.'

'I can show you the spot, but I'm afraid we've already cemented it up.'

Mr Flinders shook his head reproachfully. 'You shouldn't have done that,' he pronounced. 'That'll make it difficult for me to act, that will.'

'Why?' asked Peter.

Mr Flinders looked coldly at him. 'I ought to have been called in before any evidence of the crime had been disturbed,' he said.

'There wasn't a crime,' Peter pointed out.

This threw the constable momentarily out of his stride. He thought again for some time, and presently asked: 'And you don't suspect no one in particular?'

Peter glanced at Charles, who said: 'Rather difficult to

say. I haven't any good reason to suspect anyone, but various people have been seen hanging about the Priory at different times.'

'Ah!' said Mr Flinders. 'Now we are getting at something, sir. I thought we should. You'll have to tell me who you've seen hanging round, and then I shall know where I am.'

'Well,' said Charles. 'There's Mr Titmarsh to start with.'

The constable's official cloak slipped from his shoulders. 'Lor', sir, he wouldn't hurt a fly!' he said.

'I don't know what he does to flies,' retorted Charles, 'but he's death on moths.'

Mr Flinders shook his head. 'Of course I shall have to follow it up,' he said darkly. 'That's what my duty is, but Mr Titmarsh don't mean no harm. He was catching moths, that's what he was doing.'

'So he told us, and for all I know it may be perfectly true. But I feel I should like to know something about the eccentric gentleman. You say he's above suspicion . . .'

He was stopped by a large hand raised warningly. 'No, sir, that I never said, nor wouldn't. It'll have to be *sifted*. That's what I said.'

'. . . and,' continued Charles, disregarding the interruption, 'I can't say that I myself think he's likely to be the guilty party. How long has he lived here?'

Mr Flinders thought for a moment. 'Matter of three years,' he answered.

'Anything known about him?'

'There isn't nothing known *against* him, sir,' said the constable. 'Barring his habits, which is queer to some folk's way of thinking, but which others who has such hobbies can understand, he's what I'd call a very ordinary gentleman. Keeps himself to himself, as the saying is. He's not married, but Mrs Fellowes from High Barn, who is his housekeeper, hasn't never spoken a word against him, and she's a very respectable woman that wouldn't stop a day in a place where there was any goings-on that oughtn't to be.'

'She might not know,' Peter suggested.

'There's precious little happens in Framley that Mrs Fellowes don't know about, sir,' said Mr Flinders. '*And* knows more than what the people do themselves,' he added obscurely, but with considerable feeling.

'Putting Mr Titmarsh aside for the moment,' said Charles. 'The other two men we've encountered in our grounds are a Mr Strange, who is staying at the Bell, and a smallish chap, giving himself out to be a commercial traveller, who's also at the Bell.' He recounted under what circumstances he had met Michael Strange, and the constable brightened considerably. 'That's more like it, that is,' he said. 'Hanging about on the same side of the house as that secret entrance, was he?'

'Mind you, he may have been speaking the truth when he said he had missed his way,' Charles warned him.

'That's what I shall have to find out,' said Mr Flinders. 'I shall have to keep a watch on those two.'

'You might make a few inquiries about them,' Peter suggested. 'Discover where they come from, and what Strange's occupation is.'

'You don't need to tell *me* how to act, sir,' said Mr Flinders with dignity. 'Now that I've got a line to follow I know my duty.'

'There's just one other thing,' Charles said slowly. 'You'd probably better know about it.'

'Certainly I had,' said Mr Flinders. 'If you was to keep anything from me I couldn't act.'

'I suspect,' said Charles, 'that whoever got into the Priory has some reason for wishing to frighten us out of it.'

Mr Flinders blinked at him. 'What would they want to do that for?' he asked practically.

'That's what we thought you might find out,' Charles said.

'If there's anything to find you may be sure I shall get on to it,' Mr Flinders assured him. 'But you'll have to tell me some more.'

'I'm going to. A few nights ago a picture fell down at the top of the stairs, and when we went up to investigate my wife found the upper half of a human skull on the stairs. My brother-in-law and I then discovered a priest's hole in the panelling where the picture had hung, and in it a collection of human bones.'

The effect of this on the constable was not quite what they had hoped. His jaw dropped, and he sat staring at them in round-eyed horror. 'My Gawd, sir, it's the Monk!' he gasped. 'You don't suppose I can go making inquiries about a ghost, do you? I wouldn't touch it – not for a thousand pounds! And here's me taking down in me notebook what you told me about Mr Titmarsh and them two up at the Inn, and all the time you've seen the Monk!' He drew a large handkerchief from his pocket, and wiped his brow with it. 'If I was you, sir, I'd get out of that house,' he said earnestly. 'It ain't healthy.'

'Thanks very much,' said Charles. 'But it is my firm belief that someone is behind all this Monk business. And I suspect that that skeleton was put there for our benefit by the same person who got into the cellars.'

'Hold hard!' said Peter suddenly. 'It's just occurred to me that we didn't hear the groan of that stone-slab being opened on the night the picture fell.'

They stared at one another for a moment. 'That's one up to you,' Charles said at length. 'Funny I never thought of that. We couldn't have missed hearing it, either. Then...' he stopped, frowning.

The constable shut his notebook. 'I'd get out of the Priory, sir, if I was you,' he repeated. 'The police can't act against ghosts. What you saw that night was the Monk, and the noise you heard...'

'Was caused by the stone-block opening,' finished Charles. 'We proved that.'

Mr Flinders scratched his chin again. A solution dawned upon him. 'I'll tell you what it is, sir. Maybe you're right, and what you saw in the cellars was flesh and blood. I shall get on to that, following up the line you've given me. But there wasn't any flesh and blood about that skeleton.'

'I'm thankful to say that there wasn't,' said Charles. 'Dry bones were quite enough for us.'

'What I meant,' said Mr Flinders, with a return to his official manner, 'was that no human being caused that skeleton to be put into this hole you speak about. What you've done, sir, is you've found out the secret of the Priory. That's what you've done. Now we know why it's haunted, and my advice to you is, "Pull it down."'

'You won't mind if we don't follow it, will you?' Charles said, sarcastically.

'That's for you to decide,' said Mr Flinders. 'But how you've got to look at it is like this: When this stone, which you have improperly sealed up, opened, it made a noise which could be heard all over the house. Following on that, the person or persons that nefariously broke into the Priory by that way couldn't do it without you knowing. That's fact, that is. The police have to work on facts, sir, and nothing else. Now you say that when this picture fell down you hadn't heard that stone open. From which it follows that no person or persons did open it that night. That's logic, isn't it, sir?'

'I'll take your word for it,' said Charles. 'And here's a second way for you to look at it: It is just possible that there is another entrance to the Priory which we don't know anything about.'

🌸
CHAPTER V

The immediate effect of the visit to Constable Flinders was a visit to the Priory paid by that worthy individual the very next day. Celia received him with a flattering display of relief, and the constable, a shy man, flushed very red indeed when she told him she was sure everything would be cleared up now that he had taken the matter in hand. However, he knew that she spoke no less than the truth, and said as much. He then requested her to show him the priest's hole.

'I will, of course,' she said, 'but I wish my husband or my brother were in, because I can hardly bear to open that ghastly panel.'

Following her delicately up the stairs Mr Flinders said that he could quite understand that. When she had succeeded in locating the rosette which worked the panel, and had twisted it round, he peered inside the dark recess almost as fearfully as Celia herself. There was nothing there, but it smelled strongly of Lysol. After deliberating for a while, the constable announced his intention of climbing into the hole. He succeeded in doing this, not without inflicting several scratches on the panelling, and once inside he very carefully inspected the walls. Celia watched him hopefully, and wondered whether the scratches could be got rid of.

Mr Flinders climbed out again, and picked up his helmet from the floor where he had placed it. 'Nothing there, madam,' he said.

'What were you looking for?' inquired Celia.

'There might have been a way in,' explained Mr Flinders. 'Not that I think so meself,' he added, 'but the police have to follow everything up, you see.'

'Oh!' said Celia, a little doubtfully. She closed the panel again. 'Is there anything else you'd like to see upstairs?'

Mr Flinders thought that he ought to make a reconnaissance of the whole house. He seemed depressed at being unable to explore Mrs Bosanquet's room, but when he learned that that lady was enjoying her afternoon rest he said that he quite understood.

A thorough examination of the other rooms took considerable time, and Celia grew frankly bored. Beyond remarking that the wall-cupboards were a queer set-out, and no mistake; that a thin man might conceivably get down the great chimney in the chief bedroom; and that a burglar wouldn't make much trouble over getting in at any one of the windows, Mr Flinders produced no theories. On the way downstairs, however, he volunteered the information that he wouldn't sleep a night in the house, not if he was paid to. This was not reassuring, and Celia at once asked him whether he knew anything about the Priory hauntings. Mr Flinders drew a deep breath, and told her various stories of things heard on the premises after dark. After this he went all over the sitting-rooms, and asked to be conducted to the secret entrance to the cellars.

'I'll tell Bowers to take you down,' said Celia. 'He knows, because he helped seal it up.'

In the kitchen she left him in charge of Mrs Bowers, a formidable woman who eyed him with complete disfavour. An attempt on his part to submit her kitchen to an exhaustive search was grimly frustrated. 'I don't hold with bobbies poking their noses where they're not wanted, and never did,' she said. 'It 'ud take a better burglar than any I ever heard of to get into my kitchen, and if I find one here

'I shall know what to do without sending for you.'

Mr Flinders, again very red about the ears, said huskily that he had to do his duty, and meant no offence.

'That's right,' said Mrs Bowers, 'you get on and do your duty, and I'll do mine, only don't you go opening my cupboards and turning things over with your great clumsy hands, or out you go, double-quick. Nice time I should have clearing up after you'd pulled everything about.'

'I'm sure the place does you credit,' said Mr Flinders feebly, with a vague idea of propitiating her. 'What I thought was, there might be a way in at the back of that great dresser.'

'Well, there isn't,' she replied uncompromisingly, and began to roll and bang a lump of pastry with an energy that spoke well for her muscular powers.

'I suppose,' said Mr Flinders, shifting his feet uneasily, 'I suppose you wouldn't mind me taking a look inside the copper? I *have* heard of a man hiding in one of them things.'

'Not in this house, you haven't,' responded Mrs Bowers. 'And if you think I'm going to have you prying into the week's washing you're mistaken. The idea!'

'I didn't know you'd got the washing in it,' apologized Mr Flinders.

'No, I expect you thought I kept goldfish there,' retorted the lady.

This crushing rejoinder quite cowed the constable. He coughed, and after waiting a minute asked whether she would show him the cellars. 'Which I've been asked to inspect,' he added boldly.

'I've got something better to do than to waste my time trapesing round nasty damp cellars at this hour,' she said. 'If you want to go down I'm sure I've no objection. You won't find anything except rats, and if you can put those great muddy boots of yours on one instead of dirtying my clean floor with them you'll be more use than ever I expected. Bowers!'

In reply to this shrill call her husband emerged presently from the pantry, where it seemed probable that he had been enjoying a brief siesta. Mrs Bowers pointed the rolling-pin at Mr Flinders. 'You've got to take this young fellow down to the cellars and show him the place where the master made all that mess with the cement yesterday,' she said. 'And don't bring him back here. I've never been in the habit of having bobbies in my kitchen and I'm not going to start at my time of life.'

Both men withdrew rather hastily. 'You mustn't mind my missus,' Bowers said. 'It's only her way. She doesn't hold with ghosts, and things, but I can tell you I'm glad to see you here. Awful, this place is. You wouldn't believe the things I've heard.'

By the time they had explored the dank, tomb-like cellars, and twice scared themselves by holding the lamp in such a way that their own shadows were cast in weird elongated shapes on the wall, Bowers and the constable were more than ready to confirm a sudden but deep friendship in a suitable quantity of beer. They retired to the pantry, and regaled themselves with this comforting beverage until Bowers found that it was time for him to carry the tea-tray into the library. Upon which Constable Flinders bethought himself of his duty, and took his departure by the garden-door, thus avoiding any fresh encounter with the dragon in the kitchen.

It was at about the same moment that Margaret, returning from a brisk tramp over the fields, emerged on to the right-of-way, and made her way past the ruined chapel towards the house. The sight of someone kneeling by one of the half-buried tombs apparently engaged in trying to decipher the inscription, made her stop and look more closely. Her feet had made no sound on the turf, but the kneeling figure looked round quickly, and she saw that it was Michael Strange.

She came slowly towards him, an eyebrow raised in rather puzzled inquiry. 'Hullo!' she said. 'Are you interested in old monuments?'

Strange rose, brushing a cake of half-dry mud from his ancient flannel trousers. 'I am rather,' he said. 'Do you mind my having a look round?'

'Not at all,' Margaret said. 'But I'm afraid you won't find much of interest.' She sat down on the tomb, and dug her hands into the pockets of her Burberry. 'I didn't know you were keen on this sort of thing.'

'I know very little about it,' he said, 'but I've always been interested in ruins. It's a pity this has been allowed to go. There's some fine Norman work.'

She agreed, but seemed to be more interested in the contemplation of one of her own shoes. 'Are you staying here long?' she asked.

'Only for another week or so,' he replied. 'I'm on holiday, you know.'

'Yes, you told me so.' She looked up, smiling. 'By the way, what do you do, if it isn't a rude question?'

'I fish mostly.'

'I meant in town.'

'Oh, I see. I have my work, and I manage to get some golf over the week-ends. Do you play?'

'Very badly,' Margaret answered, feeling baulked. She tried again. 'What sort of work do you do?'

'Mostly office-stuff, and very dull,' he said.

Margaret decided that further questioning would sound impertinent, and started a fresh topic. 'If you're interested in old buildings,' she said, 'you ought to go over the Priory itself. It's the most weird place, full of nooks and crannies, and rooms leading out of one another.'

'I noticed some very fine panelling when I took you home the other night,' he said. 'Have you any records of the place, I wonder?'

'No, funnily enough we haven't,' she answered. 'You'd think there ought to be something, and as far as I know my uncle didn't take anything out of the house when Aunt Flora died, but we can't find anything.'

'Nothing amongst the books?'

'There aren't many, you know. No, nothing. Celia was awfully disappointed, because she thought there was bound to be a history, or something. And we should rather like to find out whether there's any foundation for the story of the haunting.'

Strange sat down beside her on the tomb. 'How much store do you set by that tale?' he asked. 'Do you really believe in it?'

'I don't really know,' she said, wrinkling her brow. 'I haven't seen the famous Monk, and until I do – I'll reserve judgment.'

'Very wise,' he approved. 'And if you *do* see it I wish you'd tell me. I should like to have first-hand evidence of a real ghost.' He chanced to glance up as he spoke, and his eyes narrowed. 'Oh!' he said, in rather a curt voice. 'So you did call in the police after all?'

Margaret looked quickly in the same direction. Mr Flinders was tramping down one of the paths, very obviously on his way from the house back to the village. Without quite knowing why, she felt slightly guilty. 'Yes. We – we thought we'd try and get to the bottom of our ghost.'

He turned his head, and looked directly at her. 'You've made up your minds to keep whatever you've seen, or heard, to yourselves,' he said abruptly. 'You're scared of this place, aren't you?'

She was startled. 'Well, really, I – yes, a bit, perhaps. It's not surprising considering what tales they tell about it round here.'

'You'll think me impertinent,' he said, 'but I wish you'd leave it.'

It was her turn now to look at him, surprised, rather grave. 'Why?' she said quietly.

'Because if the place is haunted, and you saw anything, it might give you a really bad fright. Where's the sense in staying in a house that gives you the creeps?'

'You're very solicitous about me, Mr Strange. I don't quite see why.'

'I don't suppose you do,' he said, prodding the ground between his feet with his walking stick. 'And I daresay I've no right to be – solicitous about you. All the same, I am.'

She found it hard to say anything after this, but managed after a short pause to remark that a ghost couldn't hurt her.

He made no answer, but continued to prod the ground, and with a nervous little laugh, she said: 'You look as though you thought it could.'

'No, I'm not as foolish as that,' he replied. 'But it could scare you badly.'

'I didn't think you believed in the Monk. You know, you're being rather mysterious.'

'I believe in quite a number of odd things,' he said. 'Sorry if I sounded mysterious.'

She pulled up a blade of grass, and began to play with it. 'Mr Strange.'

He smiled. 'Miss Fortescue?'

'It isn't what you sound,' she said, carefully inspecting her blade of grass. 'It's – things you do.'

There was an infinitesimal pause. 'What have I done?' Strange asked lightly.

She abandoned the grass, and turned towards him. 'Last night, at about one o'clock when we had summer lightning, I – it woke me.'

'Did it? But what has that got to do with my mysterious behaviour?'

She looked into his eyes, and saw them faintly amused.

69

'Mr Strange, I got up to close my window, in case it came on to rain. I saw you in one of the flashes.'

'You saw *me*?' he repeated.

'Yes, by the big rose bush just under my window. I saw you quite clearly. I didn't say anything about it to the others.'

'Why not?' he said.

She flushed. 'I don't quite know. Partly because I didn't want to frighten Celia.'

'Is that the only reason?'

She was silent.

'I was in the Priory garden last night,' he said. 'I can't tell you why, but I hope you'll believe that whatever I was doing there – I'd – I'd chuck it up sooner than harm you in any way, or – or even give you a fright.' He paused, but she still said nothing. 'I don't know why you should trust me, but you seem to have done so, and I'm – jolly grateful. Can you go on trusting me enough to keep this to yourself?'

She raised troubled eyes. 'I ought not to. I ought to tell my brother. You see, I – I don't really know anything about you, and – you must admit – it's rather odd of you to be in our grounds at that hour. I suppose you can't tell me anything more?'

'No,' he said. 'I can't. I wish I could.'

She got up. 'I shan't say anything about having seen you. But I warn you – you may be found out, another time. You want to get us out of the Priory – and we aren't going. So – so it's no use trying to frighten us away. I – I expect you know what I mean.'

He did not answer, but continued to watch her rather closely. She held out her hand. 'I must go, or I shall be too late for tea. Good-bye.'

'Good-bye,' Strange said, taking her hand for a moment in his strong clasp. 'And thank you.'

The rest of the family noticed that Margaret was rather

70

silent at tea-time, and Mrs Bosanquet asked her if she were tired. She roused herself at that, disclaimed, and, banishing Strange from her thoughts for a while, gave her attention to Celia, who was recounting the proceedings of Constable Henry Flinders.

'And as far as I can see,' Celia said, 'there those scratches will remain.'

'You would have him,' Charles reminded her. 'You despised our efforts, and now that you've got a trained sleuth on to the job you're no better pleased.'

'What I'd really like,' Celia said, 'and what I always had in mind was a detective, not an ordinary policeman.'

'You don't appreciate friend Flinders,' Peter told her. 'He may not be quick, but he's thorough. Why, he even inspected the bathroom, didn't he?'

'That's right,' said Charles. 'Dogged does it is Henry's watchword. He won't leave a mouse-hole undisturbed. You wait till he comes down our chimney one night to see if it can be done, before you judge him.'

But during the next two days, as fresh evidence of the constable's devotion to duty was continually forthcoming, he became even less popular. On the first day of his watch, Jane, the housemaid, was with difficulty persuaded to rescind her 'notice,' which she promptly gave on discerning the constable crouched under a rhododendron bush. She was on her way home, soon after sundown, and this unnerving sight induced her to give way to a strong fit of hysterics under the drawing-room window. Celia and Peter rushed out in time to witness the aghast constable endeavouring to reassure Jane, while Mrs Bowers, first upon the scene, divided her attention between scolding the distraught damsel, and predicting the future that awaited those who could find nothing better to do than to frighten silly girls out of their wits.

When Constable Flinders had stumbled over a cucumber-frame in the dark, and smashed two panes of

71

glass with the maximum noise, got himself locked in the gardener's shed by mistake, and arrested Charles on his return from a game of billiards with Colonel Ackerley, it was unanimously agreed that his energy should be gently but firmly diverted. In spite of his incorrigible habit of doing the wrong thing they had all of them developed quite an affection for the constable, and it was with great tact that Peter suggested that a watch on the Priory was useless, and that Mr Flinders would do well to turn his attention to the possible suspects.

The constable, whom only the strongest sense of duty induced to patrol the dread Priory after dark, was not at all hurt, but on the contrary much relieved at being dismissed from his heroic task, and thereafter the Priory saw him no more. Celia, who had been the bitterest in denunciation of his folly, even confessed to missing him. During his guard he had been quite useful in giving her horticultural advice and he had very kindly weeded three of the flower-beds for her, incidentally rooting up a cherished cutting of hydrangea, which he assured her would never flourish in such a spot.

It was not long, however, before they heard of Mr Flinders' new activities, for Charles encountered Mr Titmarsh in the village street, and Mr Titmarsh, catching sight of the constable some way off, remarked fretfully that he did not know what had come over the fellow.

With a wonderful air of blandness Charles inquired the reason of this sudden remark. Mr Titmarsh said with asperity that the constable was apparently running after his parlour-maid, since he was forever stumbling over him, either waiting by the gate or prowling round the house. 'And apparently,' said Mr Titmarsh, 'he thinks it necessary to enlist my sympathy by exhibiting a wholly untutored interest in my hobby. He has taken to bringing me common specimens for my opinion, and last night when I was out with my net I found the man following me. Most irritating performance, and I fear I spoke a little roughly to him. However, it seems he is genuinely anxious to observe the methods I employ, and really it is of no use to lose one's temper with such a simple fellow.'

When this was recounted to the others it afforded them considerable amusement, but when Peter said: 'I never met such an ass in my life,' Charles reproved him. 'He's doing well,' he said, selecting a walnut from the dish. 'Much better than I expected. I admit his Boy Scout stunts are a little obvious, but look at his ready wit! When old Titmarsh discovered him in ambush, did his presence of mind desert him? Not at all. He said he wanted to look for moths too. That's what I call masterly.'

'I think myself,' said Mrs Bosanquet, carefully rolling up her table-napkin, 'that we were very wise to call him in. Not that I consider him efficient, for I do not, but ever since he took the matter in hand we have heard nothing out of the way in the house. No doubt whoever it was who caused us all the annoyance knows he is on the watch and will trouble us no more.'

'No one could fail to know it,' said Peter. 'During the three days when he sojourned with us he so closely tracked and interrogated everyone who came to the house that the whole countryside must have known that we'd called him in. I'm beginning to feel positively sheepish about it. The villagers are all on the broad grin.'

'I don't care what the villagers think,' Celia said. 'We did the only sensible thing. Other people don't grin. The Colonel told me he thought it was a very wise precaution.'

'You didn't tell him why we did it, I hope?' Peter said.

'No, but I don't really see why we should keep it so dark. I merely said we'd heard noises, and Bowers was getting the wind-up so much that something had to be done.'

'The reason why we should keep it dark,' explained her brother patiently, 'is, as I've told you at least six times...'

'Seven,' said Charles. 'This makes the eighth. And I've told her three – no, let me see...'

'Shut up!' said Celia. 'I know what you're going to say. If we tell one person he or she will repeat it, and it'll get round to the person who did it all. Well, why not?'

'I should be guided by what your husband says, my dear,' said Mrs Bosanquet. 'The least said the better, I am sure. And if the Colonel's coming in to coffee and bridge with you this evening we had better move into the drawing-room, for he may arrive at any moment.'

The party accordingly adjourned, and in a few minutes Bowers announced Colonel Ackerley.

'Upon my soul,' the Colonel said, accepting the coffee Peter handed him, and a glass of old brandy, 'I must say I hope you people won't allow yourselves to be scared away from the Priory. I had almost forgotten what it was like to have any neighbours.' He bowed gallantly to Celia. 'And such charming ones too.' He sipped his liqueur. 'It's a great boon to a lonely old bachelor like myself to be able to pop in for a quiet rubber in the evenings.'

'Think how nice it is for us to have such a friendly neighbour,' Celia smiled. 'So often people who live in the country get stuffy, and won't call on newcomers till they've been in the place for years.'

'Well, when one has knocked about the world as I have, one gets over all that sort of rubbish!' replied the Colonel. 'Never had any use for stand-offishness. Aha, Miss Fortescue, I see you are preparing for the engagement. What do you say? Shall we two join forces and have our revenge on Mr and Mrs Malcolm?'

Margaret had swept the cards round in a semi-circle. 'Yes, do let's!' she agreed. 'We owe them one for our awful defeat last time we played. Shall we cut for seats?'

They took their places at the table, and as the cards were dealt the Colonel bethought himself of something, and said with his ready laugh: 'By the way, what have you done with your watch-dog? Give you my word I was expecting him to pounce out on me at any moment, for I strolled across the park to get here.'

'Oh, we've diverted him,' Charles answered. 'Our nerves wouldn't stand it any longer.'

'Besides, he's done the trick,' Celia said. 'Bowers, whose faith in him is really touching, seems to be settling down quite happily. If I did this, I shall say a spade.'

The game proceeded in silence for some time, but at the end of the rubber the Colonel reverted to the subject, and cocking a quizzical eyebrow in Charles' direction said: 'By the by, Malcolm, have you been setting your sleuth on to old Titmarsh? Oh, you needn't mind telling me! *I* shan't give you away!'

'We had to get rid of him somehow,' Peter said. 'So we thought Titmarsh would keep him well occupied.'

This seemed to amuse the Colonel considerably, but after his first outburst of laughter he said: 'But you don't think old Titmarsh has been playing jokes on you, do you?'

'Not at all,' said Peter. 'It was our Mr Flinders who thought he ought to be watched. All very providential.'

'Well, if he discovers anything against the old boy, I'll eat my hat,' the Colonel declared.

Shortly after eleven he took his leave of them, and in a little while the girls and Mrs Bosanquet went up to bed. Having bolted the drawing-room windows, the men prepared to follow them, and in another hour the house was dark and silent.

Mrs Bosanquet, who had been troubled lately with slight insomnia, was the only one of the party who failed to go to sleep. After lying awake for what seemed to her an interminable time she decided that the room was stuffy, and got up to open the window, which she still kept shut in case anyone should attempt to effect an entrance by that way. 'But that is all put a stop to now,' she told herself, as she climbed back into bed.

The opening of the window seemed to make matters worse. At the end of another twenty minutes sleep seemed farther off than ever. Mrs Bosanquet felt for the matches on the table beside her bed, and lit her candle. She looked round for something to read, but since she was not in the habit of reading in bed there were no books in the room. It at once seemed to her imperative that she should read for a while, and she sat up, debating whether she should venture down to the library in search of a suitable book, or whether this simple act demanded more courage than she possessed. There was a tin of sweet biscuits in the library, she remembered, and the recollection made her realize that she was quite hungry. 'Now I come to think of it,' Mrs Bosanquet informed the bedpost, 'my dear mother used always to say that if one could not sleep it was a good plan to eat a biscuit. Though,' she added conscientiously, 'she did not in general approve of eating anything once one had brushed one's teeth for the night.'

The tin of biscuits began to seem more and more desirable. Mrs Bosanquet lay down again, sternly resolved to think of something else. But it was no use. Biscuits, very crisp and sweet, would not be banished from her mind, and at the end of another ten minutes Mrs Bosanquet would have faced untold dangers to get one.

She got out of bed and put on her dressing-gown. It occurred to her that she might wake Peter, whose room was opposite hers, and ask him to go down to the library for her, but she dismissed this pusillanimous idea at once. Mrs Bosanquet was a lady who prided herself upon her level-headedness; she did not believe in ghosts; and she would feel very much ashamed to think that anyone should suspect her of being too nervous to walk downstairs alone in the middle of the night.

'Nerves,' Mrs Bosanquet was in the habit of saying severely, 'were never encouraged when I was young.'

'I shall go quietly downstairs, get a biscuit to eat, and select a book from the shelves without disturbing anyone,' she said firmly, and picked up her candle.

The lamp had been turned out in the passage, and since there was no moon the darkness seemed intense. Another woman might have paused, but Mrs Bosanquet was not afraid of the dark. 'What would alarm me,' she reflected, 'would be a light burning; for then I should know that someone was in the house.'

But the ground-floor was as dark as the upper storey. Mrs Bosanquet went cautiously downstairs with one hand on the baluster-rail, and the other holding her candle up. The stairs creaked annoyingly, and in the stillness each creak sounded abnormally loud. Mrs Bosanquet murmured: 'Tut-tut!' to herself, and hoped that Celia would not be awakened by the noise.

The library door was ajar; she pushed it open, and went in. The biscuit-tin, she remembered, stood on a small table by the door, and she peered for it, blinking. Yes, there it was. She set the candle down and opened it, and slipped two of the biscuits into the pocket of her dressing-gown. She had quite recovered from her rather shame-faced feeling of trepidation, for no skulls had bounced at her feet, or anything else of such a disturbing nature. She picked up the candle again, and turned to the bookshelves that ran along the wall opposite the fireplace. It was very hard to see far by the light of one candle, and she knocked her shin on a chair as she moved across the room.

The difficulty was to find anything one wanted to read. She held the candle close up to the row of books, and slowly edged along in front of the shelves, surveying a most unpromising selection of titles. '*Meditations on Mortality*,' read Mrs Bosanquet. 'Dear me, how gloomy. *The Sermons of Dr Brimley*. That might send me to sleep, but I really don't think... *Tyndall on Light*... Ah, this is better!' She came opposite a collection of novels, and reached up a hand to pull one down from the shelf. Then, just as her fingers had half-pulled the volume from its place an unaccountable feeling of dread seized her, and she stayed quite still, straining her ears to catch the least sound. All she could hear was the beating of her own heart, but it did not reassure her. Mrs Bosanquet, who did not believe in nerves, knew that something was in the room with her.

'It's nonsense,' she told herself. 'Of course there isn't. Of *course* there isn't!' She forced herself to draw the book out from its place, but her unreasoning conviction grew. It seemed as though she dared not move or look round, but she knew that was absurd. 'I've *got* to turn round,' she thought. 'It's all nonsense. There's nothing here. I can't stand like this all night. I *must* turn round.'

Fearfully she began to edge towards the door. She found that it had become almost impossible to breathe, and realized that her terror was growing.

'It's always worse if one turns one's back on things,' Mrs Bosanquet thought. 'Suppose it crept up behind me? Suppose I felt a hand touching me?'

The leap of her heart was choking her; she felt as though she might faint if she went on like this. She stopped, and very cautiously peered over her shoulder. There was nothing. Yet what was that vague, dark figure by the fireplace? Only the tall-backed arm-chair, of course. She was so sure of it that she took a step towards it, and lifted her candle to see more clearly.

The dark shape grew distinct in the tiny light. A cowled figure was standing motionless by the fireplace, and through the slits in the cowl two glittering eyes were fixed upon Mrs Bosanquet. She stood as though paralysed, and even as she stared at it the figure moved, and glided towards her with one menacing hand stretched out like the talon of a bird of prey.

The spell broke. For the first time in her life Mrs

Bosanquet gave a wild, shrill scream, and crumpled up in a dead faint on the floor.

❧
CHAPTER VI

Mrs Bosanquet groped her way back to consciousness to find the room full of lamp-light, and the rest of the family gathered solicitously about her. Someone had laid her upon the sofa, someone else was bathing her forehead with water, while a third held a bottle of smelling-salts to her nose. She opened her eyes, and looked up, blankly at first, into Celia's concerned face. She heard a voice saying: 'It's all right: she's coming round,' and by degrees her recollection came back to her. She opened her eyes again, and struggled up into a sitting posture, unceremoniously thrusting aside the smelling bottle and the brandy that Margaret was trying to give her. 'Where is it?' she demanded, looking round her suspiciously.

'Where is what, Aunt Lilian?' Celia said soothingly. 'Are you feeling better now?'

'I am perfectly well. No, my dear child, I never touch spirits. Where did it go? Did you see it?'

Celia patted her hand. 'No, dear, we didn't see anything. I woke up, hearing you scream, and when we got downstairs we found you had fainted. Did you feel ill in the night, Aunt, or what?'

'I came to get a book and a biscuit,' Mrs Bosanquet replied. 'Was there no one but myself in the room?'

'Why no, darling, how should there be? Did you think you saw someone?'

'Think!' said Mrs Bosanquet indignantly. 'Do you suppose I should scream for help merely because I thought I saw someone? I did see it, as plainly as I can see you.'

Charles came forward, ousting his wife from her place by the invalid's side. 'What did you see, Aunt Lilian?' he asked. 'Do you feel well enough to tell us about it?'

'Certainly I am well enough to tell you,' she said. 'My dears, it is all perfectly true, and I am not ashamed to own that I have been wrong. The house *is* haunted, and the first thing to be done in the morning is to summon the Vicar.'

Celia gave a gasp of horror, and clasped her brother's arm nervously. 'Oh, what have you seen?' she cried.

Mrs Bosanquet took the glass of water from Margaret, and drank some. 'I have seen the Monk!' she said dramatically.

'Good Lord!' Peter exclaimed. 'You haven't really, have you? Are you sure you didn't imagine it?'

A withering glance was cast at him. 'It is true that I so far forgot myself as to scream, and faint, but I can assure you, my dear Peter, that I am not such a fool that I would imagine such a thing. It was standing almost exactly where you are now, and it began to move towards me, with its arm stretched out as though it were pointing at me.'

Celia shuddered, and looked round fearfully.

'Just what did it look like?' Charles asked quietly.

'Like a monk,' said Mrs Bosanquet. 'It had a cowl over its face, and I trust I am not a fanciful woman, but there was something indescribably menacing and horrible about it. I can see its eyes now.'

'Where?' shrieked Celia, clutching Peter again.

'In my mind's eye. Don't be foolish, my dear, it is not here now. Its robe was black, and so were its hands – at least the one that pointed at me was. I daresay I am stupid, but that seemed to me to make it even more unnerving.

Charles turned quickly towards Peter. 'That settles it! Gloves! Now how did he make his get-away?'

'Almost any way,' Peter said. 'He'd have had plenty of time to get across the hall before any of us reached the stairs.'

'It is no use being obstinate about it,' Mrs Bosanquet said. 'It was no man, but an apparition. I am now convinced of the existence of such things. Perhaps it was sent to open my eyes.'

'All dressed up in a Dominican habit and black gloves,' said Charles. 'I hardly think so. Take a look at the front door, Peter.'

'Bolted, and the chain in position. I happened to notice. What about this window?'

Charles strode across to it, and flung back the curtains. 'It's bolted – no, by Jove, it's not!' He turned to Bowers, who up till now had been a scared auditor. 'Bowers, do you remember if you bolted this to-night?'

Bowers shook his head. 'No, sir. At least, I don't think so. Begging your pardon, sir, but the mistress always likes it left open till you go up to bed. I thought you bolted it.'

'That's right,' Peter said. 'And to-night we sat in the drawing-room. That's how it got forgotten. Cheer up, Aunt Lilian! What you saw was someone dressed up to give you a fright, and that's how he got in.'

'No, my dear, you are wrong,' Mrs Bosanquet said firmly. 'It had no need of doors or windows. For all we know it is still present, though now invisible.'

Celia gave one moan of horror, and implored Charles to take her back to town at once.

'I think we'd all better go back to bed for the rest of the night, and discuss it in the morning,' Charles said. 'I don't see that we shall do much good trying to search the garden now. We'll bolt this window, though. And what about having Margaret to sleep in your room, Aunt? Would you prefer it?'

'Not at all,' she replied. 'If it re-appeared, Margaret would be of no assistance to me, or any of you. I shall go quietly up, and to sleep, for I feel I shall not see it again to-night.'

On account of the night's disturbance breakfast was put back next morning for an hour, but contrary to everyone's expectations Mrs Bosanquet was the first down. When Celia, Margaret, and Peter appeared they found her looking as placid as ever, and reading the morning paper. 'Good morning, my dears,' she said, laying the paper down. 'I see there has been fresh trouble in China. I feel one has so much to be thankful for in not being Chinese.'

'Darling Aunt Lilian!' said Margaret, twinkling. 'You really are a marvellous person!'

'On the contrary I fear I am a very ordinary one. And why you should think so merely because I remarked...'

'Oh, I didn't! But after what you went through last night I wonder you can be so calm.'

'I lay awake and thought about that for some time after you had left me,' said Mrs Bosanquet. 'Do you know, I have come to the conclusion that I behaved very foolishly?'

Celia looked up hopefully. 'Do you mean you may have imagined it after all?'

'No, my dear, certainly not. I am not at all imaginative. In fact, your uncle used very often to say I was too mundane. But then he was extremely imaginative himself, and could tell the most entertaining stories, as I daresay you remember.'

'Then how did you behave foolishly?' asked Peter, helping himself from one of the dishes on the sideboard.

'In screaming in that uncontrolled manner. I realize now that my proper course would have been to have challenged the apparition, and commanded it to tell me what it wanted. For, on thinking it over, I am convinced it manifested itself for some good purpose. Thank you,

Peter, yes, I will have an egg.' She began to tap the shell briskly. 'It is obviously an unquiet spirit, and when you consider that it no doubt belongs to the remains you discovered in that very nasty, airless little cupboard, one can hardly wonder at it.'

'I do wish you wouldn't, Aunt!' begged Celia. 'Even in broad daylight you give me the creeps.'

'Then you are being very silly, dear child. Good morning, Charles. I hope you slept well to make up for your loss of sleep earlier in the night.'

Charles took his seat at the head of the table. 'I am grateful for the inquiry, Aunt, but no, I didn't. I might have, but for the fact that I was constrained to get up three times; once to look under the bed, once to open the wardrobe, once to demonstrate to your niece that the noise she persistently heard was the wind rustling the creeper outside the window.'

'Well, I'm sorry, darling,' Celia said, 'but after what happened you can't be surprised that I was nervous.'

'Surprise, my love,' responded her husband, 'was not the emotion I found myself a prey to.'

'Perhaps it'll convince you that the only thing to do is to go back to town this very day,' Celia said pleadingly.

'I confess that a prospect of any more such nights doesn't attract me,' said Charles. 'But what's the opinion of Aunt Lilian?'

'I was about to say, when you came in,' answered Mrs Bosanquet, 'that I have considered the matter very carefully, and come to the conclusion that we should be doing wrong to leave the Priory.'

Charles paused in the act of conveying a piece of toast from his plate to his mouth, and stared at her. 'Well, I'm damned!' he said inelegantly. 'Give me some coffee, Celia: I must drink Aunt Lilian's health.'

'Very wrong indeed,' nodded Mrs Bosanquet. 'Perhaps we have it in our power to set the ghost free. It probably wants us to do something, and to that end it has been endeavouring to attract our notice.'

'I see,' said Charles gravely. 'And probably it can't make out why we all seem so shy of it. I wonder how it'll try to – er – attract our notice next? It's already knocked a picture down, and thrown a skull at our feet, and made you faint. It must be getting quite disheartened at our failure to appreciate the true meaning of these little attentions.'

'It is all very well for you to make a mock of such things, Charles,' Mrs Bosanquet said with dignity, 'but I am perfectly serious. So much so that I am determined to do my best to get into communication with it. And since Margaret is going to town on Thursday to see her dentist I shall ask her to call at my flat, and request Parker to give her my planchette board, which is in the old brown trunk in the lobby.'

Celia was regarding her in fascinated horror. 'Are you really proposing to sit with a planchette in this house?' she asked faintly.

'Not only I, my dear, but all of us. We sit round in a circle, laying the tips of our fingers on the board, and wait for some message to be transcribed.'

'Nothing,' said Celia vehemently, 'would induce me to take part in any such proceeding! The whole thing's bad enough as it is without us trying to invoke the Monk.'

'Very well,' said Mrs Bosanquet, not in the least ruffled, 'if that is how you feel about it it would be no good your attempting to sit with us. But I for one shall certainly make the attempt.'

'This means you won't go back to town!' Celia said unhappily. 'I knew what it would be! No, don't tell me I can go without you, Charles. I may be a bad wife, and wake you up to look in the wardrobe in the small hours, but I am not such a bad wife that I'd go away and leave you with a ghost and a planchette.'

'I wish you would go back to town, old lady,' Charles said. 'I don't mean that I don't appreciate this self-immolating heroism, but it's no use scaring yourself, and nothing dire is at all likely to happen to me. If I thought there was any danger,' he added handsomely, 'you should stay and share it with me.'

'Thanks,' said Celia. 'I might have known you'd joke about it. I don't know whether there's what you call danger, but if you're going to ask for trouble by putting your hands on Aunt's horrible planchette I shan't leave your side for one moment.'

'Cheer up!' Charles said. 'I don't mind giving the board a shove to please Aunt Lilian, but last night has completely convinced me that the Monk is as real as you are. In fact, if Margaret is going to town on Thursday she can rout out my service revolver, and the cartridges she'll find with it, and bring them back with her.'

'If you think that I should be pleased by you deliberately pushing the board, you are sadly mistaken,' said Mrs Bosanquet severely. 'Moreover, I have the greatest objection to fire-arms, and if you propose to let off guns at all hours of the day I shall be obliged to go back to London.'

She was with difficulty appeased, and only a promise extracted from Charles not to fire any lethal weapon without due warning soothed her indignation. Breakfast came to an end, and after Celia had had a heart-to-heart talk with her husband, and Margaret had begged Peter not to do anything rash, such as shooting at vague figures seen in the dark, the two men left the house, ostensibly to fish.

'What we are going to do now,' said Charles, 'is to carry on some investigations on our own.'

'Then we'd better drift along to the Bell,' said Peter. 'We may as well put in some fishing till opening time, though. If you want to pump old Wilkes you won't find him up yet.'

Charles consulted his watch. 'I make it half-past ten.'

'I daresay you do, but friend Wilkes takes life easy. He's never visible at this hour. Not one of our early risers.'

'All right then,' Charles said. 'We might fish the near stream for a bit.'

Sport, however, proved poor that morning, and shortly before twelve they decided to give up, and stroll on towards the inn. They were already within a few minutes' walk of it, and they arrived before the bar was open.

'Have you been into the courtyard yet?' Peter asked. 'You ought to see that. Real Elizabethan work; you can almost imagine miracles and moralities being played there. Come on.' He led the way through an arch in the middle of the building, and they found themselves in a cobbled yard, enclosed by the house. A balcony ran all round the first storey, and various bedroom windows opened on to this. A modern garage occupied the end of the building opposite the archway into the street, but Mr Wilkes had had this built in keeping with the rest of the inn, and had placed his petrol pump as inconspicuously as possible. Some clipped yews in wooden tubs stood in the yard, and the whole effect was most picturesque. Having inspected the older part of the house, and ascertained that the original structure did indeed date from the fourteenth century, they wandered into the garage, which they found stood where the old stables had once been. Michael Strange's two-seater was standing just inside the entrance and one of the garage hands was washing it down. Charles, under pretext of examining the car, soon fell into easy conversation with the man, and leaving him to extract what information he could, Peter strolled off to where he could hear the throb of an engine at work. He had some knowledge of such machines, and a great deal of interest. He easily located the engine-room, went in, leaving the door open behind him, and found, as he had thought, that the engine drove the electric light plant. No one was there, and the first thing that struck him was the size of the plant. Puzzled, he stood looking at it, wondering why such a powerful machine and such a large plant had been installed for the mere purpose of supplying light for the inn. He was just about to inspect it more closely when someone came hurriedly into the room behind him.

'Oo's in 'ere?' demanded a sharp voice.

Peter turned to find Spindle, the barman, at his elbow. The man looked annoyed, but when he saw whom he was addressing he curbed his testiness, and said more mildly: 'Beg pardon, sir, but no one's allowed inside this 'ere engine-room.'

'That's all right,' said Peter. 'I shan't meddle with it. I was just wondering why...'

'I'm sorry, sir, but orders is orders, and I shall 'ave to ask you to come out. If the boss was to 'ear about me leaving the door unlocked I should get into trouble.' He had edged himself round Peter, obscuring his view of the plant, and now tried to crowd him out. Somewhat surprised Peter gave way, and backed into the yard again.

'You seem to be afraid I shall upset it. What's the matter?' he said.

Spindle was locking the door of the place, and until he had pocketed the key he did not answer. Then he said: 'It's not that, sir, but we 'ave to be careful. You wouldn't believe the number of young fellers we've 'ad go in and start messin' about with the plant, to see 'ow it worked. Cost Mr Wilkes I wouldn't like to say 'ow much money to 'ave it put right once, sir. Not that I mean you'd go for to 'urt it, but I've 'ad me orders, and it's as much as my place is worth to let anyone in.'

'Oh, all right,' said Peter, still surprised at the man's evident perturbation. 'But why has Wilkes installed such a large plant? Surely it's generating far more electricity than you can possibly use?'

'I couldn't say, sir, I'm sure. And begging your pardon, sir, it's opening time, and I've got to get back to me work.' He touched his forehead as he spoke and scuttled off into the inn again, leaving Peter to stare after him in still greater bewilderment.

Charles came across the yard from the garage. 'Did I hear certain magic words? I move that we repair to the bar forthwith. What have you been up to?'

'I went to look at the electric-light plant, only that ass, Spindle, hustled me out before I'd had time to see much. I must ask Wilkes about it.'

Charles groaned. 'Must you? I mean, we didn't come to talk about amps and dynamos, and I know from bitter experience that once you get going on that soul-killing topic...'

'I want to know why Wilkes has got such a powerful plant. I hadn't time to look closely, but from what I could see of it it was generating enough electricity to light the whole village.'

'Well, perhaps it does,' Charles suggested. 'Can we get into the bar without going back into the street?'

'Yes, through the coffee-room.' Peter opened a door which led into a dark little passage, with kitchens giving on to it. At the end of the passage was the coffee-room, and they walked through this to the frosted glass door that opened into the taproom itself.

There was no one but Spindle in the taproom when they entered, but they had hardly given their orders when Wilkes came in from his private sanctum, and bade them a cheery good morning.

'Hullo, Wilkes! Just up?' Peter twitted him.

The landlord smiled good humouredly. 'Now, sir, now! You will have your joke. Two half-cans was it? Come on, Spindle, look alive! There you are, sir!' He seized the tankards from his henchman, and planked them down in front of his guests.

'Very quiet this morning, aren't you?' Charles said.

'Well, we're only just open, sir. They'll start coming in presently. I see you've been fishing. Bad weather for it to-day.'

'Rotten. No luck at all.' Charles took a draught of beer. 'How's business with you?'

'So-so, sir, so-so. We get a fair sprinkling of car people in to lunch, but there's not many as stays the night.'

'I see Mr Strange is still here.'

'Yes, sir, he's here. And there's Miss Crowslay and Miss Williams, down for their usual fortnight, and Mr Ffolliot. Artists, sir, great place for artists and such-like, this is.'

'Still got your commercial?'

'In a manner of speaking I suppose I have, but he's one of them as is here to-day and gone to-morrow, if you know what I mean. Well, it's the nature of his business, I daresay, but I'd rather have someone more regular, so to speak. That Mr Fripp, well, you never know where you are with him because some days he has to go off and spend the night away, and others he's back to supper when you wasn't expecting him. However, as my missus was saying only this morning, it's all in the way of business, and I'm sure times are that bad I'm glad to get anyone staying in the house.'

Peter put down his tankard. 'I say, Wilkes, what's the meaning of that monstrous electric plant you've got outside? You can't need a thing that size, surely?'

The landlord coughed, and looked rather sheepish. 'I'm sorry you've seen that, Mr Fortescue, sir.'

'Yes, but why? Spindle pushed me out before I'd time to do more than glance at the thing. He seemed in a great way about it.'

Spindle looked deprecatingly at the landlord, and withdrew to the other end of the bar.

'Spindle's a fool, sir,' said Mr Wilkes, not mincing matters. 'Though mind you, you wouldn't hardly believe the number of people there are that ain't to be trusted anywhere near a delicate bit of machinery. I do have to be strict, and that's a fact. Of course, I know you're different, sir, and that's why I'm sorry you saw it.' He went through the form of wiping down the bar, which seemed to be a habit with him. 'You see, sir, in a manner of speaking I was a bit had over that plant.'

'I should think you were,' Peter said. 'You could supply the whole village with it.'

'Well, I don't know about that, sir,' Mr Wilkes said cautiously. 'It ain't such a powerful machine as what it looks. Still, I don't deny it's bigger nor what I want. Not but what we use a lot of power here. Because, mind you, I had the whole place wired for heating as well, there not being any gas laid on, and then there's the refrigerators, and vacuum cleaners and what not.'

'Rot!' Peter said, 'you don't need a plant that size for the amount of electricity you use in heating.'

Mr Wilkes once more wiped down the bar. 'True enough, sir, I don't. But when I took over this house I don't mind telling you I hadn't ever had anything to do with electric plants, me having always lived in a town. I didn't know no more about it than what half the young gentlemen do, who try and meddle with it. And I did have a notion to run a laundry off it, just by way of a side-business, as you might call it. So what with one thing and another I let myself be talked into putting up a plant that cost me a mint of money, and ain't, between ourselves, as cheap to run as what the smooth-tongued fellow that sold it me said it would be. Excuse me, sir, half a moment!' He hurried away to attend to a farmer who had come in, and Charles and Peter went to sit down at a table in the window.

The taproom began to fill up, and soon there were quite a number of people in it. They were mostly villagers, and there was no sign of Strange, or his odd associate. But a few minutes before one o'clock a man came in who was obviously no farm-hand. He attracted Peter's attention at once, but this was not surprising, since his appearance and conduct were alike out of the ordinary. Artist was stamped unmistakably upon him. His black hair was worn exceedingly long; he had a carelessly tied, very flowing piece of silk round his neck; his fingers were stained with paint; he had a broad-brimmed hat crammed on to his head; and was the owner of a pointed beard.

'Good Lord, I thought that type went out with the 'Nineties!' murmured Peter.

The artist walked rather unsteadily up to the bar, and leaning sideways across it, said with a distinct foreign accent: 'Whisky. Double.'

Wilkes had watched his approach frowningly, and he now hesitated, and said something in a low voice. The artist smote his open hand down on the bar, and said loudly: 'My friend, you give me what I say. You think I am drunk, *hein*? Well, I am not drunk. You see? You give me...'

'All right, Mr Dooval,' Wilkes said hastily. 'No offence I hope.'

'You give me what I say,' insisted M. Duval. 'I paint a great picture. So great a picture the world will say, why do we not hear of this Louis Duval?' He took the glass Wilkes handed him, and drained it at one gulp. 'Another. And when I have painted this picture, then I tell you I have finished with everything but my art.' He stretched out a hand that shook slightly towards his glass. His eye wandered round the room: his voice sank to the grumbling tone of the partially intoxicated. 'I will be at no man's call. No, no: that is over when I have paint my picture. You hear?'

Mr Wilkes seemed to be trying to quieten him by asking some questions about the picture he was painting.

'It is not for such as you,' M. Duval said. 'What have

92

the English to do with art? Bah, you do not know what feelings I have in me, *here...*' He struck his chest. 'To think I must be with you, and those others – *canaille!*'

'Gentleman seems a little peevish,' remarked Charles, *sotto voce*.

His voice, though not his words, seemed to reach M. Duval's ears, for he turned, and stared hazily across the room. A smile that closely resembled a leer curled his mouth, and picking up his glass he made his way between the tables to the window, and stood leaning his hand on the back of a chair, and looking down at Charles. 'So! The gentleman who dares to live in the haunted house, not?' He shook with laughter, and raising his glass unsteadily, said: '*Voyons!* a toast! *Le Moine!*'

Charles was watching him under frowning brows. He went on chuckling to himself, and his eyes travelled from Charles' face to Peter's. 'You do not drink? You do not love him, our Monk?' He pulled the chair he held out from the table, and collapsed into it. '*Eh bien!* You do not speak then? You do not wish to talk of *Le Moine?* Perhaps you have seen him, no?' He paused; he was sprawling half-way across the table, and the foolish look in his eyes was replaced by a keener more searching gleam. 'But you have not seen his face,' he said with a strange air of quite sudden seriousness. 'There is no one has ever seen his face, not even I, Louis Duval!'

'Quite so,' said Charles. 'I haven't. Do you want to?'

A look of cunning crept into the artist's face. He smiled again, a slow, evil smile that showed his discoloured teeth. 'I do not tell you that. Oh, no! I do not tell you that, my friend. But this I tell you: you will never see his face, but you will go away from that house which is his, that house where he goes, *glissant*, up and down the stairs, though you do not see, where he watches you, though you do not know. Yes, you will go. You will go.' He fell to chuckling again.

'Why should we go?' Peter asked calmly. 'We're not afraid of ghosts, you know!'

The artist swayed with his insane giggling. 'But *Le Moine* is not like other ghosts, my friend. *Ah non*, he is not – like – other ghosts!'

The landlord had crossed the room, and now threw an apologetic glance at Peter. But he spoke to the artist. 'You'd like your usual table, moossoo, wouldn't you? You'll take your lunch in the coffee-room, I daresay, and there's as nice a leg of lamb waiting as ever I saw.'

The artist turned on him with something of a snarl. 'Away, cattle! You think you can tell me what I shall do and what I shall not do, but it is not so!'

'I'm sure, sir, I never had no such idea, but your lunch'll be spoiled if you don't come to eat it, and I've got some of the green peas cooked the French way you like.'

'I do not eat in this place, where you cook food fit for pigs. Yes, you wish that I go, but I do not go till I choose, and you dare not speak, my gross one, for me. I am Louis Duval, and there is not another in the world can do what I do! Is it not so? *Hein?* Is it not so?'

The landlord had an ugly look in his eye, but to Charles' and Peter's surprise he said soothingly: 'That's right, sir. Wonderful your pictures are.'

M. Duval looked at him through half-shut eyes; his voice sank; he said almost in a whisper: 'Sometimes I have thoughts in my head, gross pig, which you do not dream. Sometimes I think to myself, has no one seen the face of *Le Moine*? Has not Wilkes seen it? Eh? You do not like that, perhaps. Perhaps, too, you are afraid, just a little afraid of poor Louis Duval.'

'Me seen it?' echoed the landlord. 'Lor', Mr Dooval, I'm thankful I haven't, and that's a fact. Now you give over talking of spooks, sir, do. You've got half the room listening to you, like silly fools, and these gentlemen don't want to hear them sort of stories.'

Contrary to Peter's expectations the drunken artist allowed himself to be helped out of his chair, and gently propelled across the bar to the coffee-room door. Those villagers who still remained in the bar watched his exit with grins and nudges. When he had disappeared, and Wilkes with him, Peter addressed a solid-looking farmer who was seated near to him. 'Who's that chap?' he asked.

'He's a furriner, sir,' the farmer answered. 'An artist. I daresay you've seen his cottage, for it ain't far from the Priory.'

'Oh, he lives here, does he? Which is his cottage?'

'Why, sir, it's that white cottage with the garden in front that's a sin and shame to look at, it's that covered in weeds.' He began to sketch with a stubby finger on the table before him. 'Supposing the Priory's here, sir, where I've put my thumb. Well, you go on down the road, like as if you was coming to the village, and there's a bit of a lane leading off a matter of a quarter of a mile from this inn. You go up there not more'n a hundred yards, and you come right on the cottage. That's where he lives.'

'I see. Yes, I know the place. Has he lived there long?'

The farmer rubbed his ear. 'I don't know as I could rightly say how long he's been here. Not more'n five years, I reckon. We've kind of got used to him and his ways, and I never heard he did anyone any harm, bar walking over fields while the hay is standing. Mind you, it ain't so often you see him like he is to-day. He gets fits of it, so to speak. Now I come to think on it, it hasn't had a bout on him for a matter of three months. But whenever he gets like this he goes round maundering that silly stuff you heard. Enough to get on your nerves it is, but he's fair got the Priory ghost on the brain.' He got up as he spoke, and wishing them a polite good-day, made his way out.

'Quite interesting,' Charles said. 'I think it's time we made a move.'

On their way home down the right-of-way they talked long and earnestly over all that the drunken artist had said.

'It is well known,' Charles said at last, 'that you can't set much store by what a drunken man may say, but on the other hand it's always on the cards that he'll let out something he didn't mean to. I feel that M. Louis Duval may be worth a little close investigation.'

'What surprised me,' Peter remarked, 'was the way Wilkes bore with him. I expected to see Duval kicked out.'

'If he's in the habit of eating his meals at the Bell you can understand Wilkes humouring him. And apparently he's not always tight by any means. The most intriguing thing about him was his interest in the Monk. I don't know what you feel about it, but I should say he knew a bit about monks.'

'I'm all for getting on his tracks,' Peter answered. 'At the same time, he was so dam' fishy and mysterious that I'm inclined to think it was a bit too sinister to mean anything. Think he is the Monk?'

'Can't say. If I knew what the Monk was after I should find this problem easier to solve.'

They walked on for some time in silence. Peter broke it by saying suddenly: 'I don't know. It was typical drunken rot when you come to think of it. All that stuff about the Monk walking up and downstairs though we don't see him, and watching us though we don't know it. You can't get much sense out of that. Ghost-twaddle.'

'I was thinking of something else he said,' Charles said slowly. 'I'd rather like to know what he meant by no one ever having seen the Monk's face, not even himself. That wasn't quite the usual ghost-talk we hear in this place.'

'N-no. But I'm not sure that it's likely to lead anywhere. Still, I agree he wants looking into.'

They had reached the Priory by this time, and agreeing to say nothing of the morning's encounter to the others they went in, and found the three women already seated at the lunch-table.

'Did you have any luck?' Margaret asked.

'No, there's too much sun,' Peter answered. He paused in the act of helping himself to salad, and lifted his head. 'What's the strange noise?'

There was a distinct and rather unpleasant sound of humming that seemed to proceed from somewhere above. Margaret laughed. 'Ask Celia. She let us in for it.'

They looked inquiringly at her. 'Sounds like a vacuum cleaner or something,' said Charles.

'It is,' Celia confessed. 'I couldn't help it, though. Really, he was so persistent I hadn't the heart to go on saying no.'

'I think it's a very good plan,' said Mrs Bosanquet. 'I'm sure there must be a great deal of dust in all the carpets, and this will save having them taken up, which I was going to suggest.'

'But what do you mean?' Peter demanded. 'We've no electricity here, so how can you...'

'Oh, it isn't an electric one! It's some new sort of patent affair, but I really didn't pay much attention, because I've no intention of buying it. Only the man was so anxious to show me the amount of dust it would draw out of the carpets and chairs that I let him demonstrate. After all, it's costing us nothing, and it seems to please him.'

'A man, with a vacuum-cleaner for sale,' Charles repeated. 'A man...' He looked at Peter, and as though by common consent they both got up.

'Well, what on earth's the matter?' Celia asked. 'You don't mind, do you?'

'I'm not at all sure,' said Charles. 'I'll tell you when I've seen this clever salesman.' He threw down his table-napkin, and went quickly out of the room, and up the stairs. The droning noise came from Mrs Bosanquet's room, and he went in. Busily engaged in running a cleaner over the floor was the shifty-eyed commercial staying at the Bell Inn.

CHAPTER VII

For a moment they eyed one another in silence. Then the man with the vacuum-cleaner said: 'Good morning, sir. I wonder whether I can interest *you* in this here cleaner? No electric power required. Practically works itself, needing only the 'and to guide it. Like this, sir, if you will kindly watch what I do.' He began to run it over the carpet, still talking volubly. 'You can see for yourself, sir, 'ow easy to work this here cleaner is. Sucks up every speck of dust, *but* does *not* take off the nap of the carpet, which is a thing as can't be said of every cleaner on the market. We claim that with this here cleaner we 'ave done away with all servant trouble. Cheap to buy, and costs nothing to run. I will now demonstrate to you, sir, what it has done, by turning out the dust at present contained in this bag, which you see attached to the cleaner. All of which dust, sir, 'as been sucked out of this very carpet.'

'Don't trouble,' said Charles. 'I'm not buying it.'

The little man smiled tolerantly. 'No, sir? Well I don't know as how I should expect a gentleman to be interested in this here cleaner, not but what I 'ave sold to bachelors many a time. But I hope when your good lady sees the dust and dirt which this here cleaner has extracted from all carpets, upholstered chairs, curtains, and etcetera, she'll be tempted to give me an order, which the firm which I 'ave the honour to represent will execute with their custom'ry dispatch.'

'And what is the name of the firm you have the honour

to represent?' Charles inquired blandly.

If he expected the invader to be embarrassed he was disappointed.

'Allow me, sir!' beamed the little man, and inserting a finger and thumb into his waistcoat pocket he drew out a card, which he handed to Charles.

It was an ordinary trade-card, bearing the name and address of a firm in the city, and purporting to belong to a Mr James Fripp.

'That's me name, sir,' explained Mr Fripp, pointing it out. 'And I 'ope that when ordering you will 'ave the goodness to mention it, supposing I can't tempt you to give me an order now, which I 'ope I shall do when you 'ave seen for yourself that this here cleaner is all that we claim it to be.'

Charles put the card carefully into his pocket-book. 'We'll see,' he said. 'Do I understand that you propose to clean all the rooms of the house for us?'

'I'm sure I shall be pleased to, sir, but if you're satisfied, 'aving seen what 'as been effected under your own eye. . .'

'Oh no!' Charles said pleasantly. 'For all I know it might break down before it had gone over half the house.' Mr Fripp looked reproachful. 'This here cleaner,' he said, 'is constructed in such a way that it can't go wrong. I should mention that we give a year's guarantee with it, as is usual. But I shall be pleased to take it over every room in the 'ouse, to convince you, sir, of the truth of all I say.'

'Excellent,' said Charles. 'And in case I make up my mind to buy it I'll send my man up to watch you, so that he will know in future how to manipulate it.'

'That,' said Mr Fripp, 'is as you like, sir, but I should like to assure you that a child could work this here cleaner.'

'Nevertheless,' said Charles, stepping to the bell-rope, and jerking it sharply, 'I should like Bowers to – observe what you do.'

Those quick-glancing eyes darted to his face for an instant. 'I'm sure I shall be pleased to show him all I can, sir,' Mr Fripp said, not quite so enthusiastically.

Charles' smile was a little grim. When Bowers appeared in answer to the bell, he told him that he was to accompany Mr Fripp from room to room, and closely to watch all he did. Mr Fripp looked at him sideways.

'Yes, sir,' Bowers said, a trifle perplexed. 'But I haven't served the sweet yet, sir.'

'Never mind,' said Charles. 'We'll manage on our own. You stay with Mr Fripp – in case his cleaner goes out of action. And just see that he doesn't knock the panelling with it. We don't want any scratches.'

'No, sir, very good,' Bowers said, and resigned himself to his fate.

But the look that Mr Fripp cast on Charles' vanishing form was one of something bordering on acute dislike.

In the dining-room Charles was greeted by a demand from his wife to explain what on earth was the matter with him.

'If,' said Charles, resuming his seat, 'you would occasionally employ your brain, dear love, you might realize that the last thing we desire is a stranger let loose in the house. Oh, and if anyone wants any pudding he or she will have to get it for themselves, as Bowers is otherwise engaged.'

'It's on the sideboard,' Celia said. 'But really, Chas, I don't quite see what harm a man selling a vacuum-cleaner can do. And I asked him for his card, just to be on the safe side.'

'Was it our friend at the Bell?' Peter asked.

'It was. I am happy to think that I've given him a nice, solid afternoon's work.' He inspected Mr Fripp's card again. 'Yes. I think this is where one calls for a little outside assistance.'

Celia pricked up her ears. '*Not* Flinders again!' she begged.

'No, not Flinders,' Charles said. 'I should be loth to interrupt his entomological studies. But I feel a few discreet inquiries might be put through.'

'If you're going to call in Scotland Yard, I for one object,' Peter said. 'We've no data for them, and they'll merely think us credulous asses.'

Charles slipped his table-napkin into its ring, and got up. 'I can hardly improve on the favourite dictum of Mr Flinders,' he said with dignity. 'You don't need to tell *me* how to act.'

'Well, what are you going to do?' Margaret asked.

'Write a letter,' Charles answered, and went out.

Peter presently ran him to earth in the small study at the front of the house. 'Why the mystery?' he inquired. 'Are you getting an inquiry agent on to James Fripp?'

'I am,' Charles said, directing the envelope. 'There's a chap I've once or twice had dealings with who'll do the job very well.'

'What about Strange? Think it's worth while setting your sleuth on him?'

'I did consider it, but I think not. As far as Fripp's concerned it ought to be fairly easy, since I've got his card. Brown can get on to this firm he apparently works for. But regarding Strange we've nothing to give Brown to start on. If he's a wrong 'un it's highly unlikely that Strange is his real name. The man we want now is friend Flinders.'

Peter groaned. 'Do we? Why?'

'To find out a little more concerning M. Louis Duval. I'm rather surprised Flinders hasn't mentioned him.'

But the reason for this omission was soon forthcoming. Flinders, when they visited him in his cottage later that afternoon, said with considerable hauteur that they had only asked him questions about the gentry. 'And that Dooval,' he added, 'ain't gentry, besides being a furriner. You've only got to look at the place he lives in. Pig-sty ain't in it. What's more, he does for himself. Ah, *and* in more ways than one!' He permitted himself to give vent to a hoarse crack of laughter at his own wit. 'But what I *meant* was, he doesn't have no one up to clean the place for him, nor cook his breakfast.' He shook his head. 'He's a disgrace to the neighbourhood, that's what he is. He goes round painting them pictures what no one can make 'ead nor tail of as I ever heard on, and half the time he's drunk as a lord. Getting worse, he is. Why, I remember when he first come here, barring the fact of his being a furriner, there wasn't really much you could take exception to about him. Very quiet, he used to be, and you never saw him in drink more'n was respectable, though there *are* some as say that it ain't only drink as is *his* trouble.'

'Drugs?' Charles said. 'I rather suspected as much.'

'Mind you, I never said so,' Mr Flinders warned him, 'nor I wouldn't, me knowing my duty too well. But Mrs Fellowes, what I told you about before – her as is housekeeper to Mr Titmarsh – she spread it about that Dooval was one of those dope-fiends you read about in the *News of the World*. And the reason she had for saying it was on account of her working for a gentleman in London once, what was in the 'abit of taking drugs, which she said made her reckernize it right off.'

'By the way,' Peter interrupted, 'how is Mr Titmarsh getting on?'

The constable shook his head. 'Ah, now you're asking, sir. Well, I don't mind telling you that when you first came here asking me questions about him, I didn't set much store by it. But I been keeping a close watch on him, sir, like I said I would, and I'm bound to say he's fishy.'

'What's he done?'

'That,' said Mr Flinders cautiously, 'I couldn't go so far as to say, him having got into the habit of giving me the slip. Behaves like as if he knew he was being followed, and didn't wish for anyone to see what he was up to.' An odd sound proceeding from Charles made him turn his head inquiringly. 'You was saying, sir?'

'Nothing,' Charles replied hastily. 'At the moment I'm more interested in Duval than in Titmarsh. Does Duval go down to the inn every morning?'

'He eats his dinner there most days,' Flinders answered. 'Though when he's got one of his fits on him I don't believe he touches a bite. You'll see him at the Bell most evenings, but he's painting one of these 'orrible pictures of his now, and he's out most of the day.'

'What's he painting?' Charles asked.

'Pink rats, I should think, sir, judging from what I see of him last night,' said the constable facetiously. 'What's more, if he told me he was painting pink rats I'd believe him a lot easier than what I do when he says he's painting the mill-stream. Because anything more unnatural I never did see. Looks like a nightmare, if you ask me.'

'The mill-stream. That's past the village, isn't it?'

'That's right, sir. If you was to think of taking a look at the picture you'll find him painting it on the near bank, just below the mill.'

'I rather think I'll wander along that way,' Charles said.

'I take it you don't want me?' Peter asked him.

'N-no. Might perturb him if two of us rolled up. I'll see what I can find out.'

They took their leave of the constable, and drove on to the village. At the Bell, Charles got out of the car and proceeded on foot down the street to the fields that lay beyond.

It was no more than a ten minutes' walk to the mill, and as Flinders had predicted, Charles was rewarded by the sight of M. Duval at work on his sketch.

Charles approached from behind him, and thus had leisure to observe the artist before his own presence was detected. The man looked more of a scarecrow than ever, but if he was under the influence of drink or drugs this was not immediately apparent. He seemed to be absorbed in his work, and it was not until Charles stopped at his elbow that he looked round.

There was suspicion in his nervous start, and he glared up at Charles out of his bloodshot eyes.

'Good afternoon,' Charles said pleasantly. 'I apologize for being so inquisitive. If I may say so, you are painting a very remarkable picture.'

This was no less than the truth. Privately Charles thought that Flinders' strictures were not without reason. The sketch before him was weird in the extreme, yet although it could hardly be said to represent the old mill, even Charles, no connoisseur, could see that it was executed with a certain perverted skill.

The artist sneered, and said disagreeably: 'What do you English know of art? Nothing, I tell you!'

'I'm afraid you're right,' Charles agreed. 'But this, I take it, is not destined for our Academy? You exhibit in the Salon, no doubt?'

This piece of flattery found its mark. 'It is true,' M. Duval said. 'With this picture, my *chef-d'œuvre*, I make my name. The world will know me at last.' The momentary fire died out of his face. He shrugged, and said with a return to his sullen manner: 'But how should you appreciate a work of genius?'

'What strikes me particularly,' Charles persevered, 'is your treatment of shadows. In fact...'

'I see them red,' M. Duval said sombrely. 'Dull red.'

'Very few people have the eye to see them like that,' said Charles truthfully.

He soon found that no flattery was too gross to please M. Duval, and he proceeded, as he afterwards told Peter, to spread himself. At the end of twenty minutes the artist had mellowed considerably, and when Charles said solemnly that Framley was fortunate indeed to have attracted one who was so obviously a genius, he threw down his brush with a gesture of bitter loathing, and cried out: 'You think I live here because I choose? Ah, *mon Dieu*!' He leaned forward on his camp-stool, and the hand which held his palette shook with some overpowering emotion. 'I think all the time how I shall get away!' he said tensely. 'Five years I have lived here, five years, m'sieur! Figure to yourself! But the day comes when I see it no more. Then – pouf! I am gone, I am free!' He seemed to recollect himself, and a smile of weak cunning showed his discoloured teeth. 'You think I talk strangely, *hein*? Not like you English, who are always cold, like ice. To those others I am nothing but a mad Frenchman, but you, my friend, you have seen that I have a genius in me!' He slapped his chest as he spoke. 'Here, in my soul! You have admired my picture; you have not laughed behind my back. And because you have sympathized, because you have recognized the true art, I will tell you something.' He plucked at Charles' sleeve with fingers like talons, and his voice sank. 'Take care, m'sieur, you who think to live in that house which is the home of *Le Moine*. I warn you, take care, and do not try to interfere with him. I tell you, it is not safe. You hear me? There is danger, much, much danger.'

'Thanks for the warning,' Charles said calmly. 'But I don't really think a ghost could do me much harm, do you?'

The artist looked at him queerly. 'I say only, take care. You have tried to find *Le Moine*, I think, because you do not believe in ghosts. But I tell you there is great danger.'

'I see. You think I should be unwise to try and find out who he is?'

'There is no one who knows that,' M. Duval said slowly. 'No one! But maybe this poor Duval, who paints pictures that the world laughs at, maybe he might – one day – know – who is – *Le Moine*.' He was smiling as he said it, and his eyes were clouded and far away. His voice sank still lower till it was little more than a whisper. 'And if I know, then, then at last I will be free, and I will have revenge! Ah, but that will be sweet!' His claw-like hands curled as though they strangled some unseen thing.

'Forgive me,' said Charles, 'but has the Monk done you some injury?'

His words jerked Duval back from that dreamy, half-drugged state. He picked up his brush again. 'It is a ghost,' he muttered. 'You have said it yourself.'

Seeing that for the present at least there was little hope of getting anything more out of the artist, Charles prepared to take his departure. 'Ghost or no ghost,' he said deliberately, 'I intend to find out – what I can. You seem to have some idea of doing the same thing. If you want my assistance I suggest you come and call on me at the Priory.'

'I do not want assistance,' Duval said, hunching his shoulders rather like a pettish child.

'No? Yet if I were to say one day that I had seen the face of the Monk....?' Charles left the end of the sentence unfinished, but its effect was even more than he had hoped.

Duval swung round eagerly. 'You have seen – but no! You have seen nothing. He does not show his face, the Monk, and it is better if you do not try to see it.' He fixed his eyes on Charles' face, and said in a low voice: 'One man – saw – just once in his life. One man alone, m'sieur!'

'Oh? Who is he?'

'It does not matter now, m'sieur, who he is, for he is dead.'

Charles was half-startled, and half-scornful. 'What did he die of? Fright?'

The artist bent his gaze on his sketch again. 'Perhaps,' he said. 'Yet me, I do not think he died of fright.' He

107

began to squeeze paint from one of his tubes. 'You will go back to your Priory, m'sieur, but you will remember what I say, is it not?'

'Certainly,' Charles said. '*And* I shall hope to see your picture again when it is more finished, if you will let me.'

There was something rather pathetic about the way Duval looked up at that, unpleasant though the man's personality might be. 'You like it enough to wish to see more? But I have many pictures in my cottage, perhaps not so fine as this, but all, all full of my genius! One day perhaps you come to see me, and I show you. Perhaps you will see something you like enough to buy from me, *hein*?'

'That was what I was thinking,' lied Charles.

The Monk was forgotten; avarice gleamed in the artist's eye. He said swiftly: '*Bon*! You come very soon, and I show you the best that I have painted. Perhaps you come to-morrow? Or the day after?'

'Thanks, I'd like to come to-morrow if I may. Shall we say about this time?' He consulted his wrist-watch. 'Half-past three? Or does that break into your working hours?'

'But no! I am quite at your service,' M. Duval assured him.

'Then *au revoir*,' Charles said. 'I'll see you to-morrow.'

M. Duval's farewell was as cordial as his greeting had been surly. Charles walked briskly back to the village, trying as he went to separate the grain of his talk from the chaff.

One thing seemed clear enough: unless the man were a consummate actor, he was not the Monk. It seemed improbable that, in his half-drugged condition, he could be acting a part, but on the other hand that very condition made it dangerous to set too much store by what he said. Much of it sounded suspiciously like the waking dreams experienced by drug-addicts, yet when he had spoken of the Monk, Charles thought that he had detected a look of perfectly sane hatred in his eyes. He had not been talking of a ghost: that much was certain. To Duval, the Monk was real, and, apparently, terrible. It was possible, of course, that in a state that resembled delirium his mind had seized on the idea of the ghostly inmate of the Priory, and woven a story about it. Possible, Charles admitted, but hardly probable.

If one accepted the provisional hypothesis that the Monk was no ghost, one was immediately faced with two problems. The first, Charles thought, was the reason he could have for what seemed a senseless masquerade; the second, which might perhaps be easier to solve if the first were discovered, was his identity.

Since they had had, so far, no means of identifying any single thing about him, he might be any one of the people with whom they had become acquainted, or, which was quite possible, someone whom they had never seen.

The artist apparently knew something, but how much it was hard to decide. Charles hoped that on the following day he might, by buying one of his pictures, induce him to disclose more. If he was weaving a fanciful tale out of his own clouded mind it would be merely misleading, of course, but Charles felt that for the sake of the remote chance of discovering the Monk's object in haunting the Priory, this must be faced.

He had reached the Bell Inn by this time. The bar was not open, but on the other side of the archway into the yard there was a draughty apartment known as the lounge. Here he found his brother-in-law seated in an uncomfortable leather chair, and chatting to Colonel Ackerley. The Colonel's golf clubs were propped against one of the tables, and he was wearing a suit of immensely baggy plus-fours.

'Aha, here's Malcolm!' he said, as Charles entered the room. 'Sit down, my dear fellow! Been fishing? I'm on my way back from my day's golf! Noticed your car outside and looked in to see which of you was trying to get a drink out of hours. Found you out, eh?'

'It cannot be too widely known,' said Charles, 'that I am more or less of a teetotaller.'

'But mostly less,' Peter interpolated.

The Colonel was much amused by this, and repeated it. 'More or less – that's very good, Malcolm. I must remember that. Might mean either, what? But what have you been doing? Calling on the Vicar's wife?'

'I regard that as a reflection on my sobriety, sir,' Charles said gravely. 'No. I've been watching a very odd specimen paint a still odder picture.'

The Colonel lifted his brows. 'That French johnny? Can't say I understand much about art, but I've always thought his pictures were dam' bad. I'm a plain man, and if I look at a picture I like to be able to see what it's meant to be. But I daresay I'm old-fashioned.'

'I should rather like to know,' said Charles, 'what he's doing here. Know anything about him, sir?'

The Colonel shook his head. 'No, afraid I don't. Never really thought about it, to tell you the truth.'

'He's not exactly prepossessing,' Peter remarked. 'He may be a bit of a wrong 'un who finds it wiser not to return to his native shores.'

''Pon my soul, you people have got mysteries on the brain!' exclaimed the Colonel. 'First it's poor old Titmarsh, and now it's what's-his-name? – Duval. What's he been up to, I should like to know?'

'Intriguing us by his conversation,' said Charles lightly. 'Making our blood run cold by his sinister references to our Monk.'

The Colonel threw up his hands. 'No, no, once you get on to that Monk of yours I can't cope with you, Malcolm. Now really, really, my dear fellow, you don't seriously mean to tell me you've been listening to that sodden dope-fiend?'

Charles looked up quickly. 'Ah! So you think he's a dope-fiend too, do you?'

The Colonel caught himself up. 'Daresay one oughtn't to say so,' he apologized. 'Slander, eh? But it's common talk round here.'

He glanced over his shoulder as someone opened the door. Wilkes had put his head into the room to see who was there. He bade them good afternoon, and wanted to know whether he might tell John, the waiter, to serve them with tea. They all refused, but the Colonel detained Wilkes. 'I say, Wilkes,' he called, 'here's that artist fellow been maundering to Mr Malcolm about the Priory ghost. Is he drunk again?'

Wilkes came farther into the room, shaking his head. 'I'm afraid so, sir. Been carrying on something chronic these last three days. First it's the Monk, then it's eyes watching him in the dark, till he fair gives me the creeps, and yesterday nothing would do but he must tell me how there was a plot about to keep him from being reckernized. If you ask me, sir, he's gone clean potty.'

'Dear, dear, something will have to be done about it if that's so,' Colonel Ackerley said. 'You never know with these drug fiends. He may turn dangerous.'

'Yes, sir, that's what I've been thinking,' Wilkes said. 'He's got a nasty look in his eye some days.'

'Better keep your carving-knife out of reach,' the Colonel said laughingly.

At that moment Peter chanced to look at the window. 'Hullo!' he said. 'There's your pal, Fripp, Chas. Looks a trifle jaded.'

Charles glanced round, but Fripp had passed the window. 'I daresay. There are quite a lot of rooms at the Priory,' he remarked.

The Colonel pricked up his ears. 'Fripp? Fripp? Seem to know that name. Wait a bit! Is he a fellow with some sort of a vacuum-cleaner?'

111

'He is,' said Charles. 'He has been spending the afternoon demonstrating it at the Priory. In fact, all over the Priory.'

'Perfect pest, these house-to-house salesmen,' fumed the Colonel. 'Came to my place the other day, but my man sent him about his business.'

'I told him he wouldn't do no good in these parts,' Wilkes said. 'What I can't make out is how he comes to be making this place his headquarters, so to speak. Don't seem reasonable, somehow, but I suppose he knows his business. You're sure you wouldn't like tea, sir?'

'We must be getting along at any rate,' Peter said, rising. 'When are you coming in for another game of bridge, Colonel? Why not come home with us now, and have some tea, and a game?'

The Colonel said that nothing would please him more, and accordingly they all went out together, and drove back to the Priory to find Celia in ecstasies over the dustless condition of the house, and quite anxious to send an order for a cleaner at once.

CHAPTER VIII

On the following afternoon Peter went off with Colonel Ackerley to play golf on the nearest course, some four miles away on the other side of the village. Margaret, whose appointment with the dentist fell on this day, had taken the car up to London, so that Charles, no believer in such forms of exercise, was compelled to walk to M. Duval's cottage.

He found it easily enough, but even the farmer's disparaging remarks upon it had not quite prepared him for anything so tumbledown and dreary. It had an air of depressing neglect; the garden was overgrown with docks and nettles, every window wanted cleaning, and in places the original white plaster had peeled off the walls, leaving the dirty brown brick exposed.

The hinges of the gate were broken, and it stood open. Charles made his way up the path to the door of the cottage, and knocked on the blistered panels with his walking stick. After a few moments footsteps approached, Charles heard a bolt drawn, and the door was opened by M. Duval.

It was plain that he had made an effort to tidy not only the living-room of his abode, but also his own person. His shirt was clean, and he had evidently done his best to remove some of the stains from his coat. Also he was sober, but he betrayed by his nervousness, and his unsteady hand, what a hold over him drugs had obtained.

He was almost effusive in his welcome, and insisted that

Charles should take tea with him as a preliminary to any negotiations they might enter into. The kettle, he said, was already on the stove. He seemed so anxious to play the host to the best of his ability that Charles accepted his offer.

'I will make it on the instant,' Duval told him. 'I do not keep a servant, m'sieur. You will excuse me?'

'Of course,' Charles said. 'And while you're getting tea perhaps I may take a look at your work?'

Duval made a gesture that swept the little room. 'You see my work, m'sieur, before you.'

All manner of canvases were propped against the walls, some so weird that they looked to be no more than irrelevant splashes of colour, some a riot of cubes, one or two moderately understandable.

'Look your fill!' Duval said dramatically. 'You look into my soul.'

For the sake of M. Duval's soul Charles hoped that this was an exaggeration. However, he bowed politely, and begged his host not to mind leaving him. Thus adjured, the artist disappeared into the lean-to kitchen that was built out at the back of the cottage, and Charles was left to take stock of his surroundings.

These were miserable enough. The cottage, which bore signs of considerable antiquity, had but the one living-room, from which a precipitous staircase led up between two walls to the upper storey. At the back a door led into the kitchen; at the front were lattice windows and the principal door of the house, and on one side a huge fireplace occupied almost the entire wall. The ceiling was low, and a wealth of old oak formed worm-eaten beams, in between which the cobwebs of years had formed. Charles judged that originally the room had served as kitchen and living-room combined, for from the great central beam one or two big hooks still protruded, from which, doubtless, flitches of bacon had hung in olden days.

The furniture was in keeping with the dilapidated building itself. A strip of dusty carpet lay across the floor; there were two sound chairs, and one with a broken leg that sagged against the wall; a table, an easel, a cupboard, and a deal chest that stood under the window, and which was covered with a litter of tubes, brushes, rags, and bits of charcoal.

There remained the pictures, and until Duval came back with the tea-pot Charles occupied himself in trying to make up his mind which he could best bring himself to buy.

Duval reappeared shortly, and set the tea-pot down on the table. He suggested, not without a hopeful note in his voice, that perhaps his guest would prefer a whisky and soda, but this Charles firmly declined.

'Eh *bien*, then I give you sugar and milk, yes? So? You have looked at my pictures? Presently I will explain to you what I have tried to express in them.'

'I wish you would,' Charles said. 'I can see that they are full of ideas.'

No further encouragement was needed to start the artist off on his topic. He talked volubly, but rather incoherently, for over half an hour, until Charles' head reeled, and he felt somewhat as though he had stepped into a nightmare. But his polite questions and apparently rapt interest had the effect of banishing whatever guard the artist had set upon his tongue and he became expansive, though mysterious on the subject of his own enforced sojourn at Framley.

Realizing that in all probability any attempt to question Duval as to his obscure meaning would drive him into his shell, Charles contented himself with sympathizing.

'Whoever is to blame for keeping you here,' he said solemnly, 'is a criminal of the deepest dye.'

This pleased. 'Yes he is wicked. You do not know,

m'sieur! But I shall have my revenge on him, perhaps soon. I tell you, I will make him suffer! He shall pay. Yes, he shall pay and pay for the years which I have spent in exile.' A little saliva dribbled from the corner of his mouth; he looked unpleasantly like a dog drooling at the sight of a bone.

With a feeling of disgust, and more than half convinced that he was wasting his time on a madman, Charles turned to the pictures, and soon made his choice. M. Duval seemed disappointed when he fixed on the least Futuristic of his works, but after an attempt to induce Charles to buy 'Sunset in Hades' he consented to roll up the more innocuous 'Reapers.'

Outside the sky had for some time been growing steadily more overcast, and as Charles prepared to take his leave, a flash of lightning lit up the darkening room, to be followed in a very few moments by an ominous rumble of thunder. The rain did not seem to be far off, and since he had no overcoat Charles was reluctantly compelled to postpone his departure.

The artist seemed to become more restless with the approach of the storm, and as the light went he took to glancing over his shoulder as though he expected to see someone. When a second and much louder clap of thunder came he jumped uncontrollably, and muttered something about fetching a lamp. He went through into the kitchen, and came back presently with a cheap oil-lamp which he set down on the table.

'I do not like the darkness,' he said. 'Perhaps you think I am strange to say that, but when one lives always alone, m'sieur, one has fancies.' He gave a little shiver, and his eyes stared into Charles' for a moment. 'But there are things which are not fancies.' Again he looked round, then leaning towards Charles he said hardly above a whisper: 'I know that there is one who watches. I have felt his eyes through my window, I bolt my door, but when I go out

116

he follows. I have heard his footsteps, but when I look there is no one there. Sometimes I think I cannot bear it, for at night, m'sieur, it is so still, and I am alone. Sometimes I think maybe I shall go mad one day. But I am not mad. No, I am not mad yet.'

'Who watches you?' Charles said quietly. 'Have you any idea?'

Duval shook his head. 'I do not know. Sometimes I think – but I do not say.'

'I hope,' said Charles, 'that it is not our Monk?'

The artist gave a start, and grew sickly pale all at once. 'No, no!' he said. 'But do not speak so loud, m'sieur! You do not know who may be listening.'

Since a heavy rain was now beating against the windows it seemed absurd to suppose that anyone could be lurking outside, but Charles saw that it was useless to reason with one whose nerves were so little under control. To humour the artist, he lowered his voice. 'It is unwise, then, even to mention the Monk?' he asked.

Duval nodded vigorously. 'For me, yes. There are those who listen to what I say though they seem to be deaf. M'sieur, I tell you it is too much! Sometimes when I am alone in this house I think it would be better to give it all up, not to attempt – I have not the courage, he is clever, ah, but clever!'

'My friend,' Charles said, 'I think someone has some sort of a hold over you. Don't be alarmed: I'm not asking what it is.'

The thunder crashed above their heads, and involuntarily Duval winced. 'Yes, he has what you call a hold, but what if I get a hold over him? What then, *hein*?' His fingers curled and uncurled; he looked so haggard that once more Charles found himself pitying him against his will.

'Forgive me if I say that I think you would do well to get away from this lonely life of yours. It has preyed too much on your mind.'

The artist's eyes stared wildly at him. 'I cannot get away!' he burst out. 'I am tied, tied! I dare not speak, even! What I could tell! Ah, m'sieur, there are things I know that you would give all to learn. Yes, I am not a fool; I know what you are seeking, you and that other. You will not find it, but I – I might! You do not believe? You think I talk so because perhaps I am drunk? You are wrong. It is true that sometimes I have drunk too much. To-day, no! What is it you desire to see? You will not answer? But I know, m'sieur! You desire to see the face of the Monk.'

Charles would have spoken, but he swept on, as though a spate of words had been loosed in him. 'You will not. But I desire it also, and I tell you the day comes when I shall see it. And if I see it, only for one little minute! one little, little minute, what shall I do? Shall I tell you? Ah no, m'sieur! No, no, no, I tell no one, but I am free! And it will be for me then to revenge myself, for me to be master!'

A flash of lightning made Charles blink. There was the scrape of a chair. Duval had sprung up, and was staring towards the window. 'What was that,' he gasped. 'What was that, m'sieur? A face? A face pressed to the glass?'

'Nonsense,' Charles said calmly. 'It was nothing but that sunflower blown against the window. Look!'

The sweat stood on Duval's forehead. 'Truly? Yes, yes, I see. It was nothing. Yet for a moment I could have sworn I saw – something. It is this accursed storm. I do not like the lightning. It makes me what you call on edge. Sometimes I fear I have not the courage to go on with what I have made up my mind I must do to be free. For when I am here with the darkness I remember that other who died.' He went to the cupboard and opened it, and pulled out a whisky bottle, half-full, and two thick glasses. 'You will take a little drink with me? This storm – one's nerves demand it.'

'Not for me, thanks,' Charles answered. 'May I suggest that if you've reason to think someone is watching you your best course is to inform the police.'

Duval cast a quick, furtive look at him. The whisky spilled into his glass. He tossed it off, neat, and seemed to regain what little composure he possessed. 'No, I do not do that. You will not listen to me: I talk folly, *hein*? Me, I am Louis Duval, and I am not afraid.'

The rain had practically ceased by now, and Charles got up. 'Then since the storm seems to be passing over you won't mind if I say good-bye, will you?' He picked up the picture he had bought. 'I shall – er – value this, I assure you. And if at any time you'd like to take me rather more into your confidence you know where I'm to be found, don't you?'

'I thank you. And for this' – he held up Charles' cheque – 'I thank you also.' With his self-command his arrogance too was creeping back. 'The day comes when you will congratulate yourself that you were once able to buy a picture of Louis Duval's for so small a price.'

That view was not shared either by Charles, or by any of his relatives. When he exhibited the painting at the Priory an astonished silence greeted it.

'Yes,' he said blandly, 'I thought you'd be hard put to it to find words to express your emotions.'

Peter breathed audibly through his nose. 'You were right,' he said.

'Nice piece of work, isn't it? I particularly like the woman's splay feet. Where shall we hang it?'

'I suggest the coal-cellar,' said Peter.

Mrs Bosanquet was regarding the picture through her lorgnette. 'What an exceedingly ill-favoured young person!' she remarked. 'Really, almost disgusting. And what is she waving in her hand, pray?'

'Since I am informed that the title of this masterpiece is

"Reapers" I should hazard a guess that it must be a sickle,' Charles replied.

Celia found her tongue. 'Charles, how *could* you?' she demanded. 'Have you gone mad, or something?'

'Not at all. I'm supporting modern art.'

'You don't know anything about art, ancient or modern. I can't get over you going out and wasting your money on an awful thing like this! You don't suppose that I could live with it on my walls, do you?'

'Shove it up on the stairs,' suggested Peter. 'Then the next time the Monk goes *glissant* up and down, though we do not see, it'll give him something to think about. After all we owe him one for that skull.'

'My dear,' said Mrs Bosanquet gravely, 'you should not make a jest of these things. When Margaret returns from London with my planchette board I shall hope to convince you as I myself have been convinced.'

'Aunt, you promised you wouldn't talk about the Monk!' Celia said uneasily. 'Just when I was beginning to forget about it too!'

'It was not I who started it, dear child,' Mrs Bosanquet pointed out. 'But by all means let us talk of something else. I do trust, Peter, that you are not serious in wishing to hang that very unpleasant picture on the stairs.'

'Well, we shall have to hang it somewhere,' Peter said. 'Old Ackerley will want to see it. When he asked me where you were, Chas, and I told him you'd gone to buy one of Duval's pictures, I thought he'd throw a fit.'

'You can jolly well tell him then that you didn't buy a picture after all,' Celia said. 'I won't have you making yourself a laughing-stock. It'll be all over Framley that you've been had.'

Charles listened to this with a suspicious air of interest. 'Do I understand you all to mean that you feel these walls are unworthy to bear the masterpiece?' he inquired.

'You can put it like that, if you choose,' Celia said.

'Very well,' he replied, and began carefully to roll it up again. 'I've always wanted to see my name in the papers as one who has presented a work of art to the nation. I wonder where they'll hang it? It would go rather well amongst the Turners.'

'And the worst of it is,' Celia said later to her brother, 'he's quite capable of sending it to the National Gallery, if only to tease me.'

Peter was more interested in the result of Charles' visit than in the fate of the picture, but it was not until he was dressing for dinner that he had an opportunity of speaking to him alone. Charles came in while he was wrestling with a refractory stud, and sat down on the edge of the bed.

'Good. I hoped you'd come in,' Peter said. 'God damn this blasted laundry! They starch the thing so that... Ah, that's got it! Well, did you discover anything, or is he merely potty?'

'A bit of both,' Charles said. He selected a cigarette from his case, and lit it. 'From a welter of drivel just one or two facts emerge. The most important of these is that unless Duval is completely out of his mind, which I doubt, the Monk is a very real personage. Further, it would appear that he has some hold over Duval, who, with or without reason, fears him like the devil. It seems fairly obvious that the Monk – and very likely Duval too – is engaged in some nefarious pursuit, and I rather gathered from what our friend said that he – I'm talking now of Duval – is only waiting for the chance to blackmail him.'

'What about?' Peter asked, busy with his tie.

'God knows. I couldn't arrive at it. It sounds absurd, but everything seemed to hinge on the Monk's face.'

'Talk sense,' said Peter shortly.

'Quite impossible,' Charles replied, flicking the ash off his cigarette. 'I'm giving you the gist of Duval's conversation. Put plainly, the Monk is strictly incognito.

121

According to Duval the only man who ever saw his face immediately died. Manner not specified, but all very sinister.'

'Doesn't say much for the Monk's face,' Peter commented. His eyes met Charles' in the mirror, and he saw that Charles was frowning slightly. He turned. 'Look here, how much faith do you place in this rigmarole?'

Charles shrugged. 'Can't say. After all we had ourselves decided that the Monk was no ghost.'

Peter picked up his waistcoat and put it on. 'Neither you nor I have so far set eyes on this precious Monk,' he reminded Charles. 'We know there's a legend about a monk haunting this place; we've had a skull drop at our feet, and we suspect – suspect, mind you – human agency. Not necessarily the Monk. The only person to see it is Aunt Lilian. I admit she's not the sort of person likely to imagine things, but you've got to bear in mind that it was late at night, and she, in common with the rest of us, had probably got the Monk slightly on the brain. She got the wind up – admits that herself. Started to "feel" things. Works herself into a state in which she's ripe for seeing anything. She has a candle only, and by its light she sees, or thinks she sees, a cowled figure.'

'Which according to her account, moved towards her,' Charles interpolated.

'True, and as I say, she's not nervous or given to imaginative flights. I don't say she didn't see all that. But I do say that some trick of the shadows cast by a feeble light held in her probably not very steady hand, coupled with her own quite natural fears, may have deceived her. The only other thing we've got to go on is the ravings of this artist-bloke, in whom you can't place much reliance.'

'Not quite,' Charles said. 'We know that there is something queer about this house. I don't want to lay undue stress on all that has happened, but on the other hand I don't want to run to the other extreme of pooh-

poohing undoubtedly odd proceedings. There was the episode of the groaning stone; there was the exceedingly fishy conversation we overheard between Strange and Fripp. Without that proof that someone is taking an extraordinary interest in the Priory I might easily discount everything Duval said. But we *know* that someone broke into the place by a secret entrance; we know that Strange had something to do with it. What he's after I don't pretend to say, but it's fairly obvious that he is after something. Given those facts I don't feel justified in brushing Duval aside as irrelevant. In fact, I'll go so far as to say that I have a strong conviction that he is perhaps the most relevant thing we've struck yet.'

Peter tucked a clean handkerchief into the breastpocket of his dinner-jacket. 'But the whole thing seems so utterly fantastic,' he complained. 'I daresay Duval is in someone's power: I always said he looked a wrong 'un. But what the hell has it got to do with the Priory?'

'That,' said Charles, 'is what we've got to find out.'

'Thanks very much. And just where do we start? The most likely explanation advanced so far is hidden treasure. Well, if you want to spend the rest of our stay prising up solid stone slabs in the cellar, you've more energy than I've ever yet seen you display.'

Charles threw the end of his cigarette out of the open window. 'If it's buried treasure the field isn't as narrow as that. Fripp, to my mind, wanted a chance to explore the rest of the house.'

'Well, that settles it. You can't take up the floorboards in every room, and go twisting every bit of moulding in the panelling in the hope of discovering another priest's hole. If we'd a history of the place no doubt we should find out all about it. But we haven't.'

'No,' said Charles. '*We* haven't. And, do you know, I find that rather surprising.'

Peter stared. 'Do you mean someone may have pinched

it?'

'Hasn't that occurred to you? This place obviously has a history – must have had. You'd expect to find some record in the library.'

'Well, yes, you might, but on the other hand the house has changed hands a lot since the place was a monastery. It may have got lost, or bought by a collector or something like that.'

'Quite so. But there's something more to it than that. When the point was first raised it struck me as being curious. I thought it worth while to drop a line to Tim Baker, and ask him to see whether a history of this place existed in the British Museum library. To-night I had his answer.' He drew a letter from his pocket, and opened it. 'There is a history, and a copy of it is in the Museum. And two pages have been torn out. What do you make of that?'

'Good Lord!' Peter said blankly. 'I say, things do begin to look a bit sinister, don't they? What do you propose we do about it? Call in Scotland Yard?'

'I've been playing with that idea for some days, but I'm not in love with it. I don't quite see myself spinning this yarn to some disillusioned official. If we'd any real data to give the Yard, well and good. But I ask you, what does our tale sound like, in cold blood? A hotch-potch without one solid fact to go on. We hear noises, we discover a skeleton, we listen to what a drunken Frenchman has to say, and see various people wandering about the grounds. The only fact we've got is that someone broke into the cellars, and that's a matter for the local police to deal with. It's not good enough.'

Peter nodded. 'That's what I feel myself, I must say. At the same time we're not getting anywhere – principally because we don't know where to start. If this inquiry agent of yours throws any discreditable light on Fripp's past, what do you say to running over to Manfield, and having a chat with the District Inspector?'

A gong chimed in the hall below them. Charles got up. 'We can do that, of course. Personally, I'm rather pinning my faith to Duval. I rather think he'll let something out sooner or later which may give us a line on it.'

They went slowly down to the library, where Celia and Mrs Bosanquet were awaiting them.

'Margaret not back yet?' Charles said.

Celia prepared to go in to dinner. 'No, but I was hardly expecting her. She said if Peggy Mason was free she might have an early dinner with her in town, and get back here about nine-thirty, before it's quite dark.'

'I hope,' said Mrs Bosanquet, 'that she will not have forgotten to call at my flat for the planchette.'

CHAPTER IX

Margaret spent a successful day in London. The dentist did not keep her waiting more than a quarter of an hour, and his excavations were not too painful. In the afternoon she visited the flat Peter and she owned in Knightsbridge, and unearthed his service revolver from a trunk in the box-room. Next she drove to Celia's house in Kensington, and after prolonged search located Charles' revolver. There remained only Mrs Bosanquet's planchette, and this the maid she had left in charge of her flat was easily able to find. By the time all these commissions had been executed Margaret was feeling ready for tea, and after that she had some shopping of her own to do. This occupied her till six o'clock, and then, somewhat weary, but with the consciousness of having left nothing undone, she drove to her club, and sat down to await the arrival of her friend, Peggy Mason.

She did not expect Mrs Mason before seven o'clock, so that she had almost an hour to while away. Under the disapproving glare of one of the more elderly members of the club she ordered a cocktail, and curled herself up in a large arm-chair with an illustrated journal, a cigarette, and her Bronx.

The journal was, as usual, full of pictures of sunburnt people snapped on the Lido, but the odd thing about it was that though the legend under the snapshots might read: 'Lord So-and-so and Miss Something-else in a happy mood,' Lord So-and-so's face became unaccountably the face of Michael Strange. Information concerning the doings of all these leisured people changed to such irrelevant scraps as: 'But what was he doing in the garden at that hour?' and: 'Could he really have been in our cellars that day we tried to locate the groan and saw him by the drawing-room windows?'

Margaret told herself severely that she was thinking a great deal too much about Michael Strange, and applied herself to the *Tatler* with a firm resolve to think about him no more.

But excellent though the resolve might be it was impossible to keep to it. Margaret gave up all pretence of doing so after five minutes, and permitted her refractory mind to do as it pleased.

Except for a brief infatuation for her drawing-master which attacked her at the age of sixteen she had never been in love. Her mother had died when she was still at school, her father three years later, and since that time she and Peter had kept house together. They were a very devoted couple, and so far Margaret had not felt in the least tempted to leave him for any one of the several suitors who had wished her to marry them. In the nicest possible way she had refused all offers, and it said much for her that these rejections never interfered with her friendship with the young man in question, nor, which was more important, with his friendship with her brother. One or two continued to cherish hopes, but when the most importunate of her suitors consoled himself eventually elsewhere, Margaret, no dog-in-the-manger, was unaffectedly glad and promptly made a friend of his bride, the very lady who was to dine with her this evening.

Until she met Michael Strange she was almost sure that she was not the sort of girl who fell in love. She wasn't at all cast down by this conviction; she didn't want to fall in love. People in love became sloppy, she thought, and they were a nuisance to all their friends, which was a pity. A girl had once told her raptly that she had known as soon as she had set eyes on the young man of her affections, that she would either marry him or no one. Margaret had considered this not only absurd, but sickly.

But during the past week she had somewhat modified her judgment. Not that she would ever be such a ninny as to fall flat in front of a man in that nauseating fashion, she told herself. Still, without going to such extremes she was bound to acknowledge that Mr Michael Strange had done something very queer indeed to her.

As to falling in love, that was rot, of course. One didn't fall in love with complete strangers, and certainly not with strangers who behaved as oddly as he was behaving. But the fact remained that from that very first meeting, when he had changed one of the wheels of the car for her she had, in her own words, 'taken to him,' as she could not remember ever having 'taken to' anyone before. There was something about his smile, which lost nothing by being rather rarely seen, that attracted her. He was good-looking too, but she didn't think that had much to do with it, for she knew men far better-looking, and she hadn't 'taken to' them in the least. No, it wasn't anything she could explain, but she just liked him very much.

She was in the habit of being as honest with herself as she could, and at this point she paused. There was rather more to it than just liking him very much. She had a suspicion that the same romantically-minded girl who had rhapsodized over her own emotions, would have described the effect of Mr Michael Strange on her friend as 'thrilling.' Margaret was not in the habit of being thrilled by young men, however personable, and she felt slightly affronted to think that such an idea had even crossed her mind. Then a really shocking thought reared up its head: she wouldn't mind if Mr Michael Strange tried to kiss her. Quite disgusted with herself, she realized that so far from minding she would rather like it. For one who had the greatest objection to stray embraces, this was unheard of. Margaret put the thought hurriedly aside: in every other way she prided herself on her modernity, but when it came to letting men maul you about – no!

But leaving that out of the question, there was no denying that Michael Strange had made her feel that she would like to see more of him.

Then had come the surprise of finding him in the Priory garden. When she had seen who he was she had instantly acquitted him, in her mind, of having had anything to do with the groan they had heard. But Charles and Peter, both likely, she realized, to be more impartial than herself, had thought his presence suspicious. They had not been reassured either by his explanation or the manner in which he gave it. Thinking it over she was bound to admit that he had sounded mysterious. At Colonel Ackerley's dinner-party, moreover, she had tried to find out more about him, and he had evaded her questions. Then there was the occasion when she had discovered him apparently studying half-obliterated inscriptions on the tombs in the ruined chapel. She had taxed him openly that time with having been in the Priory garden one night. She had known, with an unaccountable feeling of disillusionment, that he was going to deny it, and unreasonably, just because somehow she could not bear that he should lie to her, she had said quickly that she had recognized him. It would have been useless for him to deny it after that, and he had not done so. But neither had he given her any explanation of his conduct.

Margaret was no fool, and her reason told her that had there been an innocent explanation he must have given it. Since he had not done so she was forced to face the probability of his being engaged upon some discreditable business. What it could be she had no idea, but she had the impression that her presence at the Priory discomposed him. He did not want her there; he had tried to persuade her to go away. Just as though he did not want her to find out what he was doing; as though her presence made him regret what he meant to do.

He had asked her to trust him, saying frankly that there was no reason why she should. And against her reason she had trusted him, even to the extent of never mentioning his presence by night in the garden to her brother or to Charles.

Was he a crook? one of those master-crooks of fiction, who had such address and charm that no one ever suspected them? Was it possible that he was some sort of a cat-burglar who had used the empty and reputedly haunted Priory as a *cache* for his hauls? Had he hidden jewels or bank-notes in some secret hiding-place at the Priory, pending their disposal? Or was he the head of some large criminal organization who had made a haunted house their headquarters? That might account for the attempts it seemed fairly certain he had made to frighten the new tenants away, but she could not help feeling that a less risky proceeding would have been to have changed his headquarters.

An idea flashed into her mind. She glanced at her wrist-watch: ten minutes to seven. It was too late to catch Mr Milbank at his office, but he would not mind if she rang him up at his home. She got up, hesitating. It might be better if she went round to see him after dinner; he lived in town, and she knew that both he and his wife would be delighted to see her, for both had known her almost from the cradle.

She picked up her gloves and her handbag and left the lounge. She found a telephone-box disengaged, and after painstakingly reading all the alarming information about pressing buttons A and B, dropped two pennies into the slot, and gave the number she wanted. She was soon connected, remembered to press the right button, and asked whether she might speak to Mr Milbank.

130

'Speaking,' Mr Milbank's voice replied.

'Oh, is that you?' Margaret said. 'This is Margaret Fortescue... Yes, I've been up for the day. I'm speaking from the club . . . I say, I'm awfully sorry to be a pest, and I know I ought to have thought of it earlier, but would it be a ghastly nuisance if I came round to see you after dinner just for a few moments?... What?... It's frightfully sweet of you both, but I can't. You see, I've got a friend dining with me here. Could I blow in about half-past eight or nine?... Well, I shall try and make it as early as I can, because I don't want to be late getting home, but you know what it is when you have anyone to dinner... Righto, then, I'll come along as soon after dinner as I can. Thanks awfully! *Au revoir!*' She hung up the receiver, and went back to the lounge, where she found Peggy Mason awaiting her, and a diminutive page loudly chanting her name.

Margaret kissed her friend. 'Hullo! I say, wait a minute till I stop that youth howling for me. Do you ever recognize your own name when you hear it shouted like that?' She darted off to intercept the page, who having failed to obtain response to his call, was on the point of passing on to the dining-room. When she came back Peggy greeted her with a great many questions, and items of news, and these proved so absorbing that Michael Strange was forgotten for a while.

It was nearly ten minutes to nine when Margaret remembered to look at the time. 'Peggy, you brute, you've kept me talking twenty minutes longer than I meant to. Look here, I've got to go.'

'That's right,' said Mrs Mason, 'throw your guest out. Where were you brought up?' She pulled on her gloves. 'You are a mutt not to come and spend the night with me as I suggested. Sure you won't change your mind? You can ring the Priory up, can't you?'

'Not on the telephone. No, really I can't, Peggy. I've

131

got to go and see our solicitor too: that's why I'm pushing you off.'

'Solicitor be blowed,' said Mrs Mason inelegantly. 'Who ever goes to see solicitors at this hour? All right, my girl, I'm going. I shall tell Bill when he gets back from France that you had an assignation with some man you kept very dark.' Her sharp eyes detected a rising blush in Margaret's cheeks. 'Hul-*lo*!' she said, surprised. 'Don't say I've hit the nail on the head? Is there someone?'

'No, of course not, you idiot. I'm going to see my solicitor and his wife at their house in Chelsea. Can I drop you?'

'As I live in the wilds of Hampstead, which fact you are well aware of, I regard that offer as a clear proof that you are dithering. And the only explanation for that...'

'Will you shut up?' said Margaret, and dragged her forth.

A quarter of an hour later her car drew up outside the Milbanks' house on the Embankment. She was ushered at once into the drawing-room on the first floor, and found both Mr and Mrs Milbank there. They both gave her a warm welcome, and for a little while they were all engaged in the usual conversation of old friends. But when Margaret had set down her coffee-cup, Mr Milbank said: 'Well, what is it you want to see me about, Margaret? Have you been run in for furious driving?'

'Certainly not!' said Margaret indignantly. 'I may not be one of the world's best drivers, but at least I've never been had up. It really isn't anything frightfully important, but I thought that since I happened to be in town I might as well drop in and ask you about it.'

Mrs Milbank began to fold up the work she had started to embroider. 'Is it private, Margaret? Would you like me to vanish, with a plausible excuse?'

'No, not a bit! Please don't go! I wanted to ask you, Mr Milbank, whether you can remember the name of the man who wanted to know if the Priory was for sale.'

The solicitor wrinkled his brow. 'I'm not sure that I can. The file is at the office, of course, and I can let you know to-morrow. Rather an ordinary name, as far as I remember. I think it was Robinson.' He gazed up at the ceiling. 'Yes, I'm nearly certain it was. George Robinson. But I won't swear to it.'

'I see. You didn't actually meet him, did you?'

'No, he wrote, and I distinctly remember that I sent your answer to a poste-restante address, as he explained that he was on a motor tour. Why? Have you reconsidered your decision?'

'No, but we – we rather wanted to know who it was. We don't mean to sell the Priory yet.'

'I'm rather relieved to hear you say that,' smiled the lawyer, 'for I had another man in making inquiries, and turned him down.'

Margaret looked quickly towards him. 'Another man? Wanting to buy the place?'

'I imagine he must have had some such idea, though he didn't actually say so. I told him that you had no intention of selling.'

'Who was he?' Margaret asked. 'Anyone we know?'

'I shouldn't think so. He never told me his name, because, as I say, things never got as far as that. He was a youngish man – between thirty and thirty-five, I should say. Nice looking, very dark, fairly...'

'Dark?' Margaret faltered.

'Yes, very dark. Black hair and eyebrows, rather a tanned complexion, fairly tall. My dear, what *is* all this about? Why are you so anxious to know what he looked like?'

'Well! – well, we – we met someone at a party who – who seemed rather interested in the Priory, and we suspected he wanted to buy it,' Margaret explained. 'Did he seem keen to when you saw him?'

'Not to the extent of badgering me to forward an offer. He didn't even make one.'

'I wish you'd tell me just what he did say,' Margaret begged.

'I'll try, since you make such a point of it,' Mr Milbank said, still rather surprised. 'He said he had been asked to make some inquiries about a house which he understood had been standing empty for several years. I assumed he was acting for someone else, but of course he may have merely put it that way. Lots of people do, if they don't want you to think they're set on buying a thing. He said he hoped he was not too late in coming to see me, as he had heard that someone else had been after the house.'

Margaret's eyes were fixed intently on the solicitor's face. 'Oh! He'd heard that, had he? Did he say how?'

'No, and I'm afraid I didn't ask him. I told him that you had no thought of selling. Let me see: what did he say next? Yes, I think he said: "Then there's no truth in what I heard – that the present owners are considering an offer they have received?" I assured him that you were entertaining no such idea, that you had, in fact, definitely refused to sell. After that I think he chatted for a few minutes about the place. Something he said about having seen the house from his car made me suspect that he might be this man, Robinson, or whatever his name is, trying a new way of getting the Priory. I asked him whether I was not right in supposing he had written to me before concerning this matter. Whether it was he, or someone behind him who wrote I really don't know, but I distinctly remember that he did not answer for a moment. Which made me all the more certain, as you can imagine. However, I wasn't particularly interested, so I didn't go into it. He said it was quite possible that his friend had written to me, but no doubt I'd had a great many such letters, or something of the sort. I'm a busy man, as you know, and I thought I'd wasted enough time on the matter. So when he said that in the event of your wishing to sell after all, he hoped I'd let him know before you accepted any other offer, I fear I rather cut him short, and told him that I did not think he need worry himself, as for one thing you had no wish to sell the Priory, and for another the only other offer I had received on your behalf was entirely tentative. He still didn't seem satisfied, and even went so far as to request me not to advise my other client of any change in your decision before letting him know. So I told him that in any case it would be quite out of my power to do so since I had only an old poste-restante address to write to. That did seem to settle him, and he went off – quite forgetting, by the way, to leave me his address!'

'I see,' Margaret said slowly. 'Yes – I think that sounds like the man we thought was after the place. Thanks awfully for telling me.'

'I may be very inquisitive,' Mr Milbank said, 'but I do wish you'd tell me why you're so anxious to hear all this.'

She smiled. 'Sheer curiosity, Mr Milbank. I – I wondered whether he'd have the cheek to come and interview you about it. Apparently he had.' She glanced at the clock, and started up. 'Oh, Lord, I shall be hideously late if I don't start.'

She took her leave of them both and went down to her car. Mr Milbank accompanied her to the front door, wondering what lay behind her visit, and waved farewell to her from the top of his steps. She let in the clutch, and the car slid forward.

Her suspicion had been a true one, but this afforded her very little satisfaction. It seemed to be just one more link in the chain of evidence against Strange.

'And I ought to tell Peter,' she said to herself, slipping past a tram. 'It's absolutely wrong of me not to. Michael Strange is nothing to me, nor ever likely to be, and for all I know he may be planning something perfectly dreadful.

And it's no good getting sloppy and sentimental, and thinking how a Good Woman's Love might reclaim him, because that's the sort of rot that makes me sick. Besides, I'm not in love with him.'

'Aren't you?' Conscience inquired. 'Then are you going to tell Peter all you know?'

'I promised I'd say nothing,' Margaret argued. 'I may have been wrong to do so, but I did, and that's that.'

'You didn't promise not to say anything about this visit to Milbank,' Conscience pointed out.

'If I see any reason to of course I shall tell Peter,' Margaret decided. 'But for the present I mean to tackle Strange myself. And it's no good thinking he's the Monk because I don't believe it, and what's more I won't believe it.'

'What about him saying that you might get a bad fright?'

'That doesn't prove anything at all. Anyway, I don't believe he'd be the one to frighten me.'

'Doesn't it throw a little light on the fact that he seemed so anxious to get you away from the Priory?'

'No, it does not,' Margaret muttered crossly, and took a corner recklessly wide.

The interminable argument went on throughout her drive back to the Priory. Only one clear point emerged from it, and that was that she didn't want to give Charles and Peter any fresh grounds for suspecting Strange unless she were absolutely forced to. Whereat Conscience said very nastily: 'What price Loyalty, eh?'

Since she had not left the Milbanks' house until a few minutes before ten there was no hope of reaching the Priory till after eleven. Margaret knew that Celia, remembering her dinner engagement, would not be likely to worry over her lateness, but she was not quite at ease about it herself. It was true there was a moon, but all the same she did not relish the prospect of that drive up from the gates to the house. Even in daylight there was something rather eerie about woods, and the avenue led through unmistakable woodland. She and Celia had gone into ecstasies over it, for they had seen it first in bluebell time, but they had not then known that it had a reputation for being haunted.

The nearer she got to Framley the less inclined she was for the drive up the avenue, but by dint of telling herself she was not at all afraid, and thinking very hard of all sorts of things not even remotely connected with ghosts, she achieved a certain stoicism about it, and turned in at the iron gates quite determined to drive boldly and quickly up to the house, and not to peer furtively ahead.

And then the worst happened. The entrance to the drive was an awkward one, and the gates rather narrow. The avenue curved sharply just inside them, and was flanked on either side by a ditch that kept it drained. Margaret turned in at the gates much too boldly, and jammed the car. She said: 'Damn!' under her breath, and proceeded to back. After some not very skilful manœuvring she succeeded in clearing the gates. In she swept, misjudged the bend in the avenue, swung the wheel round too late and too hard, and skidded gently into the ditch.

She was too much annoyed with herself to think about ghosts. Feeling glad that Peter was not present to mock at her bad driving, she changed down into first and tried to get the car back on to the avenue. But the heavy storm of the day before had made the surface rather slimy, and the ditch, judging from the squelch which her back wheel made as it descended into it, was full of mud. The engine roared fruitlessly, and after several more attempts Margaret was forced to give it up. The car would have to be pulled out; and meanwhile she was faced with a lonely walk up to the house.

It serves me right for being such a fool, she thought. And it's no use sitting here getting cold feet about it. Out

137

you get, you idiot!

She stepped out, and collected her handbag and coat. She eyed the planchette board dubiously, but decided to leave it, in company with her own purchases, and the two revolvers, which she had hidden under the back seat. She slipped on the coat to save having to carry it, and digging her hands into its capacious pockets, set off up the avenue.

She had rounded the second bend, and only one more separated her from the sight of the house when she saw the Monk. Straight ahead of her, gliding across the avenue in the cold silver light, was that sinister, hooded figure. She stopped dead in her tracks with a gasp of horror. She saw it plainly, caught a glimpse of a cowled face that was somehow more terrifying than all the rest, and then it melted into the shadows on the other side of the avenue.

Her instinct was to turn and run back the way she had come. The figure had vanished, but it might be there, in the shadows, waiting for her to come up to it. She stood as though chained to the spot, her knees shaking under her.

I can't go on! she thought. Where am I to go to if I run back? What shall I do? What *shall* I do?

It might be anywhere amongst the dark trees that surrounded her. It had come towards Mrs Bosanquet, menacing her with an outstretched hand. If it had seen her it might even now be flitting up to her unseen in the shadows. It would be better to dart on to the house than to turn back. Perhaps someone would hear her if she screamed for help; no one would hear if she ran the other way.

A little rustle behind her decided the matter. Not daring to look round, or to shout for help, she ran as though for her life down the avenue towards the house. As she sped past the place where she had seen the Monk disappear she had an awful feeling that the cowled figure was following her. Sobbing dryly from sheer fright she gained the last bend and saw the house ahead of her.

Then immediately ahead of her a form stepped out from the shadow of a great rhododendron bush. She was breathless, and panting, but she gave one faint, desperate cry of 'Peter!'

The figure seemed to leap towards her, she tried to call again, but a hand was clapped over her mouth, and a strong arm thrown round her shoulders. 'Don't scream!' an urgent whisper commanded, and almost fainting from shock she stared wildly up into the face of Michael Strange.

CHAPTER X

For a moment he continued to hold her, then he removed his hand from her mouth, and said coolly, under his breath: 'Sorry, but I couldn't let you give the alarm. Tell me quickly, what did you see?'

Irrationally, her fright had left her the instant she had recognized him. But her head whirled. What was he doing there? Was it possible that his had been the figure she had seen? And if so what had he done with his disguise?

His hand grasped her wrist, not roughly, but compellingly. 'What did you see? You must tell me.'

She looked at him, trying to read his face in the moonlight. 'The Monk,' she answered, in a low voice.

'Damnation!' Michael muttered. 'Where?'

She pointed the way she had come, and as though by doing it she conjured up a presence, footsteps came to their ears.

Without ceremony Michael pulled her quickly into the shadow of the rhododendron bush. She glanced at him, and saw that his eyes were fixed on the bend in the avenue. A moment later a figure in a large ulster came into sight, peering about.

'Miss Fortescue!' called Mr Ernest Titmarsh. 'Miss Fortescue! Is there anything the matter? Tut, tut, I made sure I saw her!'

The grip on Margaret's wrist was removed; there was a movement beside her, she looked quickly round, and found that she was alone. As silently and as unexpectedly

140

as he had appeared, Mr Michael Strange had vanished.

Feeling utterly bewildered, and not a little shaken, Margaret stepped out into the moonlight, and waited for Mr Titmarsh to come up with her. 'I'm here,' she said, with the calm of reaction.

He hurried up, butterfly net in hand. 'Dear, dear, I did not at once perceive you. But what is the matter? I heard you call out, and saw you running. I do trust you did not catch sight of me, and take me for a ghost?'

'Mr Titmarsh, did you cross the avenue down there a moment ago?' she asked. 'Going towards the chapel?'

'By no means,' he answered. 'I was pursuing an oak-eggar just by that swampy patch of ground on the other side of the avenue. Surely you have not seen someone unauthorized prowling about the park?'

'Yes. That is – it was the Monk. I knew I couldn't be mistaken. That horrible cowl. . . ! I'm sorry, but really I feel rather groggy. Would you mind coming with me as far as the house?'

'My dear young lady! Of course, of course, but your eyes must have deceived you. Pray take my arm! Quite impossible, Miss Fortescue. I saw no monk, and surely I must have done so had there been one.'

She shook her head. 'You might not. There are so many bushes. I couldn't have been deceived. I saw it plainly.'

'Nerves, my dear Miss Fortescue, nothing but nerves. You must not let yourself believe in these silly ghost-tales. Why, you are quite upset by it! This will not do at all! Now I will pull the bell, and in a moment you will be inside, and quite safe.'

The bell clanged noisily in answer to Mr Titmarsh's vigorous tug, and almost at once quick steps sounded within, and Peter himself opened the door. 'That you, Margaret? I began to think you must have had a – good Lord, what's the matter?'

She grasped his coat weakly, and gave a small uncertain

laugh. 'Oh Peter, I've seen the Monk! For goodness sake let me sit down; I feel like a piece of chewed string.'

Mr Titmarsh clucked rather like an old hen. 'I saw Miss Fortescue running up the avenue, and went at once to her assistance. I am afraid she is a little over-wrought: she seems to have caught sight of something which she took for the Monk. Possibly a shrub, or even, though I should be grieved indeed to think so, myself.'

Peter slipped his arm round Margaret. 'Come in, sir. Very good of you to escort her. Buck up, old lady: it's all right now.' He half-led, half-carried her into the library, and put her down into the nearest chair. 'Like a drink, Sis? Feeling all right?'

Celia sprang up. 'Margaret! What's the matter, darling? Oh, good heavens, don't say *you've* seen it!'

The colour was coming back to Margaret's face. She sat up. 'Sorry, all of you. No, I'm perfectly all right now, Peter. Truly. Yes, I have, Celia. The Monk. And I made a dash for the house, and – and then – Mr Titmarsh came up.'

'And I am much distressed to think that I may have been the innocent cause of your alarm,' Mr Titmarsh put in. 'If I had not obtained permission from your good brother-in-law to pursue my search in his grounds, I should be even *more* distressed.'

'No, it wasn't you,' Margaret said. 'It was a cowled monk, just as Aunt Lilian described.' She looked round. 'Where is Aunt Lilian?'

'She had a headache, and went up to bed early,' Celia replied. 'But darling, how awful for you! Oh, we *can't* stay any longer in this beastly, hateful house!

'But Margaret, where's the car?' Charles asked. 'Why were you on foot?'

'I ditched it,' said Margaret fatalistically.

'Oh!' said Charles. 'I suppose it seemed to you to be the only thing to do, but – don't think I'm criticizing –

why?'

This had the effect of making her laugh, and a great deal of her self-possession was restored. 'I didn't do it on purpose. I made a muck of the turn at the gates, and one of the back wheels skidded into the ditch. It'll have to be pulled out. So then I had to walk up to the house. And all this happened.' She got up. 'I say – do you mind if I don't talk about it any more to-night? I feel a bit queer still, and I think I'd like to go up to bed.'

'Of course you shall,' Celia said instantly. 'Don't worry her with questions, you two. Come along, darling.'

At the door Margaret looked back. 'Oh, I got the revolvers. They're under the back seat. I thought I'd better tell you.'

'Revolvers?' said Mr Titmarsh blinking. 'Dear me, sounds very bloodthirsty. Really I do not think I should advise you to use them, Mr Malcolm. Tut, tut, there is no knowing whom you might not shoot by mistake.'

'Well I can safely promise not to shoot you by mistake,' said Charles.

However, this assurance did not relieve Mr Titmarsh's alarms. He seemed genuinely perturbed, and tried once more to convince the two men that Margaret had been the victim of a hallucination. Neither of them attempted to argue the point, and at last, after refusing the offer of a drink, Mr Titmarsh took his leave, and made off again down the avenue.

As he shot the bolts of the front door home, Peter looked at Charles. 'I think this is where we talk to the District Inspector,' he said. 'I still don't believe that Titmarsh is the man we're after, but his presence in the grounds at just that moment is a little too significant to be brushed aside.'

Charles nodded. 'All right, we'll go over to Manfield to-morrow.'

It was long before Margaret fell asleep that night. She

143

had omitted any reference to Michael Strange in her account of what happened. Until she started to tell the others all about it she had meant to keep nothing back. And then somehow or other she had left that gap, and at once had been horrified at herself for not telling the whole truth. Only the moment the words 'and then Mr Titmarsh came up' had passed her lips, it had seemed impossible to add, 'but before that Michael Strange appeared, and clapped his hand over my mouth.' It would look so odd not to have told that first of all. She asked instead to be allowed to go to bed, with a vague idea of thinking the whole situation over. She now realized that it would be far more impossible to say at breakfast next day: 'By the way I quite forgot to tell you that Michael Strange was there too.'

But on one point her mind was made up. Unless he gave some explanation of his conduct he could not expect her to go on blindly trusting him. She would see him without fail next day, and demand to know what he was doing in the Priory grounds at that hour.

On this resolve she at last fell asleep. When she awoke next morning she did not feel quite as guilty as she had the night before. After all, she thought, if Strange refused to explain himself, it would not be too late to inform the others, and she had no doubt she would be able to think out some plausible reason for not having done so before.

To the questions that Charles and Peter put to her during breakfast she returned perfectly composed replies, but when she learned that they intended to put the matter now into the hands of the County Police she rather changed colour. If a police-inspector were to question her it would be very difficult to know how to answer him. Like most people who have never had any dealings with it she had a somewhat nervous dread of the Law, and a hazy idea that you got had up for not telling the police all you knew. However, it was no good meeting your troubles half-way, and the main thing now was to tackle Michael Strange.

Mrs Bosanquet, in spite of her own terrifying experience, was quite annoyed to think that Margaret and not she had encountered the Monk. She told Margaret she had missed a great opportunity, and when Charles made a dry reference to the manner in which she had greeted the opportunity when it came to her, she said severely that there were some things that were better forgotten. She was happy in the possession of her planchette, and she proposed that they should have a sitting that very evening.

'In the evening?' Celia said. 'Not for worlds! I might summon up enough courage to sit in daylight, but not after dark, thank you!'

'I doubt very much whether we should get any results by day,' Mrs Bosanquet said dubiously. 'I know that for some reason or other which I never fathomed spirits seem to find it easier to manifest themselves in the dark.'

'Look here!' said Peter, 'are we expected to sit round in the dark like a lot of lunatics with our hands on that board?'

'Not, I trust, like a lot of lunatics,' Mrs Bosanquet said coldly.

'I won't do it,' Celia announced. 'I know what it'll be. Either Chas or Peter will start pushing just to frighten us.'

'What I was really thinking of,' said Charles meditatively, 'was appearing in a false nose and some luminous paint. But I won't if you don't care for the idea.'

'Charles,' said Celia quite seriously, 'unless you swear to me you won't play the fool I'll walk out of this house here and now.'

'My dear child,' Mrs Bosanquet said reassuringly, 'if you feel any alarm it would be much better if you didn't attempt to sit at all. And of course Charles is only making fun of you.'

'But if you're all going to sit I shall *have* to,' Celia said.

'I couldn't stay by myself while you conjured up ghosts. I should die of fright.'

'I have been told,' remarked Mrs Bosanquet, 'though I must say I never experienced anything of the sort myself, that sometimes the spirits actually lift tables off their legs, and give one quite hard knocks to manifest their presence.'

'In that case,' said Charles, 'you can count me out. I'm not going to sit and allow myself to be buffeted about in this or any other cause.'

'I think,' Mrs Bosanquet replied, 'that we are unlikely to get any results at all if you approach the subject in a spirit of levity.'

When breakfast was over Charles and Peter went off to see what could be done about hauling the car out of the ditch. They had no sooner gone than Margaret announced her intention of cycling into the village to buy darning-silk. Celia seemed inclined to accompany her, but since she had promised to go for a sedate walk with Mrs Bosanquet, she had to give up the idea. She wrote out a list of groceries to be ordered at the village store, and said that she and Mrs Bosanquet might stroll to meet Margaret on her way home.

Margaret's first house of call was not the village store, but the Bell Inn. She inquired of the porter whether Mr Strange was in, and while he went to find out, she sat down in the lounge, and watched two rather nondescript females collect their sketching paraphernalia preparatory to setting out. They eyed her with the usual faint air of hostility displayed to one another by most English people, and after ascertaining that they had not forgotten the sandwiches or the camp-stools, or the thermos, soon left her in sole possession of the lounge.

She had not long to wait before the door at one end of the lounge was opened, and Michael Strange came briskly into the room. He did not seem surprised to see her, but said without preamble: 'I'm sorry to have been so long, Miss Fortescue: I was just finishing my breakfast. Won't you sit down?'

'I hope I didn't interrupt you,' she said stiffly.

'Not at all. It's a disgraceful hour at which to be breakfasting in any case. But I had a very late night.'

Margaret fairly gasped. Of all the cool, calm cheek! she thought. She remained standing, and looking him squarely in the face, said: 'Mr Strange, I think you must know why I've come to see you this morning.'

The hint of a smile touched his mouth. 'I can guess,' he said. 'I wish you hadn't seen me last night, but you did, and the mischief's done.'

Her heart sank. 'Then you are the Monk!' she cried sharply.

His brows seemed to snap together over the bridge of his nose. He looked quickly round, and said quietly: 'Please don't raise your voice. You don't know who may be listening.'

'I don't care,' she said.

'But I do,' he answered, and moved softly to the door and opened it.

She watched him look down the passage and go to the other door and open that too. 'You probably have good reason to care,' she shot at him.

'I have,' he said imperturbably. He shut the door and came back into the room. 'I wish you would sit down,' he said. 'And just remember to keep your voice lowered.' He pulled a chair forward, and reluctantly she did sit down. 'Now then! I suppose if I say I am certainly not the Monk you won't believe me?'

'How can I?' she said. 'I saw it last night, and it disappeared into the shadows on the same side of the avenue as you emerged from two minutes later.'

He nodded. 'It does look black, doesn't it? I don't think I'll waste time in trying to prove my innocence. What I do

147

want to say is this: get out of the Priory, and get out quickly! Never mind why, but just go. I say this as one who – thinks a great deal of your safety. You saw something last night: if you stay you may see much more, and Marg – Miss Fortescue, believe me, I don't want you to run even the slightest chance of getting hurt or frightened.'

He spoke with such evident sincerity that she found herself saying in a much friendlier tone: 'Mr Strange, can't you explain yourself? You must see that I can't possibly believe you when you won't – give me any reason for your conduct.'

'I can't!' he said. His hand opened and shut. 'You mustn't ask me, Miss Fortescue. I'd give anything to be able to take you into my confidence, but it's impossible. For one thing I – well, it's no good: I daren't tell you.'

'Daren't?' she repeated. 'You are afraid that I should give you away?'

He did not answer for a moment. Then he laid his hand on hers, and clasped it. 'Look here, I've undertaken something, and come what may I must carry it through,' he said. 'When I took it on I didn't bargain for *you*, but I can't let you make any difference. Only I wish to God you'd clear out of the Priory!'

She withdrew her hand. 'Then I am right in thinking that all along you've wanted to get us out of the house?'

'Yes, I have wanted to.'

'Why?' she said directly.

'I've told you. It's not safe, and I can't be answerable for what may happen.'

'It is not by any chance because our presence interferes with what you are doing?'

'It does interfere, but that is not why I'm so anxious you should go. Miss Fortescue, I don't think there's much I wouldn't do for you, but if you persist in remaining at the Priory I can't guarantee your safety. Do you understand? You'll be running a risk of – danger, and I can't stop it, and I might not be able to help you. And God knows if anything were to happen to you...' He broke off.

She found herself saying: 'Well?'

He looked quickly towards her. 'I think you must know what I – what I feel about you,' he said.

Her eyes fell. 'I only know that you don't trust me, though you expect me to trust you,' she answered, almost inaudibly.

'It isn't that I don't trust you, but I *can't* tell you – Oh, damn it all, why did I ever take this on?' He got up abruptly, and began to pace up and down the room.

She watched him in silence for a moment. He was frowning, and when he frowned he did look rather sinister, she thought. 'Have you considered that if – that if you think... Have you considered that you might give it up?' she said, stumbling badly.

'No!' he threw over his shoulder. 'Not that it would be any good if I did.'

There was another short silence. Margaret tried again. 'Is what you're doing of such vital importance?' she asked.

'Yes, of vital importance.' He came back to her side. 'Margaret, if I were at liberty to take you into my confidence I would, but too much hangs on it. I can't do it. I know things look black: they *are* black, but will you believe that it's not what you think?'

'I don't know quite *what* to think,' she said.

'You've seen me in some odd circumstances, you've seen me do things that look more than suspicious. I don't deny it, and I may have to do things that will seem far more suspicious. But I swear to you I've a good reason for all I do, even though I can't tell you what it is. Margaret, I've no right to ask you, as things are, but will you try and trust me a little longer? Will you trust me sufficiently to do as I beg of you, and leave the Priory till I've finished the job I've undertaken?'

She found it hard to meet his eyes, and felt a wave of colour rise in her cheeks. 'Even though I – said yes, my brother and brother-in-law wouldn't go.'

'If you can't persuade them they can take their chance,' he said. 'But will you go? You and your sister, and your aunt?'

She shook her head. 'No, I can't do that. You couldn't expect me to go away and leave my brother in danger. And nothing would induce Celia to leave Charles.'

He said impatiently: 'Good God, haven't you had enough happen in that house to make you see the only thing to do is to clear out?'

At that she looked up. 'What do you know about anything that has happened at the Priory?' she asked gravely.

He bit his lip. After a moment she said: 'Were you responsible for – things that have happened?'

'I can't answer you, and I don't want to lie to you,' he said curtly. 'I can only tell you that from me you stand in no danger whatsoever. But I'm not the only one mixed up in this.' He made a little gesture of despair. 'It's no good going on like this. If you won't go, you won't. But I have warned you, and you can believe that I know what I'm talking about.'

She began to twist the strap of her handbag round her finger. 'I do believe that you – wouldn't hurt me, or any of us,' she began.

He interrupted her. 'Hurt you! My God, no! Can't you understand, Margaret? I – I *love* you!'

She bent her head still lower over the absorbing strap. 'Please – you mustn't...!' she said inarticulately.

'I know I mustn't. But you don't know what it's like for me to see you here... I wish to God I'd met you under other circumstances!' He ran his fingers up through his crisp black hair. 'And yet I don't know that

I'd have had a better chance,' he said despondently. 'The whole thing seems hopeless, and it's no good for anyone in my – line of business – to think of a girl like you.'

In a very muffled voice Margaret said: 'If I – if I knew it was honest – I – I shouldn't care – what your line of business was.' She tried to achieve a lighter note. 'As long as it isn't keeping a butcher's shop, or – or anything like that,' she added with a wavering smile.

He made a movement as though he would take her hand again, but checked it. 'I've no right to speak at all till I can – clear up all this mess,' he said. 'But to know that you – well, one day I hope I shall be able to say all the things I want to say now. One thing I must ask you though: Will you trust me enough not to mention to anyone that you saw me in your grounds last night?'

All the reason she possessed told her to say 'No,' but something far stronger than reason made her say instead: 'All right, I – I will.'

'My God, you are a wonderful girl,' he said unsteadily.

She got up. 'I must go. But I'd like to warn you of something. I didn't tell my people that you were there last night. You guessed I hadn't, didn't you? But Peter and Charles have motored into Manfield to-day, to tell the County Police what has been happening at the Priory. And – I think they'll tell the inspector to keep an eye on you.'

'Thank-you,' he said. His smile flashed out. 'Don't worry your head over me,' he said. 'The police aren't going to get me.'

She held out her hand. 'I should be – very sorry if they did,' she said. 'Good-bye.'

He took her hand, looked at it for a moment as it lay in his, and then bent his head and kissed it.

CHAPTER XI

Having extricated the car from the ditch with the aid of a farm-horse, Charles and Peter drove it into Manfield, the market town that lay some six miles to the east of Framley. Here was the headquarters of the County Police, and in the red-brick police-station they found the District Inspector.

This individual was of a different type from Constable Flinders. He was a wiry man of medium height, with foxy hair and a moustache meticulously waxed at the ends. He had a cold blue eye and a brisk manner, and his air of business-like competence promised well.

He listened without comment to the story Charles unfolded, only occasionally interrupting to put a brief question. His face betrayed neither surprise nor interest, and not even the episode of the discovered skeleton caused him to do more than nod.

'One had the impression,' Charles said afterwards, 'that such occurrences were everyday matters in this part of the world.'

'You say the picture fell,' the inspector recapitulated. 'You have a suspicion someone was responsible. Any grounds for that, sir?'

'None,' said Charles.

'Except,' Peter put in, 'that we can neither of us see how the falling picture could have knocked the rosette in the panelling out of place.'

The inspector made dots on his blotting-pad with the

point of a pencil he held. 'Very hard to say that it could not, sir, from all you tell me. You haven't tested it?'

'No,' said Charles, 'funnily enough we haven't. Though there are quite a lot of pictures in the house, and if we'd smashed one in the test we could always have tried another.'

The first sign of emotion crept into the inspector's face. The cold blue eyes twinkled. 'Very true, sir,' he said gravely. 'Now there is the entrance into the cellars. You say you heard this move on several occasions, and on the last you went down and saw someone make his escape that way. Did you recognize this person?'

'No,' Charles said. 'There was hardly time for that.'

'Very good, sir. And since you have sealed up that entrance no further attempt has been made to break into the house?'

'On the contrary. My aunt encountered the Monk in the library.'

The inspector made more dots. 'The lady being, I take it, a reliable witness?'

'Most reliable. Moreover, up till then she had no belief in the story that the Priory is haunted.'

'Quite so, sir. And on that occasion you discovered the window into the library to have been open?'

'Unbolted. It was shut, however.'

'But I understand it could be opened from outside?'

'Yes, certainly it could.'

'And this – Monk – would have had plenty of time to escape by that way, pausing to shut the window behind him, in between the time of the lady's falling into a faint, and your arrival on the scene?'

'Plenty of time. So much so that neither my brother-in-law nor I thought it would be of any use to search the grounds.'

'I see, sir. And since that occasion no one has, to your knowledge, been in the house?'

'Not to my knowledge. But last night, as I told you, my sister-in-law distinctly saw the Monk in the grounds. A moment later Mr Ernest Titmarsh ran up to her.'

The inspector nodded. 'If you don't mind, sir, we'll take the people who have acted suspiciously in your opinion, one by one. Ernest Titmarsh: that's the first?'

'No. The first was a fellow who's staying at the Bell Inn, in the village.'

'Name, sir?'

'Strange, Michael Strange. He is the man whom we found wandering close to the house when we first heard the stone move. He's a man I'd like you to get on to.'

'Inquiries will be made, sir.'

'He is also the man whom we overheard talking in an exceedingly suspicious manner to James Fripp, traveller for Suck-All Cleaners. About whom I have received the following information.' He took a letter from his pocket-book, and handed it to the inspector.

The inspector read the letter through. The inquiry agent had not been able to discover very much about James Fripp, for the firm for which he worked had engaged him only a month previously, and knew nothing about his former occupation. But the agent gave, for what it was worth, the information that before the war a man going under the name of Jimmy Fripp, and corresponding more or less with Charles' description of the commercial traveller, had been on two occasions imprisoned for burglary. His last incarceration took place in 1914; he had been released shortly after war broke out, and had joined the army. Since the end of the war he had been lost trace of, nor could the agent discover what type of work, honest or otherwise, he had been employed in. It seemed possible that the Fripp in question might be the same man, but no proof of this was forthcoming.

The inspector folded the letter, and gave it back to Charles. 'Thank you, sir. You don't need to worry about him; we've got our eye on him all right.'

'The man I'm really worrying about,' Charles answered, 'is Strange. We know he's in collusion with Fripp, and that being so there can be little doubt that Fripp is working under his orders.'

The inspector nodded, but again repeated: 'You don't need to worry. We'll look after Mr Strange too.'

Peter was not quite satisfied with this. 'Yes, I know, but what do you propose to do? We're getting a little tired of this mystery, and we'd like a stop put to it.'

'Well, sir, I'm sure I can understand that, and you may depend upon it we shall do our best. And if I might suggest something, I wouldn't advise either of you gentlemen to mention to anyone that you've been to see me about this. Whoever it is that has been annoying you, we don't want to put him on his guard, and once you tell one person a bit of news it has a way of spreading.'

'Quite so,' Peter said. 'We have been rather careful all through not to talk of what has happened. But you still haven't told us what you mean to do. Are you going to put a man on to watch the Priory?'

'Yes,' Charles said, flicking a speck of cigarette ash off his sleeve, 'and if you do, need he smash the cucumber frames? It isn't that they contain any cucumbers, but...'

The inspector's lips twitched. 'I quite understand, sir. But...'

'And he's not to frighten the housemaid,' Charles continued. 'Also, I may be unreasonable, but I have a constitutional dislike for being arrested in my own grounds. If I can't come and go unchallenged I shall become unnerved, and the consequences may be hideous.'

'My brother-in-law,' said Peter, thinking it time to intervene, 'is referring to the well-meaning efforts of Constable Flinders.'

'Yes, sir. Very annoying, I'm sure. But you won't be worried in that way again. If you will leave the matter in our hands, I think I can promise we shall be able to clear it all up in a very short while.'

'Well, I must say I hope so,' Peter remarked, gathering up his hat and stick. 'We came down to Framley for a quiet holiday, and so far we've had no peace at all.'

'Just a moment,' Charles said. 'What about Duval?'

The inspector fingered the tips of his moustache. 'I've made a note of all you told me about him, sir.'

'Yes, I know: I saw you. But doesn't it strike you that he might, if interrogated skilfully, throw a good deal more light on the matter?'

'He might, sir, and of course we shall have to consider that. But on the other hand you never know with these dope-maniacs. Still, I shall go into it. You can safely leave it to me.'

Peter looked at Charles. 'I think that's all, isn't it? There's nothing else we wanted to ask the inspector?'

Charles' expression of rather sleepy boredom had been growing steadily more marked. 'I can't remember anything else,' he replied. 'Unless you think we might invite him to come and take part in our séance to-night? Or do you think the presence of a stranger might make the Monk shy?'

'Yes, I do,' said Peter hastily, and edged him towards the door.

The inspector held it open for them, and they went through into the charge room. A man in a felt hat and a light raincoat was standing by the counter that ran across the end of the room, and as the door opened he glanced over his shoulder. For a fleeting instant his eyes encountered Charles', then he turned his back again, and bent over some form he appeared to be filling in. But quickly though he moved Charles had had time to recognize him. It was Michael Strange.

'Oh, half a minute!' Charles said. 'I think I've left my gloves on your table, inspector.'

'Gloves? You didn't have any, did you?' Peter asked.

'Yes, I did,' Charles said, and went past him, back into the room. He motioned to the inspector to close the door, and as soon as this had been done, he said softly: 'No gloves at all, but I've just seen the very man we've been discussing. Strange.'

'Have you, sir? Here?' the inspector asked.

'Outside, filling up some form. He didn't want me to recognize him, for he turned his back at once. I should like very much to know what he's doing. It looks to me as though he followed us here, to find out what we were up to.'

The inspector nodded. 'Good job you saw him, sir. Now you go out, will you, quite naturally, and I'll have a word with this Mr Strange, just casually, you understand. I shall soon find out what he came for.' He pulled the door open again. 'That's right, sir. And you'd be surprised the number of pairs of gentlemen's gloves that get lost. Not but what you could hardly leave them in a better place than the station-house, could you? Good morning to you, sir.'

Outside Charles looked round for Strange's car, but it was not visible. Since it seemed improbable that he had walked to Manfield it was clear that he had parked it somewhere where it would not be seen. Charles got into his own car, and waited for Peter to take his place beside him. As he let in the clutch Peter said: 'Well, where are the gloves?'

'In the top right-hand drawer of my dressing-table so far as I know,' Charles answered. 'That, my boy, was a blind.'

'Was it indeed? Why?'

'Did you see that fellow who was waiting in the charge room?'

'No – that is, yes, I believe I did notice someone, now you come to mention it. I can't say I paid much attention

157

to him, though. What about him?'

'Michael Strange.'

'No!' Peter said. 'Are you sure?'

'Positive. He turned his head as I came out of the inspector's room. That inspector-fellow is going to ask what his business is. With all due deference to Inspector Tomlinson I could have told him the answer. He'll dish up some cock-and-bull story of having lost something, but if he didn't follow us to try and find out just what we were going to tell the police, I'm a Dutchman.' He hooted violently at an Austin Seven which was wavering undecidedly in the middle of the road. 'And I wouldn't mind betting that he overheard every word we said in that room.'

'It does look like it, but wasn't there a bobby in the charge room?'

'There was when we came out, but do you suppose a clever fellow couldn't have got rid of him for quite as long as he wanted?'

'Might, of course. But how the devil did Strange know we were coming here to-day?'

'Well, we've talked about it pretty freely, haven't we?'

'In our own house, Chas!'

'Also while we were getting the car out of the ditch. You said: "If they don't buck up with that horse we shan't have time to get to Manfield and back before lunch."'

'I didn't say anything about the police-station, did I?'

'I don't remember. But whatever you said it looks as though you were overheard, and Mr Michael Strange thought it worth his while to follow us.'

Peter sat pondering it for a while. 'Of course he might have been concealed in the wood, but, dash it! he must be pretty acute if he connected a visit to Manfield with the police! Why, half the countryside goes to shop there! No, it looks to me as though someone told him.'

'Who?'

'The housemaid! She could have heard us talking at breakfast.'

'My dear Peter, she's no crook's accomplice!'

'She's a dam' silly girl though, and if Strange wanted to pump her he could.'

They had emerged from the outskirts of the town into the open country, and Charles put his foot on the accelerator. 'Yes, that's possible, of course. One thing that seems to me quite obvious is that Strange is going to be more than a match for Inspector Tomlinson.'

Peter waited until the car had swung round a bend in the road before he spoke. Charles' driving, skilful though it might be, kept his passengers in a constant state of breathlessness. 'Do you think Tomlinson means to do anything, or does he discount all we say in favour of the ghost theory?'

'The impression I got was that he gave us the benefit of the doubt, but privately considered us a fanciful pair who'd got the wind up. He'll send a man over to lurk about the place for a couple of days, and that'll be the end of it.'

'Give him a trial,' Peter said. 'I must say he didn't seem to be overburdened with ideas, but he may have kept them to himself.'

They reached the Priory to find the others just getting up from lunch. 'Oh, Charles!' Celia exclaimed, 'the tennis-net has arrived, and Bowers and Coggin have been putting up the stop-netting all the morning. And if you'll come and do the measuring I'll mark the court out, and we can play after tea.'

This programme was faithfully carried out, and not even the depressions and the bumps in the court damped Celia's enthusiasm. 'It adds to the fun,' she said, when Charles failed to reach a ball that bounced unaccountably to the right.

When they came off the court after a couple of hours play they were pleasantly weary, and, as Margaret said, were beginning to get to know the peculiarities of the ground. It was just as Charles had announced his intention of spending a lazy evening that Celia remembered to break a piece of news to them all which put an end to such dreams.

'I forgot to tell you,' she said guiltily, 'that I've given Bowers leave off, and I said they could have the car. They're going to the cinema in Manfield, and I said it would be all right if they just put a cold supper on the table – and – and we'd clear it away, and wash up.'

'Did you indeed?' said Charles instantly. 'Now isn't that a pity? Because I've just remembered that I shall have to go out directly after supper, so I shan't be able to…'

'Liar,' said Celia, without heat.

'Besides,' Margaret put in, 'you can't go and desert us. We've promised Aunt Lilian we'll try out her planchette.'

Celia's face clouded. 'Margaret, if we talk hard about something else, don't you think she might forget about it?'

'No,' said Margaret, considering this. 'It would only be a case of putting off the evil hour. I think we'd better do it once, just to please her, and then when nothing happens she'll probably get bored with it.'

'But supposing something *did* happen?' Celia pointed out.

'Well, it 'ud be rather interesting, I think,' Margaret said coolly.

Celia was so far from agreeing with her that she did her best to keep Mrs Bosanquet's mind off the subject all through supper. But it was to no avail. When the meal had been cleared away, and the family had repaired to the library, Mrs Bosanquet produced her board, and said: 'Well, my dears, shall we have our sitting?'

'I wish you wouldn't talk as though we were a

collection of fowls,' Charles complained. 'Provided I am supplied with a comfortable chair I don't mind lending what I feel sure will be powerful assistance.'

Celia looked at him suspiciously. 'If that means that you're going to fool about...'

'Hush!' said her husband reprovingly. 'For all you know I may be a strong medium. In fact I shouldn't be surprised if I went into a trance. Time will be as nothing to me. All the secrets of the future will be revealed to me.'

'Yes, dear, quite possibly you are a natural medium,' Mrs Bosanquet said. 'But when people come out of trances they don't remember anything that happened to them while they were in the trance. At least, so I have always understood.'

'In that case,' said Charles, 'I charge you all the instant you see me fall into a trance to ask me what's going to win the 3.20 to-morrow. And see you write down the answer.'

'If you go into a trance,' said Peter, 'that isn't the only thing we'll ask you. There are lots of things about your past I've long wanted to know.'

Mrs Bosanquet was arranging chairs round a small table. 'That will do, my dear,' she said. 'You know it is no use approaching this in a spirit of levity. Now let us all take our places round the table, and then I'll turn the light down.'

Celia was already showing a tendency to cling to Charles' hand. 'Not right out, Aunt!' she implored.

'No, I will leave just a glimmer. I don't think we need draw the curtains, do you, Margaret? There doesn't seem to be any moon to-night. And it will make the room so stuffy. Now, are you all ready?'

'Wait a moment!' Celia begged. 'Charles, you've got to sit by me!'

'Celia, you goose!' Margaret said softly. 'You don't really expect anything to happen do you?' She took the seat on her sister's left, and Peter sat down beside her.

161

Mrs Bosanquet turned the central lamp out, and lowered the wick of the one that stood on a table by the fireplace, until only a tiny flame showed. Then she groped her way to the empty chair between her nephews and sat down.

'Oh, isn't it dark and horrible?' shuddered Celia.

'You'll get used to it,' Margaret said soothingly. 'Already I can just see, vaguely. What do we have to do, Aunt Lilian?'

Mrs Bosanquet, happy in having induced them to take part in the séance, at once assumed the rôle of preceptress. 'First, you must be quite comfortable in your chairs,' she said.

'That knocks me out,' Charles interrupted. 'No one could be comfortable in a chair like this. There are already three knobs pressing into my spine.'

By the time he had solemnly tested three other chairs, and decided in favour of a Queen Anne upholstered chair with slim wooden arms, even Celia had begun to giggle.

With unimpaired patience Mrs Bosanquet started again. 'Now, are you all settled?'

'Yes,' Margaret said, before Charles had time to speak. 'Go on, Aunt, what next?'

'We all lay just the tips of our fingers on the board, taking care not to press or lean on it.'

'Here, who's going to hold my arms up?' demanded Charles, having tried the effect of obeying these instructions.

'No one, my dear. You just sit with them extended. Now you must all of you try to make your minds a blank...'

'That oughtn't to be difficult for some of us,' said Peter.

'True,' agreed Charles, 'but to think this was the one occasion when Flinders would have been really useful, and we weren't warned in time to call him in!'

'Shut up, Chas!' Margaret said severely. 'All right,

Aunt. Anything else?'

'No, dear. Only when the board begins to move you must on no account push it, or in any way seek to influence it. Think of something else, and just keep your hands perfectly steady. Have you all got your fingers on the board? Then we will be quite quiet now, and wait.'

Dead silence fell. In the dim light they could just perceive one another, but Celia could not keep her eyes from peering fearfully into the darkness beyond. After perhaps three minutes, Charles said suddenly: 'What happens if I sneeze?'

"Sh!' said Mrs Bosanquet.

Another silence fell. This time it was Peter who broke it. 'I say, are you sure this is right?' he asked. 'Isn't it only one person who manipulates a planchette? Or am I thinking of a ouija board?'

"Sh!' said Mrs Bosanquet again.

Time crept by. Margaret's arms began to feel rather numb, and still the board did nothing but tremble slightly with the involuntary muscular twitches of all their hands. She became aware of a sound, and listening intently, identified it as somewhat stertorous breathing. She tried to see the faces of her companions, and at that moment Mrs Bosanquet herself spoke: 'My dears!' she said impressively, 'I do believe Charles was right, and he's gone into a trance. His hands are no longer on the board, and he is breathing just like a medium did whom I once visited. Charles! Can you hear me?'

A slight, but unmistakable snore answered her. 'Kick him, Celia!' said Peter. 'The blighter's gone to sleep.'

Celia promptly shook her husband, who grunted, yawned, and sat up. 'Charles, you're not to go to sleep! It's too bad of you!' she scolded.

'Asleep?' said Charles. 'Did I seem to you to be asleep?'

'You did,' said Peter grimly. 'Snoring like a pig.'

'Nonsense,' Charles replied. 'And I warned you what

163

might happen! You've gone and roused me out of what might have proved to be a valuable trance.'

Mrs Bosanquet said worriedly: 'We shall never get any results like this!'

'It's all right, Aunt Lilian,' Celia reassured her. 'I'll see he stays awake.'

'Well, I do trust there will be no more interruptions,' Mrs Bosanquet sighed.

Under her breath Celia said: 'It isn't fair to tease her, Chas. Do behave decently!'

Thus adjured Charles again placed his hands on the board, and they sat in another hopeful silence.

This time the silence was of such long duration that even Mrs Bosanquet began to feel sleepy. But just as she had decided that her arms were aching too much, and she had better suggest a postponement of the séance, the board moved quite an inch across the paper underneath it.

'Peter, you pushed!' Margaret said.

'I swear I didn't!'

"Sh!' Mrs Bosanquet begged.

Once it had started the board seemed to grow quite energetic, and began to describe circles, and make jerky darts in every direction.

'It keeps on leaving me behind,' Charles complained. 'There it goes again! Now I've lost it.'

'Charles, you must keep your hands on it!' Mrs Bosanquet told him.

'I can't; it doesn't seem to like me.'

'It's all jolly fine,' Peter remarked, as the board made a dash to one side, 'but it can't be writing! It keeps going backwards.'

'It's drawing a plan of the Priory,' Charles prophesied. 'Yes, I thought so; that's that corner by the garden-hall, I'll bet.'

'It often starts like this,' Mrs Bosanquet said. 'It will settle down, if we are patient.'

'I hope you may be right,' Charles answered. 'I've taken enough exercise to-day without having to chase this blinking board all over the table now. Ah, the beggar nearly got away from me that time!'

'You know, if no one is pushing it, it really is rather wonderful,' Margaret said.

'Listen! What was that?' Mrs Bosanquet exclaimed. 'Did you hear a sharp sound rather like a rap?'

'Sorry,' Celia said. 'It was me. One of my earrings has dropped on to the floor.'

At that moment Peter cried: 'Ouch!' and Mrs Bosanquet said quite excitedly: 'There! I knew something would happen! Did you feel anything, Peter?'

'*Feel* anything?' he exploded. 'That brute...'

'Fancy Peter being singled out!' marvelled his brother-in-law. 'Sit still, Peter: the Monk is probably trying to attract your attention. You may feel something else if you wait.'

'If I feel anything else,' said Peter savagely, 'I'll scrag you!'

'But my dear, what has it got to do with Charles?' Mrs Bosanquet asked. 'You really *must* try and keep calm.'

'You don't suppose any spirit was responsible, do you?' Peter said. 'That brute Charles kicked me on the shin.'

'If you did do anything so inconsiderate, Charles, I must beg you not to repeat it. And *please* don't talk any more!'

She sounded so hurt that Charles repented, and relapsed once more into silence.

The board continued to move jerkily over the paper. Celia began to yawn. Then, startling them all into rigidity, two sharp raps sounded somewhere in the room.

Celia drew in her breath sharply, and shrank against Charles.

'Quiet, all of you!' whispered Mrs Bosanquet. 'I will speak to it!'

165

Two more raps sounded: Peter's chair slid softly backwards.

Mrs Bosanquet uplifted her voice. 'Whoever you may be, I charge you, answer me! Rap once for Yes, and twice for No, and then we shall understand you. Do you wish to communicate with us?'

'Oh don't! Please stop!' Celia gasped.

An apologetic voice spoke out of the darkness, and both Charles and Peter sprang up. 'Well yes, Mum, in a manner of speaking I do,' it said. 'But if I got to stand rapping on this 'ere window, I don't see as how I shall ever get much forrader, as they say.'

A shout of laughter broke from Charles. 'Flinders!' he cried. 'I might have known it!'

CHAPTER XII

He stepped to the lamp and turned it up. Standing just outside the open French window was Constable Flinders.

'How very disappointing!' said Mrs Bosanquet. 'I'm afraid that has broken the thread.'

Celia, whose cheeks were still ashen with fright, began to laugh.

'Come in, Flinders,' Charles said. 'And what on earth are you doing, creeping round the house?'

The constable removed his helmet, and having looked round to be quite sure there was no mat on which he ought to wipe his feet, stepped into the room. 'I'm sure I beg your pardon, sir, if I gave you a start, but when I went and knocked on the back door there wasn't no one there, and I see the kitchen all dark. So I come round to the front and happening to see this here window open, and a bit of a light burning, I thought as how I would take the liberty of seeing if you was in here. Because,' he added, with a touch of severity, 'if you wasn't I should have had to warn you not to go leaving windows open on the ground floor.'

'But what do you want?' Peter demanded. 'And how did you manage to come right up to the window without us hearing you?'

The constable looked gratified. 'I do move quietly, sir, don't I? I've had rubbers put on my boots, that's what I've done. Just to be on the safe side, so to speak.'

'They'll be asking you to join the C.I.D. soon,' Charles said admiringly. 'Sit down, and tell us what you came about.'

'Thank you, sir.' Mr Flinders selected the straightest chair he could see, and sat down on the edge of it. 'Well, sir, it's like this. After what you told me about that furrin chap – that Dooval – I give the matter a lot of thought, and I come to the conclusion the best thing I could do was to watch him as much as I could, without losing sight of Mr Titmarsh. And I can tell you, sir, he's one man's work, he is. I lorst him again the other night, and it's my belief he gave me the slip on purpose. Well, sir, this very evening when I was trailing Mr Titmarsh, who should I see but this Dooval?'

'Where?' Charles said.

'Right here, sir. That is, up by the ruin, me being on the right-of-way at the time, wondering where that old – where Mr Titmarsh had got to. I don't mind telling you, sir, that it gave me quite a turn, seeing him. "My Gawd!" I says to myself. "Is that the Monk?" Then I got my lamp on to him, and I see who it was. I called out to him, but before you could say "knife" he'd done a bunk, sir. Scared out of his life, he was. So I thought the best thing I could do, seeing as I was so handy, was to come right up on to the house and tell you.'

'Quite right,' Charles said. He turned, as Margaret, who had slipped out of the room a minute or two before, came back with a tray. 'Good idea, Margaret,' he approved. 'You'll have a glass of beer, after your labours, Flinders?' He got up and unscrewed the top of the bottle. It made a pleasant hissing sound. The constable watched the golden liquid froth into the glass, and his eye glistened. Charles held out the glass.

'Not supposed to take anything when we're on duty, you know, sir,' the constable said, accepting it.

Charles poured out two more glasses. 'You can't be on duty at this time of night,' he said.

'Well, sir, since you make a *point* of it,' said Mr

Flinders, and raised the glass. 'Here's your very good health, sir.'

'Same to you,' said Charles.

Celia spoke. 'Charles, you must tell this French person you will *not* have him wandering about in our grounds. Really, it's a bit too thick! Apparently the whole countryside regards this place as common land. I won't put up with it any longer!'

'What can he be doing here, anyway?' Margaret wondered.

'Looking for the Monk, like the rest of us,' answered Charles. 'Let's form a society, shall we?'

'No,' said Celia crossly. 'We shan't. I'm sick to death of the Monk!'

'Well, I'll go and have a chat with Duval to-morrow,' Charles promised.

He had no particular desire to set foot inside the artist's dreary little cottage again, so on the following morning he cut short his fishing, and strolled on to the Bell Inn in the hope of meeting Duval there. He was rewarded by the sight of the artist seated alone in the taproom at a table in the corner. He had a glass of whisky before him, and he was sitting in a slack attitude, with his hands clasped between his knees, and his eyes staring moodily at the ground. He looked up as Charles came across the room, and a furtive expression crept into his face.

Charles sat down on the settle beside him, and having ascertained that the only two people within earshot were busily discussing fat stock, he said: 'Good morning. I was looking for you.'

'I do not know why,' Duval said sullenly. 'I will not tell you anything. It is better that you go away and leave me alone.'

'Oh yes, I think you do know,' Charles replied. 'Last night you were seen in our grounds.'

The artist gave a shiver, and one of his claw-like hands

169

grasped Charles' knee under cover of the table. 'Be quiet!' he muttered. 'Have I not said even the walls have ears?'

'It is not a very original observation,' Charles remarked. 'Moreover, no one is listening to us. What I want to say is this: I can't have you pursuing your search for the Monk in my grounds. Sorry if I seem obstructive, but there are too many people already in the habit of treating the place as though it were their own.'

'Speak that name again, and I leave you!' Duval said. His hands were shaking. 'If it were known – if someone saw me with you, I do not know what might happen. If you must talk with me, talk of my art.'

He raised his voice to an unnatural pitch, and said boisterously: 'Yes, my friend, it is true I have the eye for colour, even as you say. I see colour like no one else has ever seen it.'

Two people had come into the taproom together, and both looked round. They were Wilkes and Michael Strange. Strange, after one glance, turned away, but Wilkes kept his eyes on the pair in the corner for a moment or two, and made an involuntary grimace of annoyance.

Again the artist's fingers closed on Charles' knee. 'Be careful!' he said, so softly that Charles only just caught the words. 'Look who has entered! For the love of God, m'sieur, guard your tongue! If that one knew that I had spoken with you of – of the things we both know of...!' He broke off, passing his tongue between his lips.

Michael Strange, a tankard in his hand, was making his way towards a seat by the window. He bestowed a curt nod on Charles, and sitting down began to scan the columns of a newspaper. The length of room separated him from the corner table, and Charles said: 'I've no wish to upset you, but do you understand that I cannot permit you to haunt my grounds?'

The artist got up. 'I go. I speak with you another time.

Here, it is not safe. I come up to speak with you to-night perhaps, when no one can see.' Once more he raised his voice, in unconvincing joviality: 'Ah, you are too good, m'sieur! But it is true: I have revolutionized the art of painting.'

The landlord came up to them. ''Morning, sir. 'Morning, moossoo. Got everything you want, sir? What, you off, moossoo? Well, this is a short visit you've paid the Bell to-day, and no mistake.'

The artist clapped him on the shoulder. 'My friend, this gentleman has bought from me a picture! He is not an artist, no, but he is a connoisseur!'

'That's very nice, sir, I'm sure,' Wilkes said, and passed on.

Duval picked up his hat, and without another word to Charles went out of the bar. After a few moments Charles followed him, and went rather thoughtfully home.

So far Inspector Tomlinson had been as good as his word: they were not worried by any apparent supervision. As far as Charles could make out no one had come over to Framley either to watch or to make inquiries, and his suspicions that the inspector had not taken the matter very seriously began to grow stronger.

At lunch-time Celia asked whether he had seen Duval and forbidden him to come any more to the Priory. When she heard that the artist proposed to pay them a visit that night she was anything but pleased. 'He can't come to-night!' she said. 'You know we've got the Rootes and Colonel Ackerley dining with us.'

'I can't help it,' Charles replied. 'I don't propose to ask him to dinner. If he does turn up I'll tell Bowers to push him into the study. I shall soon be able to get rid of him.'

Margaret said, without raising her eyes from her plate: 'You didn't ask Mr Strange to dinner too?'

'I did not,' said Charles with emphasis.

'I wondered,' Margaret explained off-handedly, 'because

I thought Celia wanted him invited.'

Her brother regarded her intently. 'Celia? I was under the impression that it was you who seemed keenest about it.' He waited to hear what she would say, but she said nothing at all. 'Look here, Sis, I know you've got rather a soft corner for that fellow, but you can take it from me that there's something very fishy about him. And if you happen to meet him at any time, I'd like you to be very much on your guard. See?'

Margaret flushed scarlet. 'What do you mean? Why should I meet him? And I don't know why you should think I have a soft corner for him simply because I won't leap to conclusions as you're doing.'

'All right, keep your hair on,' Peter recommended. 'But I don't mind telling you that yesterday this precious Mr Strange of yours somehow or other got wind of our visit to the police, and followed us. I just mention it so that you shall see there is a real need for you to be on your guard when talking to him.'

Startled grey eyes flew to his face. 'Followed you?' Margaret said. 'To – to Manfield?'

Peter nodded. 'How he got wind of it we don't know, but it seems fairly certain that he did.'

She knew only too well from what source Michael Strange had obtained his information. She felt guilty and unhappy, knowing that she was doing wrong to withhold her own discoveries from her relations. She finished the meal in silence, aware of her brother's scrutiny, and took care to avoid a tête-à-tête conversation with him afterwards. This was an easy matter, as they all played tennis again during the afternoon, and there was no opportunity for him to speak to her alone in between the last set and the arrival of their guests.

She lingered over her dressing, and did not go down to the drawing-room until she had heard one of the visitors arrive. She entered the room at length to find Colonel

Ackerley apparently discussing whooping-cough with the doctor.

'I'm afraid there's no doubt about it,' Roote was saying. 'But it oughtn't to interfere with you, Colonel.'

Celia turned as Margaret came in. 'Oh, Margaret, isn't it a nuisance for the Colonel? His butler's little boy has developed whooping-cough!'

'All the fault of these cinemas,' grumbled the Colonel, shaking hands with Margaret. 'Time and again I've said people had no business to let their children go to those germ-ridden holes. But you might as well talk to a brick wall as to that housekeeper of mine. Silly fools, both she and her husband.'

Dr Roote drank his cocktail in a gulp. 'Well, I don't see what you're worrying about,' he said. 'All kids go through it, and it isn't as though this one lives in your house.'

'No, but I shall have him whooping all over the garden if I know anything about it. Never wanted a couple with a child, but like a fool I gave way and let 'em live over the garage. Ought to have stuck to my original intention, and barred children.' He put down his glass, and seemed to make an effort to throw off his annoyance. 'Well, well, you'll say I'm a crotchetty old bachelor, eh, Mrs Malcolm?'

'Not a bit,' Celia assured him. 'I say instead that you'll take a brighter view after dinner.'

It was not until shortly before ten o'clock that Bowers came in to announce the arrival of M. Duval. Charles had cut out of the bridge four, and was standing behind the Colonel, watching him play, with considerable skill, a difficult hand. Bowers came up to him, and said softly: 'M. Duval, sir. I've shown him into the study.'

'No spade, Colonel?' Celia asked quickly.

The Colonel, frowning over the dummy she had laid down for him, glanced at his own cards again. 'Bless my

173

soul, did I pull out that club? Thanks, partner.' He picked the club up again and followed suit. The third player seemed to be wool-gathering. The Colonel said impatiently: 'Come on, Roote!'

The doctor, who had been looking at Charles, started. 'Sorry, sorry! What's led?' He played, and again looked at Charles. 'Didn't know you'd struck up a friendship with Duval, Malcolm.'

'I shouldn't describe my dealings with him exactly as a friendship,' Charles answered. 'I allowed myself to be inveigled into buying one of his pictures, and since then he's been trying hard to make me buy another. All right, Bowers, I'll come.'

He followed the butler out, and went across the hall to the study.

The artist was standing peering out of the window into the darkness. He started round as the door opened, and Charles saw that he was in one of his most nervous moods. No sooner was the door shut than he said hurriedly: 'M'sieur, you permit that I draw the curtains?'

'Certainly, if you like,' Charles replied.

'I must not be seen here,' Duval said, pulling the curtains across the window. 'Once I thought I heard a step behind me, but when I looked there was no one. I do not think I am followed here, but I am not sure. Sometimes I hear noises, but perhaps they are in my head. For it is very bad, m'sieur, ah, but very bad!'

'I'm sorry,' Charles said. 'Now what is it you want to see me about?'

The artist drew closer to him. 'There is no one outside? You are sure? No one can hear?'

'No, no one.'

Duval cast a glance round the room. 'I do not like this house. I do not know where the stairs are, but he goes up them like a ghost, m'sieur, and he can hear.'

'The stairs,' said Charles patiently, 'are at the other end

of the hall, and since each step has its own creaking board I defy anyone to go up like a ghost. The only people in the house are ourselves, my family, my servant and his wife, and three guests, who are playing bridge in the library.'

Duval said suspiciously. 'Those three? Who are they?'

'Dr and Mrs Roote, and Colonel Ackerley.'

Duval seemed satisfied, but he sank his voice even lower. 'M'sieur, I will be quick. I come to say to you that you must not set your *gendarme* to watch me. You must tell him there is no harm in poor Duval. M'sieur, it is true! I do not do you any evil when I am in your garden, and I must go there, though I fear greatly, yes greatly! It is there I think I find the Monk. Something I have discovered. But your *gendarme* he challenge me, and I go away before I have discovered the great mystery. M'sieur, I implore you permit that I search here.'

'My dear fellow,' Charles said, 'I really can't have you prowling about the grounds. My wife doesn't like it, and I warn you I've got a revolver, and I'm liable to shoot if I see anyone suspicious lurking near the house.'

This threat did not have much effect. 'But me you know, and you would not shoot me after all your so great kindness. No, no, I know better. And I tell you it is of importance – of importance unheard of that you do not let that *gendarme* follow me. If I am watched what can I do? And he, that imbecile, he goes so clumsily he can be heard, and it is not only Duval who hears him.'

'You mean you think you're on the track of the Monk.'

The guarded look came creeping back into the artist's wild eyes. 'I do not say.'

'Then in that case I fear *I* do not call off my watchdog.'

'But, m'sieur, I have told you I do no harm! I would not hurt you, or those others. What do I care for them? But nothing!'

'Look here,' Charles said, 'why all this mystery? You've already said you expect to find the Monk in these grounds.'

The artist passed his hand across his brow. 'Sometimes I do not know quite what I say. I do not wish to tell you that, for you understand it is no use if someone else finds him. I must be that one. M'sieur, think! For years I have waited. At first I did not care: I was content. But now I am not any longer content, and I think that it is better to have courage than to go on like this. For me, I have genius, and I will not be what you call underdog all my life. Better dead, m'sieur! Yes, I have thought that. Better dead! But I do not mean to die. Not like that other. For see, m'sieur! I am armed.' He showed Charles a wicked-looking knife, and grinned fiendishly. 'That would slip between the ribs, *hein*? Softly, oh but softly! When I hear footsteps in the dark, I take hold of him, my little knife, and courage comes to me.'

'Indeed?' said Charles, beginning to think that the man was really mad. 'And do I understand that that is meant for the Monk?'

Duval nodded. 'Yes, but I do not wish to kill him. No, that is not good. I wish only to see his face, for once I have seen it, m'sieur, he is in my power, and I hold him like that.' He closed his fingers tightly.

'Well, when he's in your power,' Charles said, 'perhaps you'll be so good as to tell him to cease haunting this house.'

'Yes, perhaps I do that for you, m'sieur, if you let me search as I please. For I have made up my mind that even if I must go down amongst the dead to do it I will find him.'

'Let's hope no such journey will be necessary,' Charles suggested, and was surprised to see that leering secret smile twist the artist's mouth again. 'In the meantime, I don't think you need worry about Constable Flinders.'

'And I may search? You will not forbid me?'

'Well, we'll see about that,' Charles said, bent only on getting rid of him. 'And now I'm afraid I shall have to ask you to go, because I can't leave my guests any longer.'

The artist clutched his wrist. 'You will not tell the *gendarme* to arrest poor Duval?'

'No, I won't do anything like that,' Charles promised, and opened the door. He saw Duval out into the porch, and watched him dart out of the beam of light thrown through the open door. With a shrug of the shoulders he shut the door again, and went back to the library.

As he entered the room Celia looked up as though she were about to say something, but encountering a warning frown changed her mind.

'Well, Malcolm, bought another picture?' the Colonel chaffed him. 'You know, you haven't yet shown us the first one you bought.'

Charles shook his head. 'I never show it to people after dark,' he said. 'It upsets them. Did you make your contract, by the way? That four spade one you were playing when I left you?'

'Yes, we made it,' Ackerley replied. 'Oughtn't to have, but Roote discarded a diamond. Aha, Roote, caught you napping that time, didn't I? Can't think why you held on to the heart.'

Dr Roote merely grunted. He had embarked on his third whisky since dinner, and though still perfectly sensible was looking slightly hazy. In a little while his wife, seeing him look round for the decanter again, gave the signal for the party to break up. Colonel Ackerley stayed on for about twenty minutes after the Rootes had gone, and then he too took his departure.

Gathering up the scattered cards, Celia said: 'I'm sorry for that little woman. I should divorce you, Charles, if you got fuddled every evening.'

'I do not at any time approve of drunkenness,'

announced Mrs Bosanquet, 'and when a doctor falls into the habit of taking rather too much, I consider it most reprehensible. Now, if one of us was attacked by appendicitis in the middle of the night, what would be the use of sending for Dr Roote? Mrs Bowers was telling me that they say in the village that he can't be got out of bed at night to attend to anyone, and we all know what that means.'

'If you get attacked by appendicitis, Aunt, we'll send for Ponsonby, from Manfield,' Peter promised.

'Yes, my dear, I hope that you would. But my appendix was removed some years ago,' said Mrs Bosanquet with mild triumph.

An hour later, as Peter was about to blow out his candle, and go to sleep, his door opened softly, and Charles came in, fully dressed.

'Hullo!' Peter said. 'Anything wrong?'

'No, but I've got a fancy to do a little sleuthing myself. Do you feel like accompanying me?'

Peter raised himself on his elbow. 'Who are you going to track?'

'Friend Duval. Unless he's clean cracked, he thinks he's on to the Monk's trail, and I can't help feeling it might be worth our while to follow him.'

The bed creaked in the adjoining room, and in a moment Margaret appeared in the open doorway with her dressing-gown caught hastily round her. 'If you don't want to be overheard you'd better see that the door's shut in future,' she said. 'Go on. What did Duval say to-night?'

Charles gave them a brief résumé of the artist's conversation. Peter sat up when he had finished. 'The knife business makes it look as though he's mad,' he said, 'but if we don't try and find out what he's up to we're a couple of fools. If you'd like to clear out, Sis, I propose to dress.'

'You can take your clothes into my room,' said his

178

sister disobligingly. 'I want to hear some more. Who did he think was following him, Charles?'

'I don't know. The Monk, presumably. I have an idea he's afraid of Strange.'

Conscious of her brother's sidelong scrutiny Margaret said calmly: 'Why?'

Charles told her what Duval had said that morning when Strange had entered the taproom with the landlord. She nodded. 'I see.' She watched Peter swing his legs out of bed, and sat down, folding her dressing-gown more tightly round her.

Peter collected his clothes, and disappeared into her room. Through the open doorway his voice reached them: 'What about Celia?'

'She doesn't like it, but she says if Margaret will go and keep her company and I promise to run no risks I may go just this once.'

Margaret raised her eyes. 'What are you going to do, Charles?'

'It all depends,' he answered. 'I don't propose to run any unnecessary risks, and from Duval's account the Monk is a dangerous customer. But if by following Duval we can get a sight of the Monk it's worth doing.'

'You mean, you'd follow the Monk, and see where he went to?'

'That's the general idea.'

Margaret looked straight ahead of her for a moment, as though she were considering. 'Yes,' she said at last. 'I think perhaps you ought to. But don't shoot, Charles. Either of you. You don't want to land yourselves in a mess, and you mustn't forget that you don't know what the Monk is after. He may not be doing anything criminal.'

'The only shooting I'm likely to do will be in self-defence,' Charles replied.

Peter came back into the room in his shirt-sleeves.

'Don't you worry, Sis. We shan't get into trouble.'

'You might get excited, and do something you wouldn't do in cold blood,' she insisted. 'And I've got a sort of idea that the Monk doesn't want to hurt any of us.'

Peter got into his coat, and buttoned it. 'Where did you get that idea from, if I may ask?'

'I don't know. But I do feel that you oughtn't to leap to conclusions.' She got up. 'Well, I'll go along to Celia now. Good luck, you two.' She went out, leaving her brother to frown after her.

'Strike you that Margaret takes an unduly sympathetic interest in the Monk?' he said. 'I don't quite like it. That fellow, Strange, has been getting at her, if you ask me.'

'She's too sensible,' Charles said. 'Are you ready?'

Together they went downstairs, and let themselves out by the front door. The night was rather overcast, but the waning moon shone fitfully through the clouds.

'Good: shan't need our torches,' Charles said, slipping his into the pocket of his tweed coat. 'The chapel is our goal, I think. That's where Flinders saw Duval.'

They made their way to the ruin, and cautiously inspected it. No one was there, and a deep silence brooded over the place. They searched the ground all about it without success, and at last Peter said: 'Look here, it's no use wandering aimlessly through the woods. It 'ud be more sensible if we walked down to Duval's cottage to see whether he's there or not. If he's tucked up in bed I think we can safely write him down a lunatic. If he's not there – well, he may still be a lunatic, but we can lie in wait for him on the road and see which direction he comes from. That'll narrow the field for us to-morrow night.'

'All right,' Charles said reluctantly. 'Not that I think it helps much, but I agree we shan't do much good going on like this.'

They started to walk down the right-of-way. 'What's more,' Peter pointed out, 'it's just possible that he may not have ventured out yet. After all, he knew we had a dinner-party, and since he seems very loth to let anyone catch sight of him he'd be bound to give the party some time to break up.' He flashed his torch on to his wristwatch. 'It's only just on midnight. Duval might well think we should still be up.'

'True,' Charles agreed. 'Anyway, we can but try your idea.'

They walked on in silence, until they came to the place where the right-of-way joined the main road into Framley. A few yards up the road the lane that ran past Duval's cottage branched off. They turned into this, and went softly up it till they saw the broken gate that led into the cottage garden. They paused in the lee of the untrimmed hedge, and craned their necks to obtain a glimpse of the tumble-down building. No light shone from either of the upper windows, but they thought they could see a dim glow in the ground floor.

'How many rooms?' Peter whispered.

'One downstairs, besides the kitchen.'

Peter stole to the gate, from where he could get a clear view of the cottage. He rejoined Charles in a minute or two. 'There is a light burning downstairs,' he whispered. 'But I think the curtains are drawn. I move that we walk up past the place and wait under the hedge to see whether he comes out or not. If he does he's bound to come this way, and he won't see us if we're the other side of the gate.'

Charles nodded, and followed him to a distance of a few yards beyond the gate. A ditch, with a bank surmounted by a hedge, flanked the lane, and they sat down on this bank in silence.

No sound came from the house on the other side of the ditch. After perhaps twenty minutes Charles yawned. 'We must look uncommonly silly,' he remarked. 'I don't believe he's in. Or else he's gone to bed, and left a light burning.'

Peter stood up. 'I'm going to try and have a look inside,' he said.

'You can't go spying in at a man's windows,' Charles objected.

'Can't I?' Peter retorted. 'Well, you watch me, and see. I've no compunction about spying on Duval whatsoever. The trouble with you is that you've got a legal mind. I don't somehow see Duval & Co. displaying a like punctiliousness where we're concerned.'

He carefully lifted the sagging gate out of position, and stole up the tangled path to the house. Charles saw him apparently listening at the window; then he crept round to the back, and was gone for some time.

He rejoined Charles presently. 'Can't hear a sound,' he said. 'But there's certainly a light. Just you come up, will you?'

Charles sacrificed his principles, and followed Peter up to the front door. He stood listening intently. It was just as Peter had said: not the smallest sound came from the room on the other side of the door.

'I believe you're right,' Charles whispered. 'He's either out, or asleep. If he's asleep I propose to wake him.'

Before Peter could stop him he had raised his hand and knocked smartly on the door.

'You ass!' Peter hissed. 'If he's there we don't want to disturb him!'

'If he's there his talk was all moonshine, and it doesn't matter whether we disturb him or not,' Charles replied. He knocked again.

The answering silence was a little uncanny. They waited, then Charles knocked louder than ever.

'By Jove, I believe he is out!' Peter said. 'Take care he doesn't come back suddenly and see you.' He moved boldly towards the window, and set his eye to the dirty glass where the curtains inside just failed to meet.

Suddenly he spoke in a sharp, uneasy voice. 'Charles, just come here a moment. There's something . . . Here, take a look. What's that thing you can just see?'

All his scruples forgotten Charles pressed his face up against the glass. 'I can't quite – it looks like an arm. Yes, it is. Then someone must be standing there! But – damn this curtain!' He pressed closer, staring between the narrow gap in the curtain. The thing that was just discernible was unmistakably an arm in an old tweed sleeve, and below the edge of the frayed cuff a hand hung slackly. Charles stood still, trying to see more, but the gap was too small. But all the time he watched the hand never moved, and no sound broke the silence.

He turned. 'There's something wrong here,' he said. 'We've got to get in. Try the door.'

Peter put his hand on the latch. 'Bound to be bolted – unless he's out.'

But the latch lifted, and no bolt held the door in place. He pushed it cautiously open and peered in. Then a startled exclamation brought Charles up quickly to look over his shoulder. 'Oh, my God,' Peter cried on a note of horror.

For there, in the centre of the squalid little room was Louis Duval, quite dead, and hanging from one of the hooks in the beam that Charles had noticed.

CHAPTER XIII

The body hung horribly limply, and the face which was turned towards them was slightly discoloured as though death had resulted from strangulation rather than dislocation. The mouth hung open, and between lids that were almost shut the whites of the eyes gleamed in the lamplight.

Peter's hand fell from the latch of the door which he was still holding. He felt sick, but conquering the rising nausea he went up to that still figure, and touched one of the drooping hands. It felt chilly, and with a feeling of loathing he let it fall. The arm swung for a moment and then was still.

'Dead . . .' Charles said. 'Poor chap!'

Peter was looking round the room; it was untidy, and a dirty plate with a knife and fork stood on the table, but there were no signs of any struggle having taken place. The only thing that seemed significant was a fallen chair, and from its position it looked as though Duval had kicked it from under his feet when the rope was round his neck. 'Think the whole affair got on his nerves so badly that he – did himself in?' Peter said, instinctively lowering his voice.

Charles shook his head. 'I don't know. It's possible; he was pretty distraught to-night. But I can't help thinking of what he said about the other man who died.'

Peter jumped and looked round. 'You don't think – the Monk did this?'

Charles did not answer immediately. 'He was trying to find out who the Monk is,' he said after a short pause. 'He was scared out of his life; he was afraid he was being followed. So much was he afraid that he carried a fairly murderous knife on him. Now we find this.' He made a gesture towards the hanging corpse.

'No sign of a struggle,' Peter said, again scanning the room. 'And his hands are free, and there's that chair which he obviously stood on.'

'His hands might have been bound,' Charles said. 'No, don't touch them. This is a matter for the police. Come on, let's get out of this: we can't do anything here. We'd better go on to the Inn, and ring up the police-station at Manfield.'

'Charles, we can't leave him hanging there!' Peter said, impelled by his horror of that dangling corpse.

'He's been dead for at least an hour from the look of it,' Charles said. 'We can't do any good by cutting him down, and the police won't thank us for interfering. Come on: let's get out, for God's sake!'

Peter followed him into the garden. As Charles shut the door he said: 'Door was unbolted. It looks damned black to me.'

'Why should he bolt the door if he meant to kill himself?' was Peter's answer.

Charles did not say anything. Both he and Peter were glad to be out of that dreadful room, and they set off at a brisk pace towards the village.

The Inn was only some ten minutes' walk distant from the cottage, and they soon reached it. The place was in darkness, but they pressed the electric bell, and heard it ring somewhere inside. After a short interval the door was opened, and the barman's startled face looked out.

'I want to use your telephone,' Charles said curtly. 'It's urgent, so let me in, will you?'

Spindle seemed reluctant to let him pass, but Charles

pushed by him without ceremony. 'Where is it?' he asked impatiently.

'What – what's happened, sir?' Spindle said. 'I 'ope – no one's taken ill?'

'Never you mind,' Charles said. 'Where's the telephone?'

'There's a box outside the coffee-room, sir. But I don't know as – I don't know as Mr Wilkes...'

'Rubbish! Wilkes can't possibly object to having his telephone used. Where is he?'

'He's gorn to bed, sir. I'll show you where the 'phone is, and call 'im.'

He led the way down the passage to a telephone box, and casting another wondering look at them made off in the direction of the back premises.

Charles found the number he wanted, and stepped into the box. Peter remained at his elbow, listening. He supposed the landlord's room must be reached by way of the back stairs since Spindle had gone in that direction, but a moment later Spindle reappeared, and saying that he would rouse Mr Wilkes at once, went quickly up the stairs that ran up at the front of the house.

Charles had at last got himself connected with the police-station, and was endeavouring to make an apparently sleepy constable understand. 'Hullo! Hullo, is that Manfield Police Station?... Yes? This is Malcolm speaking – *Malcolm*... M.A.L.C.O.L.M. – yes, *Malcolm*, from Framley... No, *Framley*. Is Inspector Tomlinson there?... Damn! Look here, you'd better send a man over at once. There's been an accident... No, I said there's been an accident... Yes, that's right... What?... Well, it's either suicide, or murder, and the sooner you get a man over here the better... You'll what?... Oh good, yes!... I'm speaking from the Bell Inn, and if you call for me here I'll take you to the place. Right, good-bye.' He hung up the receiver, and turned to tell Peter what the constable had said. 'He's going to get hold of Tomlin...' He broke off, staring past Peter. The front door was open, and on the threshold, his hand on the latchkey which he had not yet withdrawn from the lock, was Michael Strange, standing as though arrested by what he had heard, and looking directly at him.

Peter turned quickly, following the direction of Charles' gaze. 'Strange!' he ejaculated. 'What the hell are you doing?'

Strange drew the key out of the lock, and shut the door. 'I might echo that question,' he said coolly. He came towards them, and they saw that he was looking decidedly unpleasant. 'What have you found?' he said.

Charles laid a restraining hand on Peter's arm. 'Do you know, that is something we propose to tell the police,' he said. 'I don't immediately perceive what it has to do with you.'

Strange looked at him under frowning brows. 'Look here,' he said harshly, 'if you're wise you'll stop poking your nose in where it's not wanted.'

Charles' brows rose in polite surprise. 'Is that a threat?' he inquired.

'No, it's not a threat. It's a warning, and one which you'd do well to follow.' He swung around on his heel as he spoke and went up the stairs without another word.

Peter had started forward as though to pursue him, but again Charles checked him. 'Leave it,' he said. 'We've no right to detain him. All we can do is to tell the police.'

'While you stand on ceremony he'll get clean away!' Peter said hotly.

'I don't think it,' Charles answered, 'if he had anything to do with what we found to-night I'm pretty sure we've discovered who the Monk is. And he's a damned cool customer – much too cool to give himself away by bolting.' He glanced up the staircase. 'I don't know bout you, but I feel as though I could do with a stiff peg. What on earth's Wilkes up to all this time?'

As though in answer to his question the landlord came into sight at the top of the stairs. 'Sorry to keep you waiting, sir,' he said, 'but I stayed to pop on my clothes. Spindle says you wanted to use the telephone, urgent, sir. I do hope nothing's wrong up at the Priory?' He came down as quickly as a man of his bulk might, and they saw that he was fully clothed and that his placid countenance had taken on a look of anxiety.

'No, there's nothing wrong at the Priory,' Charles answered. 'It's that fellow, Duval. We've just been up to his place, and – he's dead.'

The landlord fell back a pace. '*Dead?*' he echoed. 'Dooval? So that's...' A cough broke off what he was about to say. He went on again when the spasm was at an end: 'So that's why he never turned up to-night like he generally does,' he said. 'How – what happened, sir? Was it the drugs he takes, do you think? Perhaps he ain't actually dead. I have heard as how they often goes into a kind of a stupor.'

'He's dead right enough,' Charles said grimly. 'We found him hanging from his own ceiling.'

The landlord's rosy cheeks turned suddenly pale. 'Hanging?' he whispered. 'You mean – someone – did him in?'

'No, it looks like suicide on the whole. I say, can you get us a drink? We feel we need one after this.'

Wilkes turned mechanically towards the bar. 'Yes, sir. That is, it's after hours, you know, sir, but I can stretch a point seeing what the reason is. I – I take it you wanted to ring up the police?'

'Naturally. They'll be over in about half an hour, I should imagine. Can we sit and wait here till they come?'

'Yes, sir, certainly. Will you have a whisky? And I'd be glad if you'd keep it quiet that I served you after hours, if you don't mind, sir.' He measured out two tots, still

188

looking rather pale about the gills. Charles told him to pour a third for himself, and he did so. 'Hanged!' he repeated. 'My Gawd, sir, I can't get over it! Regular shock it is, when I think how he took his dinner here this morning same as usual. He did seem a bit queerer than usual now I come to think of it, but there, he was always such a one for going off into one of them silly fits that I didn't set any store by it.'

'What about the soda, Wilkes?' Peter interrupted.

The landlord started. 'I'm sure I beg your pardon, sir.' He produced a siphon, and squirted the soda-water into the glasses. 'It's given me such a turn I don't hardly know what I'm doing.' He sat down limply. 'To think of him – dead! And like that too. It must have upset you, finding him,' he shuddered.

'Yes, not a pretty sight,' Charles said.

They remained seated in the bar, until the noise of a car approaching roused Wilkes from his awe-struck meditations. The car drew up outside, and he hurriedly concealed the tell-tale glasses. 'I'll go and let 'em in, sir,' he said, and went out to the main door.

Charles and Peter followed him. Inspector Tomlinson was standing in the entrance, and at sight of Charles he said briskly: 'Very good of you to wait, sir. Hope we haven't kept you. If you'll come out I've got a car here, and you can tell me what has happened while we go along to this place. Where is it, sir?'

'Only a stone's throw. I'll direct you.'

'Who's the dead man, sir? Do you know him?'

'Duval. The artist I spoke to you about.'

'I remember, sir,' the inspector said. As usual he displayed nothing but a business-like and detached interest in the occurrence. 'Will you get in beside Sergeant Matthews in the front, sir, and tell him the way? This is Dr Puttock, the Divisional Surgeon. Can you find room behind, Mr Fortescue? I'm afraid it's a tight fit.'

Peter managed to wedge himself between Dr Puttock and the inspector, and the car started forward. In a few minutes it turned into the rough lane, and drew up outside the cottage.

'I shall have to ask you gentlemen to come in with me,' the inspector said. 'Hope you don't mind, sir.'

'No, it's all right,' Charles said, and got out of the car.

They went into the cottage, and the sergeant, producing a note-book began to write in it, his eyes lifting from it from time to time to observe everything in the room. None of the three men paid any attention to Charles or Peter for some time, but when the body had been taken down and laid on the floor, the inspector seemed to become aware of them again, and said kindly: 'Not very pleasant for you two gentlemen, but we shan't keep you very long, I hope... Note the position of that chair, Matthews. Looks as though deceased must have stood upon it, doesn't it?' He glanced down at the doctor who was kneeling beside the body, making some sort of an inspection. 'Clear case of suicide, eh, doctor? As soon as the ambulance comes we'll get the body away.'

The doctor spoke over his shoulder. 'Hand me my bag, will you, inspector?' He opened it, and took out a pair of forceps. As far as Peter could see, from his place by the door, he was doing something inside the dead man's mouth. Then the doctor shifted his position slightly, and Peter could see only his back. At length he got up, and closely scrutinized something that his forceps had found. He took a test-tube from his case, and carefully dropped the infinitesimal thing the forceps held into it. Then he corked it tightly.

The inspector watched him with the air of an inquisitive terrier. 'Got something, doctor?'

'I shall want to do a more thorough examination,' the doctor replied. He glanced down at the body. 'You can cover it, sergeant. I've finished for the present.' He replaced the test tube in his case. 'I'm not satisfied that this is a case of suicide,' he said. 'I found a scrap of cotton wool in the deceased's nostrils, very far back.'

The inspector pursed his lips into a soundless whistle. 'Nothing in the mouth, doctor?'

'Nothing now,' said the doctor significantly.

'Better go over the place for finger-prints,' the inspector said. 'Now, Mr Malcolm, if you please, I'd like to hear just how you happened to find the body.'

Charles gave him a clear and concise account of all that had passed that evening, up to the time of the discovery of the corpse. He neither omitted any relevant point nor became discursive, and at the end of his statement Sergeant Matthews, who had taken it down, looked up gratefully.

'Thank you, sir,' the inspector said. 'If more witnesses were as clear as you are the police would have an easier time.'

Charles smiled. 'I'm not exactly new to this sort of thing,' he said.

The inspector cast him a shrewd glance. 'I thought I'd spotted you, sir. I saw you at the Norchester Assizes about six months ago, didn't I?'

'Quite possibly,' Charles said. 'Now there's one other thing I'd like to mention. When my brother-in-law and I reached the Bell Inn, the barman went to rouse Wilkes, the landlord, while I was ringing you up. As soon as I had finished speaking to the station, I turned round to find that Strange had come in with his own latchkey, and had been listening to all I'd said.'

The doctor looked up sharply. 'Strange?' he repeated.

'Yes, doctor, we've got a note about him,' the inspector said. 'Go on, sir.'

'He asked us what we had found, and upon my refusing to tell him, he seemed distinctly annoyed, and said, as near as I can remember, that he advised us to stop poking our noses where they weren't wanted. I asked whether that was a threat, and he replied that it was a warning which he advised us to take.'

'That's very interesting, sir,' the inspector said. 'You say he came in from the street?'

'Yes, using his own key.'

'Then Strange was not in the Inn when this happened,' the inspector said. 'I think I'll be having a word with him.' He nodded to the sergeant. 'You'd better run these gentlemen back to their home, Matthews. I take it they know at the Inn where we are, sir?'

'Wilkes knows, yes.'

'Then he'll direct the ambulance on. Now, sir, I don't think there's any need for me to keep you standing about here any longer, but if you could make it convenient to come over to the station to-morrow we may have something more to ask you. And we'd like you to read through your statement, which we'll have put into long-hand by then, and sign it. Sergeant Matthews will drive you home now. I hope what you've seen won't keep you awake.' He went out with them to the car, and saw them off. The police car backed down the lane to the main road, and in a very short time deposited them at their own front door.

Celia and Margaret were both awake, and no sooner had the two men entered the house than Margaret leaned over the banisters, and asked them to come up at once and tell them what had happened.

Celia was sitting up in bed with a shawl round her shoulders. 'Thank goodness you're back!' she sighed. 'You've been away such ages we've imagined all sorts of horrors. Did you discover anything?'

Charles and Peter exchanged glances. 'They're bound to know when the inquest comes on,' Peter said. 'Tell them.'

'Inquest?' Margaret said sharply. 'Who's dead? You haven't – no, of course you haven't.'

'It's Duval,' Charles explained. 'We didn't find him in our grounds, so Peter suggested we should go down to his cottage. And we found him there, dead.'

'Murdered?' Celia quavered, gripping her shawl with both hands.

'We don't know,' Charles answered, sitting down on the edge of the bed. 'Apparently he hanged himself, but we shan't know definitely whether it was suicide or not till the inquest, I imagine.'

'But what a ghastly thing!' Margaret said. 'Who can – oh, surely it wasn't murder? Why should anyone think so?'

'Well, perhaps it isn't,' Charles said consolingly. 'Peter and I have got to go over to the police-station to-morrow, and we may hear something fresh then. At present we only know that the doctor wasn't satisfied, and is going to conduct a post mortem.'

'Please tell us just what happened!' Margaret begged.

Charles made the story as short as possible, and he did not mention the doctor's discovery. At the end of his tale Celia said: 'If anyone killed him it was the Monk, and now we know for certain he's not a ghost. Well, I always said I wasn't scared of flesh and blood, but do you think it's safe for us here?'

'Yes, I think so,' her brother replied. 'If the Monk did murder Duval it's fairly certain he did it because Duval had discovered his identity. Or even because he knew Duval had been talking to us. He isn't likely to try to do any of us in. Too risky, for one thing, and for another, no motive.'

'How could he have known that Duval had talked to us?' Margaret asked. 'Do you think he followed him here this evening?'

'Duval undoubtedly thought that possible. It would be easy for him to find out that we'd had dealings with Duval without that, though. I never made any secret of the fact

193

that I visited him, and all sorts of people have seen me talking to him at various times,' Charles said. 'Wilkes, Ackerley, the Rootes – they all knew, not to mention various locals who've seen Duval and me together at the Bell.'

'And, from what you told us to-day, Mr Strange as well,' Margaret said, meeting her brother's eye.

'Yes, Strange, too.' Charles glanced at his watch. 'Well, I don't know how the rest of you feel, but I'm all for bed.'

Margaret got up rather reluctantly. 'Yes, I suppose we'd better try and get some sleep,' she agreed. 'But I do wish we weren't so much in the dark still. Well, good night, you two. Coming, Peter?'

Brother and sister went out together, and soon quiet descended on the house.

The two men drove over to Manfield on the following morning. It was a Sunday, and the market-town had a forlorn appearance. Even the police-station seemed rather deserted, and the constable in charge ushered them immediately into the inspector's office. Here in a short time the inspector joined them.

He bade them good morning, thanked them for coming over in such good time, and sat down behind his desk.

'Discovered anything fresh?' Charles asked, drawing up his chair.

The inspector shook his head. 'Looks like a nasty case against someone, sir,' he said. 'The inquest will be held on Tuesday, and I'm afraid both you gentlemen will have to give evidence.'

'Of course,' Charles said. 'We were quite prepared for that. Can you tell us anything more?'

'Well, sir, strictly speaking I ought not to, but seeing how much you know already, I don't mind telling you that the Divisional Surgeon has just finished his post mortem, and there doesn't seem to be much doubt that it's murder. I needn't ask you not to repeat this, sir, I know.'

'Of course not. What did he discover?'

'It's that piece of cotton wool, sir. Looks as though Duval was chloroformed, and then strung up. Dr Puttock found traces of chloroform still lingering. And during his examination he found various abrasions on the deceased's body as though there had been a bit of a struggle, and in it Duval had knocked against things – the table, maybe, or something like that. Then, sir, the doctor found a bit of skin in one of his finger-nails, as though he might have clawed at someone's face, or hand, or whatever it may have been.'

'Any finger-prints?' Charles asked.

'No, sir. Only the deceased's on that plate you saw, and the glass, and such-like. Whoever did this job took care to wear gloves.' He unlocked a drawer in his desk, and took out an envelope. From this he shook a black bone button. 'After you'd gone, I had a good look round and I found this lying under the coal-box. Must have rolled there.'

Charles and Peter inspected it. It was about the size of a farthing, a cheap-looking button with a pattern stamped on it. 'Looks like an ordinary glove-button,' Peter said.

'Just so, sir. Made in France, too, but that doesn't tell us much. But I went through all the deceased's belongings, and there wasn't a single pair of gloves in the house, let alone one lacking a button. It doesn't prove anything, but it's something to go on.' He put it back into the envelope.

'You're not producing that at the inquest, are you?' Charles asked.

'Oh no, sir,' the inspector replied, smiling. 'The police aren't as thick-headed as that, you know. Our course is to ask for an adjournment. You've never seen anyone wearing gloves with this type of button, I suppose?' They shook their heads. 'No, well, I didn't expect you would have, but there was just a chance of it.' He locked it away again. 'You won't mention that to anyone, if you please, sir.'

'Certainly not.' Charles looked round as the door opened. A man came in with a typewritten document, which he laid before the inspector.

'That's right, Jenkins,' the inspector said. 'That'll be all. Now, sir, would you please read through what you said last night, and see that we've got it down right? And if you'd just tell me your part of the story, Mr Fortescue, I'll take it down, and we shall have everything ship-shape.'

Peter briefly recounted his share in the night's happenings. When he had done Charles put down the typewritten sheets. 'Yes, that's right,' he said. 'Want me to sign it?' He drew out his fountain pen, and scrawled his name at the bottom of the statement. As he screwed the cap on again, he said: 'I don't think, inspector, that when we came to see you the other day you set much store by our tale, but has it occurred to you just where all this points?'

'Yes, sir, it has,' the inspector replied at once. 'And you'll pardon me, but I did set considerable store by what you told me. If I hadn't I wouldn't have been quite so open with you this morning. But you see, what you told me wasn't the first thing I'd heard about the Priory Monk. I've been remarkably interested in him for some time.'

'No good asking you what your previous information was, I suppose?' Charles asked.

'No, sir, I'm afraid it's not. But you can be quite sure I'm not taking the matter lightly. I know what you think. You think that it was the Monk who murdered Duval. Well, it's not for me to give my opinion, lacking any proof, but I would like you, if you will, sir, to try and remember just what Duval said to you about the Monk.'

As well as he could Charles gave the gist of Duval's remarks, but as he warned the inspector, Duval had made so many vague references to that mysterious figure that he found it hard to recollect them all. But on one point his memory was perfectly clear: Duval believed that the only man who had ever seen the Monk's face had been murdered, and he knew that in trying to discover the Monk's identity he was running a great risk. 'So much so,' Charles said, 'that he had taken to carrying a business-like looking knife about with him.'

'Yes, and that raises a question,' Peter put in. 'If he was murdered last night, there must have been a bit of a struggle. The fragment of skin proves that. And you can't chloroform a man without overpowering him first. If the Monk did it, why didn't Duval draw his knife? He must have had time, because as soon as he set eyes on the Monk he'd have been on his guard. The Monk can't have taken him unawares in his own house. Was the knife on him?'

'Yes, sir, it was. But you can look at it in another way. We know from what Duval said to Mr Malcolm here the very night he died that he hadn't seen the Monk's face then. He'd discovered something, but it seems fairly plain it wasn't the Monk. If you think it over, he had precious little time to discover who the Monk was in between the time when Mr Malcolm says he left the Priory, and you found him hanging in his cottage. From the fact of his evidently having been taken by surprise, since he never got the chance to draw his knife, doesn't it look as though whoever it was who went to his cottage didn't go in his disguise of a Monk? Looked at in that light, my reading of the thing is that the person who visited Duval didn't rouse any suspicion in him. He didn't know who the Monk was; some man whom he didn't suspect at all came to his house, possibly with a plausible excuse. He let him in, and before he knew where he was this person had clapped the pad over his face. We'll say there was a struggle: it looks as though the murderer was a pretty strong man. Duval was a bit of a weed, besides being weakened by the dope he took, but you try holding a handkerchief over a man's face when that man's struggling. It's not easy, and a struggle there must have been. But you can understand

Duval trying too hard to wrench his assailant's hand away from his mouth to have time to try and get at his knife. For what it's worth, I found a broken plate in the kitchen, but the place was such a pig-sty there's no saying it was put there by the murderer. Still, it might have been, and we know he set the room to rights when he'd finished Duval. One of the cold-blooded ones, he is: you do find 'em sometimes. He staged the whole thing to look like a suicide, and it's the doctor's opinion he was cute enough to remove any of the pad that may have got into Duval's mouth. But that scrap you saw the doctor extract from Duval's right nostril he missed. The doctor only found it with his forceps. If it hadn't been for that it *would* have looked like a clear case of suicide, especially with a man of Duval's temperament. But a man don't chloroform himself when he sets out to commit suicide by hanging, and even if he did, that's ruled out by the fact that there was no trace of the bottle, nor the pad either. No, it's murder right enough, and if you ask me, murder by some person whom Duval didn't dream was likely to attack him.'

Both men had listened to him in attentive silence. 'If that is so,' Charles said slowly, 'it seems to exonerate Strange. For if I'm not very much mistaken Duval was afraid of Strange.'

'But did he suspect him of being the Monk?' Peter asked.

'No, I don't know that he did, but he thought Strange had something to do with the Monk. At least, so I infer from what he said when he saw Strange come into the bar yesterday morning.'

The inspector was fingering the typewritten statement. 'I wouldn't go about saying Strange did this, sir,' he said slowly.

'Well, naturally not, but you must admit things look pretty black against him. Did you see him after we'd left you last night?'

'Yes, sir, I saw him. You'll understand I can't tell you anything about him, but you can set your mind at rest on one point: there's nothing Strange can do that we shan't know about. So in case you were feeling that we are leaving any dangerous person at large you can be sure that his doings are known to us, and you don't stand in danger from him.'

'I must say, I'm glad to hear you're keeping a watch on him,' Charles said, preparing to get up. 'Well, we mustn't waste your time. If there's nothing else you want me to tell you I think we'd better be pushing off.'

'No, sir, nothing else, only to remind you again not to talk of this. The inquest will be held here at eleven-thirty on Tuesday.'

Charles nodded. 'We'll be here. I take it I shan't be wanted to speak about Duval's fears of the Monk?'

The inspector came as near to a wink as so staid an individual could. 'The coroner won't want to hear any ghost stories, sir,' he said meaningly.

CHAPTER XIV

The news of Duval's death had spread round the neighbourhood as such news does spread, and when it was known that the people to discover the corpse were Charles Malcolm and Peter Fortescue, not only Roote and Colonel Ackerley, but Mr Titmarsh as well, all found excuses to call at the Priory on the chance of picking up some fresh news. The Colonel, who knew the family best, was entirely frank. 'Sheer curiosity, Mrs Malcolm,' he twinkled. 'That's what's brought me up to see you.' But even he could extract nothing more from Charles and Peter than was already known.

Mr Titmarsh said that he had come to inquire how Margaret was after her experience on Thursday; Dr Roote thought that he had left his scarf at the Priory on Saturday evening. And both gentlemen tried their hardest to pump Charles, and went away dissatisfied. On Monday morning Celia met Mrs Pennythorne, the Vicar's wife, in the village shop. Mrs Pennythorne was far too adroit to ask questions, but she greeted Celia most effusively, and said that she had been meaning for some days to ask the whole Priory party over to dinner. As Celia was perfectly well aware of the fact that Mrs Pennythorne did not like her, she was not taken in by this, and she declined the invitation to dine at the Vicarage on the following evening on the score of the inquest, which might last till late. Not to be baulked, Mrs Pennythorne begged her to choose her own day, and she was so persistent that Celia was forced to accept an invitation for Wednesday.

When she broke the news to the family there was an outcry from all but Mrs Bosanquet, who said reprovingly that the Vicar was a most interesting man, and she should be glad of an opportunity of consulting him as to the best method of exorcizing unquiet spirits.

'All right,' Charles said. 'You go, and say the rest of us have developed smallpox.'

'You and I have simply got to go,' Celia said. 'I'd have got out of it if I could, but she just wouldn't take no for an answer. But I really didn't see that it was fair to let you all in for it, so I said I couldn't speak for the rest of you. If Aunt Lilian wants to go surely three of us'll be enough. You don't want to, do you, Margaret?'

'Not much!' Margaret said. 'You're a true friend and sister, Celia. Peter and I will spend a tête-à-tête evening.'

'She may be a true sister, but as a wife she's a stumer,' Charles announced. 'Anyone with a grain of resource would have said that I was so unnerved by finding Duval's body that only complete quiet could restore me.'

'I hardly think she'd have been convinced,' Celia replied. 'By the way, Margaret and I can come to the inquest, can't we?'

'If you like,' Charles answered. 'But it won't be at all interesting.'

Mrs Bosanquet assumed her most disapproving expression. 'If you take my advice, my dears, you will stay quietly at home with me. You do not want people to think you are some of these sensation-hunters we hear so much about nowadays. In my opinion, inquests and murder trials are not things that can interest women of breeding.'

'But this is different, because Chas and Peter are mixed up in it,' Celia objected. 'Besides, everyone's going, even Mr Titmarsh. Colonel Ackerley said that though he didn't want to seem heartless, Framley hasn't had anything so thrilling happen since he came to live here.'

'That may be, my dear, but the Colonel is not a female. Quite the reverse, in fact, for being a soldier I've no doubt he holds human life very cheaply.'

Later in the day Constable Flinders paid them a visit, and shook his head broodingly. 'You ought to have sent for me, sir,' he said reproachfully. 'It would have been a nice case for me to handle, and there's no denying there's precious little scope in Framley for a man who has ambition.'

'Sorry,' Charles said. 'But I thought you were watching him.'

'I can't be everywhere at once, sir, can I? I go and take my eye off him for half a moment, just to make sure that Mr Titmarsh wasn't getting up to mischief, and I'm blessed if he don't go and hang himself. I suppose the next thing'll be I'll find while I been about my ordinary duties that tiresome old bug-hunter – Mr Titmarsh, I should say – has gone and done himself in with his own killing-bottle.'

'Well, that'll give you a case anyhow,' Charles consoled him.

The constable said austerely: 'You mustn't get it into your head, sir, that the police want people to go about killing themselves. All I said was, it's a bit hard that when a Framley man commits sooicide them chaps from Manfield get called in before I hear anything about it. Not that I'm blaming you, sir,' he added handsomely. 'No doubt you done as you see fit, and it isn't everyone who keeps his head on his shoulders when he goes and finds a thing like a corpse.'

The inquest, as Charles had predicted, was not particularly interesting to Celia and Margaret, but those outside the family who had not imagined that any other verdict than suicide would be forthcoming, were in a positive buzz of speculation and wonderment.

Charles and Peter recounted all that they had done, both citing as their reason for visiting Duval's cottage his suspicious presence in their grounds on the night before. The inspector was called, and also Dr Puttock, and the inspector then asked for an adjournment, pending further police inquiries. This was granted, and for the time being the case was over.

'And I vote,' said Peter, 'that we ask old Ackerley in for some tennis this afternoon, and try to get the taste of all this out of our mouths.'

They waited for the Colonel outside the court-room, and when he appeared he readily accepted the invitation. 'I won't ask questions now,' he said, 'but I warn you, I'm all agog to hear a bit more. If you don't want to fall into Mrs Pennythorne's clutches, you'd better get away before she catches you. I saw her making for the door fairly bursting with curiosity.'

'Then let's clear out at once,' Peter said. 'Half-past three suit you, Colonel? We ought to tell you that the court's a terror, and full of docks.'

'Be able to blame it then for my bad shots,' the Colonel said.

They escaped just as the Vicar's wife emerged from the court-room, and drove back to the Priory in time for a late lunch. The Colonel arrived punctually at half-past three, and proved to be a player of considerable standing.

'What a pity we couldn't have got another man!' Celia said when they repaired to the terrace for tea. 'But Dr Roote doesn't look as though he'd be any good, and I can't see Mr Titmarsh standing up to you, Colonel.'

'Give me a mixed double every time,' the Colonel said. 'Much better fun! But I'm out of practice. When I was in India I used to play a lot. I've rather given up of late years.'

'What part of India were you stationed in?' Peter asked. 'I've got a cousin who's just had the luck to be sent to

Wellington.'

'Oh, I've been all over the place,' the Colonel answered. 'But I didn't come here to talk about India, young man. Out with it! Did you know the police thought it was murder?'

'Now then, sir, you ought to know better than to try and drag information out of us,' Charles said. 'Of course I need hardly say that the police perceiving at once that we had missed our vocations, entrusted us with all their secrets. In fact, we're considering entering the force on the strength of it.'

'Yes, yes, but you needn't be so close,' the Colonel said. 'What I can't understand is, who in the world should want to murder that French fellow? Seemed harmless enough, I always thought.'

'I've got a theory about it,' said Charles, helping himself to a cucumber sandwich. 'Who knows but what he may have possessed an oleander hawk-moth? We are all aware that Mr Titmarsh is expending untold energy in his pursuit of this elusive specimen. Very well, then. He found that Duval had one, and so...'

'Really, Chas, I don't think you ought to joke about it,' Celia said. 'It's not exactly decent.'

'Well, why was he in your grounds?' the Colonel asked, not to be put off. 'Was that what he came up to see you about Saturday evening? You know, you're being quite maddening, and it's my belief you know a lot more than you pretend.'

'Of course I do,' said Charles. 'Didn't I say so?'

'Oh, I give you up!' the Colonel said hopelessly. 'All I can say is, I hope it hasn't given you a distaste for the Priory.'

'Not at all,' Charles said, demolishing another sandwich. 'Why should it?'

'I don't know, but after all the business about the ghost which you spoke of some time ago, I was afraid finding a corpse – must have been a bit of a shock, eh? Glad I didn't stumble on it – might rather put the lid on it.'

'A new theory,' Peter remarked. 'The Priory ghost killed Duval. You'll be making my sister nervous, if you're not careful, sir.'

'Well, I wouldn't do that for the world,' said the Colonel gallantly, and began at once to talk of something else.

But it seemed as though no conversation could for long steer clear of the problems besetting the owners of the Priory. The Colonel's talk led to a description of a round of golf he had played the day before, and since his partner had been Michael Strange it was not surprising that he began to talk about him. 'Seems a nice chap,' he said. 'How do you get on with him?'

'We hardly know him,' Celia replied.

'He's played golf with me once or twice,' the Colonel said. 'Retiring sort of fellow, but I always feel sorry for people taking a holiday by themselves. Dull work, what? What's his job by the way? Haven't liked to ask him outright since he seemed so uncommunicative. Wondered whether, like so many poor fellows since the war, he's had to take up some rotten thing like selling from house to house. Distressing, the number of sahibs who are doing jobs they wouldn't have touched in 1914.'

'I'm afraid we can't tell you anything about him,' Celia said. 'We've really only met him to talk to once, and that was at your party.' She looked round. 'Will anyone have any more tea? No? Then what about another set?'

The next day passed quietly enough, and was only marred, Charles said, by the prospect of having to go to dinner with the Pennythornes. He spoke bitterly on the subject of people who shirked their clear duty, but his words made not the slightest impression on either Peter or Margaret.

'We shall be with you in spirit,' Peter told him, but so

far from consoling Charles this assurance provoked him to embark on a denunciation of his brother-in-law's character, which was only stopped by Celia hustling him upstairs to change into his dress clothes.

Peter and Margaret enjoyed a tête-à-tête meal, and sat down afterwards in the library to play piquet together. After three hard-fought rubbers they gave it up, and to Margaret's dismay Peter, instead of retiring as he usually did, into a book, showed a disposition to talk. She had a shrewd idea whither his conversation would lead, and she was not mistaken. In a very short time Peter, busy with the filling of a pipe, tackled her bluntly. 'I say, Sis, mind if I ask you a question?'

She minded very much indeed, but she had to say No.

'We've always been pretty frank with each other,' Peter said, 'or I wouldn't ask. But aren't you a bit more interested in that fellow Strange than you pretend to be?'

Margaret reflected gloomily on the manifold failings of the male sex, and decided that the worst of these was the appallingly blunt questions men asked. 'I don't think so,' she replied. 'I must say I do rather like him. I'm sorry you've got such a down on him. Does he wear the wrong kind of tie?'

Peter refused to be put off by such flippancy. 'I don't want to be officious,' he explained painstakingly, 'and I don't say for a moment that you aren't quite capable of looking after yourself, but I have got a distinct impression that Strange has got on your soft side. Am I right?'

'Very seldom,' Margaret retorted. 'But I've already said I like the man. Perhaps that's partly your fault, because you and Chas run him down so much.'

'Rot!' Peter said sweepingly. 'All Charles and I have said is that Strange behaves in a way that can't be described as anything but fishy. You must admit that he does.'

Margaret was silent. Peter struck a match and said

between puffs: 'I've a suspicion you've seen rather more of the fellow than I have. Has he ever told you anything about himself?'

She could answer that quite truthfully. 'No.'

'Well, has he ever said anything to make you think that we're on the wrong track about him?'

She thought for a moment, wondering how much she could divulge without breaking her word to Strange. Peter had always been her confidant, more so than Celia, who was older, and who no longer lived with them, and never till now had she kept anything from him. It was uncomfortable to be so torn between two feelings, uncomfortable and unaccustomed. Yet something deeper than her friendship with her brother now had her in its hold, and even while one part of her longed to tell him everything, the other prompted her to keep silence. She looked up to find that Peter was regarding her steadily. She coloured, and said: 'It's very hard to say. But from – things he has said to me I do feel perfectly sure that whatever he may be doing he doesn't want to hurt or alarm us in any way.'

Peter's brows rose. 'Really? Then he admits he's at the bottom of our mystery?'

'No. He never said that. But he did say that he wished we would leave the Priory. I think I can safely tell you that.'

'Did he, indeed? Any reason?'

She hesitated. 'N-no. Only that – he didn't want us to be in any danger.'

'Think he was responsible for that skeleton?'

'I don't know, Peter,' she said honestly.

He smoked in silence for a while. At last he said: 'Don't you see, Sis, that what you've told me practically proves that my suspicions aren't by any means groundless?'

'In a way I do, but... Look here, Peter, you know I'm not the sort of silly fool who gasses about intuition and all that sort of rot, don't you?'

He grinned. 'Yes, thank God!'

'Well, I'm not, but I don't mind admitting that about Strange I have got an absolute conviction that he isn't out to harm any of us. I agree he's being mysterious, and I agree that for some reason or other he may want to get us out of this place. But I don't believe the reason is a bit what you think.'

'My dear girl, I don't know what to think!'

'No, but you've got an idea that he's a wrong 'un. And that's where I think you're mistaken. If he wants to get possession of this house it's for some purpose we've none of us guessed.'

He hunched his shoulders lower in his chair. 'Quite sure you aren't being a bit led away by a personable exterior?'

'Ever known me fall for a handsome face?'

'I haven't, but I shouldn't like to swear that you never would. And I grant you Strange is a nice-looking chap, and a powerful-looking one too, which as far as I can make out is what most women like in a man.'

'Well, if that's the line you mean to stick to it's not much good my arguing,' Margaret said with some asperity.

Conversation showed a tendency to flag after that. Presently Peter said: 'One thing that seems to me to stand out a mile is that you're keeping something up your sleeve. Not cricket, Sis.'

'Oh, shut up!' Margaret said crossly. 'Even supposing I were I don't see that it makes much odds now that you've told the police the whole story.'

'If you know anything about Strange that we don't, it might help the police considerably.'

'I haven't the smallest desire to help the police,' Margaret replied. 'I hate policemen: they come nosing round after wireless licences, and tell you you don't know how to drive your car just because you misunderstand their silly signals. Anyway, I don't want to talk about Michael Strange any more.' She gave a little shiver. 'I say, don't you think it's beastly cold?'

'It is chilly,' he agreed. 'Wind's in the north. Like me to shut the window?'

'You might push it to just a bit. It'll get airless if we have it completely shut. I've half a mind to put a match to the fire. Look and see if there's any coal in the scuttle.'

He lifted the lid. 'Empty. We can soon get some though, if you really want a fire. Seems ridiculous in July, I must say.'

'Nothing's ridiculous with the English climate. Honestly, wouldn't you rather like a fire?'

'I don't mind one way or the other. If you're cold, have one.' He reached out a hand to the bell-pull, and tugged it.

'It's broken,' Margaret informed him. 'Celia didn't think it was worth while having it mended. If you take the scuttle out to the kitchen Bowers'll fill it, and bring it back.'

'All right,' he said obligingly. 'Though you're a pest, you know.' He dragged himself out of his chair and picked up the scuttle. 'This is where an electric heater would come in handy.'

'Oh no, think how cheery it'll be to see a blaze!' Margaret encouraged him.

He went out, and she picked up the matches and knelt down before the wide grate. A fire had already been laid, and enough coal to start it had been arranged on top of the wood. Margaret lit the edges of the newspaper, and had the satisfaction of hearing, in a few seconds, a promising crackle. The wood was dry, and caught easily, and Margaret, seeing that no frenzied fanning was going to be necessary, got up from her knees. She put out her hand to help herself up by one of the projecting bits of the moulding that ran round the fireplace, and to her surprise the carved wooden apple that her fingers had grasped twisted right round. She stared at it, and then quickly looked round the room, remembering the rosette that had moved to slide back the panel of the priest's hole.

Beside the fireplace a dark cavity yawned in the panelling.

She scrambled up, and forgetting that Peter had gone through the door that led to the servants' quarters, called to him. 'Peter, come here quickly!'

Then she remembered that he could not hear her, and she stood for a minute, looking at the gap in the panels. Not for worlds, she thought, would she venture inside until Peter came back, but sheer curiosity impelled her to tiptoe towards it, and try to peep in.

It was so dark that she could only see that it seemed to be a narrow stone stairway, leading up in the thickness of the wall. The central lamp threw its light so that it only illumined the step immediately in a line with the opening, and the stone wall beyond. Margaret could not see more than the dim outline of another step leading downwards. She was half afraid that some horrible skeleton might be inside, but she could not perceive anything of that nature. Holding with one hand to the edge of the panel, she ventured to step just inside, in the hope of being able to see where the stairs led. Leaning her other hand against the wall she craned forward trying to pierce the darkness below her. She moved her right hand from the wall to feel ahead of her, wondering whether she was really standing on a staircase, or whether it was only another priest's hole. Her hand did not, as she had half expected, encounter another wall, but to her annoyance a gold bangle that she wore and whose clasp she had been meaning to have strengthened, came undone, and fell with a tinkle on to the second step, which she could just perceive. Involuntarily she stooped to pick it up, but to reach it she had to let go of the panel she still held, and take one step down on to the second stair. Her fingers had closed on the bangle and she was about to step back on to the level of the library floor when she was startled to see the shaft of light cast by the lamp in the room disappearing. She turned like a flash, and saw to her horror that the panel was sliding noiselessly back into place.

She flung herself forward, but she was too late. The panel had closed, and she was in utter darkness.

In the terror of finding herself a prisoner she lost her head, and shrieked for her brother, beating wildly on the back of the panel, trying to tear it open. She only succeeded in breaking a finger-nail, and her panic grew. She screamed, 'Help! help! Peter, Peter, Peter!'

Somewhere below her she heard a soft, padding step, and the hush of a robe brushing against the wall. Like a mad woman she clawed at the panel. 'Quick! oh quick! Peter, *help*!'

Then in the darkness a gloved hand stole across her mouth, and an arm in a wide sleeve was round her, holding her in a vice.

She tried to break free, to jerk her head away, but her arms were clamped to her sides and that horrible gloved hand was like a gag over her mouth.

She felt herself slipping into unconsciousness, and through the sudden roaring in her ears she heard as though from a great distance Peter's voice calling: 'Margaret, what is it? Where are you?'

A low, inhuman chuckle sounded immediately above her head, and there was something so gloating and fiendish in that soft sound that terror such as she had never known seized her. Then the waves met over her head and she fainted.

CHAPTER XV

As he came into the hall from the servants' wing Peter heard Margaret's scream. It sounded muffled, but he heard her shriek his name, and crossed the hall in three bounds.

'Margaret, what is it?' he cried. 'Where are you? Margaret! Margaret!'

The room was empty, and no answering call came to him. He stared round, then sprang instinctively to the window, only to find that the falling bolt was as he had left it, just holding the double windows together. She could not have gone that way, and hardly knowing what he did he tore the curtains apart and dragged the big leather screen aside. But she was not in the room. Yet a moment before he had heard her voice coming from this direction: she could not have gone far!

'Think! think!' drummed his brain. 'Don't lose your head! Think!'

He came back into the middle of the room, and as he once more glared round for some clue to her whereabouts his eye caught sight of a crumpled handkerchief lying near the wall beside the fireplace. Quickly he crossed to where it lay, and picked it up. It was one of the flimsy scraps of crêpe-de-chine she always used; he had returned it to her twice already this evening, for she invariably dropped it about.

His thoughts raced. She had been sitting on the other side of the fireplace all the evening; if she had dropped her handkerchief here she must for some reason or other have moved to this spot after he had left the room. What could have taken her there? His eyes ran swiftly over that side of the room. Not a book, for the shelves were on the opposite wall; nor the coal-scuttle, for he had taken that away. She must have stepped close up to the wall, too, for the handkerchief had been touching the wainscoting. Light began to break on Peter. She hadn't gone out by the window; she hadn't gone by the door, since when she screamed he had just come back into the hall, and must have seen her had she left the room by that exit. There remained only one solution: somewhere in the room was a secret entrance that they had none of them discovered.

He at once inspected the panelling, and went to the place where the handkerchief had lain, and sounded the panels all along that side of the fireplace. It was hard at first to detect a difference, but by dint of repeated banging on two panels he was almost sure that one had a different, and more hollow note. It was probably padded on the inside to disguise it, he guessed, and he began to feel all round the beading for any catch there might be. Some echo of Margaret's frantic cry still seemed to sound in his ears, and his hands moved with feverish haste over the woodwork. She must have accidentally discovered the moving panel, and then – what had happened? A rather sickening fear stole into him; his fingers tore fruitlessly at the beading; he even set his shoulder to the panel in a vain attempt to break it down. His reason checked him once more. It was no use getting desperate: he must think, and think quickly. How had she discovered the panel? Not by design, that much was certain. By accident it must have been, and what could she have been doing that led her to put her hand on the spring that worked it?

His gaze, searching the room, fell on the fire, which was now burning brightly. Of course! She had been lighting the fire! What a fool he was not to have remembered that earlier! He strode up to the grate, and as he bent to scrutinize it there flashed into his mind the recollection of the rosette that had moved to slide back the panel into the priest's hole at the top of the stairs. If another such hole existed it was almost certain that it was worked by the same sort of device.

He fell on his knees, wrenching and twisting at the carved surround of the grate. It was a garland in a design of apples and pomegranates and leaves. Inch by inch he went over it, his heart sinking as leaf after leaf, fruit after fruit remained immovable under his probing fingers. Then, when only one more cluster remained untested he found the wooden apple that turned, and almost let out a yell of triumph as it slid in his hold.

His eyes were fixed on the panel he suspected, and even as he turned the apple, he saw it glide back to reveal the same dark cavity that had startled Margaret.

He sprang to his feet. His only thought was to get to his sister; even had it entered his head in that moment of anxiety he would not have paused to fetch his revolver, upstairs, locked in a drawer of his dressing-table. Without stopping to consider he was through the aperture, and standing on the first step. 'Margaret!' he shouted. 'Margaret, Margaret! Where are you?'

There was a faint movement behind him, he started round, but just a second too late. Something struck him a stunning blow on the head, and he fell without a sound, sprawling down the narrow stairs. A moment later a cowled figure moved across the aperture, and then once more the panel slid back into place, and the library was empty and silent.

Five minutes afterwards Bowers came into the room with the coal-scuttle. He looked round, rather surprised to see no one, but concluded that Peter and Margaret had either strolled out into the moonlight, or were in some other room. He made up the fire, and then went over to draw the curtains. He wondered why they had been pulled aside, for he distinctly remembered drawing them while his young master and mistress were still in the dining-room. As he pulled them together he noticed the position of the double French windows, which though open, had been set so that the falling-bolt just held them together, and prevented them swinging wide into the room. If Peter and Margaret had gone out, it was not by that way. He supposed they must have gone by the front door, perhaps meaning to stroll down the avenue to meet the rest of their party who would soon be returning from their dinner engagement. Funny tastes people had, Bowers reflected. As for him he'd do anything sooner than walk down that avenue after dark.

He began to tidy the room, shaking up cushions, and emptying the ash trays. The screen seemed to be out of place; he adjusted it carefully, and straightened the position of one of the chairs. Glancing at the clock he saw that it was already after ten, and time for him to bring in the usual tray of glasses, whisky decanter, soda-siphon and lemonade. With a final look round the room he went away to the pantry to prepare the tray. By the time he had collected the decanter from the dining-room, and returned to the library, ten minutes had gone by. Since there was still no sign of Peter or Margaret it seemed certain that they must have gone out. In which case, Bowers thought, remembering his friend Flinders' warning, it was very unwise of them to have left the window open. He moved across to it, and not only shut it, but bolted it as well. Then he went back again to the kitchen, where Mrs Bowers was folding up her crochet-work preparatory to going to bed.

'Locked everything up, Bowers?' inquired that martial woman.

'All but the front door,' he replied. 'Lot of use it was me having to go down those cellar stairs for a scuttle-full of coal! They've gone out.'

'Gone out?' Mrs Bowers echoed. 'At this time of night?'

'Must have. Neither of them was in the library when I went in with the scuttle, nor when I took the tray in.'

'Well, that's not like Miss Margaret to want a fire one moment and then go trapesing out in the garden the next,' remarked Mrs Bowers. 'They're probably in the study.'

'What would they go and sit there for, when they've lit a fire in the library?' Bowers demanded.

'Don't ask *me*!' his wife abjured him. 'But if that's what they are doing all I can say is Miss Margaret'll catch her death, and start one of her coughs, for it's the coldest room in the house. I think I'll go along and see what she is up to.' She got out of her chair, not without effort, for she was a lady of ample proportions, and sailed away to scold Margaret for her imprudence.

But the study was in darkness, and Mrs Bowers' opening gambit of 'Now, Miss Margaret, you know you didn't ought to sit in this cold room,' was cut off short. Mrs Bowers went across to the library; that was empty too, and so were both the drawing and dining-rooms.

Bowers had followed his wife into the front part of the house by this time, and he again repeated his own conviction that they had strolled out.

'What, after Mr Peter saying Miss Margaret was feeling shivery, and would like a fire? Stuff and nonsense!'

'Well, if they haven't gone out, where are they?' Bowers asked reasonably. 'Perhaps Mr Peter thought a walk would warm his sister up.'

'If he thought anything so silly he'll have a few straight words with me when he comes in, grown up or not!' declared Mrs Bowers with a look in her eye that all the Fortescues had been familiar with since babyhood. 'Bowers, my man, just you pop up and knock on their bedroom doors to make sure they're not there.'

'Well, they aren't, because they haven't taken their candles,' said Bowers, pointing to the array on the hall table.

'Never you mind whether they've taken candles or not, you go up and see,' commanded his wife.

Sighing, Bowers obeyed, but he soon reappeared with the intelligence that it was just as he had said: no one was upstairs. 'I tell you what,' he said. 'They've gone to meet the others, and they wanted the fire lit for when they come in.'

'It does look like it,' Mrs Bowers admitted. 'And if that's what they have done, I'm not going up myself till they're in. I know Miss Margaret, none better! Never was there a child like her for catching colds, and the first thing she'll do when she gets in is to pop right into bed with a hot bottle, or my name's not Emma Bowers.' With that she proceeded majestically back to the kitchen, and resumed her seat by the fire. She picked up her crochet again, but her eyes kept lifting to the clock on the mantelpiece, and when the hands pointed to eleven, she could no longer contain herself. 'I'll give Mr Peter a piece of my mind when he comes in!' she said wrathfully. 'When did you take that scuttle to the library, Bowers?'

'I dunno. Bit after ten, I think,' Bowers answered, deep in the racing columns of a newspaper.

'Then they've been out a full hour! I never did in all my life! Hark, was that the front door? For the love of goodness, stop reading that nasty trash!'

Bowers put the paper down meekly, and listened. Voices sounded in the hall. 'That's the master I can hear,' he said.

Mrs Bowers once more arose and sallied forth. In the hall Mrs Bosanquet was unwinding the inevitable tulle from her head. As Mrs Bowers came into the hall Charles said: 'Ten o'clock would have been a godly hour at which to have taken our leave. I shall never forgive you, Aunt Lilian. Never.'

'I'm sorry if you were anxious to go, my dear,' was the

placid reply, 'but I was in the middle of a very interesting discussion with the Vicar. I found him most enlightened: not in the least hide-bound, as I had feared might be the case.'

Celia saw Mrs Bowers. 'Hullo, still up, Emma?' she said.

'Miss Celia, where's Miss Margaret and Mr Peter? Didn't you meet them?'

'Meet them? No, did they set out to look for us?'

'That's what we don't know, madam. Bowers thought so, but I said all along they wouldn't do a thing like that on a night as cold as this is. All I do know is, they aren't in the house.'

'What's that?' Charles stopped arguing with Mrs Bosanquet, and stepped to his wife's side. 'When did they go out?'

'It must have been about ten o'clock, sir, from what Bowers tells me.'

'But how funny!' said Celia. 'What in the world can have possessed them? Do you suppose they got bored, and went to look up the Colonel?'

'Well, Miss Celia, they may have done so, but all I can say is it's not like Miss Margaret to go ordering a fire to be lit if she means to go out the moment it's done.'

'A fire? Did she order a fire?' Charles asked.

'Yes, sir, she did. Mr Peter came out to the kitchen with the library scuttle, which was empty.' She looked over her shoulder at Bowers. 'Round about ten o'clock that would have been, wouldn't it, Bowers?'

'Just about then, or maybe a minute or two after,' Bowers agreed.

'But you say they went out at ten,' frowned Charles.

'So they must have, sir,' Bowers replied. 'Because it didn't take me more than five minutes to fill the scuttle, and when I took it back to the library, which I did straight away, there wasn't a sign of either of them. I

218

didn't set much store by it, but when I came back with the tray ten minutes after that, and they still weren't there, I did think it was a bit funny, and I mentioned it to Mrs Bowers, just in a casual way.'

'Perhaps Margaret has induced her brother to walk up to the ruin by moonlight,' suggested Mrs Bosanquet, who had caught perhaps half of what had been said. 'It is a very clear night, but I must say I think it was imprudent of the dear child to go out with the wind in the north as it is.'

'My dear Aunt Lilian, they wouldn't spend an hour at the chapel!' Charles said.

'An hour! No, certainly not. But have they been gone for so long as that?'

Celia was looking at her husband. 'Charles, you're worried?'

'I am a bit,' he confessed. 'I can't see why they should want to go out like that. No one came to the house during the evening, I suppose?'

'No, sir, no one to my knowledge. That is, no one rang the front-door bell, nor yet the back either.'

'They *must* have gone to the Colonel's!' Celia said.

'Then what did they want a fire for, Miss Celia?' struck in Mrs Bowers.

'Perhaps they thought it was such a sudden change in the weather that we might be cold after our drive,' Celia suggested.

'No, madam, they never thought that, for as I was just saying to Bowers, Mr Peter brought that scuttle out, and said Miss Margaret was feeling shivery, and was going to light the fire. Which she must have done – unless you did, Bowers?'

'No, I never lit it,' Bowers answered. 'It was burning up fine when I brought the scuttle in.'

Charles strode over to the library, and went in. 'Windows been shut all the evening?' he asked.

'No, sir. When I came in I found them just held

219

together. I'll show you, sir.' He drew back the bolts, and placed the windows as Peter had left them. 'Like that, sir.'

'I see. With the bolt holding them together?'

'Yes, sir. I particularly noticed that, because I saw by it that they couldn't have gone out on to the terrace.'

'You didn't notice anything else out of the ordinary? Nothing was disturbed?'

'Well, sir, things were a bit untidy, but only in a natural way, if you understand me. Ash trays full, and the paper on the floor, and the cushions a bit squashed. Nothing else, sir.'

Celia laid her hand on Charles' arm. 'Charles, you don't think anything can have happened to them, do you?' she asked anxiously.

'I hope not, but I don't quite like the sound of it. Can you think of any reason for them wanting to go out at ten o'clock?'

'No, I can't. Unless Aunt Lilian's solution is the right one. After all, we never did go up to the chapel by moonlight, and Margaret more than once said she'd like to.'

'I'd better go up and take a look,' Charles decided. 'You others might search the house – though why they should conceal themselves I can't imagine.'

'Charles, take your revolver!' Celia called after him, as he left the room.

'I'm going to,' he said over his shoulder.

It was quite a little walk to the chapel from the house, and he did not come back for nearly twenty minutes. They had heard his voice occasionally, shouting the names of the missing couple, but no answering call had come to their ears. Both Celia and Mrs Bosanquet were feeling very anxious by the time he returned, and when he shook his head in answer to their eager inquiries they began to look rather scared.

'But it is quite ridiculous!' Mrs Bosanquet said. 'They

must be somewhere!'

'Undoubtedly,' said Charles. 'But where? You've been all over the house?'

'Yes, there's no sign of them,' Celia replied. 'You – don't think they can have gone up to the ruin, and – and found the Monk, and he – did something to them?'

'I should hope it would take more than that dratted Monk to tackle the pair of them!' snorted Mrs Bowers.

But the idea was taking hold of Celia. 'Supposing he had a gun?'

'If Peter had any sense he wouldn't take Margaret up to the chapel at night without his revolver,' Charles said. 'I'll go and look in his room, and see if it's in his dressing-table. That's where he keeps it.' He went out, but this time he was soon back again, and in his hand he carried Peter's revolver. Looking distinctly grim he laid it down on the table.

Celia's fingers gripped the arms of the chair she had sunk into. 'Then they were unarmed! Charles, it's the Monk! I know it's the Monk! Oh, fool, *fool* that I was to suggest they should stay here alone this evening.'

'Steady!' Charles said. 'Don't leap to conclusions, Celia. For all we know they had a perfectly good reason for going out, and they'll walk in any moment. They may even have walked down the road to meet us, as Bowers suggested, and we missed them.'

'How could we miss them?'

'Easily. We were all talking, and I for one never scrutinize pedestrians.'

'But they'd have stopped us!' Celia pointed out.

'Not necessarily. You must remember that our head-lights were on, and the glare would prevent them recognizing the car till it was abreast of them. And I was driving pretty fast, too. They may have called to us, and failed to make us hear.'

Celia looked at the time. 'But, darling, it's a quarter to

twelve, and we've been in three-quarters of an hour! They must have got back by now. Why, if they set out at ten they've had time to get as far as the Vicarage and back again by now!'

'No, not quite,' Charles said. 'Not that I see either of them walking all that distance just to meet us. I'll tell you what: I think I'd better get the car out of the garage again, and run back as far as the Vicarage, just in case they were cracked enough to walk as far as that, and have met with some accident. Sprained ankle, or something of that sort. Then if I don't find them I'll go in to Ackerley's place, and ring up the police-station from there, and bring Ackerley himself along to help me search.' He picked up Peter's revolver. 'Bowers, you know how to handle this, don't you?'

'Yes, sir,' Bowers answered, taking it.

'I want you to stay in this room with Mrs Malcolm and Mrs Bosanquet, and on no account to leave them. Quite understand?'

'Don't you worry, sir!' Mrs Bowers said, picking up the poker. 'I just wish that Monk *would* come in, that's all! I'd Monk him!'

Celia nodded bravely. 'Yes, that will be best. Don't waste any time, Charles: we shall be all right. There's nothing we can do while you're gone, is there? It's so awful to have to sit here so helplessly.'

Charles was buttoning up his overcoat again. 'I'd rather you stayed all together in this room,' he said. 'I daresay there's no reason for me to be alarmed about you, but I'm not taking any more risks. I'll be back as soon as I possibly can.' He bent and kissed Celia's pale lips. 'Keep your pecker up, old lady. I shall probably meet them in the avenue.' He hurried away as he spoke, and the next instant they heard the front door bang behind him.

Charles went quickly round to the garage, and got the car out. He laid his revolver on the seat beside him, and

222

after backing and turning the car, drove off down the avenue to the gates.

The Vicarage lay on the other side of the village, and Charles drove through the narrow, deserted street at a pace that made a solitary pedestrian leap out of harm's way. There was no sign of Peter and Margaret anywhere along the road, and since they had pleaded a previous engagement as their excuse for not joining the dinner-party that evening, they would certainly not have gone into the Vicarage. Moreover the house was in darkness, and seeing this, Charles turned the car, and started to drive back the way he had come.

In the village street he overtook a bicyclist, and his powerful headlights showed this late plodder to be Constable Flinders. Charles drew up beside him. 'I've got your case for you, Flinders,' he said. 'Can you leave that bicycle, and come up to the Priory?'

Mr Flinders stared at him. 'Lor', sir, what's happened?'

'Mr and Miss Fortescue have disappeared, and I'd like you to go up and stand guard over my wife and aunt. Leave – no, shove it on the back seat. Can you?'

'Me bike, sir? It'll dirty your cushions, won't it?' the constable said dubiously.

'What the hell does that matter? Lift it in.'

'Well, if you say so, sir, I will,' the constable said, and hoisted his bicycle into the back of the car. He then got in beside Charles, and instinctively grasped the seat with both hands as the car shot forward. 'Sir,' he said solemnly, 'if I was on dooty and saw you driving like this I should have to run you in. I should really, sir.'

'No doubt, but I happen to be in a hurry. Now look here, this is what has happened.' Briefly he told Flinders of his brother's and sister-in-law's unaccountable disappearance.

The constable listened in open-mouthed astonishment, and at the end of it collected his wits sufficiently to say:

'Well, one thing I can tell you, sir. It ain't Mr Titmarsh, for he's not been out of his house the whole evening.'

'I didn't suppose it was,' said Charles impatiently.

'No, sir,' said the constable, rather hurt, 'but it narrows it down, so to speak, don't it, when we know for certain it wasn't him?'

'When we get to the Priory,' Charles said, paying no heed to this, 'I'll put you down, and you can cycle up to the house and wait for me there. I'm going on to Colonel Ackerley's house to telephone to Manfield, and I hope to bring the Colonel back with me to help search the grounds.'

'Do I understand you to mean, sir, that you mean to call in them chaps at the police-station?'

'You do.'

The constable coughed. 'In a manner of speaking, sir, that should have been left for me to do, if I see fit.'

'I'm afraid you'll have to overlook the irregularity for once,' Charles replied, pulling up at the Priory gates.

The constable got out, and extricated his bicycle from the back of the car. 'Very irregular, sir, that's what it is,' he said. 'I don't hardly know what to say about it.'

'Think it out on your way up to the house,' Charles advised him, and drove on while this retort was slowly filtering through to the constable's brain.

No light shone from any window in the White House, but since it was now some time past midnight Charles had hardly expected the Colonel to be still up. He drove to the front door, switched off his engine, and got out, thrusting his unwieldy gun into the deep pocket of his overcoat. He found the electric bell, and pressed it. He heard it ring somewhere inside the house, and kept his finger on it for some time.

Nothing happened. Charles rang again, and beat a loud tattoo on the door with the rather ornate knocker. There was still no answer. The Colonel must be a heavy sleeper,

Charles thought, and remembered that Ackerley's butler and cook slept over the garage, a few yards from the house. He stepped back into the drive, and scanned the upper windows, wondering which was the Colonel's room. Setting his hands to form a funnel round his mouth he shouted: 'Colonel! Colonel Ackerley!'

No answer came from the house, but a light showed above the garage, and presently a window was thrown up there, and a voice called: 'Who is it? What do you want?'

Charles walked along till he stood under this window. The Colonel's butler was leaning out. 'I want to use the Colonel's telephone,' Charles said. 'It's very urgent. Is he in?'

'I'm sure I don't know, sir,' the butler answered rather sulkily. 'Who *are* you?'

'Charles Malcolm, from the Priory. I can't make the Colonel hear at the house. Think you could come down and let me in?'

The butler's voice changed. 'Mr Malcolm! I beg your pardon, sir: I didn't recognize you. Yes, sir, I'll be down in just a moment if you wouldn't mind waiting.'

He drew in his head, and Charles paced up and down in front of the house in a fret of impatience. Presently the butler came down, having pulled on a pair of trousers and a coat. 'Sorry to keep you, sir. You wish to use the telephone? I hope nothing serious, sir?'

'It is rather. Is the Colonel out, or just a heavy sleeper?'

'I expect he's out, sir. He very often goes out after dinner. I believe he plays bridge at the County Club at Manfield, sir.'

'Very late to be still at the club, surely?'

'The Colonel never goes to bed much before midnight, sir. And, of course, I don't know when he comes in, as I don't sleep in the house.' He inserted a key into the Yale lock of the front door, and turned it. 'If you'll excuse me, sir, I'll go first and switch on the light. The telephone is in the study, sir. This way, please.'

He ushered Charles into the Colonel's sanctum, and discreetly left him there, shutting the door as he went out.

It did not take Charles long to get connected with the police-station and he was lucky enough to find someone intelligent on duty. This officer said that he would get on to the inspector at once, and he promised that a couple of men should be sent off to the Priory as soon as the inspector was informed of what had occurred.

Charles hung up the receiver, and was just about to leave the room when an idea struck him, and he lifted the receiver off its hook again. When the exchange spoke he gave the number of the Bell Inn, and waited.

After a considerable pause, he heard Spindle's unmistakable voice. ''Ullo! Bell Inn. 'Oo is it?'

'Malcolm speaking, from the Priory. Would you please ask Mr Strange to come to the telephone?'

''Old on, please,' said the voice.

Another, and longer pause, followed. Then Spindle spoke again. ''Ullo, are you there? Mr Strange is not in his room, sir. Can I take a message?'

'Are you sure he's not in the lounge?' Charles asked.

'No, sir, I've bin to see. Mr Strange is out.'

'Where's he gone?'

'I couldn't say, sir. 'E 'as 'is own key, you see, because 'e told Mr Wilkes 'e'd got friends in Manfield, and 'e'd be visiting them a good deal, and staying late. Lots of gentlemen prefers to 'ave a key, because I go off duty at one o'clock, sir, you see.'

'I see,' Charles said. 'No, there's no message, thanks. Sorry to have bothered you. Good-bye.' He hung up the receiver again, and went out into the hall, where the butler was waiting.

'That's all,' Charles said. 'Will you explain to the Colonel that I had to telephone very urgently? I'm sure he'll understand. And thanks very much for coming down to let me in.'

'Thank *you*, sir,' the butler said, pocketing the douceur. 'The Colonel will be sorry he wasn't in, I know.' He accompanied Charles out into the drive again, and watched him get into the car. Charles bade him good night, and set off again for home.

He did not put the car in the garage this time, but left it standing outside the front door. In the library Constable Flinders was trying to avoid Mrs Bowers' indignant glare, and at the same time to prove himself master of the situation.

Celia looked up anxiously. 'No luck?'

'None. I got on to Manfield, and they're sending over at once. Then I rang up the Bell Inn, and asked to speak to Strange.' He took off his overcoat, and Celia saw that his good-humoured countenance was looking decidedly grim. 'And Strange,' he said, 'is not there.'

CHAPTER XVI

Someone was calling him. Peter could hear his name being spoken, but the voice was very far away. He became aware of a dull ache in his head, and opened his eyes with a groan. The voice sounded nearer; he identified it gradually as his sister's, and as the mist cleared from before his eyes he saw her face above him. Puzzled, he stared up at her. She was stroking his cheek. 'Darling, you're better now, aren't you? Peter, speak to me, please speak to me!'

He blinked; his head was splitting, he thought. He said thickly: 'Hullo... Margaret! What – what's happened?'

She appeared to be crying. 'Oh, thank God!' she said. 'I thought you were dead. Oh, my dear, how did he get you?'

He moved his head, staring round him. He was lying on a bare stone floor, in a queer cell-like room which he never remembered to have seen before. His brain felt clogged, but bit by bit his memory was returning. He struggled up on his elbow, grasping Margaret's wrist. 'You called me!' he said. 'I couldn't find you. Then I . . .' He broke off, as the whole scene came rushing back to him. 'My God, where are we?' he said. 'What happened to you?' He put his hand to his head feeling it tenderly. 'Lord, my head! Something must have knocked me out. How did I get here? How did you get here?'

She helped him to his feet. He was still feeling sick and dizzy, and was glad to sink down on to a chair by the plain deal table, and to rest his head in his hands. Margaret knelt beside him. 'It was the Monk,' she said.

'I heard you call,' he said. 'Couldn't find you. Then I saw your handkerchief.'

'Where?' she asked.

'By the panel. Made me think. Realized there must be a way we hadn't found. Got on to the moulding. An apple. Did you twist it?'

'Yes, yes. By the fireplace. And then?'

'Saw the panel move. So anxious about you, like a fool never stopped to think. Dashed in. Shouted to you. Then...' He stopped, frowning. 'Yes, I heard something behind me. I think I turned round. I don't remember anything else. What happened to you? How did you get here? Who brought me here?'

She glanced fearfully over her shoulder at the door of their prison. It was shut, but a steel grille at the height of a man's head was let into it. A sort of shutter with round holes cut in it was drawn across the grille on the outside. She turned back to Peter, and slid her hand into his. 'When you'd gone I knelt down and lit the fire. Then I started to get up, and you know how you put out your hand to steady yourself? Well, I did that, and caught on to the apple in the carving. It moved, and I saw the opening in the wall, just as you did. I called you, but you'd gone. I never meant to go in, but there didn't seem to be anything there, and I did just step inside, holding on to the panel all the time. Peter, it was a staircase! Did you realize that?'

'Yes, I remember thinking in a flash how that was what Duval must have meant when he said the Monk went up and down the stairs though we didn't see. Go on: what happened next?'

She shuddered. 'It was so awful...my bangle – you know the one – came undone, and fell on to the second step. I didn't stop to think: I never dreamed – anyone was there. I let go the panel and just stepped down one stair to pick it up.' Her fingers clung suddenly to his hand. 'Peter, I saw the light going, and I turned round, and the panel was closing! Peter! I nearly went mad! I couldn't stop it, and that's when I screamed. I tried to tear it open; it was pitch dark, and I couldn't see any catch, or feel anything. I shrieked for you again and again. Then – then I heard something moving.' She was shaking like a leaf. He put his arm round her, clumsily patting her shoulder. 'A sort of padding footstep, coming nearer and nearer. And I couldn't see, couldn't move that awful panel. Then – I felt something creep over my mouth. It felt horrible, horrible! Then I knew it was a hand in a glove. It gripped my face so that I could hardly breathe, and an arm grasped me round above the elbows. I couldn't move, I heard you call out to me from the library, and then – then, there was a fiendish sort of chuckle, quite soft, but so utterly wicked, and cruel, that it just finished me, and I fainted. When I came to I was in this place, quite alone. I didn't know how I got here, or who that hand belonged to – or – or how long I'd been here till the door opened, and I saw the Monk standing there. He didn't speak; he looked at me for a moment through those slits in his cowl, then he turned and bent down and started to drag something in. It was you, Peter, and oh, I thought you were dead, I thought you were dead! He just let you fall on the floor, and went out. I hadn't any water or anything to bring you to. I undid your collar, and when you didn't move, I was so desperate I shrieked for someone to come and at least let me have some water. But no one did and no one answered. Only this awful roaring noise went on.'

He lifted his head. 'Then there is a noise? It's not just in my head?'

'No, it's never stopped all the time I've been here.'

He sat for a few minutes trying to collect his thoughts. 'Poor kid!' he said. 'Ghastly for you. And a fat lot of good I've been to you!'

She laid her cheek against his arm. 'You're here, and that's all I care about. You don't know what it was like to be alone. At least we're together now.'

'If only my head didn't ache so much I might be able to think,' he said. He looked round, and blinked. 'Where the hell are we?' he said. 'Electric light?'

She glanced up at the bulb that had caught his attention. 'So it is. I haven't had time to notice it till now. Then we can't be in the Priory, can we?'

He got up, and began to move round the small room. It was like a square cave cut out of solid stone, all except the door which was made of thick wood. 'No window,' he said. 'We must be underground.' He went to the door, and slipping his hand sideways between two of the bars of the grille, tried to push back the shutter by inserting a finger into one of the ventilation holes. He could not move it, nor could he manage to see anything through the holes.

'If we're underground that accounts for the coldness and the smell of damp,' Margaret said. 'Peter – you don't think – they're going to leave us here – to starve?'

'Of course not,' he said instantly. He stood by the door, listening. 'That noise,' he said. 'That's a machine and an electric one, or I've never heard one!' He stared across at his sister, dawning suspicion in his eyes. He seemed about to speak, then checked himself, and went up to one of the walls, and closely inspected the stone blocks that formed it. 'I believe we're under the cellars,' he said. 'I'm no geologist, but this looks to me exactly the same sort of stone as that one that moved and we sealed up. We are in the Priory!'

'Right under the ground?' she asked. 'Below the cellars even?'

'I'm not sure, but I think we must be. The place feels like a tomb, much more so than the cellars did.' He looked round again. 'Why, what fools we've been not to think of it! Didn't those old monks often have underground passages leading from the monastery to the chapel?'

'Yes, I believe they did,' she said. 'You think that's where we are? But this is a room!'

'Cut, if I'm not much mistaken, in the foundations of the house. I don't know much about monasteries, but I suppose the monks must have had a use for an underground room or so. Storing valuables in times of stress, and all that sort of thing.'

'But the light!' she objected. 'There's no electricity at the Priory.'

'It must be worked by a plant. Good God!'

'What?' she said quickly.

'At the Bell! That big plant I saw there! But it can't possibly...' He broke off, utterly bewildered.

'Did you see a plant there? You never told me.'

'I forgot about it. It was one day when Charles and I were there. I got into the engine-room, and I was just thinking what a ridiculously big machine it was for the work it had to do when Spindle hustled me out. Yes, by Jove, and I wondered at the time why he seemed so upset at finding me there. But Wilkes gave a plausible sort of explanation, and I never thought any more about it. Why, good Lord, do you realize that if I'm right, and it's that plant that produces this light, and works the machine we can hear, Wilkes must be in this, up to the eyes?'

'Wilkes?' she repeated incredulously. 'That fat, smiling landlord? He couldn't be!'

'I don't know so much. And that throws a fresh light on it. Strange! He's staying at the Bell. For all we know he and Wilkes are hand in glove over this.'

'Oh, no!' she said. 'It isn't Michael Strange! It can't be! Not after what he said to me! No, no, I won't believe that!'

He did not press the point. He stood still, listening to

the throb and the muffled roar of the machine, trying to think what it could be. The noise it made stirred some chord of memory in his brain. Margaret started to speak, and he signed to her to be quiet, with a quick frown and a finger held up.

Suddenly he remembered. Once, a couple of years before, he had been shown over a model printing works. He swung round, and exclaimed beneath his breath: 'Margaret! I believe it's a printing press!'

She waited, searching his face. He seemed to be listening more intently than ever. 'I don't see...' she began.

'Forgers!' he said. 'I can't see what else it can possibly be – if it is a press.'

'Forgers?'

'Probably forgers of bank-notes. I don't know.' He came back to the table and sat down on the edge of it. 'Let's get this straight. I believe we've hit on the secret of the Priory. If there's a gang of forgers at work here that would account for the efforts to get us out of the house. Jove, yes, and what a god-sent place for a press! Empty house, reputation for being haunted, only needed a little ghost-business to scare the countryside stiff, *and* to scare the former tenants out! I can't think why we never even suspected it.'

'But Peter, it's fantastic! How could a gang of forgers know of this underground passage, and that sliding-panel?'

'Not the gang, but the man at the head of it. The man who stole the book from the library, and tore the missing pages from the copy at the British Museum. The Monk, in fact.'

'You mean Michael Strange, don't you?'

'I don't know whether I mean him or not, but it's clear that the Monk's no ordinary forger. He's someone who knew something about the Priory, someone who's devilish thorough and devilish clever.'

She caught his hand, pressing it warningly. The bolts were being drawn back from the door of their cell. Peter thrust her behind him, and turned to face the door.

It opened, and the first thing they saw was the blunt nose of an automatic. A rough voice said: 'Keep back, both of you.'

They obeyed; there was nothing else to do. The door opened farther, and they saw a man standing there in the rough clothes of a country labourer. A handkerchief was tied round the lower half of his face, and a cloth cap was on his head. He had a bottle of water in his left hand, and this he set down on the floor. 'Keep as you are!' he warned them, and took a step backwards, feeling behind him. He pulled a second chair in, and thrust it into the cell. 'You can have that, and the water,' he said. 'And I wouldn't waste my breath shouting for help, if I was you. No one'll hear you, not if you shout till you're black in the face.'

'Where are we?' Peter said, not that he had much hope of getting an answer.

'You're where no one'll ever think to look for you,' the man replied.

Margaret said: 'But you can't keep us here! Oh please, don't go! You couldn't leave us here to starve!'

'It's none of my business,' was the callous answer. 'And there's precious little the Monk stops at, I can tell you. You've interfered with him. *That's* what happens to people as cross the Monk's path.' He drew his thumb across his throat in a crude descriptive gesture.

'Look here,' Peter said, 'I'm a pretty rich man, and if you get us out of this there's a fat reward waiting for you, and no awkward questions asked.'

The man laughed. 'Me? No bloody fear! Know what happened to Dooval? I've got no wish to go the same road, thank you kindly.'

'I'll see nothing happens to you.'

'Oh, you will, will you? Think you could stop the Monk? Well, there ain't a soul that knows him, and if you had a guard of fifty policemen he'd still get you. You wouldn't clear out of the Priory, you kept on nosing round after the Monk. And he's got you, and you talk about escaping! You won't do that, my fine gentleman, don't you fret. Nor no one won't recognize you if ever they finds you, for you'll be no more'n a skeleton. You crossed the Monk's path.' With that he gave another of his brutal laughs, and went out, and shot the bolts home again.

Margaret sat down limply. 'Peter, he can't mean that! No one could be as awful as that!'

'Of course they couldn't, Sis. Keep a stiff upper lip. Even supposing they do mean to clear out and leave us to rot, do you suppose Charles is going to do nothing?'

'But he said – no one would ever think to look for us here. Oh, Peter, why ever didn't we leave the Priory as Celia wanted?'

'Nonsense!' he said bracingly. 'When Charles finds we've disappeared he'll pull the Priory down stone by stone. Listen, Sis! Don't give way! Already Charles knows there's something odd about the place. You don't suppose he and Celia would calmly give us up for lost when they must guess we're somewhere in the house? They'll have Scotland Yard on to it, and the whole countryside will be up. There isn't the slightest doubt that they'll find us.'

She pointed out the water-bottle. 'And we've got that – to last us till they do find us. It might take them weeks. Or perhaps the Monk will do as that man meant, and kill us.'

'If he were going to kill us he'd hardly have bothered to let us have any water, or a second chair,' Peter pointed out. 'Sis, if you let go of yourself, you're not the girl I take you for. We may even find a way out ourselves. My

235

dear kid, people don't get buried alive in the twentieth century!'

She knew that he was talking more to reassure her than from any real conviction, but she pulled herself together. 'Yes. Of course. Sorry. Do you suppose this machine goes on all day, or will they all go away?'

'Go away, I should think. Too risky to work by day. When they've cleared off we can try and force that shutter back. I might be able to reach the top bolt, and that would give us a better chance of breaking the door down. Or I might be able to drive the wood in with the help of one of the chairs. What we've got to do is to keep our spirits up and talk of something else till the gang has gone. Wonder how they ventilate this place?'

She tried to follow his lead. 'Yes, they must have some sort of ventilation, mustn't they? And though it's musty, and sort of close, it isn't airless, is it? How would they do it?'

'Don't quite know. If they've got power enough to work a machine they've probably rigged up some system of fans, same as they have in mines. But there must be an outlet somewhere, and that's what I can't make out.'

They speculated on this for some time in rather a half-hearted fashion. Then Peter produced his cigarette-case, and they lit up, and smoked for a while, trying to think of something cheerful to talk about.

It was not only damp, but also cold, in the stone room, and Margaret had no coat. Peter saw her shiver, and began to take off his coat. 'Sis, why didn't you sing out? You must be frozen in that thin dress. Here, put this on.'

She demurred, but he insisted, and at last she put it on gratefully: Peter looked at his watch. 'Nearly one o'clock. I'd give something to know what old Chas is doing.'

'Celia will be dreadfully worried,' Margaret said. 'I wonder what they thought when they found us gone? Oh, Peter, suppose they were late, and just jumped to the conclusion we'd gone to bed, and didn't bother to look?'

'You're forgetting Bowers,' he reminded her. 'He went to get the coal, and when he got back to the library and found no trace of us, he must have thought it a trifle odd. I'll tell you what, Sis, that fire of yours was a stroke of genius. Because when the others hear how we took the trouble to light it they're bound to smell a rat. They can't think we went to bed, or strolled out for a walk, or anything like that.'

These cheerful surmises occupied them for another half-hour, each one producing fresh reasons why Charles and Celia must guess what had happened. But they could not keep it up for ever, and again silence fell between them, and they sat busy with their much less cheerful thoughts.

Peter was chiefly anxious on the score of time. Though he spoke optimistically to Margaret he was less certain in his own mind that the Monk would not leave them to starve. He could not but remember Duval's fate, and the cold-blooded way in which that murder had been carried out. He did not doubt that before he gave up hope of finding the missing pair Charles really would demolish the Priory, but it might be too late by then. They could hardly hope that Charles too would hit on the panel in the library, for thinking it over, Peter realized that no one could guess that they had been kidnapped there. It would be much more likely that Charles would think they had gone out into the grounds. One thing Peter felt sure about: Charles would connect Michael Strange with this. Therein lay the greatest hope of a swift deliverance, for Strange might be made to talk.

Margaret's thoughts were by no means so reasoned or consecutive; she was still shaken by the terrifying experience she had gone through, and it seemed as though her brain could do nothing but repeat scraps of what Strange had said to her that day at the Inn. He had said it was no use supposing that she would ever look at a man in his 'line of business.' But he had said that from him she stood in no danger. Yes, but had he not added that he was not the only person mixed up in this? He had said too that there was danger, and that he might be powerless to help her. Unless he was the most accomplished and heartless liar he could not, on the face of it, be the Monk. It was possible that he was working under the Monk's orders, and if that were so Margaret felt convinced that the Monk had some unbreakable hold over him. He had told her that he *must* go on with the job he had undertaken. What else could that mean?

Peter's voice broke into her thoughts. 'Margaret, you say the Monk lugged me in here. What did he look like?'

She gave a shiver. 'You've seen pictures of those Inquisition people? Well, like that. He's got a long black robe on, with a cord round the waist, and a cowled hood drawn right down over his head and face. And do you remember what Aunt Lilian said about the black hand that pointed at her? Well, that was true. He wears black gloves, sort of cotton ones, with buttons, only he doesn't do them up. That was the only bit of him you could see for the disguise – his wrists. I particularly noticed, because it was the only thing about him that looked human. There was a button off one glove, too. Isn't it funny what stupid little things one fixes on?'

'A button off,' Peter said. 'Well, I thought as much.'

'Why? What did you think?'

'Nothing. Something the police told us, and we weren't to repeat. Could you see what sort of build he was?'

'No, not very well with that loose robe on. Fairly tall, but not out of the way. A powerful man, because he managed to drag you to this place, and I couldn't see anyone else helping him. And his arm felt like steel when he held me.'

'And he didn't say anything?'

'No. That seemed to make him even more sinister.

That, and the dreadful chuckle.'

'Doesn't really help us much,' Peter said. He looked at his watch again. 'Half past two. Look here, Sis, I think you'd better try and get some sleep. You've had a very strenuous time, and you're looking fagged out. And you mustn't forget we shall have a busy time ahead of us when this crowd clears off. Suppose you were to sit on my knee. Think you could snooze a bit with your head on my shoulder?'

She shook her head. 'I couldn't, Peter. And I'm not a light weight, you know. I should wear you out.'

'Oh no, you wouldn't!'

'Really, I'd rather not. I'm not sleepy. Anything but. Let's play some guessing game to keep ourselves occupied. Animal, vegetable, or mineral. You start.'

'All right,' he said. There was a pause. 'I've thought. Go ahead.'

The game seemed dreary beyond relief, but they kept on at it valiantly for nearly an hour. Then Margaret gave it up, and they began to wonder again what Charles and Celia were doing.

It was nearly four o'clock when the noise of the engine suddenly ceased. Margaret instinctively felt for Peter's hand. They sat in silence, listening, and presently they heard a door open and a murmur of voices. They could distinguish no voice they knew, nor could they catch what was said. Footsteps sounded retreating in the distance, and when these had died away they heard a key grate in a lock. Someone had remained behind, and there could be little doubt who that someone was.

Peter gently pulled Margaret to her feet, and led her to the wall alongside the door, so that she should be out of range of a shot fired through the grille. He placed himself as near to the door as he dared, determined to make a fight for it if the Monk came into the room.

But no one came. They heard the padding footstep

which Margaret had described, and it died away as the others had done.

After the noise of the machine the silence that now hung over the tomb-like place was so profound that Margaret felt that she knew at last what was meant by 'hearing a silence.' Nothing broke it, and she realized with a feeling of panic how completely buried alive they were. She felt she dared not speak, but presently Peter turned and said: 'Gone. We'd better wait a bit before we get to work.'

She nodded. The palms of her hands felt cold and sticky. She had an awful fear that the Monk might be still there, listening to them, waiting.

The minutes crept by. Peter whispered: 'I'm going to give him half an hour's grace, just in case he hasn't gone. We've got loads of time. Let's sit down again. But if I say "move" get back to this wall again. See?'

'Yes,' she replied. 'We'd – we'd better go on talking, hadn't we?'

'That's the idea. Let's play *I love my love with an A*, as we used to when we were kids.'

This programme was faithfully carried out, and since neither of them seemed to be able to think of drinks beginning with D, or attributes beginning with Q it took them more than half an hour to struggle through the alphabet. When they had at last come to the end, Peter got up. 'I think it's safe enough now,' he said. 'If he were coming to do us in he wouldn't wait all this time. You sit still. I'm going to try and move that shutter.'

For perhaps twenty minutes he tried by every means he could think of to force it open, but it was of no avail. He banged on the door, to test the thickness of the wood. It sounded very solid, but he could at least try to break through. He picked up one of the chairs, and drove it with all his might against the door until one of its legs broke, and he was forced to pause for a while to get his breath.

He sat down on the table, wiping the sweat from his face. 'Well – I'm warm enough now, anyway,' he said, trying to coax a smile into Margaret's wan countenance.

She did smile, but it was a pathetic effort. He patted her hand. 'Cheer up, Sis: we'll get out all right.'

He sat still for a few minutes, trying to think what other implements he could use against the door. He felt Margaret's hand gripping his arm, and glanced down at her. Her eyes were fixed on the door, and she was white as death. He looked quickly in the same direction, and saw what had attracted her attention. Inch by inch the shutter was sliding back.

'Move!' Peter said under his breath, but it seemed as though she either did not hear him, or dared not stir. He slipped in front of her, shielding her; there was no time to force her over to the wall.

The panel slid still farther; they saw a cowled face behind the grille, and through the slits in the cowl eyes glittered as the light caught them.

Peter stood perfectly still, and his mouth felt unpleasantly dry all at once.

The sinister face disappeared; there was a sound of bolts being drawn, and the door was opened. On the threshold stood the Monk, an automatic in his right hand. He put up his other hand, and pulled the cowl back from his head.

A bitter cry broke from Margaret. 'My God! *You*!' she gasped.

For the Monk was none other than Michael Strange.

CHAPTER XVII

For an instant they all three stared at one another. Then Strange said in a voice of blank surprise: 'How the devil did you get here?' His eyes travelled to Margaret's tense face, and he took a quick step towards her. 'Please don't look like that! It's all right, Miss Fortescue.'

Peter decided that he could not have recovered from the blow on his head so completely as he had thought. 'How did we get here?' he repeated. 'That won't quite do, Master Monk! I don't know what your little game is, but...'

Strange said impatiently: 'I'm not the Monk. Oh, I know I'm togged up in the same disguise, but you can't really think I'm he!'

Margaret leaned forward eagerly. 'You're not? Oh, I said you couldn't be!'

His eyes softened. 'You believe me, Miss Fortescue? Without proof? In spite of appearances?'

She nodded. 'If you tell me so,' she said quite simply.

It seemed as though he was going to take her hand, but he did not. He said only: 'Thank you.' Then he turned to Peter. 'I told you you'd get yourself into a mess if you didn't stop poking your nose into my affairs,' he remarked cheerfully. 'I'm not the Monk, and my name isn't Strange. I'm Inspector Draycott, of the C.I.D.' He thrust his hand into the front of his robe. 'I've got a card somewhere, in case you still don't believe me.'

'Draycott!' Peter said. 'You don't mean you're the man

who handled that big case against Williams last year?'

'I did, yes. Who told you? Malcolm? I was always afraid he might spot me.'

'I don't think he ever saw you till we came down here,' Peter said, feeling rather limp. 'Then are you after the Monk?'

'Of course. I've been after him for months.'

'And you've known about this place all the time?'

'I've suspected it, but I only found the way in to-night. Look here, I think we'd better reserve my story till we're out of this, don't you? Miss Fortescue must be worn out. How did you get here?'

'Through the panel in the library!' Margaret said. 'I found it by accident.'

'Then there is an entrance from the Priory!' Michael exclaimed. 'But you didn't come down here just for fun, did you?'

'No, no!' Margaret said, and quickly told him all that had happened to them.

He listened frowningly. His comment, which made Margaret laugh, was: 'Damn. From my point of view this is the worst thing that could possibly have happened.'

He saw her eyes dancing, and smiled ruefully. 'Yes, I know, but don't you see that when the Monk finds you're gone to-morrow night he'll know this place is discovered, and clear out. And the devil's in it that I don't know where his get-away is.' He shrugged. 'Well, I shall have to find it during the next twelve hours, that's all. The first thing to do is to get you out of here.'

'By the way, where are we?' Peter asked.

'You're under the Priory.'

'I thought as much! But did you get in by the panel in the library?'

'No, I never knew of that. I got in through the cellars of the Bell Inn. The passage leads right under your grounds. I suppose neither of you have the faintest idea how you came here, after the Monk caught you?' They shook their heads. 'Then we shall just have to search till we find the way. I can take you back to the Bell easily enough, but it'll mean walking home from there, as I daren't get my car out of the garage for fear of rousing Wilkes or Spindle. And I should say you've had about enough for one night.'

'No, we haven't, have we, Peter?' Margaret said. 'I agree that we ought to find the way back to the library, but we're quite game to do what you want us to. You didn't come down here just to look for us, did you?'

'I didn't. I came to reconnoitre, and to find where the press is.'

'Then before we try and find the way out let's get on with the reconnoitring,' Margaret said briskly. 'I don't feel done-up at all now.'

Michael looked at her uncertainly, but Peter clinched the matter. 'I'm damned if I'll go meekly home at this stage!' he said. 'I was right then? It is a printing press?'

'Yes, it's a press all right. I want to locate it first, and make sure how many ways there are of getting into it. I've found one, I think.' He led the way out of the square cell, and they found themselves in a low, vaulted passage in which Peter could not stand fully upright.

Turning to the right Michael stopped in front of a stout door similar to the one they had come through, except that it boasted a lock. He tried it, but it did not open. 'I think I'll go and get Jimmy Fripp,' he said. 'He's much cleverer at opening doors than I am, and we shall waste less time in the long run. You'd better come along too, just in case of accidents. Mind your heads.' He went before them up the passage, his torch showing them the way. Once a rat scuttered off almost under their feet, but Margaret had gone through too much to be discomposed by a mere rodent.

As they proceeded down the passage the air became noticeably fresher, and the reason for this was soon made

244

apparent, for they saw a square opening in the side of the passage. No light could be seen through it, but it was obviously a window. Peter stopped Michael to point to it. 'Ventilation? But aren't we underground?'

'Yes, and that was one of my main difficulties – to find how this place, if it really did exist – was ventilated. Not very easy with all you suspicious people on the watch. Remember that night you saw me, Marg – Miss Fortescue?'

'Margaret will do,' she said. 'Yes. Were you looking for it then?'

'I was, but I didn't find it till later. Have you ever looked down the well in that bit of the garden that looks as though it were once a sort of pleasaunce?'

'The well? Oh, I know! No, I hate looking down wells. I don't think any of us found it for quite a long time, did we, Peter?'

'I don't think we did. But I'm afraid I never even thought about it.'

'You might easily fail to see it unless you happened to stumble on it as I did,' Michael said. 'The weeds have grown up all round it, and it only sticks up a couple of feet out of the ground. That's it.' He pointed to the opening. 'Cut right down in the side of the well. Clever, isn't it? Come along; we'll get hold of Jimmy before we start talking.'

'Fripp?' Peter said, following at his heels down the passage. 'Do you know Charles and I once heard you holding a most suspicious conversation with that fellow?'

'Did you? Yes, it's his one fault, and I can't break him of it. He will talk where he can be overheard.'

'Charles set an inquiry agent on to him. Look here, is he an ex-burglar or not?'

'Yes, he's an old lag,' Michael answered. 'He was my batman during the war, and I took a fancy to him, and kept him on as my servant when we were both demobilized. He's a useful sort of chap on a job like this.

Pick any lock under the sun.'

Margaret chuckled. 'Aren't you afraid to leave anything about?'

'Not a bit. He's one of the very few who do really turn over new leaves. Sorry he upset you. How much did your inquiry agent get hold of?'

'Precious little. But if he's your servant how does he find the time to travel for Suck-All Cleaners?'

'He doesn't. That's a put-up job. The head of the firm is a pal of mine, and he employed Jimmy to oblige me. It's answered fairly well on the whole, though Marson – that's the head of Suck-All Cleaners – was very dubious. Said Jimmy wasn't the right type at all.'

'I don't know about that,' Peter said. 'He very nearly sold a cleaner to my elder sister.'

Michael looked over his shoulder, grinning. 'I know. I don't think he'll ever forgive Malcolm. You know, I'm sorry to have to say so, but you people have been the most ungodly nuisances I ever came across. If you had let Jimmy alone in the house he'd probably have found that sliding panel.'

'If it comes to that,' Margaret retorted from the rear, 'if only you'd told us who you were we shouldn't have got in your way.'

'You don't know how much I wanted to. But I couldn't. I was acting in absolute secrecy. I didn't even know at first that you mightn't be mixed up in this. And you must see that for me to have told you all about myself would have been most dangerous. You might have talked, or let something slip out unwittingly.' He paused, and signed to them to stand still. They saw that they had reached the end of the passage, and were confronted by a flight of worn stone steps. 'Will you stay here?' Michael said. 'And don't talk, because I'm going to open the trap.' He went softly up the steps, and they waited in silence for him to reappear.

Presently they saw the torch-light approaching again; Michael came into view, and behind him was James Fripp. This individual greeted them with a headshake. 'Well, this is a fine set-out, and no mistake,' he remarked, with an entire disregard of the manners usually required of a gentleman's servant. 'Some people don't seem able to keep out of trouble, and that's a fact.'

'Shut up,' said Michael. 'Some people can't keep their mouths shut, and you're one of them. Do you know, Mr Fortescue heard you talking once, and set an inquiry agent on to you?'

'That's a nice thing!' exclaimed Mr Fripp indignantly. 'Set one of them busies on to me? Why, I'm as innocent as a babe unborn! And if anyone told you different they're a liar. Most of the police are, barring Mr Draycott, who ain't as bad as some,' he added gloomily.

'Come and see if you can open a door without damaging the lock,' Michael interrupted, and began to lead the way back.

Mr Fripp said, with an air of unconvincing virtue: 'I'll do what I *can*, just to oblige, but you needn't talk as though I was in the 'abit of picking locks, sir.'

'Don't be an ass,' Michael said. 'Mr and Miss Fortescue know all about you.'

'No one don't know all about me,' Mr Fripp announced firmly. 'There's always people ready to swear a man's life away, and I've come across more than most in my time. You didn't ought to pay attention to everything you 'ear, miss.'

Margaret assured him that she never paid attention to malicious reports. Mr Fripp said that it did her credit.

They walked on in single file until they reached the locked door. Peter judged the distance to be about a quarter of a mile, and realized that the passage must run straight beneath the Priory grounds to the Inn.

Mr Fripp bent down, and turned his torch on to the

lock. Then he felt in his pockets for some slim-looking tools, which he laid on the ground. One of these he inserted gently into the lock.

'Can you do it without any damage?' Michael asked.

Mr Fripp forgot his rôle of injured innocence. 'Lor' yes, sir! If you'd seen some of the locks I've picked you wouldn't ask me whether I could open this one. It ain't worthy of me, this ain't.' He worked in silence for a short while, and then, turning the instrument he held, he pushed the door. It opened without a sound, for it had no other fastening than the lock.

Michael flashed his torch into the room. They saw a press in the centre, and some smaller machines round it. The room was a fair size, and contained only the machines, a few wooden stools, and a safe.

'Electric light and all!' said Mr Fripp admiringly, and switched it on. 'Do themselves proud, don't they? There's no denying it don't pay to be honest, no matter what they say.'

Peter and Michael were both inspecting the press. Margaret sat down on one of the high stools, and listened to their highly technical comments. Mr Fripp stood beside her, and seemed to take as little interest in the press as she did. 'Wonderful how they can make it out, ain't it, miss?' he said affably.

She agreed. 'Is it all printed by that big machine in the middle?' she inquired.

Michael heard her. 'No, this is where they roll it off. Come and look.'

She went up to him, and he showed her an engraved plate. 'See? That's the plate. The paper goes between those rollers and when the current's turned on, that plate slides backwards and forwards, while the rollers press the paper on to it, and shoot it out this end, roughly speaking.'

'I see. It's like looking-glass writing, isn't it? What are the other machines?'

'One of them cuts the paper. This one. I don't understand all of them.'

'Neat little affair,' Peter said. 'I suppose this is the engraver's corner. Wonder who does it?'

'Unless I'm much mistaken, Duval was the engraver,' Michael answered. He looked round the room. 'Only the one door. Better test the walls, though. Where you find one moving stone-block you're likely to find another.'

Peter looked up quickly. 'Oh, so it was you, then?'

'Yes. Sorry if I gave you all a scare. It wasn't me you saw in the cellars, though. That was Fripp. He was trying to find a way into this place from there.'

'Look here!' Peter said. 'Have we also to thank you for our skeleton? Because if so . . .'

'What skeleton?' Michael asked, moving along one wall, testing as he went.

'That one we found in the priest's hole.'

'I never knew you did. No, that must have been one of the Monk's attentions.'

'But, Michael, you said that day at the Inn that you were responsible for what had happened at the Priory!' Margaret objected.

'I don't think I said that, did I? If I did I thought you were referring to the groaning stone. Anything that side, Jimmy?'

'Not that I can find, sir. Nothing there, Mr Fortescue?'

'Nothing,' Peter said, dusting his hands.

'Well, that's something, anyway,' Michael said. 'They can't get out of this room by any other way than the door. If I can only find the Monk's own entrance I may get him yet.'

Margaret was puzzled. 'But doesn't he come in through the Inn? What's that entrance for, then?'

'The rest of his gang. I watched them go down this evening, and I watched them come up. At neither time was the Monk with them, and from what I heard they none of them, with the possible exception of Wilkes, know his way in or who he is.'

'By Jove!' Peter said. 'Then I'll bet that's what Duval had discovered! You know, he came up to see Charles the very night he was murdered, and he told him that though he hadn't found out who the Monk was – "seen his face," was the way he put it – he had found out something.'

'I think there's no doubt he did find the Monk's way, and that's why the Monk murdered him. What's more, I still believe it comes out at the chapel.'

Margaret remembered something. 'Peter, didn't Charles say Duval talked about finding the Monk if he had to go down amongst the dead to do it?'

'Yes, I believe he did. We thought he was cracked. Have you tried to find an entrance in the chapel, Strange – I mean Draycott?'

'Till I'm sick of the sight of masonry,' Michael replied. 'And unless I find it I can't be sure that is his way in, so that I daren't make a raid in case he gets away by some passage we don't know of. The rest of the gang's no use unless I can get the Monk. No, there's no other entrance here. We'd better try and find the secret stairway. If we can't, I'll nip back to the Inn, and go to the Priory, and attack it from that side. Come along, Jimmy, and take care how you lock the door.'

They went out again into the passage, switching off the light. While Fripp locked the door, Michael bolted the one into the Fortescues' late prison, and fixed the shutter in position again.

'Now as far as I can make out,' he said, 'we must be standing at the moment either on the level of the cellars, or below them. Probably below, judging from the depth of that opening into the well. And we mustn't forget that on the library side of the Priory the cellars are on the level of the ground. Moreover, if that machine was only just below the sitting-room you must have heard it. The

250

question is what part of the house are we under? If the Inn is there' – he pointed up the passage – 'then the chapel ought to be more or less in *that* direction. Well, we'll see where the passage leads this way.' He led them on, flashing his torch ahead. The passage ended in an archway and through this they went, finding themselves in another of the cell-like apartments. It was bare of furniture, and out of it led yet one more.

'Talk about the 'Astings Caves!' said Mr Fripp. 'They aren't in it with this.'

'Try for a moving block,' Michael said. 'Time's getting on, and I must be back at the Inn before anyone's up. Fortescue, you take that wall, will you? Just run along it: never mind about the upper blocks. Get on with it, Fripp! Don't stand mooning about!'

They started once more to try and move one of the stone blocks that made up the wall. 'The things the perlice get up to!' Mr Fripp remarked. 'Give me an honest job of burglary, that's what I say! Well, it ain't 'ere, sir. If we've got many more of these rooms to go over you'll have to send me to one of them sanatoriums where you lay out on a nice balcony the whole blooming day.'

But only one other room led out of the one they were in, and it was comparatively small. They started to test its walls, but before Peter had got more than half-way along his side of the room Michael said: 'Got it!'

He set his shoulder to the block, and it swung easily and silently on its hidden pivot.

'Took the trouble to oil this one,' commented Mr Fripp. 'Now mind what you're about, sir. Let me 'ave a look!'

'It's all right,' Michael said, drawing his head and shoulders back into the room. 'Only be careful how you step, Margaret. We're right on the staircase. Can you get through if I go first, and give you a hand?'

'Good Lord, yes!' she said. As soon as he had clambed

through the gap, she scrambled after him, and found herself standing on the narrow stone stairway. They seemed to be somewhere in the middle of it, for the stairs went down as well as up.

The other two squeezed through the opening, and Michael pressed the block back into position. The light of his torch showed nothing to distinguish this block from any of the others.

'We shall have to count the stairs,' Michael said. 'I propose to explore downstairs after I've deposited you two at the Priory. Mind how you step, Margaret: the stairs are very steep and narrow.'

They climbed in silence, each of them counting to themselves as they went. Margaret's legs were aching badly by the time they came to a halt; and she was thankful to get even a short rest.

Michael's torch was playing over the wall that flanked the staircase on the right, and they saw that the stone had ended, and they were standing behind rough brick. Michael moved on again.

'There! If I haven't lorst count!' said Mr Fripp disgustedly.

The brick gave place to what looked like a wooden partition of thick deal.

'Clever,' Michael said. 'Nailed the deal on behind the oak panel to deaden the hollow sound. Here we are!' His torch showed a plain round knob past the panel. He went on up two more stairs, and twisted it. Nothing happened. 'That's odd!' Michael said. 'It surely must be this knob that corresponds to the apple in the carving the other side. You didn't do anything but turn it, did you, Margaret?'

'No, nothing.'

He asked abruptly: 'Did the Monk come up or down?'

'Up. I was standing on the second stair, where Peter is now, when the panel closed.'

'There's no knob farther down,' Michael said. An idea

occurred to him. 'I wonder – get off that stair, will you, Fortescue?'

Peter moved, and as Michael once more turned the knob the panel slid back.

'Clever little dodge,' Michael remarked.

He was interrupted by a strangled shriek from within the library. 'Charles, look! look!' Celia cried.

'Seventy-three, counting this one,' Peter said. 'It's all right, Celia: it's us!'

CHAPTER XVIII

He stepped through the opening into the library, as he spoke, and found himself confronting Charles' levelled revolver. Celia and Mrs Bosanquet were gazing with startled fixity at him, and Inspector Tomlinson had just lowered a Colt automatic.

Charles put down his revolver, and swallowed twice before he spoke. Then he said: 'Oh, hullo! Just back?' His flippancy deserted him. 'Gosh, you have given us a fright! Where's Margaret? What happened?'

Margaret came through the aperture, and at sight of her Celia jumped up and flew to embrace her. 'Oh, darling, I've been thinking you dead ever since ten o'clock!' she said, half-crying. 'Who found you? Did you escape by yourselves?'

By this time both Michael and Fripp had come into the room. Charles wrung Michael's hand. 'Good man! Yes, we know all about you. The inspector had to split on you.'

There was a positive babel of talk. After a while Mrs Bosanquet made herself heard above it. 'But surely that is the man who cleaned all the rooms so thoroughly?' she said in a bewildered voice, and pointed at Fripp.

'Yes, ma'am,' said Fripp with feeling, 'and if I was you I wouldn't have one of them cleaners in the house, not if I was paid to. They're enough to break your heart.'

Michael, who had been speaking to Inspector Tomlinson, now glanced at his watch. 'Good Lord, it's almost five o'clock! Fripp and I had better hurry, or we shall run into one of the servants at the Inn. Look here, you people, the best thing you can do is to go to bed, and get what sleep you can. I'll come back after breakfast, tell you some of the things you're all dying to know, and set about the job of finding that other entrance. Now that you've discovered this panel it ought to be easy. There's only one other thing: Fortescue and his sister have got to keep themselves hidden. No one must know that they've been found. See? No one. In fact you must give the impression to anyone you happen to see that you're worried to death, and are sure that they must have gone out, and got kidnapped in the grounds, or something of that sort.' He looked at Mrs Bowers rather dubiously, but she nodded. 'Sure you understand? And don't let that housemaid of yours find them here.'

'It's her half-day,' said Mrs Bowers. 'Nor she don't turn up till nine in the mornings, and mostly late. I'll nip up and make Miss Margaret's and Mr Peter's beds before she gets here, and she don't ever go into any of the sitting-rooms.'

'Better not have her at all to-morrow,' Charles said. 'Can you get rid of her without her smelling a rat, Emma?'

She thought for a moment. 'Yes, sir. If Miss Margaret and Mr Peter aren't supposed to be here there'll only be the two bedrooms to do. I'll say she can have the whole day, since we're all at sixes and sevens. You leave it to me.'

Mrs Bosanquet had been scrutinizing Michael through her lorgnette. She now turned to Charles, and said in the perfectly audible voice deaf people imagine to be a whisper: 'My dear, you may say what you please about that young man being a detective, but it appears to me that he is the same malicious person who pointed at me in the dark.'

Michael laughed. 'I've never pointed at you, Mrs Bosanquet. I'll explain it all to you later. Come on, Fripp: we'll go back the way we came. You'll turn up again later in the morning, inspector. You understand what I want you to do?'

'Yes. Send a man over to make a lot of inquiries, and make it seem we're on the wrong track. Well, Flinders will do a bit of searching all the morning, I don't doubt, and so long as he doesn't know the truth he'll put every one off the scent. I'll get back to the station now, and be with you again about ten.'

Margaret said worriedly: 'Must you go back that way? I suppose it's safe, but I don't like to think of you down there.'

Charles opened his eyes at that, but Margaret did not notice his surprise.

'I shall be all right,' Michael said. 'You go and get some sleep. So long!' He went through on to the stair, Fripp followed him, and as Michael set his foot on the second step the panel slid into place again.

Charles went to see the inspector off the premises. When he came back Margaret was telling her story to her sister and aunt. Charles listened to it in silence, but when she had finished he drew a long breath. 'Talk about half-wits!' he said. 'Why did you want to go and step into the cavity?'

'I know it was silly, but...'

'Silly?' said Charles. 'Call a spade a spade for once. You go through the opening, drop bracelets about, shout to Peter to come and have a look at what you've found, as though it were a sovereign left over from before the war, and then you're surprised the Monk grabs you. I don't blame him, poor chap. As for Peter – can you beat it? If his face was different he'd be cut out for the hero in a popular thriller. He knew Margaret had been pinched, but did he get his revolver? Not a bit of it! After making enough noise on the panel to bring up half a hundred monks, he bursts in, all full of heroism, and very properly gets knocked on the head.'

'Well, I'd like to know what you'd have done in my place,' Peter said.

'I should at least have remembered the planchette,' Charles said.

Celia interposed as Peter was about to retort. 'No, don't bother to answer him, Peter. Come up to bed. You must both be worn out.'

Accordingly they all went upstairs, and in spite of the fact that Margaret felt she would not be able to close her eyes, so wide-awake did she feel, she dropped into a dreamless sleep almost as soon as her head had touched the pillow.

She awoke four hours later, feeling rather heavy-eyed, but not in the least inclined to stay in bed. She wondered whether it would be safe to venture out of her room, and at that moment Celia cautiously looked in. 'Oh, you're awake! Darling, will you have breakfast in bed?'

'No, rather not!' Margaret said, getting up. 'Where's Jane? Is it all right for me to go and have a bath?'

'My dear, it's absolutely providential! She's apparently so scared by the news of your disappearance, which Flinders seems to be zealously spreading round the village, that she hasn't come at all! Her father turned up at eight with a feeble excuse, and we're quite safe. I told Mrs Bowers we'd have breakfast at half-past nine. I'll go and see if Charles is out of the bathroom yet.' She withdrew, and Margaret collected her towels and sponges, and prepared to follow her.

They had just started breakfast when Michael came in. 'Hullo!' Peter said. 'Had breakfast?'

'Yes thanks, I had some at the Bell. How are you both feeling?'

'I've got a whacking great bump on my head, but

otherwise we're all right. Sit down and have a second breakfast. Did you get back safely last night?'

'Yes, but only just in time,' Michael answered, sitting beside Margaret. 'Thanks, Mrs Malcolm.' He took the coffee-cup she had handed him. 'Look here, the first thing I want to know...'

Charles, who had got up to carve some ham for him, turned. 'I beg your pardon? I admit I'm not feeling at my best this morning, but it seemed to me that you said *you* wanted to know something.'

'I do,' Michael said brazenly.

Charles returned to his chair and sat down. 'Someone else can go on carving,' he said. 'I'm not strong enough. Moreover, I don't want to give him any of that peculiarly succulent ham now. A remark more calculated to provoke a peaceful man to homicide I've never yet heard.'

'Sorry,' Michael grinned. 'But it's important. Did either you or your sister, Fortescue, get any idea of the Monk's identity?'

'What, don't you know who he is?' Charles demanded.

'Not yet.'

Charles looked round at the others. 'I don't believe he's a detective at all. Let's exorcize him. Anyone got any wolfbane, or is that only good against vampires?'

'You needn't pay any attention to Charles,' Margaret said. 'We never do. Peter didn't see the monk, and I didn't recognize him at all. He never spoke, and the disguise absolutely covered him.'

'Just one thing!' Peter said. 'There was a button missing from one glove.'

Michael's eyes brightened. 'So even the Monk slips up occasionally! That's going to be very valuable. You can't tell me anything more about him?'

'No, except that he's about your height,' Margaret said, 'and very strong.'

'I see. I hoped he might have given you some clue to his

258

identity.'

'Haven't you got any idea who he is?' Margaret asked.

'I've got a strong suspicion, but that's not quite enough.'

'Oh, do tell us,' Celia begged.

He shook his head. 'I'm afraid I can't do that.'

Charles reached out a hand for the marmalade. 'Let it be clearly understood,' he said, 'that if you don't propose to gratify our curiosity, you've obtained that ham under false pretences. Kindly let us have the whole story.'

'All right,' Michael said. 'How much did Tomlinson tell you?'

'Practically nothing. When he turned up last night I told him that I'd rung you up at the Bell, and found you out. Where were you, by the way?'

'Hidden in the cellar. Where did you ring up from?'

'Ackerley's place. He was out, but the butler let me in.'

'I see,' said Michael. 'What time was it?'

'About midnight. Well, considering everything you'll hardly be surprised when I say that I regarded your absence as fishy in the extreme. The inspector seemed extraordinarily loth to do anything, and I rather lost patience. I threatened to go to the Bell, knock them up, and lie in wait for you. That upset old Tomlinson, and after a bit he took me aside and after swearing me to secrecy, told me who you were. That rather changed the complexion of things, of course. His point was that if you weren't at the Bell you were on the Monk's tracks. Who the Monk was, or what he was up to, he wouldn't tell me. The only thing he was worrying about was to keep me from giving the alarm and thus spoiling your game. He held that nothing could be done till you turned up. I agreed to give you till this morning to put in an appearance, and then you turned up. Now let's have your story.'

'It's rather long,' Michael said, 'but I'll make it as brief as I can. It began four years ago. I wasn't on it then, of course, but about that time the French police discovered that there were a number of forged Banque de France notes circulating through the country. These notes were obviously the work of an absolute master, and it takes an expert all his time to detect them. Well, I won't go into all the early details, but it soon became apparent that whoever was responsible for the notes was a pretty cunning rogue who knew not only how to hide his tracks, but how to keep his staff in such dread of him that they'd go to gaol sooner than speak. About three years ago the French police got hold of one of the Monk's agents, but nothing they could threaten or promise had the slightest effect on him. He's serving his term now. The only thing he said from start to finish was that prison was better than what would certainly happen if he spoke.'

'Poor thing!' said Mrs Bosanquet charitably. 'Let us hope that he will see the error of his ways and reform. Though I believe the French prisons are not so good as ours in that respect. But do go on, Mr... Do you mind telling me what your name is?'

'Draycott,' he replied.

'A much better name than Strange,' she approved.

'Thank you,' he said gravely. 'Where was I? Oh yes! Well, these notes went on circulating, and to make it more difficult they were not all of one denomination, as is generally the case. The Sûreté is pretty good at its job, you know, but it was completely baffled. Whenever the police thought they were on the right track it led them to a blank wall. The man who eventually discovered the key to the mystery was a Customs official at Boulogne, who knew nothing whatever about it. There was a man called Alphonse Martin who was employed by a firm of manufacturers of cheap goods outside Paris. They turn out quantities of so-called Parisian novelties, such as you'll see in any second-class linen-draper's. Pocket combs, studded with paste, puff-boxes, and all that sort of meretricious junk that's designed to catch the eyes of city typists, and domestic servants. As you probably know, one of the chief markets for that particular class of goods is England. Most firms deal through an agent – a middleman – or rather, they used to before the war. But the middleman, though he still exists, had been getting more and more squeezed out of late years, since manufacturers have discovered that he isn't necessary, and it pays them far better to sell direct to the various stores. One of the foreign firms who had tried this, and found it was a success, was this firm for which Martin worked. Martin was a man of about thirty-five, and had been employed by the firm for years. Married man, with children, who lived at Neuilly, led a very respectable sort of life, was well known to any number of people, and was altogether above suspicion. He was a man of fair education, and he had the advantage of being able to speak English through having lived over here for some years when he was in his early twenties. This qualification, coupled with his good record, and the fact that he was apparently a very capable salesman, got him promoted to the job of acting as the firm's chief agent for England. He was known to most of the buyers of London and provincial stores, and he used to come over from time to time with suitcases full of samples. The Customs officials all got to know him, he never tried to smuggle anything through, and after a bit his baggage was never searched except in a perfunctory way.

'This might have gone on for ever if a new Customs officer hadn't been sent to the Douane at Boulogne to take the place of someone who was leaving. The fellow was a young chap, very keen to show himself smart at the job, and he didn't know Martin from Adam. Unfortunately for him Martin fell into his hands on the last of his journeys from London back to Paris. Whether the new official found anything irregular amongst the goods Martin was carrying, or whether he was merely being officious, I don't know, but at all events, he took exception to something or other, and made Martin unpack the whole of one suitcase. This is where the *douanier* really did show that he was a smart fellow, for in the course of his suspicious search through the suitcase, he noticed that the cubic content of the inside didn't correspond with the size of the case on the outside. In fact, he discovered that the suitcase had a false bottom and false sides. Martin put up some story of a specially strengthened frame; it didn't entirely satisfy the *douanier* and he talked of making further investigations. Then Martin lost his head, and tried to bolt. After that the game was up, of course. He was caught, the suitcase was examined, and a whole consignment of Banque de France notes was found to be lining the bottom and the sides. Same with the two other cases he had.

'That put the Sûreté on to the right track at last. Martin, like the other man, refused to talk, and there was nothing found on him to give the police any further clue. Or so they thought. They sent a man over to London, and this is where the C.I.D. steps in.'

'Did you take it on then?' Margaret inquired.

'No, another man was put on to it at first, but after a bit they had to transfer him to another job, and I took over.'

'You mean,' Celia said shrewdly, 'the other man failed to solve it, don't you?'

He reddened. 'I expect he'd have solved it if he'd had more time, Mrs Malcolm.'

'That's all right, Celia,' her husband said. 'This is the man behind the scenes in that big murder case you used to read religiously in all the evening papers about six months ago. He's only being bashful. Go on, Draycott: how did you get on to this place?'

'Oh, that was really a slice of luck!' Michael assured

them. 'When I went through everything Martin had had on him at the time of his capture, I found just one thing that looked as though it might be worth following up. He had his order-book, his passport, and licence, and various papers connected with his business. They didn't help. The only other things he had were a London hotel bill, a letter from his wife, a local time-table, and a small account-book in which he kept a check of his running expenses. I had a look at the time-table first. It was one of those rotten little paper books you buy for twopence at the railway station. It was a time-table of trains on the line that runs through Manfield to Norchester. Now Norchester's not a very likely spot for a traveller in Parisian novelties, and as you know, it's the only place of any size on this line. Still, it was quite possible that there was some shop there that stocked these goods.

'The next thing I got on to was the account-book. Martin was a very methodical man, and he didn't just jot down his expenses roughly. Obviously his instinct was to write down exactly what he'd spent every penny on, and the book was full of items such as "'Bus to Shepherds Bush, so much," and "Cigarettes, so much." Also he kept a strict account of his railway fares. Usually he put down the town he went to, but sometimes it was just: "Train fare, so much." At first this didn't seem to lead anywhere, but I studied the book very closely, and I found after wading through pages of that sort of stuff that though he sometimes put down "Fare to Birmingham," and some-times only "Fare to B," or even just "train fare, so much," there was one train fare that kept on recurring and never had anything more against it than the words "train fare." The sum was six and eightpence, and by good luck it was the only six and eightpenny fare he ever had. I tabulated all his various journeys, and found that there was no mention in his accounts of any town on this particular line. So then I got down to it, and studied his time-table.

It took in the Tillingford Junction areas as well, so there was a fair field. I noted the names of all the stations you could get to for six and eightpence, and those that had cheap day returns at that price. In the end I got it down to five, of which Manfield was one.'

'I call that most ingenious!' said Mrs Bosanquet, who had been listening enthralled. 'But wasn't it still very difficult?'

'It wasn't so much difficult as boring,' Michael replied. 'It was a case of nosing about at pubs, and such-like places, and trying to find out whether there were any suspicious people in any of these places. When I worked round to Manfield it was just at the time that you were moving into this house, and there was a fair amount of talk about it. When I learned that the house had been empty for years, and was supposed to be haunted, I thought I was getting warm, and I moved on to Framley. Fripp followed me, and between us we soon found out enough to make us feel we'd hit on the place we were looking for. Only' – he smiled – 'you'd taken possession of the house, your servants were already here, and it was very difficult for me to do much. But I managed to pick up a good deal of information one way and another, and when I heard of previous tenants being frightened away, and of a cowled figure being seen, I was as sure as a man can be that the Priory was the source of the false banknotes.'

'Not happening to believe in ghosts,' said Charles, with an eye on his aunt.

She was quite equal to it, and answered with complete composure: 'This has been a lesson to all of us not to be credulous, I am sure. If you remember, Charles, from the very first I said that you were imagining things. Pray continue, Mr Draycott.'

Charles seemed incapable of speech. Michael went on: 'I got on to Inspector Tomlinson at Manfield, and he was exceedingly helpful. Through him I learned what there was to know about most of the people here. Naturally Duval was the most suspicious character. I won't bore you with the stages at which I arrived at the conclusion that there was an underground passage. Suffice it that I did arrive at it. Finding that opening into the well clinched the matter. And I hit on the moving stone. That didn't lead to much, but a visit, on the off-chance, to the British Museum library disclosed one significant fact.'

'We know!' Peter interrupted. 'Two pages torn out of the history of this house!'

'Oh, did you get on to that too? Yes, that was it. That same day I went to visit your solicitor, to find out whether anyone had tried to get you to sell the house, and if so, who he was, and where he came from.'

'I found that out,' Margaret said. 'You don't know how it worried me.'

'Did it? I'm sorry.' He smiled down at her, and Celia caught her husband's eye significantly. 'I drew a blank, except that I found someone had tried to buy the place. I next got on to Wilkes.'

'Yes, what made you suspect him?' Peter asked. 'Was it that electric-plant of his?'

'Not at first. It was just one little thing after another. I found that when you traced all the Priory ghost stories back they generally came from the same source: Wilkes. The very day you arrived' – he nodded at Charles – 'Wilkes spun a very fine yarn about having seen the Monk. I don't know if you remember, but Fripp was in the bar at the time, and he recounted the whole story to me. It was a good story I thought, and there was only one flaw. Wilkes couldn't be content to confine himself to eerie feelings and shadowy figures: he had to strain after an effect, which he doubtless thought very terrifying, and say he saw the Monk standing behind him. And he then committed the crowning error of saying the Monk just vanished into thin air. That was going a bit too far, and it set me on to his tracks. Then there was Duval. He used to come every day to the Bell, and he wasn't exactly the sort of customer a landlord of Wilkes' type encourages as a general rule. When he was drunk he got talkative, and rather abusive, but so far from throwing him out Wilkes always seemed anxious to humour him. The electric light plant I couldn't get a glimpse of for quite some time, but one thing I did see: Nearly every night, at opening-time, most of the village turns up at the Bell, as you probably know. They're in and out the whole evening, and the bar's usually pretty full. I kept a watch on the various *habitués*, and I noticed that two of the men who went in I never saw come out again. Moreover, Wilkes was never visible in the early morning, and it looked very much as though he was in the habit of keeping remarkably late hours. That gave me the idea that there might be a way down to the underground passage from the Inn. As you know, the Bell is very old, and it may well have been some sort of an annexe to the original monastery. The difficulty was to locate this possible entrance, and that's not an easy matter in a public inn. You never know whom you'll run into if you start prowling about. However, I got a chance to go down into the cellars unperceived yesterday, and I seized it. It's full of bins, and I managed to hide myself successfully. It was one of the most uncomfortable evenings I ever spent, for once down I didn't dare come up again till I'd discovered all I hoped to. I saw Wilkes, Spindle and two other men come down soon after closing time, and I watched them shift a big cask that stood on top of the trap-door. All but Spindle went down, and when he had replaced the cask over the trap, Spindle went off again. He's obviously the look-out man. The night Duval was murdered, and you came to the Bell, Malcolm – do you remember what a time it took for Wilkes to materialize?'

'I do indeed,' Charles said.

'Spindle didn't go upstairs to wake him. He nipped down the back stairs, gave the signal that would summon Wilkes – there's an electric bell just inside the trap door, by the way – and nipped up again. Wilkes came hurrying back, went up the back stairs, and came down the front fully dressed. You thought that was what had taken him so long.

'But I'm wandering from the point. Where was I?'

'Behind a beer-barrel,' said Charles. 'Come to think of it, you might have chosen a worse hiding-place. Go on.'

'I wish I'd thought of that earlier,' Michael said. 'I thought it a rotten spot. I stayed there till about four o'clock when Wilkes and Co returned. Still, I was repaid, for the two strangers were full of something that had happened. Evidently they hadn't been able to give vent to their feelings down below, and they meant to talk it all over with Wilkes before they left the Inn. Duval was mentioned, and apparently neither of them had the smallest doubt that the Monk had done him in. They were in a great way about that, partly out of fear of the Monk, partly because they thought Duval's death would bring the police down on them. Then one of them said that it wasn't that so much as "what's happened to-night." They both agreed about that, and the other one said that it was too thick, and he wouldn't be a party to murder. Wilkes tried to soothe him by saying there'd be no murder, but it was plain that the milder one of the pair wasn't satisfied. He kept on saying that he wouldn't stand for it, until the other one turned on him and told him to go and tell the Monk so if he dared. He replied if he knew who the Monk was, he would, and be damned to the lot of them, and then they both rounded on Wilkes, and accused him of knowing the Monk's identity. The ferocious one said that it was his belief Duval had found "where the Monk goes," and he'd half a mind to have a shot at doing the same thing. Wilkes managed to pacify him, and I learned from what he said that the Monk meant to clear out as "soon as the run's finished," things having got suddenly dangerous. That was you, of course, but I didn't know that at the time. After a bit more palaver they all cleared out, and as soon as I dared I went up to my room, ascertained that Wilkes had gone to bed, got hold of Fripp and a perfectly good disguise – hired from Clarkson's, by the way – and went down to see what I could discover. The rest you know.' He glanced at the clock on the mantelpiece. 'Tomlinson ought to be arriving at any moment now, and as soon as he comes I want to investigate the rest of that staircase.'

'I never heard such a thrilling tale in my life!' Celia said. 'And you can say what you please, but I think you're a pretty clever detective!'

'Hear, hear!' Peter said. 'By the way, what if the Monk takes it into his head to go down some time to-day to have a look at us?'

'I thought of that,' Michael said, 'but I can't see any reason why he should. Neither Wilkes nor Spindle will: it's far too risky, besides which I've left Fripp to make himself a nuisance to Wilkes. The Monk can't go, because to be seen in daylight might give him away, and now of all times he won't take any chances.'

Bowers came into the room, and went to Charles. 'Colonel Ackerley has called, sir, and he says if you could spare a moment he would like to speak to either you or the mistress. I've shown him into the library.'

'All right, I'll come,' Charles said. 'I take it I'd better keep your presence here a secret even from him, Draycott?'

'Yes, don't tell anyone,' Michael answered.

When Charles entered the library the Colonel rose from a chair by the window. 'My dear fellow, I hope I haven't disturbed you, but I felt I must come up to inquire. My man told me about you coming up to my place to telephone last night, and this morning the milkman told him what had happened. Now is there any mortal thing I can do? Is my car any use to you? I never was more shocked in my life. Have you any idea what can have become of them?'

'None,' Charles said. 'We're worried to death about it. As far as we can make out they must have strolled out, possibly to meet us – we were dining with the Penny-thornes, you know – and what happened then, or who spirited them away, we haven't the foggiest notion. The police are on to it, of course. The whole thing's a mystery. It seems certain somebody must have kidnapped them, but who, or why, we simply don't know. My wife's in a dreadful state: expects to hear of their bodies being discovered in some wood. I can't think it's as bad as that, though. It's awfully good of you to offer to help: I hoped I'd be able to get hold of you last night.'

'I was over at Manfield. I'd have come like a shot if I'd been in. But can I do anything to-day?'

'Thanks very much, sir, but I don't think you can. Now the police have taken over, there's really nothing any of us can do. Of course we're getting on to the hospitals, and circulating a description. But it's awfully good of you to offer.'

'Good of me be damned! I'm only sorry there's nothing I *can* do. But I needn't keep you here at any rate. I know you must be wishing me at Jericho. Don't forget to call me up if you want anything at any time. I may have to run over to Norchester this afternoon, and I might be late back. But my man will let you in if you should want to telephone again. You'll convey my deepest sympathy to your wife, won't you?'

He had hardly been gone five minutes when the police-car arrived, and the inspector got out. He was shown into the dining-room at once.

'I'm afraid I'm a bit late,' he said. 'I got detained. Now,

269

what are the plans, inspector? We're all of us pretty well in your hands.'

'It'll have to be to-night,' Michael said. 'Can you manage it?'

'Yes, I've arranged for the Flying Squad from Norchester to be here. That's all right,' the inspector answered. 'I take it we've got to try and find this other entrance?'

'We're only waiting for you, to start,' Michael answered. He looked inquiringly at Peter and Charles. 'Are you game to come and help us?'

'Not only game to, but all bursting with enthusiasm,' Charles said. 'You don't mind, do you, Celia?'

'Not if Mr Draycott is going to be with you,' she said. 'If anyone else comes to inquire, what shall I tell them?'

Charles repeated what he had said to the Colonel. 'And I think Margaret ought to retire to her room,' he added. 'If anyone happened to look in at the window and see her the game would be up.'

'All right,' Margaret agreed. 'I'll stay upstairs till you get back. You'll return here, won't you, Michael?'

'Yes, if I may,' he said. 'Sorry you've got such a dull morning ahead of you, but it'll be all over by to-night.'

Five minutes later the four men were once more on the secret stair.

'We'd better go up first, and make sure where it leads to,' Michael said. 'There's obviously a way into it from the first floor.'

They followed him up the stairs until they came to a blank wooden partition. The usual knob was found, and as they expected the partition opened. Something that looked at first like a curtain was hanging just inside, but when Michael flashed the light on to it they saw that it was a dressing-gown.

'One of the cupboards,' Michael said.

A sharp voice called: 'Who's there? Come out at once!'

'Great Jupiter!' said Charles. 'It's Aunt Lilian!'

'In that case, you can go first,' said Michael, and made way for him to pass.

Mrs Bosanquet, on the other side of the cupboard-door, said quaveringly: 'I am not afraid of you, and I warn you the police are in the house, and I have rung my bell!'

'Well, stop ringing it, Aunt,' said Charles, emerging.

She was backed against the wall, but at sight of him wrath took the place of the alarm in her face. 'Well really, Charles!' she said. 'How dare you hide yourself in my wardrobe?'

'I didn't. We're all here...'

'All? Do you mean two strange men are mixed up with my clothes?'

'No, but there's a way on to the secret stair at the back of your wardrobe. Come and look.'

Mrs Bosanquet clutched at the bed-post. 'Are you telling me that I have been sleeping in this room and the whole while that Monk-person has been able to get in?' she asked faintly. 'No, I don't want to see it. And I don't want those men pushing their way through my dresses. Go away, please. I am about to transfer all my belongings into Margaret's room.'

Charles retreated, and closed the panel behind him. 'Very unpleasant shock for the lady,' the inspector said gravely.

'All things considered,' Charles said, 'I think we'd better go *down* stairs.'

'Yes, sir, I think we had. I'll post a man in that room to-night, inspector.'

'It would be as well,' Michael agreed. 'That seems to be the only entrance up here. Will you go ahead?'

'You take the lead,' Tomlinson replied, and made room for him to squeeze past.

'Take care how you tread,' Michael warned them, and began to descend.

271

They went down, and down, past the library, past the moving stone, which Michael pointed out to them. At every step the atmosphere grew colder and danker. 'I'm glad I'm not alone,' said Charles. 'I don't like it one little bit.'

'Nor do I,' confessed the inspector. 'Like going into a grave. My word, it's damp, isn't it?'

'I think in all probability we are going into a grave,' Michael said. 'Something very like it, anyway.'

'Smells filthy,' said Peter. 'I can't stand must.'

'We're at the bottom now, anyway. Look out for your heads.'

'I shall have to have someone to hold my hand soon,' Charles remarked. 'Do I understand we're likely to come out at the chapel?'

'That's what we're hoping,' Michael answered.

'Speak for yourself,' Charles recommended. 'I'm not hoping anything of the kind.'

The inspector gave a chuckle, which echoed rather eerily.

'Please don't do that again!' said Charles. 'It unnerves me. Of course we only want a few bats to complete the picture.'

'What's that ahead?' Peter asked suddenly, peering over Michael's shoulder. 'By Jove, you're right, Draycott! We've got to the crypt! Well, we always knew there must be one under the ruins.'

In a moment they were all standing in a low vaulted space. The vaults were supported by stone pillars, and as Michael's torch slowly swept the place they saw grim relics on the flagged floor. There were old worm-eaten coffins; one or two had rotted away, and a few bones, crumbling to dust, lay amongst the remains of the wooden shells. The lid of one coffin had been prised open, and when they looked into it they saw that it was empty.

'You bet that's where our skeleton came from!' Peter said. 'Gosh, what a gruesome place!'

Charles wiped his brow: 'Yes, not my idea of the ideal entrance-hall,' he agreed. 'I'm shortly going to develop the horrors.'

'Postpone them for a bit,' begged Michael. 'We've got to discover the way out. You've got torches, haven't you? Then let's get on to it.'

They set to work to explore the crypt. The first thing to attract their attention was a flight of stone steps, that had once obviously led up to the floor of the chapel, but these only mounted for a few feet before they were blocked by fallen masonry, and the earth that had accumulated on top with the passing of years. Michael tested them in vain, and sprang down again.

'Hi!' Charles called from the other end of the crypt. 'Come over here! I always said I'd missed my vocation. I've found the gentleman's front-steps.'

With one accord they all hastened to where he was standing. He played his torch up the wall where the vaulting had broken away. A set of iron rails ran up, like a ladder.

'That's it!' Michael said. He inspected the dust and the jagged bits of stone at his feet. 'What's more, that vaulting has been deliberately broken down. What do you think, inspector?'

'It looks like it,' the inspector answered. 'Especially as the roof's good nearly everywhere else.' He stood directly beneath the broken roof and turned his torch upwards. 'That's queer. There's a sort of square place forming what looks like a second roof. Can you see, Draycott?' He stepped back to make room for Michael. 'It's a good bit higher than the rest of the vaulting too. What do you suppose it can be?'

'Unless I'm much mistaken it's one of the tombs,' Michael answered. 'The whole of the bottom has been taken away, and the floor of the chapel. Good Lord, I hand it to the Monk! He's thorough. I'm going up. You might keep your torch on it, to show me the way, one of you.' He pocketed his own, and started to climb the vertical ladder. They waited anxiously for the result. 'To think of the hours I've spent examining all those beastly tombs!' Michael said from above their heads. 'I suspected them right off, but I couldn't get one of them to open. Hullo!'

'What?' came from three pairs of lips at once.

'A sort of handle. Wait a bit.' He removed his right hand from the rail above him and reached up to turn the handle. 'It seems to be something on the same sort of principle as a Yale lock,' he said, and pressed upwards. 'Yes, by Jove, it moves! Throw the light more to the side, will you? I thought so! It's hinged. That accounts for my being able to lift it. Take the light away now; I'm going to open it.'

They switched off their torches, but they were not long in darkness, for the solid stone slab that Michael was pressing, opened slowly upwards, and a shaft of daylight filtered into the crypt.

Michael climbed carefully higher, until he could see over the top of the tomb. 'It's all right. There's no one here. I just want to see how this works from outside.' He swung the slab right back, and climbed out. He was gone for perhaps five minutes, and they saw him swing a leg over the side of the tomb again, and pull the slab to after him. They heard the lock click as it shut.

He came quickly down the ladder again. 'No wonder I couldn't find it. Unless you knew exactly where to look you never would. There's a slit in the carving on the side of the tomb. Beautiful bit of work. It's just wide enough to take a very thin flat key. The Monk's put a complete lock on the lid of the tomb, and a couple of hinges. Well, I think that's settled his little hash once and for all. We've got him, inspector.'

CHAPTER XIX

When they got back to the library, after a thorough examination of the secret cellar, it was nearly one o'clock, and Celia had received several callers. Even Mrs Pennythorne had bicycled over to inquire after the missing couple, and Mrs Roote, and Mr Titmarsh had also come to offer their sympathy.

Since Charles had seen the underground passage and the rooms that led out of it he and Peter had had a quiet consultation. As a result of this Peter took Michael Draycott aside just before they all went in to lunch, and tackled him frankly.

'Look here, Draycott,' he said, 'I'm going to ask you a plain question, and I want you to answer quite honestly: isn't Margaret's and my escape from that cell going to make your job to-night rather ticklish?'

Michael hesitated. 'Well, of course, it does complicate things, I admit,' he said. 'Still, it can't be helped.'

'It might be helped,' Peter said. 'If we went back.'

'No, that wouldn't do at all, sporting of you though it is to suggest it. I couldn't allow it.'

'Don't you run a risk of failing to bring off your *coup* if we're discovered to have escaped?'

'I'm hoping for the best,' Michael answered lightly. 'If it were only you I'd ask you to go back, but to let Miss Fortescue go down again is out of the question.'

'Go down where?' Margaret had come up to them, and caught the last words.

Michael turned to her with the special smile he seemed to keep for her. 'Nowhere,' he said.

She laughed. 'What a snub! But do tell me what's out of the question?'

It was Peter who answered. 'Margaret, it has occurred to me, and to Chas as well, that us not being in that cell to-night may ruin Draycott's plans. He won't say so, but...'

'You're exaggerating,' Michael said. 'And in any case what you suggest can't be considered for a moment.'

'Inspector Tomlinson doesn't agree with you. He thinks it can.' Peter looked down at his sister. 'What we've been thinking is this, Margaret: if Wilkes and those others happened to go down to-night before the Monk and found us gone, they'd give the alarm. If the Monk goes first, which is even more likely, Draycott will have to close in on him, and let the rest of the crowd go hang. Do you see?'

Margaret looked from him to Michael. 'I hadn't thought of that. You think we ought to go back?'

'No, I don't,' Michael said.

'I leave it to you, Sis,' Peter told her. 'I know it won't be nice for you, but do you think you could screw up your courage enough to do it?'

She seemed to consider. 'Could you get hold of an automatic for me, Michael? I could hide it in my dress. If I had a gun I'd do it.'

Peter nodded. 'She's a pretty good shot, Draycott. You can trust her with a gun.'

'I can't manage the double pull of a service revolver, or I'd borrow Charles',' Margaret said.

The inspector, who had come up, and had been listening, said: 'If you'll consent to be shut up down there again, miss – and if you do I'd like to say that there's very few ladies who've got your pluck – you'll both be fitted with a couple of Colts. Not that I think you'll have any

276

need to use them. All we want you to do is to sit in that cell, as if you'd been there all day, and *keep* there till Mr Draycott gives the word for you to come out. We'll draw the bolts back as we come down the passage, but don't come out, either of you. There may be a bit of shooting, you see. While you're behind that stone wall you're safe enough, but we don't want you mixed up with the scuffle there's bound to be outside.'

Margaret smiled at Michael, who was frowning. 'At that rate I don't see that we shall be in any danger at all. It'll just be rather boring, having to wait. I'm game.'

The inspector turned to Michael. 'You're in charge, Draycott, I know, and it's for you to give the orders, but if you'll allow me to make the suggestion, the lady won't come to any harm, and it's taking a big chance if she stays up here.'

'I know,' Michael said. He hesitated. Then he laughed ruefully: 'Oh, Margaret, you *are* a nuisance!'

'No, I'm not. Peter's quite capable of looking after me – and after all, the last thing the Monk would do would be to waste time in shooting us for no reason at all. Consider it settled. When ought we to go down again?'

'Good girl!' Peter said, and went off to tell Charles.

The inspector saw Michael take Margaret's hand, and opened his eyes very wide indeed. He murmured something about going to speak to the sergeant, and withdrew.

'Margaret – I can't tell you what I think of your pluck, and your sportsmanship,' Michael said.

She blushed charmingly. 'If you're going down there – do you think I wouldn't want to – to be there too?' she asked.

For a moment he looked at her; then, without quite knowing how she got there, she found herself in his arms.

There was a loud cough in the doorway. 'Don't mind me,' Charles said. 'Of course if I were tactful I should go

277

silently away. But I want my lunch, and Celia won't start till you come.'

Both scarlet in the face, they fell apart. 'Oh – oh is it ready?' Margaret asked. 'We're just coming. And – er – Chas!'

'Yes?'

'We – Michael and I – we're going to be married.'

'What a surprise!' Charles said. 'I ought to have had warning of this.' He grasped Michael's hand. 'Congratulations! And do you mind coming in to lunch?'

Over lunch they discussed their plans, and it was decided that Peter and Margaret should descend into their prison again not later than eight o'clock, to be on the safe side. Michael, Tomlinson, Charles, and three of the Flying Squad from Norchester would take up their positions in the house. It would be Charles' duty, aided by the ubiquitous Flinders, to stand by the panel in the library, in case the Monk managed to reach it. Sergeant Matthews had already blocked up the entrance into Mrs Bosanquet's room, since they were too short of men to spare a couple to stand guard there. The sergeant and one other man were to lie in wait in the chapel, concealed amongst the ruins, and when they saw the Monk go down through the tomb they were to signal with a torch to the house, where a man would be on the look-out from one of the upper windows. Their task was then to stand by the tomb, and hold the stone slab down in case the Monk doubled back to make an escape that way. There was no hiding place in the crypt, and Michael had judged that it would be safer not to attempt to post any men inside the secret entrance. At the Inn, Fripp was to keep a lookout, and as soon as he had seen Wilkes and the two other men descend into the cellars he was to signal from his window to the police lying in wait outside. One of them would speed off at once to the Priory on his motorbicycle to tell Michael that all was well; the other three would enter the Inn, arrest

Spindle before he could give the alarm, and bottle up the second entrance.

'Do you still suspect anyone in particular?' Margaret asked Michael when he returned to the Priory shortly after six.

'I'm sure of it,' he answered. 'I found out one thing that settles it – or so I think.'

'I do think you're a tantalizing person!' complained Celia.

'I don't like him,' Charles announced. 'Don't marry him, Margaret. We can't have a policeman in the family. What about our wireless licence? He's bound to find out that it's expired.'

They dined early, and as soon as the meal was over Margaret went up to change into the frock she had worn on the previous evening. With a praiseworthy attention to detail she made her hair look tousled, and wiped all the powder off her face. As Charles remarked, in a newly engaged girl this deed almost amounted to heroism.

At eight o'clock they opened the panel and went down those cold, damp stairs, Michael leading the way. It was nervous work, for the Monk might already have entered, unlikely though this was. However, Margaret felt the butt of the Colt she carried in the pocket of Peter's coat, which she had put on, and took heart. If there was going to be any shooting, she thought, someone would get a surprise.

They climbed through the moving stone, and made their way cautiously through the two vaults to the passage. The place was eerily silent, and it was evident that no one had yet come down into it. The light was still on in their cell, and they entered. Then Michael shut them in, and bolted the door, and returned to the library.

'Ugh!' said Margaret cheerfully. 'Well, who says the age of adventure is dead? I hope we don't have to wait long.'

'Careful!' Peter said. 'The Monk moves pretty softly, and we don't want to be overheard. We'd better talk of something else.'

This they did while the slow hours dragged past. In spite of the gun in her pocket the long wait began to get on Margaret's nerves, and by eleven o'clock she had no need to assume an expression of anxiety. Her eyes had begun to look a little strained, and she was very pale.

Then they heard that padding footstep, and Margaret instinctively grasped Peter's arm. It came nearer, and then stopped. The shutter slid back, and once more they saw the cowled face at the grille. For perhaps fifteen tense seconds the eyes they could see through the slits observed them. Then, just as Peter had thumbed down the safety catch of the pistol behind him, the shutter closed again, and the footsteps passed on.

Margaret was shaking. 'I don't think I can bear it for much longer,' she whispered.

They heard the grate of a key, and knew that the Monk had unlocked the door into the printing-room. There was a long, long pause. Once they thought they heard the soft footfall again, but they could not be certain.

Another hour crept by. Margaret felt cold, and rather sick. 'It's – it's like waiting at the dentist's when you're going to have a tooth out,' she whispered, trying to smile.

Even as she said it they heard footsteps approaching, and the murmur of voices.

'The rest of the gang,' Peter said. 'Feeling all right, Sis?'

She grimaced, but nodded.

The voices drew closer: they heard the same man who had brought the water on the night previous, say: 'Well, this is my last night, and I don't care who hears me say it. Things are getting a sight too hot for me.'

Someone, probably Wilkes, Peter guessed, said something in a low voice. 'Let 'em hear!' the other replied. 'They won't hear much after to-night.' Then the voices ceased, and in a few minutes the roar of the engine started.

It seemed to the two who waited in their cell that hours

passed. Margaret looked at Peter with a scared question in her eyes. He put his lips to her ear. 'Don't forget they had to wait for the signal. 'Tisn't as long as we think, Sis. Don't fuss!'

They relapsed into listening silence again. 'Difficult to hear above the row of the engine,' Peter said.

But he too was beginning to wonder whether any hitch had occurred. Then the shutter slid back, and they saw Michael's face for a moment. Peter went to the door, and Michael whispered: 'I'm going to draw back the bolts, but whatever you do, don't come out till you're given the word.' He disappeared as he spoke; they heard the bolts drawn cautiously back, and then Peter beckoned Margaret to come and stand out of range of the grille.

Outside in the passage, the four other men had halted behind Michael. A stream of light came from the room beyond Peter and Margaret's cell, and they knew that the men were working with the door open, probably for the sake of air.

Michael gave the signal, and they crept forward.

Michael and Tomlinson reached the door together. 'Hands up!' Michael said. 'The first man who moves I shoot!'

Even as the words left his mouth there was a report, and the light went out; someone had fired at the electric bulb, and the place was plunged into sudden darkness.

But in that brief moment Michael had had time to see the whole room in one lightning glance. Wilkes was there, working the central machine; the two other men were there, but there was no sign of the Monk.

In a moment there was turmoil. A gun cracked, and the inspector's revolver answered it. Someone's torch lit up a corner of the room for a brief instant, then there was a scuffle in the doorway, another shot, and a wild struggle in the passage. Above the noise of the engine and the fight, Michael shouted: 'He's not here! Collar those men!'

281

He felt a shot whistle past his head, ducked, and ran back down the passage, a gun in one hand, his torch in the other.

Behind him the noise grew fainter and fainter; he could safely leave Inspector Tomlinson to deal with the three others but something far more important remained to be done. The Monk had not been in the printing-room. Michael had a sickening fear that there was some other entrance he had failed to discover, but the first thing to do was to race for the crypt, in case the Monk had gone that way. As he ran he cursed himself for not having taken the precaution to go up the stairs past the library before he led the police down. The Monk must have been on the stairs when they came through the panel; he might have been listening to what had been said in the library, waited for them to get through the moving stone, and then gone on down to the crypt. Well, he couldn't get out through the tomb, in any case, Michael reflected.

He reached the stone, and set his shoulders to it. It was dangerous work, for the Monk might even then be lying in wait to shoot down his pursuers. He stayed for a moment, with a leg over the barrier, and his torch lighting up the stairs. He could see nothing, but below him he thought he heard a rustle. He sprang through and went on down. There was no sign of life in the low passage that led at the foot of the stairs to the crypt, and no glimmer of light shone in the crypt itself. He reached it, and his torch flashed round, searching every corner. The crypt was empty. He sprang for the iron ladder, scrambled up, and shouted: 'All right there? No one tried to get out?'

The men outside answered: 'All right here, sir.'

He climbed down again. There must be another way out, and like a blundering fool he had allowed the Monk to escape.

He heard Sergeant Matthews' voice echoing down the passage: 'Where are you, sir? Mr Draycott! Where are you?'

'Here!' Michael called, and in a few minutes the sergeant came hurrying into the crypt.

'Has he got away, sir? We got the others. The inspector's gorn up to be sure he hasn't forced that panel at the top of the stairs. Lord, this is bad luck, ain't it, sir?'

Michael was searching the crypt for any sign of an entrance. Suddenly he stopped, his torch-light turned full on to one of the coffins. It was the coffin they had looked into that morning. Then the lid had lain beside it. But now the lid covered it.

The light swept on. Michael said: 'He's not here. We'd better get back to the library. Just a moment though: I'll make sure there's nothing behind these stairs.'

To the sergeant's astonishment instead of going to the block staircase he pulled a note-book and a pencil from his pocket, scrawled rapidly, and then said: 'Come over here and look, sergeant.'

The sergeant opened his mouth, saw Michael scowl at him, and shut it again. He went to him, and Michael thrust the open book into his hands. 'Just sound this wall,' he said, proceeding to do so.

The sergeant's puzzled eyes read: 'He's in the coffin. If we lift the lid one of us'll get shot. Pretend to go away; take shoes off in passage, creep back, crouch down at head and foot of coffin, and wait for lid to lift. Then collar him as he gets out.'

'No, there's nothing here,' Michael said loudly. 'He's gone the other way. No use keeping those two up there by the tomb. I'll send them off to search the grounds.'

The sergeant's wits worked slowly but surely. 'Right, sir: I'll give the word to them.' He stepped under the hollow tomb, and setting his hands to his mouth shouted: 'He's got away. Search the grounds!'

'Come on then!' Michael said. 'We've no time to lose.' Together they went back into the passage, and along it for some yards. At a sign from Michael the sergeant stopped and began to take off his boots. In another moment they stood up in their stockinged feet, and began to creep back to the crypt.

Michael had to take the risk of a light being seen inside the coffin; he turned his torch on for just long enough to locate the coffin. Then the light disappeared again, and in the dense darkness they went up to the coffin, and crouched down at each end.

Not a sound broke the stillness. Michael set his teeth, and tried to think what he would do if no one were in this coffin.

A creak almost made him start. The coffin lid was lifting. He stayed, ready to spring. The sound of a scrape and a thud told him that the lid had been lowered to the floor of the crypt. He heard a noise as of a body moving in the coffin; he rose stealthily. He was so near the coffin that he felt some rough material brush his cheek as he got up. It gave him the position of the Monk, and he made his spring. 'Light, sergeant!' he shouted.

A pistol shot sounded; Michael had his arms clamped round a struggling form. The sergeant's torch flashed on, and the sergeant came dashing to help.

'The gun! The gun!' Michael cried. The sergeant seized the Monk's pistol arm, and wrenched it round. The gun fell clattering to the ground and the sergeant quickly picked it up.

To and fro the struggling men swayed, and before the sergeant had time to reach them they were down on the floor, Michael uppermost.

The sergeant called: 'All right, sir!' and launched his bulk into the fray.

'Got him!' Michael panted, and there was a click as the handcuffs snapped together. 'Take him, sergeant, and be careful; he's damned strong.'

The sergeant had blown long and loud on his whistle,

and they could hear men hurrying down the passage. The Monk, once the handcuffs were on, had ceased to struggle, but stood passive in the sergeant's grip. From first to last he had not uttered a word.

The inspector dashed in, followed by a sturdy constable. 'You've got him?' he cried. 'Well done, sir! Well done! Hullo, are you hurt?'

'Only a scratch,' Michael said. 'Flesh wound. Couldn't grab his pistol hand in time. Take him up to the house.'

In the library were by this time not only Charles and Flinders, but Celia and Mrs Bosanquet as well, and the two prisoners from below, who had been escorted up, after the capture of the gang, by a solicitous policeman.

When the Monk came through the open panel Mrs Bosanquet gave a small shriek of dismay, and not even the sight of the guard about the cowled figure reassured her. She got behind a table, and commanded Charles not to take his gun off the Monk for one moment.

Michael came through the panel. 'Now then!' he said. 'Let us have a look at you.' He went up to the still figure, and pulled the cowl back from the Monk's head.

There was a gasp of utter astonishment from Celia. For the man who stood revealed was none other than Colonel Ackerley.

He made no movement to resist, and the expression on his face as he looked at the assembled company was one of sardonic scorn.

'But – but I don't understand!' Mrs Bosanquet said in a voice of complete bewilderment. 'That's the Colonel!'

Michael had taken the handcuffed wrists and jerked them up to look at the gloves the Colonel wore. As Margaret had described, they were buttoned gloves of some cotton fabric, and one button was missing. 'That was a little mistake of yours, Colonel,' he said. 'I shouldn't have expected you to slip up on a detail like that.'

285

It was plain the Colonel, not in the habit of buttoning his gloves, had not until now noticed the loss of one significant button. His eyes searched Michael's face for a moment, and a shade of uneasiness crept into his own.

None of this was betrayed by his voice, however. 'Well, Mr Strange,' he said, quite in his own manner. 'I congratulate you. You are cleverer than the others who have tried to find me out.' He looked at Charles, and his sneer returned. 'Your efforts were not quite so brilliant.' His glance went back to Michael; it was as though he felt everyone else in the room to be beneath contempt. 'As a matter of interest, how did you guess my identity?'

'When a man of your stamp is seen to be on terms of apparent intimacy with the local publican,' Michael answered, 'one is apt to draw unwelcome conclusions.'

The Colonel raised his brows. 'Indeed, Mr Strange? Or to leap to conclusions, shall we say? If you had no other reason than that for suspecting me you made a lucky guess.'

Michael smiled. 'Oh, not quite!' he said. 'When a man gives out that he is going to play bridge at the County Club in Manfield, and I discover his car to be still in the locked garage, I feel that requires a little explanation. I'm sorry I can't give you a more detailed account of all the things that led me to be sure you were the man I was after, but time is getting on. You will no doubt hear all you want to know at your trial.' He made a sign to Inspector Tomlinson, and the two attendant policemen grasped the Colonel's arms again to march him away.

He resisted, but it was only to bow to Celia. '*Au revoir*, my dear Mrs Malcolm,' he said. He turned to Margaret, who had been standing like a statue, listening. 'As for you, Miss Fortescue, I am sure that you will be relieved to know that in spite of your damnably annoying behaviour, I had very little intention of leaving you to starve as you so palpably feared. And may I give you a word of advice?

When next you escape from prison, and return to it with the idea of bluffing your captor, drink some of the water you have been supplied with. Had you thought of that you would have given your clever Mr Strange less trouble, for I might then have been in the printing-room when he surprised my staff.'

She did not answer him; he laughed shortly, and turned to Mrs Bosanquet. 'I was amused at your efforts to conjure up my wraith, madam,' he said. 'I was behind the panel at the time, and really I was almost tempted to appear. I always hate to disoblige the ladies.' He bowed again, and without so much as glancing at the men of the party, went out under escort.

There was a long silence. Then Charles sat down weakly. 'Let no one speak to me,' he said. 'I shall no doubt recover in time.'

'But *Ackerley*!' Peter stammered. 'Draycott, how the devil did you arrive at it?'

'Well, you heard some of my reasons,' Michael said. 'But the first clue I had was Time. You see these forgeries have been going on for five years, and it seemed probable that they were from the beginning carried out from this place. That ruled out Titmarsh: he only came here three years ago. Roote has been here an even shorter time; various other inhabitants round about have been here too long a time. It was only Ackerley who came to live at the White House five years ago, and I thought it significant that his arrival was shortly followed by the arrival not only of Duval, but of Wilkes also to take over the Bell Inn. Now Wilkes paid a very large sum for the Bell: too large a sum for an inn so little frequented. And by lying up in odd corners I found that a pretty close intimacy seemed to exist between the two men. Wilkes was the only one who knew who the Monk was; you might call him the Monk's chief of staff. That set me on to Ackerley, and that's where Fripp came in handy. After the murder of Duval I let Fripp break into the Colonel's house one night when the servants had gone to bed. You know that they slept over the garage. And of course the Colonel was out on his secret business. I told you Fripp was clever with locks. And he's not burdened with any scruples. He found a bottle of chloroform, which is now in my possession...'

'But didn't the Colonel miss it?' Charles demanded.

'No; for the very good reason that Fripp exchanged it for one almost identical. He also found the missing book. I'll let you have that when the trial's over; those two pages cut from the copy at the British Museum are most interesting.'

'House-breaking!' Charles said, casting up his eyes. 'Our incorruptible police!'

'Oh no!' Michael grinned. 'Jimmy's not a policeman. He would be insulted to hear you say so.'

Peter struck in: 'But an officer in the army – I suppose he wasn't, though?'

'On the contrary, he was. But he left the army under rather odd circumstances. It was hushed up, but I discovered on inquiry that his reputation was not exactly savoury. I wondered when he seemed loth to tell me where exactly he had been stationed.'

'I can't get over it!' Celia burst out. 'That cheery, sporting Colonel! He must be a *monster*!' She got up. 'I'm going to bed. My head's in a positive whirl. And Charles! All these horrible secret passages have got to be blocked up.'

'Leave it to Draycott,' said Charles. 'I'm going away for a rest-cure. And I suppose he's going to be as much an owner as I am. Not that I approve, but there! when are my wishes ever considered?' He rose and prepared to follow his wife out. Over his shoulder he said: 'And don't be more than half an hour saying good night, you two.'

But they were almost as long as that over it. Safe in

Michael's arms Margaret said: 'But why did you say I'd never look at anyone in your "line of business"?'

'Well, I was afraid you wouldn't,' he explained. 'After all, I'm only what Jimmy calls a "beastly busy." How could I dream you'd ever even think of marrying me?'

She buried her face in his shoulder. 'I said I shouldn't care as long as it was honest,' she said, muffled.

He laughed softly as he bent to kiss her, 'Or a butcher's shop!' he reminded her.

Crime fiction – now available in paperback from Grafton Books

Crime fiction – now available in paperback from Grafton Books

James Hadley Chase

One Bright Summer Morning	£1.95	☐
Tiger by the Tail	£1.95	☐
Strictly for Cash	£1.50	☐
What's Better than Money?	£1.50	☐
Just the Way it Is	£1.95	☐
You're Dead Without Money	£1.50	☐
Coffin From Hong Kong	£1.95	☐
Like a Hole in the Head	£1.50	☐
There's a Hippie on the Highway	£1.95	☐
This Way for a Shroud	£1.95	☐
Just a Matter of Time	£1.95	☐
Not My Thing	£1.95	☐
Hit Them Where It Hurts	£1.95	☐

Georgette Heyer

Penhallow	£1.95	☐
Duplicate Death	£1.95	☐
Envious Casca	£1.95	☐
Death in the Stocks	£1.95	☐
Behold, Here's Poison	£1.95	☐
They Found Him Dead	£1.95	☐
The Unfinished Clue	£1.95	☐
Detection Unlimited	£1.95	☐
Why Shoot a Butler?	£2.50	☐

To order direct from the publisher just tick the titles you want and fill in the order form.

GF2781

True crime – now available in paperback from
Grafton Books

To order direct from the publisher just tick the titles you want
and fill in the order form.   GF2581

The best of crime fiction now available in paperback from Grafton Books

John Hutten

Accidental Crimes	£1.95	☐
29 Herriott Street	£1.95	☐

Dan Kavanagh

Duffy	£1.50	☐
Fiddle City	£1.50	☐

Joseph Hansen

Troublemaker	£2.50	☐
Fade Out	£2.50	☐
Gravedigger	£1.95	☐
Skinflick	£1.95	☐
The Man Everybody was Afraid of	£1.95	☐
Nightwork	£1.95	☐

Stephen Knight

Requiem at Rogano	£2.50	☐

Rod Miller

The Animal Letter	£2.50	☐

To order direct from the publisher just tick the titles you want and fill in the order form.

GF3081

The world's greatest thriller writers now available in paperback from Grafton Books

Robert Ludlum

The Chancellor Manuscript	£2.95	☐
The Gemini Contenders	£2.50	☐
The Rhinemann Exchange	£2.50	☐
The Matlock Paper	£2.50	☐
The Osterman Weekend	£2.50	☐
The Scarlatti Inheritance	£2.95	☐
The Holcroft Covenant	£2.95	☐
The Materese Circle	£2.95	☐
The Bourne Identity	£2.95	☐
The Road to Gandolfo	£2.50	☐
The Parsifal Mosaic	£2.95	☐
The Aquitaine Progression	£3.50	☐

Lawrence Sanders

The Third Deadly Sin	£2.50	☐
The Tenth Commandment	£2.95	☐
The Second Deadly Sin	£2.50	☐
The Sixth Commandment	£2.50	☐
The Tomorrow File	£2.50	☐
The Pleasures of Helen	£2.50	☐

To order direct from the publisher just tick the titles you want and fill in the order form.

GF1881

The world's greatest thriller writers now available in paperback from Grafton Books

Len Deighton

Twinkle, Twinkle, Little Spy	£2.50 ☐
Yesterday's Spy	£1.95 ☐
Spy Story	£2.50 ☐
Horse Under Water	£2.50 ☐
Billion Dollar Brain	£2.50 ☐
The Ipcress File	£2.50 ☐
An Expensive Place to Die	£2.50 ☐
Declarations of War	£2.50 ☐
SS-GB	£2.50 ☐
XPD	£2.95 ☐
Bomber	£2.95 ☐
Fighter (non-fiction)	£2.95 ☐
Blitzkrieg (non-fiction)	£2.50 ☐
Funeral in Berlin	£2.50 ☐
Goodbye Mickey Mouse	£2.95 ☐

'Game, Set and Match' Series

Berlin Game	£2.95 ☐
Mexico Set	£2.95 ☐
London Match	£2.95 ☐

Jack Higgins

A Game for Heroes	£1.95 ☐
The Wrath of God	£1.95 ☐
The Khufra Run	£1.95 ☐
Bloody Passage	£1.95 ☐

Trevanian

The Loo Sanction	£2.50 ☐
The Eiger Sanction	£2.50 ☐
Shibumi	£2.50 ☐
The Summer of Katya	£1.95 ☐

To order direct from the publisher just tick the titles you want and fill in the order form.

GF1681

The world's greatest thriller writers now available in paperback from Grafton Books

Anthony Price

Soldier No More	£2.50	☐
The Old Vengeful	£2.50	☐
Gunner Kelly	£1.95	☐
Sion Crossing	£2.50	☐
Here Be Monsters	£2.50	☐

Julian Rathbone

A Spy of the Old School	£1.95	☐
Nasty, Very	£2.50	☐

Matthew Heald Cooper

To Ride A Tiger	£2.50	☐
When Fish Begin to Smell	£1.95	☐

Donald Seaman

The Wilderness of Mirrors	£2.50	☐

Dan Sherman

The Prince of Berlin	£1.95	☐

To order direct from the publisher just tick the titles you want and fill in the order form.

All these books are available at your local bookshop or newsagent, or can be ordered direct from the publisher.

To order direct from the publishers just tick the titles you want and fill in the form below.

Name _____

Address _____

Send to:
Grafton Cash Sales
PO Box 11, Falmouth, Cornwall TR10 9EN.

Please enclose remittance to the value of the cover price plus:

UK 60p for the first book, 25p for the second book plus 15p per copy for each additional book ordered to a maximum charge of £1.90.

BFPO 60p for the first book, 25p for the second book plus 15p per copy for the next 7 books, thereafter 9p per book.

Overseas including Eire £1.25 for the first book, 75p for second book and 28p for each additional book.

Grafton Books reserve the right to show new retail prices on covers, which may differ from those previously advertised in the text or elsewhere.